ENTICEMENTS

Also by Una-Mary Parker

Riches
Scandals
Temptations

ENTICEMENTS

Una-Mary Parker

HEADLINE

Copyright © 1990 Una-Mary Parker

Published by arrangement with
Dutton-New American Library,
a division of Penguin Books, USA, Inc,
New York, New York

First published in Great Britain in 1990
by HEADLINE BOOK PUBLISHING PLC

10 9 8 7 6 5 4 3 2 1

British Library Cataloguing in Publication Data

Parker, Una-Mary
Enticements.
I. Title
823.914 [F]

ISBN 0-7472-0278-8

Typeset by Colset Private Limited, Singapore

Printed and bound in Great Britain by
Richard Clay Ltd, Bungay, Suffolk

HEADLINE BOOK PUBLISHING PLC
Headline House, 79 Great Titchfield Street, London W1P 7FN

This is for
Baba, Robbie, Buffy and Kate
with all my love

Prologue

Marissa extended her slim hands with their scarlet-painted nails and slowly undid Edward's black bow-tie.

'I'm early,' she announced softly, her eyes never leaving his face.

Edward's smile creased his tanned face into a network of deep laughter lines, and his pale blue eyes swept languidly over the contours of her body.

'You certainly are,' he replied.

'I thought that . . . perhaps . . . before all your guests arrived . . .' Marissa's voice trailed off, leaving no doubt in his mind what she meant.

'Oh, Marissa . . . Marissa.' Her name was wrenched from his throat as he pulled her almost roughly against him. 'You know I'm crazy about you, don't you?'

She nodded, unbuttoning his white evening shirt now, her scarlet lips just a whisper away from his mouth. 'I love you too. I'll love you always.'

'Will you, darling? Will you really?' There was anxiety in his voice and fretfulness in his eyes. He couldn't bring himself to say "Even though I'm so much older than you?" Saying the words would give the thought a painful reality he wanted to deny even to himself.

'Of course I will,' said Marissa, clinging to him.

Grabbing her hand Edward led her into his bedroom and locked the door. The Park Avenue apartment had been swarming with people from the De Vere Catering Company for the past few hours: setting up tables, draping them with snowy damask cloths, arranging platters of exotic food, carting in vases of flowers and crates of extra glasses and crockery. There was no privacy anywhere, and in thirty minutes a hundred guests would be arriving to see in the New Year.

Swiftly Edward undressed, watching Marissa as she slipped out of something brief and black and sparkling, seeing only the creamy

1

velvet of her skin, the fullness of her breasts, the long curve of her thighs. With a groan of desire, he pulled her down beside him on to the kingsize bed, knowing he mustn't be selfish in his haste, knowing he must try to make it last as long as he could for her sake, but wanting her so badly it hurt.

'My love,' Marissa murmured into his ear, then sensing his acute longing she lowered herself on to him almost immediately, arching her body as she took him deep inside her, running her nails through the greying hair on his chest. Closing his eyes, trying to concentrate on prolonging the moment when he knew he'd be unable to hold back, Edward caressed her breasts with an experienced feather-like touch and listened to her little whimpers of delight.

Then she leaned forward, squeezing him so hard and tight inside her that a thousand tiny torturous arrows of fire shot through him. Gasping, he thrust with desperate urgency. He couldn't wait. It had been years since a woman had made him feel like this, years since he'd enjoyed the sexual vigour of his youth . . . years since . . . In a flooding flash it was all over, and he was lying there, breathless.

'Oh, Christ, Marissa!' he cried out. 'I'm sorry, darling. I'm sorry. I couldn't wait.'

She kissed him lovingly, gently, cradling him in her slender arms. 'It's all right,' she crooned, 'I love to feel you come like that. We'll do it again later, after the party. Then we can make it last longer.'

Edward held her close, feeling there was something very special about her. In the three months he'd known this bewitching creature he'd been swept off his feet, made to feel young again, reborn. How often did a man of his age have the chance to recapture the first flush of his sexuality? Yet Marissa, with her sweet and understanding ways, had done just that for him. Made him feel young and whole again, with his juices flowing and his batteries recharged.

Perhaps he ought to marry her. The thought struck him with all the adolescent recklessness he thought the years of responsibility had swept away. Why not? he asked himself, surrendering to the delightful fantasy. It would cause a bit of a scandal of course. Chins would wag at the Chairman of the Tollemache Trust, the most powerful British management company based in New York, marrying a girl forty years his junior; people would say Sir Edward Wenlake, the cleverest businessman of his generation, had lost his marbles. Back in England his ex-wife, the imperious Lady Wenlake, would rage that he was letting the family down, his son and daughter . . . but so what? It would be worth it.

His thoughts were interrupted by Marissa.

'Let's drink a toast,' she was saying softly, handing him the glass of champagne he'd left on the bedside table. 'Here's to a happy New Year. I think it's going to be the best one yet.'

'I'll drink to that, my darling.'

Chapter One

FLASH . . . Rebecca aimed the camera, steadied it and clicked, catching the host, Sir Edward Wenlake, as he greeted a new arrival, in that second freezing his smile on celluloid for posterity. He looked tall and elegant in a hand-made Savile Row dinner-jacket, and she admired the charm and amiability he exuded as he moved from room to room, making introductions, offering drinks and mingling with everyone; the perfect host, suave and gracious, his thick white hair groomed and gleaming under the shimmering chandeliers, his pale blue eyes languid and kindly. For a man his age he was also exceedingly attractive, and being single was on the top of every New York hostess's guest list.

FLASH . . . Rebecca focused her Leica on a tall blonde girl with long silvery hair, wearing a black sequinned mini-dress. She was reported in all the gossip columns to be Sir Edward's latest girlfriend although she was young enough to be his daughter. Even, at a pinch, his granddaughter. Rebecca clicks away, remembering that Marissa lived in the Trump Tower and that nothing else was really known about her. FLASH . . . FLASH . . . FLASH . . . Smiling broadly, Marissa poses for the camera and Rebecca sees a deep insecurity in the girl's eyes. Despite the radiant smile . . . and yet Marissa Montclare was supposed to have everything any young woman could ever wish for: beauty, great personal wealth, a palatial apartment, above all a distinguished lover. Rebecca took a final shot and moved on.

FLASH . . . Brian Norris, the forty-eight-year-old Vice-Chairman of the Tollemache Trust, posed with his wife in front of one of the apartment's marble mantelpieces, over which hung a Reynolds of a Wenlake ancestor. Of average height and build, Brian habitually looks as if he is about to pick a fight with someone. His small feet are planted aggressively wide and his chin sticks out, while his grey eyes range watchfully around the room. Unlike Sir Edward who, from the moment of birth, had moved continuously sideways on the social graph of life, from prep school and Eton

5

through to Caius College, Cambridge and thence the business world where thirty-six years previously he formed the Tollemache Trust, Brian had clawed his way up via the state school system and working in a supermarket in the north of England.

Only by taking evening classes and correspondence courses had he been able to join a southern finance company as a junior clerk. Married by this time to an ambitious girl from a background similar to his own, Brian threw himself into work and in time his street-wise business acumen came to the notice of Sir Edward. Now, fifteen years later, he'd reached the top and was determined to stay there. His wealth and power gave him a heady god-like sensation at times, a feeling that he was an early product and a perfect example of the Thatcherite philosophy: "Seek and ye shall find. Work and ye shall be rewarded." By his side, Christine, her face as carefully painted as a model's, her body tinged yellow from too many sessions under the sun lamp, Rebecca noted, seemed determined to keep up with Brian. If he could scale the dizzy heights of entrepreneurial success, so could she. Taking a look at Marissa Montclare shortly after their arrival, Christine had pronounced her to be 'dead common', but not without a hint of jealousy in her carefully modulated voice.

Rebecca continued to work the rooms steadily and methodically, a tall slim figure in dark silk trousers and mandarin-style jacket, her long brown hair held back by a black velvet bow at the nape of her neck, taking more pictures than were necessary to complete her photo-feature on Sir Edward which had been commissioned by the British magazine *Hello!*, but knowing that his New Year's Eve party was a special landmark in Manhattan's social calendar. Everyone who was anyone was present, from the cream of aristocratic society to the super-rich and the most famous celebrities of the moment. Sir Edward's address book read like a mixture of the social register and *Burke's Peerage*, with a healthy handful of artists, opera singers and ballet stars thrown in, and as Rebecca circuited the apartment it seemed that every name within it had been summoned tonight to celebrate the end of the old year and the start of the new.

They stood clustered in the library where leatherbound books filled the shelves from floor to ceiling and richly carved mahogany furniture gleamed in the apricot lamplight; they gathered in the drawing-room with its delicate French chairs and ornate gilt mirrors; and they assembled in the dining-room where a long buffet, piled high with delicacies, was placed down one side of the red-brocaded room, and the crystal chandelier cast rainbow reflections on the walls. Her camera hung on a silk cord from her neck, a black leather bag filled with extra lenses and films slung from her shoulder,

Rebecca took dozens of shots, knowing she'd have to get Sir Edward to supply the guests' names afterwards.

'Good *eve*-ning!' A middle-aged woman with fabulous rubies and diamonds and a tightly stretched face came up to her. It was Mrs Tom Dempsey, an avid socialite whose main aim in life was to be regularly featured in *Women's Wear Daily*.

Rebecca smiled politely, knowing this gushing matron's evening would be ruined if she wasn't photographed. It was as if she had to see photographs of herself in magazines to be sure she existed at all. 'Good evening.' Might as well get it over with, Rebecca thought. 'May I take a picture of you? Over here by the flowers?'

The relief at being asked made the older woman flush with pleasure. 'Oh! Do you *really* want to take my picture, my dear?' she asked coyly. 'Well . . .' She hesitated just long enough for it to look good. 'Well . . . if you *insist*!'

The picture taken, Mrs Tom Dempsey moved on, no longer as friendly. Her mission had been accomplished and it wouldn't do for her friends to see her cultivating a photographer, not even one as famous as Rebecca Kendall.

Rebecca, at twenty-five, had carved a unique niche for herself as a freelance photographer of international repute. Her rise from the obscurity of a keen amateur to the heights of professional acclaim had been meteoric. The only daughter of a New Hampshire paediatrician and his schoolteacher wife, she had been fascinated by photography ever since her parents gave her a camera for her tenth birthday. She took pictures of everything – the family dog, the cat with its kittens, and her two younger brothers whom she bribed with chocolate to sit still. Family outings and picnics were recorded in detail, and at the age of twelve she drove her whole family crazy by insisting on covering all their activities, from dawn to dusk, in order to create what she called 'A Day in the Lives of the Kendall Family'.

In due course her pocket-money went to buy a new and better camera, and she started entering contests, and winning prizes. Rebecca possessed that rare combination, an artistic eye coupled with technical ability. In that magical split second that makes all the difference between an adequate picture and a brilliant one, her sense of timing was instinctive. She would catch a swimmer at the exact moment he entered the water from a high dive, or a tennis player precisely as he lunged forward to take a low volley; she would get a shot of a cat as it leapt into the air to catch a butterfly, or a baby as it smiled fleetingly. All everyday events, but Rebecca brought to them a quality that made them outstanding photographs.

When she persuaded her parents to let her go to New York at the age of nineteen, she got a job immediately with a fashion photographer. She wasn't allowed to take many pictures but the general training, especially in the darkroom, proved invaluable. After two years she took the gamble of going freelance, and it paid off. Now, her photographs were in demand with leading newspapers and magazines all over the world; she'd even done a series of studies of the President's wife 'at home'.

At that moment Sir Edward came up to her and placed his arm around her waist.

'Everything all right, darling?' he asked, in his friendly fashion. Rebecca had realized some time before that he called all women 'darling' because he couldn't remember their names. By the same token all men were 'old chap'.

'Everything's fine,' she replied breezily. 'I've nearly finished. I'm going to take a few more "candid" shots and that'll be it.'

'Wonderful! And you will look after yourself, darling, won't you? You've been working so hard. Do have some champagne and something to eat.' With a smile he moved on, still oozing charm but in such a blatantly disarming manner that Rebecca forgave him. It was people like Sir Edward who added a little glamour to life. Disconnecting her flash unit, she re-loaded her 35mm Leica with faster film and set to work again.

Using only the available light that spilled from silk-shaded lamps or chandeliers, Rebecca was able to work more discreetly now, putting on record – mostly for her own benefit – the cream of New York society with its guard down. Not the type of shot she'd ever submit to *Vanity Fair* or *Town and Country*, she reflected, chuckling to herself as she captured coiffeured matrons beaming through their bridgework, and middle-aged tycoons relaxing their stomach muscles for a moment. One day she planned to compile a coffee-table book of all her candid shots, entitled *Private Parties*. Meanwhile she clicked away, catching those tell-tale moments when people don't think they're being observed: a newly engaged girl having another squint at her engagement ring and wishing it were bigger; a jealous wife watching her husband flirt with a beautiful bimbo; a hungry-looking woman trying to catch the eye of the man she's in love with . . . while his wife is at his side!

Through the viewfinder, Rebecca saw it all, life's little triumphs and tragedies ready to be captured on film while no one noticed what she was doing. Some time before she'd copied an idea from the world-famous photographer, Henri Cartier-Bresson, that enabled him to work discreetly and unobserved. She'd had all the shining silver parts of her camera enamelled black, so that it did not glint in the light and attract attention. Her Leica was now no more noticeable than a small, slim, black purse. For Rebecca, the great advantage was that people didn't start posing and putting on what she called their 'photogenic expressions' as soon as she appeared.

At that moment Marissa came into the room and looked around. She didn't notice Rebecca and her camera this time, and so the flashing smile was missing and the eyes were troubled as she seemed to search for a face in the crowded room. Rebecca clicked away for no better reason than the girl interested her. But then most of Manhattan was interested in Marissa. Three months ago no one had ever heard of her, and even now no one knew where she came from or who she was. But since she had become Sir Edward's latest paramour everyone wanted to find out. The town was buzzing with talk and all the gossip columns were featuring the two of them wherever they went. The cocktail party circuit was crazy with fascination and not just because the name Marissa Montclare couldn't be real, or because she was a delicious looking twenty year old and Sir Edward-ought-to-know-better-than-to-go-with-a-young-girl-at-his-age. The most surprising fact was that Marissa appeared to be a millionairess in her own right. Some people even thought she had as much money as Sir Edward. The question everyone was asking was: where the hell did she get it from?

Rebecca wandered into the master bedroom to freshen up and found a group of gossiping women sitting on Sir Edward's bed, which was set in a niche of heavily festooned cigar brown velvet and silk draperies. She shuddered. It was not her style at all. Then she remembered she wasn't here because it was her style, but because she'd been asked to do a photo-feature on a man famed for both his flamboyance and his brilliance. Shrugging, she went over to his dressing-table, noting the ivory-backed brushes inlaid with the Wenlake crest in silver, and a valuable antique dressing-case equipped with silver-topped jars and bottles, scissors, button hooks and a nail buffer, were arranged neatly on top.

Staring into the mirror, she regarded herself solemnly for a moment. Her pale skin was clear and had a luminous glow; her perfectly symmetrical bone structure, inherited from her handsome father, was enhanced by large hazel eyes fringed with long lashes. But Rebecca disregarded her own beauty. She'd always been more interested in what was going on than in how she looked, and so she nonchalantly flicked back her hair and returned to the party.

It was nearly midnight. In Times Square the giant multi-faceted steel ball would soon be lowered to signify the end of the year, and the crowds would be singing and kissing and cheering and hugging.

9

For a moment she wished she could be out there as she'd been in previous years, taking pictures of all the happy faces and being part of the scene.

After taking some more photographs in the dining-room and library, she made her way back to the drawing-room where Sir Edward was urging everyone to fill their glasses ready for the toast. There was a forced excitement in the atmosphere now, as if all the guests were bad actors who had been asked to take part in the crowd scene of a lavish Italian movie.

'Come along everyone!' Sir Edward called out jovially. He'd been drinking throughout the evening and wasn't too steady on his feet. 'Only two minutes to go! Fill up your glasses.'

Afterwards, Rebecca was to remember that it was at this moment that Marissa came hurrying across the room, pushing past people, her face a ghastly white and her eyes shocked. She rushed up to Sir Edward and tugged at his arm saying something, to which he paid no attention. He was full of jocularity, his charged glass raised and his face flushed with merriment. Rebecca couldn't hear what Marissa was saying above the conversation, but as she spoke to Sir Edward she seemed to be pleading, and there was no mistaking the fear in her eyes as she tried to make herself understood. Then he turned away to throw his arms around a friend in a bear-hug, laughing loudly as he did so, and Marissa ran out of the room, her hand up to her mouth as if to stifle a sob.

As she disappeared into the adjoining library, the antique grand-father clock in the hall started striking twelve, its pure sharp chimes cutting across the babble. Sir Edward raised his glass and shouted: 'Happy New Year!'

Like a chorus everyone took up the words. 'Happy New Year! Happy . . . Happy . . . New . . . New . . . Year . . . Year!'

With a clink of glasses and a chatter of voices they all kissed and hugged and drank champagne and wished each other well, and above all, louder than the rest, Sir Edward's voice repeatedly boomed: 'Happy New Year! Happy New Year!'

And then Rebecca heard it. A woman's scream, so piercingly agonized that she froze. It seemed to echo in her head, resounding in its awfulness. She found she couldn't move. Her feet seemed stuck to the carpet, her throat had seized up, and something deep inside her seemed to be quivering on the brink of terror. Her camera, always so busy recording everything she saw that it was like an extension of herself, hung immobile from her neck, its shutter closed. People were looking at each other with stricken faces and a pall of silence hung over them all as if the very rooms were holding

10

their breath. Then, across Rebecca's line of vision, Sir Edward seemed to float, waxen white, his eyes pools of agony.

'What's happened?' she heard him roar. Suddenly the room erupted in a garbled cacophony of cries.

'Oh, Jesus!'

'Marissa's fallen!'

'My God!'

'Christ, how did it happen?'

'She must have died instantly.'

'She was drunk.'

'She slipped.'

'She fell.'

'She was pushed!'

'It was an accident!'

'Call an ambulance!'

'Call the police!'

Rebecca struggled through the jostling crowd of instantly sobered guests and entered the library where the icy night air flowed in through an open window and people stood, dazed with disbelief, staring out into the darkness as if expecting Marissa to reappear. Distantly the faint sound of revellers, singing in the New Year, floated up from the street. The lights of Manhattan blazed frostily, and fourteen floors below Marissa Montclare lay sprawled on the sidewalk, her sequinned mini-dress glinting in the darkness.

A shining bright New Year, full of hope, had stolen across the roof-tops of the city, leaving a trail of hangovers not yet realized and good resolutions not yet broken; and a mysterious young woman had died at one of the smartest parties of the season.

Automatically, Rebecca raised her camera and started taking pictures of everyone and everything in sight. Already there were too many questions about a girl who had called herself Marissa Montclare, to go unanswered.

'Is this it? Are you sure you'll be OK?' Jerry Ribis, a young man Rebecca had met at the party, drew his car up to the kerb outside a converted warehouse where she had her apartment. It was nearly four o'clock in the morning.

'Sure. It was very kind of you to bring me home,' she replied gratefully. 'Cabs are scarce on New Year's Eve. I was going to take the subway.'

'The subway!' he exclaimed. 'You shouldn't go on the subway . . . ever. It's much too dangerous.' He looked through the car window at the picturesque old buildings of the street in which they were parked. 'I don't know this area. What's it like? This is TriBeCa, isn't it?'

Rebecca smiled in spite of the crushing tiredness that was rapidly enveloping her. This sweet young man, who'd told her he was a lawyer, obviously confined his activities to the Upper East Side of Manhattan, to clients who lived in areas like Sutton Place and Beekman Place, and to the *crème de la crème* of society.

'Yes,' she said patiently. 'It's called TriBeCa because this is the triangle below Canal Street. It's become very fashionable . . . see all those boutiques and restaurants? And there are a lot of art galleries too. It's all very trendy around here.'

'And you have an apartment in this old warehouse?' Jerry's voice sounded wondering. She could sense what he was thinking: What a strange place for a girl to live.

'That's right. I moved here two years ago. What I like about the area is that there are no skyscrapers. I think the highest building is only six floors.' She opened the car door and eased herself out, her camera bag clutched in her arms. 'Thanks again for the lift.'

'It's been a strange and dreadful night, hasn't it?' Jerry said as he got out of the car and walked her to her door. 'I feel as if yesterday was ten years ago.'

Rebecca nodded. 'I know exactly what you mean. I feel as if I haven't been to bed for ten years either. I don't think I'll ever forget tonight.'

'I don't think any of us will.' He looked thoughtful. 'She was very young to die.'

'Too young,' Rebecca replied succinctly.

The stairs creaked as she climbed to the third floor and opened the front door as silently as she could so as not to disturb her roommate, Karen Rossini. Sleep would be impossible; the events of the past few hours were so deeply etched on her mind that she still felt in shock, going over those terrible moments again and again, as if she were replaying them on a VCR: Marissa's fearful scream; the frozen silence that followed before all hell broke loose; Sir Edward's panic-stricken eyes; and then Brian Norris's strange behaviour . . . as if he saw the situation only as a potential scandal, not the tragic loss of a young life.

Going quietly into the kitchen, Rebecca put on some coffee. She decided that as she couldn't sleep she'd develop the films she'd taken at the party – although, as she'd told the police, she was unlikely to have anything pertinent to show them because she'd been in the drawing-room when it had happened. 'It', was what they all said, or 'the incident'. Nobody said 'when Marissa fell' or 'when Marissa died'.

As the percolator bubbled, her mind went back to Brian Norris and the way he'd taken charge of everything. 'Sir Edward's retired to his bedroom . . . shock, you know,' he'd murmured in an almost conspiratorial tone. 'It was a terrible accident . . . a terrible thing to happen.' He moved from group to group, soothing the horrified guests, squeezing hands, patting shoulders. 'I don't think any of us saw anything, did we? Unless we're careful this could turn into a lengthy investigation . . . and we're all busy people, aren't we? I think the less we say . . . don't you agree? None of us want to be more involved than necessary, do we?' Coaxing and persuasive, Brian repeated the phrases like a mantra, subtly briefing the guests on the line he expected them to take. When he came up to Rebecca, she looked at him stonily.

'I'm sure we can count on your discretion,' he said pointedly. 'This is going to be tough enough on Sir Edward as it is. He was very fond of Marissa. I think, for his sake, the sooner this business is wrapped up the better, don't you? I mean, nothing's going to bring her back . . . we'll probably never know what made her fall . . . but the polished floor, of course . . . a lot of champagne . . . it was very hot in the room . . .' His voice drifted off, hinting at all the possible causes of the tragic accident.

Rebecca didn't reply but she noticed there was much nodding of heads and several people looked at each other, muttering. Then it seemed that while they waited for the police to arrive, many of the guests slipped out the back door of the apartment, several leaving their fur coats behind. Rats deserting the sinking ship, she thought. The crunch had come. Sir Edward would soon know who his real friends were.

While Rebecca waited for the coffee to brew, she went into the spare bedroom she'd had turned into a darkroom. Most of the time she sent her films to a nearby laboratory to be developed and printed – they processed all her colour work, for instance – but in emergencies or when she wanted to do some experimental black and white printing, she liked to do it herself. She'd taken eight black and white films at the party; each 35mm film had thirty-two frames which meant she'd end up with two hundred and sixty shots in all. Surely one of them would hold a clue as to what had really happened that night.

'Is that you, Rebecca?' a small voice asked in the passage behind her.

'God, Karen, you scared me half to death!' Rebecca spun round and saw her roommate standing sleepily in the doorway. Karen wore a knee-length blue T-shirt with a picture of Mickey Mouse on the front. Her blonde-streaked hair hung in a tousled cloud round her face. 'I'm sorry, did I wake you?' Rebecca said contritely.

Karen yawned widely and leaned against the wall. 'It's OK. I haven't been in long myself. What are you doing in the darkroom at this hour?'

Rebecca lined up the films she'd taken in a neat row on the workbench. 'I'm going to put these through in a minute, but I'm having some coffee first. Want some?'

Karen considered for a moment, her head on one side, and then replied: 'Yeah, why not? I probably won't get back to sleep anyway.'

In the bright little kitchen, they climbed on to two high stools with red seats on either side of the narrow bar top where they ate all their meals. The fragrant aroma of coffee permeated the room as Rebecca filled two big mugs patterned with scarlet poppies.

Karen took a sip and then let out a sigh of contentment. 'Ah, that's good. I needed that. I had a fight with Tony at the party, told him I wasn't going to see him again, and it's left me all strung out.'

'Oh?' Absently, Rebecca toyed with the sugar bowl.

'D'you know what he did?' Karen was wide awake now, her grey eyes sparking with remembered anger.

'What did he do?' There was a touch of resignation in Rebecca's voice. Karen and her string of boyfriends could be a bit tedious at times. Sooner or later her relationships ended in a flurry of fights and acrimony, and Rebecca always seemed to be the one who had to intercept persistent phone calls and make excuses.

'Well, you know we were going to a party given by a girl called Caro? So we arrive and we meet a girl called Zoe, and d'you know what Tony did? He screwed her! Right at the party! IN THE NEXT ROOM! so we could hear everything! Can you beat it?' Karen wriggled indignantly and took another swig of coffee. 'I know I've only had a couple of dates with him but have you ever heard of such *gross* behaviour? Right there at the party! What a son-of-a-bitch!'

Rebecca's face registered the right amount of shock-horror to mollify Karen's wounded pride. 'What was this Zoe like?'

'I should have known what would happen as soon as I saw her,' replied Karen in disgust. 'She had that sort of look, you know? Bedroom eyes, and her clothes a sort of contrived mess. We were all sitting on the floor drinking and talking, and Zoe goes and sits in front of Tony. But I mean right in front! Between his knees! And then what does she do? She leans back against his crotch and starts rubbing her back against him! Have you ever heard of anything so crass?'

Rebecca agreed she hadn't. 'Maybe she did you a favour, though.'

Karen glared. 'What do you mean?'

14

'If Tony can be seduced as easily as all that, do you really want to hang out with him?'

Karen considered the question, and then said reluctantly: 'I suppose you could be right, but he was sort of sweet and he had the most gorgeous wavy hair.'

'Oh, Karen, *really*!' Rebecca scolded, although she was laughing. 'Anyway, how was your party? Anything exciting happen?'

'You could say that,' Rebecca replied, serious again. 'A girl called Marissa Montclare . . .'

'Who?'

Rebecca continued . . . 'She was Sir Edward Wenlake's latest girlfriend and she fell from a window of his apartment on the fourteenth floor, and in my opinion she was pushed.' Saying it, coming right out with it like that, convinced her she was right. Marissa hadn't 'fallen' or 'slipped' and it hadn't been an accident, as Brian Norris had insisted. If Rebecca was sure of anything at that moment it was that Marissa had been murdered and she'd known minutes before that it was going to happen. That's what she'd been trying to tell Sir Edward. That's why she'd run out of the room, sobbing with terror.

'What?' Karen stared at Rebecca, appalled. 'You mean, someone actually pushed her out of the window? Who?'

'I don't know. It's only a feeling I have. The police were treating it as an accident when they came to the apartment, but I think they were led to believe that by the Vice-Chairman of Sir Edward's company. He took charge of everything after it happened, obviously desperate to avoid a scandal. Perhaps for Sir Edward's sake or the company's . . . perhaps for his own.'

Karen drew in a deep breath. 'My God, how awful! Did the police question you?'

'Yes, but I couldn't help much. I'm hoping something relevant might show up on one of my films but I'm not sure what.'

'It's a terrible thing to say, but what a scoop for you! You've got real luck, d'you know that, Becky? Things seem to happen when you're around with your camera. Did you get any pictures of this girl tonight?'

'Yup.'

'There you go! You've taken the last pictures ever of her, before she died. All the papers will want them.'

Rebecca knew what Karen said was true, but she did not relish the fact that her luck tonight had been because of someone else's death. She *was* lucky, though she was sure a lot of her 'luck' was of her own making. It was she who'd convinced her parents to let her live and work in New York. It was she who'd decided that photo-journalism was what she wanted to do. Then she smiled to herself, knowing the best bit of luck had been when she'd met Stirling Hertfelder, her agent, her friend and her lover. Stirling had helped to make her successful and in time he'd make her rich as well. He owned the Hertfelder Agency, handling the work of a couple of dozen top photographers, some in fashion, some in advertising, and a few photo-journalists like herself.

'Becky, you've got it all!' Karen was saying. 'Nice family, a gorgeous boyfriend, and a brilliant career! What more does a girl want?'

Rebecca laughed. 'Right now, a good night's sleep.'

'Ha!' mocked Karen. 'Some people don't know when they're fortunate. Stirling has the looks of Tom Cruise and the personality of Dustin Hoffman – and what do *I* get? A jerk who screws another girl at the party I take him to! Right under my nose! There ain't no justice in this world.' She ran her hands through the tangle of honey-coloured curls that fell to her shoulders and gave a big sigh.

'You're right,' said Rebecca. 'Well, I'm off to the darkroom. Why don't you go back to bed?'

'I suppose I might as well.' Karen climbed off the stool, yawning again. 'Let me know if you find anything interesting.'

'You bet I will. See you for breakfast.'

Rebecca shut herself in the darkroom and automatically threw the 'No Entry' switch that turned on an amber warning light outside the door. Then she checked the mixture of hydroquinine, sodium hydroxide and sodium sulphite in which she developed the films, making sure it was at 68°F. Seating herself on a high stool, similar to the ones in the kitchen, she arranged the equipment on the bench before her. Then she turned off the ruby red safe-light, plunging the room into pitch blackness. From now on, and until the films were in the developer, she'd have to use all the skills required of a blind person. Each roll of film had to be carefully removed from its cartridge and loaded on to a steel reel, without buckling or kinking the sensitive emulsion. Feeling her way, she loaded all eight and then placed the reels into a metal rack before lowering them into the tank of chemicals. Then, with a sigh of relief because the trickiest part was over, she set the luminous timer to go off in seven and a half minutes and fixed the bakelite lid over the tank.

She worked quickly and skilfully, familiar with the layout of the darkroom she'd designed herself, with its 'wet' bench with tanks and a sink down one side, and its 'dry' bench with enlarger and printing materials down the other. She knew exactly where

16

everything was. No one else was ever allowed to touch anything.

When the timer pinged loudly she lifted the rack out of the developer and plunged it into an adjoining tank containing an acid stop bath, before finally putting the films in fixer. She had run through this routine so many hundreds of times she could almost do it in her sleep; the next step would be to submerge the rack under running water for half an hour and then the films would be ready to hang, like a line of washing, in the drying cabinet. Finally, the moment came when she would cut the strips into eight negative lengths, before printing them.

Two hours later Rebecca was looking at a sheet of contacts through a magnifying glass, realizing at that moment that she might have discovered how Marissa Montclare had died.

Chapter Two

Lady Wenlake awoke late on New Year's Day to the sounds of angry shouting beneath the bedroom window of her house in Wiltshire.

'It's a fucking disgrace!'

'You're nothing more than murderers!'

'We'll put a stop to it . . .'

'GET OFF OUR LAND!'

The last voice belonged to her son, Simon. Startled, she jumped out of bed and pulled back the rose-patterned chintz curtains. Peering through the window, anxious to keep out of sight, she drew a sharp intake of breath as a wave of anger and disbelief flowed over her. Her hands started to shake. How *dare* they? How dare those people come on to her property. Right up to her front door.

Brandishing sticks and placards with the words 'Animal Rights Activists' emblazoned on them, was a motley collection of youngish men and women. They had gathered in the front drive of Pinkney House, where Lady Wenlake's family had lived since 1745. They were yelling abuse at her twenty-six-year-old son, Simon, who stood on the doorstep, a vivid figure in his Pink Hunting coat, which contrasted vividly with the protestors' green and brown anoraks.

'Get off our land,' Angela Wenlake heard him shout again, but nobody seemed to be paying any attention.

The Howich Hunt always held its Meet at Pinkney on New Year's Day, and she wasn't going to have this tradition spoiled by a lot of stupid townspeople who felt sorry for a fox! The fox enjoyed the chase; everyone knew that. Hunting was part of England's heritage and there was no finer sight in the world than a meeting of magnificent horseflesh, mounted by people wearing proper hunting clothes, the men in their Pink coats and the women riding side-saddle, in black habits, with hounds primed to charge across fields and over fences in pursuit of their quarry.

Lady Wenlake snorted, enraged by the audacity of those whom

she considered to be dangerous fanatics. The countryside, even the suburbs, was swarming with foxes these days, and, she thought darkly, it would soon be swarming with mink as well because these activists were always creeping into places at night and releasing captive animals. They broke into laboratories too, releasing rabbits and rats and mice which were probably carriers of all sorts of dreadful diseases.

Dressing hurriedly in her usual impeccable tweeds, she ran a brush through her greying curls, permed tightly because that was how ladies, such as the Queen, had their hair done, and put on a quick dab of red lipstick. At that moment there was a knock on her bedroom door.

'Who is it?' she called.

'It's me, Mummy.'

'Come in, child. Have you seen what's going on?'

Jenny entered the room, a softer plumper version of her mother, but with her father's lazy blue eyes. Her fair hair hung without style or shape to her shoulders and she wore a skirt that was much too long and a sweater in a drab shade of green.

'What shall we do?' she asked uncertainly.

'I'll tell you what we'll do,' Angela retorted crossly, 'we'll teach these Animal Rights Activists, or whatever they call themselves, a lesson! The Howich Hunt has had its Meet here on New Year's Day for the past fifty years. I'm not going to let a bunch of dangerous lunatics stop us now.' With that she strode back to the window, and leaning far out, shouted to the people on the drive below: 'Hey! You there!'

Startled, the throng fell silent, gaping up in amazement at the autocratic face of Lady Wenlake. Her features were flushed with anger and her mouth was tight and grim.

'This is private property. Kindly leave at once or I shall call the police. You are trespassing!'

A moment's stunned silence was followed by angry jeering, and a man tried to imitate the way she talked.

'Oh, we're trespassing, are we?' he mimicked. 'Well, fancy that. Beg pardon, Your Ladyship, I'm sure!' Some of the others sniggered and moved nearer the house, but a thin pale young man with a lot of hair shook his fist and yelled: 'Murderess!'

'Call the police now,' Angela commanded Jenny, over her shoulder but loud enough to be heard by those down below. 'I will not tolerate this behaviour on my land.'

Simon, who had himself been rather stunned by his mother's outburst, felt he ought to do something dramatic to back her up.

These ghastly people, who all looked as if they came from towns rather than the country, hadn't listened when he'd shouted before so he decided to try other tactics. Going back through the portico of Pinkney House, he re-emerged a moment later with his riding crop clenched in his hand.

'Be off with you!' he thundered, his fine blond hair ruffled by the strong breeze. 'Go away! The police will be here in a minute!'

His antics had about as much effect as a dripping tap on a forest fire. The sight of him brandishing a riding crop made some of the activists angrier than ever, and for a moment Simon thought they were going to charge him with their placards.

'Get back!' he yelled, a touch of hysteria making his voice rise. 'You've no right to be here.'

At that moment about twenty mounted members of the Hunt, on a variety of valuable mounts, came trotting briskly up the long drive to the house. They were led by the Master, accompanied by the whipper-in and hounds who scurried about excitedly, sniffing the ground. Last came fifty or sixty followers on foot; people who hadn't missed a New Year's Day Meet in twenty years. They would bring their children with them, gazing in admiration at the sight of the Hunt gathering in the drive, to drink the stirrup-cup which the butler and his staff would serve in small glasses from their silver trays.

Pinkney House had originally been built in the Elizabethan era and then added on to during the reign of William and Mary. Against the elegant facade of chequered brick in shades of mellow rose and beige, the horses and riders looked as if they belonged to another age, a time when elegance predominated and the privileged classes ruled the land. The dazzling scarlet of the huntsmen's coats, always referred to as 'Pink' in deference to Mr Pink, the original tailor to have made riding habits for the élite, stood out in brilliant contrast to the white breeches and shining leather boots worn by the majority of men. Some of the older women still rode side-saddle, with cleverly draped black skirts covering their legs, their features softened by a veiled black silk top hat.

Now, as they grouped and re-grouped in the drive, the men doffing their hats to the ladies in greeting, the ladies adjusting their white string gloves as they held their reins, the horses pawing the ground impatiently, all eagerly waited for the Master's signal that the Hunt could begin. Any minute now he would blow his horn.

'A proper picture they make, don't they?' remarked a woman from the village to her friend.

'Yes, just like them table-mats,' said the other, with deep appreciation.

21

But many of the followers were angry today as they hurried up the drive, scowling at the invaders who had dared to come into their community to try and wreck something as traditional as the Meet. Some carried walking-sticks which they held purposefully before them; others spiky-looking umbrellas.

Soon the drive was packed with people on horseback, people on foot, and hounds, which the whipper-in was trying to keep away from the protestors lest they be fed with poisoned morsels. The Animal Rights Activists tried to spread out in an effort to encircle those on horseback. They waved their banners and shouted, making the horses nervous. Someone yelled something and a grey horse reared, nearly unseating the young lady on his back. A scuffle broke out between protestors and followers, and someone took one of the placards and smashed it. The mood was getting ugly. Watching from her window, Lady Wenlake felt apprehensive. Suppose one of the horses was hurt?

'The police are on their way,' said Jenny, coming back into the room.

'Why on earth didn't anyone wake me this morning?' her mother demanded irritably. 'You knew the Meet was today. I should have been down hours ago and then none of this would have happened.'

Jenny pointed to the antique table that stood by the large Empire bed, with its yellow brocade draperies and antique lace-edged sheets and pillow cases. 'There's your early morning tea. You haven't drunk it. Didn't you hear when it was brought in?'

'Obviously not.' Angela Wenlake knew the reason she'd overslept was because she'd given a big dinner-party for New Year's Eve, and had drunk a lot of champagne followed by several brandies. She looked out of the window again. The Master, an elderly titled landowner who was even more autocratic by nature than Angela, was ordering the activists to get away from the horses. They in turn were shouting abuse and throwing a few missiles. It seemed as if a skirmish would break out any minute.

'I'm going down,' said Angela. 'This thing's getting out of hand.'

'Mummy, you can't!' It was only family loyalty that prevented Jenny herself from protesting with the Animal Rights Activists. She thought hunting, and shooting and fishing for that matter, cruel and unnecessary.

At that moment they heard the sound of police sirens, and up the drive came a convoy of white cars, their blue roof-lights flashing.

The effect on the activists was startling. Some stood their ground defiantly, but the majority dropped their placards and fled, lolloping away over fences and fields.

As Lady Wenlake emerged from the house, her head held imperiously high, her son smirking bravely now the enemy was in retreat, all that could be seen of their uninvited guests was green and beige backviews, bobbing away over field and fence into the distance. The remaining few had been quietly and efficiently arrested by the police.

'Well done, m'dear!' said the Master, his white moustache bristling. He'd known Angela Wenlake since she'd been a young girl and she was a woman after his own heart: strong, capable, and unafraid. 'Give the blighters a run for their money. Damned cheek, coming on to your land like that.'

Angela nodded vigorously. 'A bunch of lay-abouts. I bet they're all living on social security. That type don't know what it is to do a proper day's work!'

The hunt was about to set off, and she watched them go with a pang of regret. If it hadn't been for a bad riding accident many years ago in which she had injured her back, she'd have been out with the Meet every week during the season.

She waved goodbye to Simon as he trotted off on Clover, the roan mare she'd given him for Christmas, and her heart swelled with pride at the sight. Vicariously, she was able to live a part of her life through her beloved son. They shared the thirty-room mansion she'd inherited from her father and she was determined they always would, even if he married. They also had the same interests and love of the countryside. More like a surrogate husband and less like a son, Simon was Angela's constant companion. In her opinion he was everything that Edward wasn't. But then, she reasoned, you moulded your children the way you wanted them to be. Husbands came as they were, for better or worse – in her case certainly for worse; sons could be shaped as they grew into perfect men.

Jenny broke in on her thoughts. 'Do you want some breakfast, Mummy?'

Angela glanced at her daughter, taking in the fair colouring and the English peaches and cream skin, noting with an unpleasant, almost painful stab, Edward's eyes, languid and torpid, looking at her.

'I'll have some coffee,' she said briskly, turning to go indoors. 'I think it's a great pity you didn't go with the hunt, it would have done you good.'

Jenny sighed softly. 'Mummy, we've been through this a thousand times. I don't like hunting. I don't even like horses very much, so what's the point of my traipsing all over the countryside for hours on end being miserable? I've a lot of reading I want to catch up with before I return to London. The Christmas holidays are short enough as it is without my doing things I don't want to do.' Jenny taught six to eight year olds at a smart private kindergarten in London, where she shared a flat with two girlfriends. She seldom stayed at Pinkney House choosing instead to visit her father in New York as often as possible during the school holidays, much to her mother's annoyance.

'Well, it's your life, I suppose,' Angela Wenlake said grudgingly. 'I still think it's a great pity. You meet some very nice young men on the hunting field.'

In silence they entered the house again and crossed the large square baronial hall, its panelled walls embellished with priceless Grinling Gibbons carving, the stone-flagged floor strewn with Persian rugs, and in the centre stood a large round oak table bearing an arrangement of flowers from the greenhouse, the morning newspapers and the post on a silver tray.

Gathering up her letters and copies of the *Times, Daily Mail* and *Telegraph*, Angela strode ahead into the dining-room. Jenny followed, and having helped herself to grilled kidneys and bacon from a silver dish on the sideboard, seated herself at the long table, which Peters the butler had laid for breakfast immediately after last night's dinner-party.

In continued silence, Jenny and her mother read the newspapers. There was a mention in *The Times* of the Tollemache Trust's acquisition of a famous brewery company. Jenny read it with avid interest.

'Have you seen this?' she asked, handing the paper to her mother. 'Daddy seems to have pulled off quite a coup.'

Angela glanced at it dispassionately. Since their divorce eleven years ago, on the grounds of his adultery with Simon's and Jenny's nanny, she'd taken only a passing interest in Edward's activities. He might be a business genius, but as far as she was concerned he was a lecherous roué who had brought disgrace on her noble family by forcing her to be its first member to seek a divorce. Adding insult to injury he was also only the son of a second baronet, whilst her family, the Ponsonby-Hadleigh-Edmunds, could trace their lineage back to 1640 when one of her ancestors had been a Lord-in-Waiting to Queen Elizabeth.

'Hmm,' she said dismissively, pouring herself another cup of coffee.

After breakfast, Angela always went to her desk in the study to attend to household matters. Running Pinkney House, with its eighteen bedrooms, library, and billiard room where Queen

Victoria's husband, Prince Albert, was reported to have played whilst visiting Angela's great-great-grandparents; its dining-room, drawing-room, study, and a whole collection of smaller rooms behind the green baize door which separated the gentry's quarters from the servants', required a certain organizational ability. In a house this size something was always needing attention, whether it was a sash cord that needed replacing or a hinge that needed oiling. Then there were the gardens and surrounding thirty acres where oaks and elders, birch, lime and copper beech grew in profusion, dominated by a cedar of Lebanon that rose from the centre of the west lawn in towering majesty.

Angela gazed out of the window now, wishing it was summer. The garden looked bleak as it slumbered through the months from November to April, but in high summer it was a dazzling mass of lilies and lavender, begonias and buddleia, and creamy roses which tumbled over the low stone walls surrounding the sunken garden. In season one side of the house became shrouded by a two hundred-year-old wistaria hung thickly with amethyst blooms. Thankfully, she thought, as she made lists of things that required attention, she had a very good indoor and outdoor staff, including Fred, who looked after the horses.

At four o'clock, Simon returned from the hunting-field, splattered with mud but triumphant. 'We ran a big fellow to his lair!' he said gleefully as he struggled out of his fine leather boots in the hall. 'We had a long chase . . . right across Highclere meadow, through Dutchling Farm, round the edge of Sutton Wood and then just as we thought we'd lost him, he was cornered by hounds in that field beyond . . . y'know, that bit of land that belongs to the Chislehursts. Then the blighter doubled back to the wood and we got him just before he vanished down his lair!'

Angela beamed. 'Well done, darling! I'm glad you had a good run.'

'I don't suppose the fox would agree,' remarked Jenny drily.

'Oh, do shut up,' snapped Simon. 'You're as bad as those morons who were here this morning. It was a great kill.' He preened himself before the long mirror, well pleased with the day's activity.

'Why don't you have a nice hot bath and then we'll have tea?' Angela suggested.

'Good idea!' He sauntered off, tapping his thigh lightly with his riding crop.

Jenny glanced at her watch. 'I think I'll give Daddy a ring and wish him a Happy New Year. He'll be having breakfast, so it's a good time.'

The rigid set of Angela Wenlake's back expressed her disapproval. Not that she'd ever prevented the children contacting Edward, but she'd much rather they didn't. Her one fear was that Jenny would want to go and live in New York permanently, and then, as Angela told her friends, 'She'll *never* find a decent husband.'

'Shall I give him your love, Mummy?' Jenny was asking ingenuously.

Angela shot her a look that spoke volumes. 'You can wish him well for the New Year,' she said drily. 'As to love . . . no doubt he's suffering from a surfeit of that already.'

Jenny ignored the barb. In her opinion her father was entitled to girlfriends; he'd never remarried, and so he could do as he liked.

A voice she didn't recognize answered the phone.

'May I speak to Sir Edward Wenlake, please?' she said.

'Who wants him?'

The voice was brusque and English. Jenny supposed her father had employed a new manservant. Not a very polite one, it seemed.

'Oh, are you the butler? This is Miss Wenlake speaking.'

There was a lengthy pause, during which she heard an irritated exclamation.

'This is *not* the butler!' the voice said stiffly. 'I happen to be Brian Norris, Vice-Chairman of the Tollemache Trust. I presume you are Jenny?'

'Yes.' She hesitated, waiting for him to offer some explanation. When none was forthcoming she asked: 'May I speak to Daddy?'

'I'm afraid he's out.'

'Oh!' Jenny was taken aback by his curtness, and the fact that this man whom she'd never liked, seemed to be installed in the Park Avenue apartment. 'Would you ask him to give me a ring? Do you know how long he'll be?'

'Er . . . well, the thing is . . .' Brian seemed to be hedging. '. . . It's like this . . .'

'He's not ill, is he?' Jenny asked, alarmed.

'No-o-o-o.' He drew the word out, as if trying to make up his mind about something. 'He's not ill,' he said at last, 'but I suppose you're going to hear about it sooner or later, so I might as well tell you now.'

'What is it?'

'There was an accident at a party he gave last night . . . no, don't get in a panic! He's all right, but one of his guests died. He's down at the local precinct, making a statement.'

'Poor Daddy! How dreadful. What happened?' Her mind was

26

filled with visions of elderly people collapsing from heart attacks.

There was a harsh edge to Brian's voice. 'Nothing for you to worry about. Just one of those unfortunate things. Naturally, we're trying to play it down because anything like this is bad PR, so I'd be grateful if you didn't mention it to anyone.'

Jenny thought to remind him that she was on the other side of the Atlantic, and that she didn't know anyone who would be particularly interested anyway, but instead she said: 'Will you ask Daddy to get in touch with me, please? I'll be at home, at Pinkney all evening.'

'OK.' The phone crashed down and the line went dead.

'And thank you, too!' Jenny muttered angrily as she replaced the receiver. Of all the rude boorish men! What on earth was her father doing with a vice-chairman like Brian Norris, for God's sake?

Angela Wenlake came out of the drawing-room at that moment, passing Jenny where she sat by the phone in the hall. She raised her finely arched eyebrows.

'What's wrong?'

Jenny shook her head. 'Nothing. Daddy's out.' She paused for a moment then added: 'He'll ring me back later.'

Angela shrugged. What Edward did was of no concern to her.

Sir Edward Wenlake clambered wearily out of the chauffeur-driven Lincoln Continental which had picked him up from the local police headquarters, and was immediately surrounded by a jostling mob of television reporters, all shouting and pointing their cameras in his direction. Ducking and dodging around them were newspaper reporters and photographers, their flashlights blinding and dazzling him, their microphones thrust into his face as he tried to make the ten yards from the kerb to the entrance of his apartment building.

'How long had you known Marissa Montclare?'

'Were you planning to marry her?'

'How do you feel about her death?'

'How do you think it happened?'

'Please!' Sir Edward raised his hand, his gold crested signet ring flashing in the morning sun, as if to shield himself from the onslaught, as if to ward off this screeching bunch of media animals who were buzzing round him in a predatory way.

'Please . . . I have nothing to say.'

They were undaunted by his curt reply. If anything it galvanized them to renew their efforts to extract every ounce of information they could from this distinguished man whose face had suddenly grown old, and whose slim elegant body seemed on the verge of collapse. Stepping on each other's feet, elbowing each other out of the way, the media returned to the attack.

'Where did you meet Marissa?'

'What are you going to do now?'

'Where were you when she died?'

'Were you planning to marry her?'

FLASH – FLASH – FLASH – clicked the cameras; BLABBER – BLABBER – BLABBER – clamoured the voices, as jabbing microphones closed in around him, imprisoning him and binding him in a tangle of wire-linked equipment. It was a zealous inquisition by an angry rabble he felt was about to devour him.

Blindly, almost savagely, Sir Edward hit out at whatever was in front of him as he struggled to move forward, his chauffeur helping on one side, the doorman from the building on the other.

'It's a disgrace,' he roared, 'that I should be hounded in this way! Who the hell d'you think you are? Let . . . me . . . go . . . you . . . bastards!' His face was scarlet now, his teeth clenched. He felt as if something was going to explode in his head. I'm an innocent person, he thought, enraged. Why should I have to endure this outrageous intrusion into my privacy? Haven't I suffered enough already, losing the woman I loved . . . having to submit to police questioning?

At last he got to the entrance, and with a final shove pushed aside the last of his tormentors.

'Are you all right, sir?' the doorman enquired solicitously.

'I'm fine,' Sir Edward assured him.

'Anything I can get you, sir?' Harvey, his chauffeur, looked pale.

'Not a thing, thank you, Harvey. I won't be going out again today, so go home and enjoy what was meant to be a day off.' Some day off! thought Sir Edward. It might be a day off for the rest of New York, at least for those who weren't swarming all over the sidewalk outside his house; but it didn't feel like a holiday to him. He hurried into the elevator and pressed the button for the fourteenth floor. If he'd been hounded by a pack of baying wolves he couldn't have felt more unnerved.

'Brian?' he called out as soon as he entered the familiar comfort of lush panelling, rich hangings, family paintings and flower-filled rooms. He'd asked his vice-chairman to wait at the apartment until he got back from making his statement, as they had much to discuss.

'I'm in the lounge,' Brian called back. Edward was so pleased to hear his voice that he didn't even wince, as he usually did, at hearing his antique-filled drawing-room referred to as 'the lounge'.

'How did it go?' asked Brian. He was sitting in front of the tele-phone at a table by the window. Before him were spread copious notes written on Sir Edward's private crested writing-paper. 'You're back sooner than I expected.'

Edward went to the Adam-style marble fireplace and pressed the small brass bell in the wall beside it.

'It was pretty hellish . . . but not as hellish as that bunch of bloody reporters down by the front door,' he replied. At that moment Scott, the manservant whom he'd brought with him from England, came quietly into the room.

'You rang, sir?'

'Yes, Scott. Bring me a very large whisky and soda please. D'you want anything, Brian?'

The Vice-Chairman hesitated. Under normal circumstances, and if he'd still been working in a supermarket in the north of England, he'd have asked for a beer, or maybe a port and lemon or a rum and coke. Now, as a representative of the Tollemache Trust, he knew something else was expected of him.

'I'll have whatever you're having.'

Sir Edward turned to Scott. 'Two large whiskies, and have there been any messages for me?'

'I've been looking after the phone,' Brian interjected. 'Your daughter rang. She wants you to ring her back.'

Sir Edward looked up sharply. 'Jenny? My God, has she heard already?' The languid blue eyes registered anxiety.

Brian shook his head. 'She wanted to wish you a Happy New Year.'

'What? Oh, my God!' Edward sank on to one of the pretty brocade sofas, crushing the pale blue silk cushions as he did so. What a bloody awful way to start the New Year! He put his hands up to his face, rubbing his forehead and eyes as if to assuage the wretchedness he felt. Here he was, a man of sixty-two, five thou-sand miles away from the country of his birth, being questioned by the police and hounded by the media because the young girl he'd been so fatally in love with had fallen to her death from his apart-ment window. The fact that he was a powerful businessman who had reached the heights of success in a career many envied did not console him at this moment; nor did the fortune he had made, nor the beautiful possessions he had acquired, nor the fact that he could count among his friends the most famous and influential people on both sides of the Atlantic – and that included royalty.

29

At this moment he felt no different from the ordinary man with no special privileges, as he realized that grief is the great leveller. For a terrible moment hot tears pricked the back of his eyes and a sob rose in his chest, but he quickly controlled his emotions. Crying was a weakness that had been knocked out of him at the age of seven when he'd been sent away to boarding-school, and he wasn't going to give way now. For one thing, it would never do to show grief in front of Brian. Their relationship was strictly professional and must remain so. Brian was useful to the company, with his acute business sense and ability to do all the distasteful jobs that others might have shirked. He must never be allowed to see a chink in Sir Edward's dazzling armour for it might give him ideas . . .

'Where the hell's that whisky?' Sir Edward growled angrily. 'What's Scott doing? Growing the damned barley first?'

Brian ignored the little outburst. It was only natural Edward should be upset; what had happened was a serious embarrassment to the Tollemache Trust. The stockholders were not going to like it at all, and in his opinion there was everything to be gained by hushing up as many of the details as possible. Christine and he had always disapproved of Edward's womanizing. Neither of them could understand why the English upper classes thought it so dashing and amusing for a man to have a lot of mistresses. Christine had been very critical of Marissa, he remembered, and she'd referred to Edward as 'a dirty old man' and predicted darkly that he'd give them all a bad reputation by going with a girl over forty years his junior. But then she was also of the opinion that Brian should be the chairman of the company . . .

'Edward's only there because of his title,' she told her husband one day. Bitchily she added: 'You could do his job standing on your head with a kipper up your arse!'

'Language, language,' Brian had cautioned her. In his opinion women shouldn't swear. Christine was apt to come out with rather coarse and common phrases. It made him nervous that she might forget herself in public. Meanwhile, the present situation had to be dealt with and, as usual, he knew the burden of coping would fall on him.

'I think I've succeeded in preventing this becoming too big a scandal,' he said. 'The important thing is to play it down.'

At that moment Scott came back into the room, carrying a silver tray with two large Waterford glass tumblers of Johnny Walker Black Label and soda.

Sir Edward took his and drank deeply. Then he cocked an eye in Scott's direction, signalling he'd want a refill very shortly.

'It's a big enough scandal already,' he observed when they were alone again. 'You should have run the gauntlet of the media downstairs. I don't know how I'm going to play it down. What do you think? Any suggestions?'

Brian looked down at his small feet in their highly polished shoes, and his mouth tightened with annoyance. How bloody typical, he thought. How bloody typical of the aristocracy to get themselves into a mess because of their own decadence, and then expect others to get them out of it again. However, he'd foreseen what would happen and he knew instantly that it would be up to him to dig Edward's path back to respectability, if only for the sake of the company and, in the long run, for his own sake as well. He didn't intend to be dragged down by a salacious scandal.

Rising from the table by the window, he came over to Edward. 'I told the police last night that Marissa slipped on the polished floor and fell out of the window which had been opened because the room was stuffy. I emphasized it was a terrible accident.'

Edward frowned. 'So you told me. I suppose that is what happened, but I still find it hard to believe.'

Brian sat down on the edge of a little Louis XIV chair and leaned forward, his elbows resting on his knees, his hands cradling his whisky and soda, which suddenly tasted rather sour.

'You didn't say that to the police, I hope?'

Edward shook his head. 'They didn't ask me what I thought, only what I'd seen and heard. But I saw nothing . . . I was in this room when . . . when . . .' His voice faltered, hearing again the terrible scream in his head.

Brian pounced, relieved. 'Exactly! You saw nothing! I, on the other hand, was able to give an account of what happened because when it happened I was in the library talking to the president of Topic Oil and his wife. They can substantiate that. Marissa went over to the window . . . slipped . . . and it was a case of Good Night, Vienna! . . . and she was gone!'

Edward's eyes opened wide, staring at Brian's pudgy face with distaste. His second-in-command's phraseology, he thought, left a lot to be desired.

'You actually saw her fall?' he asked slowly.

Brian looked startled. 'No, of course not! I think I had my back to the window at the time.'

'Then how . . . ?'

'For fuck's sake, Edward!' he exploded. 'Do you want everyone to go around saying the girl you were sleeping with was murdered in your apartment? Or so bloody miserable she topped herself? Is that what you want? Months of police enquiries? Murder suspects? A lengthy court case? And if you think the media are after you now it's nothing to what will happen if there's any suggestion that something sinister took place. The case could even be covered live on TV, from the courthouse, every morning for weeks! For Christ's sake, Edward, you're sitting on your head and thinking with your ass! Think what it would do to the company. It *has* to be an accident! Those slippery Persian rugs you insist on having . . . the window open because the room was stuffy . . . that sort of thing! If we keep our heads, it'll be OK.' There was a pause and the two men sat in silence. Then Brian continued, as if to convince himself: 'After all, Marissa *may* have fallen accidentally. Who's to know? It is the most likely explanation when you come to think of it. Who would want to kill her anyway, and why would she want to jump?'

Edward drained his whisky and soda and saw that Scott had placed another one on the little table at his elbow. He took the fresh glass and sipped at it thoughtfully.

'I have a feeling she was frightened by something just before it happened.'

Brian looked alarmed. 'What could she be frightened of, for Christ's sake?' he demanded harshly.

'I wish I could remember.' Edward shook his head. 'She said something to me . . .' He racked his brains, wishing to God he hadn't drunk so much the previous night. He could barely remember anything about the party. Until the moment he heard Marissa scream, the whole evening had passed in a blur of friendly faces and much laughter as he quaffed glass after glass of champagne and mingled with his guests. If he was completely honest he couldn't remember a single thing anyone, including himself, had said from about nine o'clock onwards.

Brian sighed heavily. 'Did you mention that to the police?'

'What? That Marissa was frightened of something?' He shook his head. 'I've only just remembered it myself. I think she said something . . . perhaps it'll come back to me later.'

'Then do us a big favour and keep it to yourself when it does,' Brian urged. 'At the moment everyone thinks it was an accident. Let's keep it like that or we'll all be in the shit.'

Edward rose and wandered over to the window that looked down on Park Avenue. Lack of sleep and the stress of the past twelve hours had made him feel light-headed. He took a quick gulp of his drink. Marissa . . . all blonde and fair, with a body as smooth as satin. But he knew it wasn't just her body and her sexuality he was going to miss. She'd been trusting, like a little kitten, and warm and generous and kind. A smile hovered over Edward's mouth as he remembered the childlike way she'd told him all about herself.

'My father was Jack Montclare,' she'd said, in a soft voice and mid-Atlantic accent he was sure had been acquired through elocution lessons. 'He made a fortune manufacturing railway lines and sleepers and that sort of thing. When he died last year, he left me all his money.' Her mother, she'd told him, had died when she was seven. The thing that had pleased him so much was the fact that Marissa obviously hadn't been interested in him for his money. She had enough of her own to live in luxury for the rest of her life.

As if by telepathy, Brian suddenly looked across at the brooding figure of his boss. A nasty thought had occurred to him.

'Did she have any family?' he asked bluntly. 'Anyone who should be informed?'

Edward's languid eyes looked sad. 'No, no one. Her mother died when she was small and her father died about a year ago. She was alone in the world, apart from me,' he added hollowly.

'Well, that's a relief!' said Brian. 'We wouldn't want relatives poking around to find out what happened now, would we?'

The family sat in the drawing-room of Pinkney House waiting for Peters to announce dinner, which he did every evening by gently drumming the brass gong that hung suspended in a black lacquer Chinese stand in the hall. Angela, seated by the fire, sipped her usual apéritif, a Manhattan cocktail made from whisky and vermouth.

This was the time of day she liked best, especially in the winter when the apricot velvet curtains were drawn and the room glowed gold in the lamplight. The drawing-room was furnished with some fine William and Mary walnut furniture, several impressive landscapes by Constable and, as always, a profusion of flowers, something she insisted on all the year round. When the greenhouse ran short she telephoned Harrods and they sent down several boxes of their best blooms.

On the other side of the fireplace Jenny sat reading a novel while Simon, changed into a dark suit for the Wenlakes only wore evening dress when they were entertaining, threw a log of apple wood on to the fire and then put the brass fireguard in position on the hearth.

At that moment the soft drumming of the gong came from the hall, loud enough to be heard but discreet enough not to annoy.

'There we are,' Simon said. He said that every evening. He was a young man of meticulous habit and became fidgety if his routine was disturbed. His bland pink face already showed a certain anxiety, a fear that some disruption was about to occur. 'There we are,' he repeated, as if to reassure himself. Then he smiled at his mother. 'I'm starving.' He always said that, too.

As they rose to leave the room, they heard the phone ringing. Jenny strained to hear Peters answer it.

'It's for you, Miss Jenny,' he announced a moment later. Without looking at Angela he added: 'It's Sir Edward, miss. Calling from New York.'

'Thank you.' She flushed with pleasure.

Angela clicked her tongue in annoyance. 'How typical of Edward to ring you now. He knows we always dine at eight.'

Simon wagged his head in agreement. 'Yes, dinner's ready,' he chided, 'and we're having pheasant. One of the ones I bagged the other day.' Turning, he followed his mother into the dining-room. 'And tell the old man,' he shouted over his shoulder, 'that I bet *he* couldn't bring down two birds with one shot!'

Jenny stared at his broad back. 'I don't suppose he'd want to,' she said coldly. Then she grabbed the receiver and heard her father's voice.

'Jenny, is that you? How are you, darling?'

She thought he sounded very tired. 'I'm fine, Daddy. How are you? I rang you earlier to wish you a Happy New Year but I heard something dreadful about your party. What happened? Who died?'

There was a pause. She could sense her father trying to control his emotions. When he spoke his voice was strained.

'A friend . . . well, she fell from a window. It's been the most hellish twenty-four hours of my life. I haven't been to bed yet.'

'Oh!' Jenny gave a gasp. 'My God!' She felt stunned, standing there in the large square hall, her eyes fixed on a painting of a landscape that hung above the telephone table: men and women harvesting in the eighteenth century, arranging great stooks of corn under a clear blue sky. She dragged her eyes away from the idyllic scene.

'Daddy, how did it happen?'

'I . . . well, I think she slipped.'

'Who was it? Anyone I know?'

'It was a young girl, younger than you. You've never met her.'

'Oh, Daddy, how dreadful! What a terrible thing to happen.' Her mind was reeling. Her father's apartment was so high up. The girl wouldn't have had a chance. But one persistent question kept

34

recurring in her mind: how could she have slipped? The window sill, Jenny recalled, came up to about the top of her thighs. The girl would have to have leaned out and even so . . .

'How awful for her parents.'

'She hadn't any parents. They're both dead,' said Sir Edward. 'Anyway, it's all in the hands of the police now.'

'Daddy, shall I fly over and stay with you? You must have had a nasty shock, and I don't have to be back at the school for another two weeks.'

'There's no need, darling.'

'But I'd like to, and I'm sure you need cheering up. Anyway, I'm stuck down here with . . .' She almost said 'with Mummy' but loyally changed it to '. . . with nothing to do. Anyway I'd love to see you.' Jenny enjoyed her trips to New York, where her father included her in his sophisticated lifestyle as if she were a close woman friend, making her feel much older than her twenty-three years. Sometimes she even acted as hostess when he entertained.

'Well . . .' He seemed to be hesitating, and then she heard him say, 'All right, why not? It would be nice to have you here for a while. When will you come?'

'Tomorrow! I'll catch a plane tomorrow.' A glamorous trip was just what she needed at this time of year, when everything was so flat and grey after Christmas.

When Jenny hurried into the dining-room Angela looked up disapprovingly. 'Your soup's cold.'

Jenny slid into her seat, which was positioned between her mother and Simon, who sat at opposite ends of the gleaming expanse of mahogany, looking at each other through a forest of silver candelabra. She pushed her fair hair back from her face. Her eyes sparkled with excitement.

'Daddy's invited me to stay until the new term begins and I'm flying to the States tomorrow.' She decided not to mention the tragedy that had prompted the trip.

'You'll miss the Hunt Ball,' Simon said accusingly.

'Yes, and the house party I'm giving that weekend,' added Angela, 'and we've got the Lancasters staying, including Freddie. You knew that, Jenny. You can't possibly go gallivanting off to New York.'

She tried to suppress a smile at her mother's transparent matchmaking. The Earl and Countess of Lancaster were old friends of the Wenlakes; Lord Lancaster had been at Eton at the same time as Sir Edward. Their son and heir, the Honourable Frederick Wareham, a jolly but vacuous young man who was in the Blues and Royals, had long been earmarked by Angela as a suitable husband for Jenny.

Jenny shrugged. 'You'll have to make my excuses then, won't you?'

'I most certainly will not.' Angela glared coldly down the table, her pearls gleaming in the candlelight. When she wanted to she could be very regal, thought Jenny.

'I'm sorry, but I'm going to New York,' Jenny insisted with unaccustomed firmness. 'I didn't invite the Lancasters or Freddie to stay for the weekend so there is no reason for me to be here. Simon can produce a girl to take my place at the Hunt Ball . . . I'm sure there are lots of young women in the county who would be thrilled to bits to partner Freddie.'

'What's he going to think?' Simon protested. 'He'll expect to escort you, not some girl he's never set eyes on before.'

'Simon's right,' said Angela. 'It will look very rude if you're not here. It will look as if you're not interested!' Her voice rose in chagrin.

'And who on earth will I get to take your place?' Simon demanded.

'Oh, you'll find someone.' Jenny smiled mischievously. 'What about Charlotte Cowan?'

Angela turned dull red with anger. Charlotte Cowan was an extremely pretty girl who lived nearby, and on a previous occasion when they'd met, Freddie had been very attracted to her. Angela had been so furious she'd sworn never to have 'that pushy girl' to the house again.

'Don't be silly, Jenny,' she said sharply. 'I think you're being very selfish going off like this. I really think you must tell your father you can't come.'

'Why has your father asked you over now anyway? You usually go in the summer,' said Simon. He never referred to 'our' father, or even just 'Father'; it was always 'your' father.

'Why shouldn't he?' Jenny retorted. 'He'd probably ask you too if you were nicer to him.'

'I wouldn't go if he begged me!' retorted Simon. 'I've nothing in common with that lecherous old rogue.'

'You're right, you haven't,' said Jenny. 'He's got brains, charm, business acumen. You've nothing in common with him at all.'

Simon flushed angrily. 'I'd rather make an honest living by farming the land here than wheeler-dealing in an office. I think it's immoral to make a fortune without ever having had to do an honest day's work for it.'

'You seem to forget that it's Daddy's so-called fortune that paid for your education, your training at Cirencester Agricultural

College, and the fact that you've got a stable full of hunters and everything else you could ever want! If his money is so immorally earned, how can you bear to touch it?'

'That's enough, Jenny,' Angela cut in sternly. 'I will not have the two of you fighting when we're having dinner.'

'But I'm right, Mummy, aren't I?' Jenny protested. 'I know Daddy paid for my education, all my clothes, the flat in London; he's been extremely generous to both of us, and I just wish Simon would at least appreciate the fact.'

Angela shot her son a faintly warning look. 'It's not very pleasant, Simon, to hear you running your father down,' she said, but in a gentle understanding voice. 'Just because he's hurt me in the past doesn't mean you have to turn against him now.'

'Exactly!' Jenny agreed, vehemently. 'We are his children.'

'After the way he treated Mama, running all over the place with his girlfriends, he deserves nothing better,' cried her brother. 'I'd let him rot in hell if I had my way!'

'That's enough, Simon,' said Angela, but she was smiling.

Jenny looked at her brother with disdain. 'Thank God Daddy *doesn't* ask you to go to the States! We wouldn't want all those smart New York girls thinking you were typical of English men, would we? It'd be enough to ruin Anglo-American relations!'

'Oh, grow up,' he snapped. 'Go to America and don't bother to come back!'

Angela looked alarmed. 'Of course she must come back. Now, for goodness' sake, let's have our dinner in peace. I'm fed up with all this quarrelling.'

They finished dinner in uneasy silence, and as soon as it was over Jenny rushed up to her room to start packing, thankful she hadn't said anything about the death of one of her father's party guests. If she had, her mother and Simon would really have had something to get their teeth into.

Chapter Three

Rebecca carefully placed the negative between the two sheets of glass in the metal negative carrier of the enlarger, switched on the powerful bulb in the lamphouse and focused the lens until the image shone down sharp and clear on the white laminated baseboard.

Karen, still in her Mickey Mouse T-shirt, peered over her flatmate's shoulder. 'What are you doing? What am I supposed to be looking at?'

'See?' Rebecca had called Karen into the darkroom as soon as she knew she was awake. She wanted her roommate's objective opinion on the negatives which she thought held a vital clue to Marissa Montclare's death. 'See this man's back . . . Leaning forward with his hands outstretched like he's going to lift something?'

Karen wrinkled her nose and peered closer. She hardly ever went into the darkroom, and she knew nothing about photography. 'I can see something,' she murmured doubtfully, 'but I'm confused by everything black looking white, and everything white looking black!'

'That's because you're looking at a negative. The image is reversed. When I do a print you'll see that everything is the colour it should be.'

'Can't you make it larger, Rebecca? All I can really see is a couple; they look as if they were talking to each other.'

Rebecca nodded. 'That's Senator Ronald Webster and his wife. Hang on a second and we'll do a blow-up of the part that matters.' Turning a knob, she raised the enlarger head until it was at the top of its supporting column. 'Now we'll change the lens,' she continued, reaching up to a shelf that ran along the wall behind the 'dry' bench. A moment later, the relevant section of the negative was enlarged, filling the baseboard.

'There!' Rebecca sounded triumphant. 'This is the first of five pictures I took with this man in the background. Each shot shows him in a different position. I'm certain he's got something to do with Marissa's death.' Moving quickly and efficiently she turned off the light in the lamphouse, took a sheet of printing paper from an Ilford box and slid it, emulsion side up, into the masking frame that formed part of the baseboard. She set the timer to seven seconds and switched it on.

Karen watched, intrigued. 'If he was doing something suspicious,' she said slowly, 'surely he wouldn't have let you take his photograph?'

The timer clicked off and Rebecca turned to the 'wet' bench on the opposite wall and plunged the sheet of printing paper into a shallow enamel dish of print developer. 'He wouldn't have known I was taking pictures,' she explained. 'I'd been using a flash all evening and doing quite a few semi-posed pictures. Then I decided to use natural light to get a few candid shots. No one realized I was still taking pictures.'

Rebecca swished the sheet back and forth, being careful to handle it by the edges only to avoid finger marks. In the dim red glow of the darkroom safe-light, they craned eagerly forward, watching for an image to appear. After a few seconds Karen let out a yelp. 'There! It's a man in a white jacket . . . I can see clearly now. What on earth is he doing? It looks as if he's got no head.'

Rebecca held up the print. 'I'll tell you what he's doing . . . he's leaning forward with his hands outstretched because he's about to open a window . . . *the* window that Marissa fell from! I recognize it because there's the edge of the library bookcase, and that's the only room with velvet curtains – the rest have brocade. He's looking out through the curtains . . . see? They're hiding his head! I'm going to print the other four shots. Now I'm certain I know what happened.'

Excitedly, she changed the negative in the carrier while telling Karen to dip the first print into the stop bath, then the fixer, and finally the large tank of running water at the far end of the bench.

'It's kinda busy in a darkroom, isn't it?' Karen observed, wiping her hands on a towel. 'How long do the pictures have to stay in that wash?'

'The same time as washing negatives – around thirty minutes. Then we'll dry them on that flat-bed dryer in the corner. I'll switch it on to heat up.' Rebecca's hands flew here and there. This was her little kingdom, where she was in complete control. Some of her happiest hours had been spent locked in this darkroom, working by the glow of the red safe-light.

At last the five relevant pictures had been printed, washed, and dried. It was eleven o'clock on New Year's Day and Rebecca had been on the go for twenty-seven hours so far.

40

'There's no doubt in my mind,' she said slowly, looking from one to another. 'What do you think?'

Karen spoke without hesitation. 'I think you should show these to the cops right away.'

Rebecca looked at Detective Tom O'Hara, a stunned expression on her face. Between them on the desk lay the five photographs.

'But it's obvious!' she protested. 'Each picture shows the sequence of events, as they happened. I remember taking them in the library on my way to the drawing-room, just before midnight.'

When she'd arrived at the police precinct she'd been informed that O'Hara was in charge. Now, as she sat looking at him, something made her feel distinctly uncomfortable. It was as if he didn't believe a word she had to say.

'So what have we got?' he demanded. 'Pictures of some guy opening a window. It don't add up to nuthin'.' In spite of his Irish ancestry, his accent was pure Bronx.

'Opening *the* window,' Rebecca corrected him. 'Look, in the first picture he's standing in front of the library window and the curtains are closed. I can prove this is the library window, the one Marissa Montclare fell from. Look at the way he's turning his head. It's obvious he's looking around to see if he's being watched.

'Here in the second picture we see him from the back, and he's reaching for the bottom of the window. In the third shot,' Rebecca pointed to the eight by ten inch glossy print, 'he's standing upright with his arms extended . . . because he's opened the window to almost shoulder height. See?

'In the fourth he's turning round adjusting the drapes so they are closed again. And the fifth is like the first . . . he's looking over his shoulder to be sure he hasn't been observed, and he's on the point of moving away. You can tell by the angle of his shoulders and arms.'

O'Hara looked at her pityingly. 'So the apartment was hot, with all those people crammed in. So a guy opens a window to let in some nice cool air. So what?' He shook his head, the dark curls at the back of his thick red neck glistening with sweat. 'It don't add up to homicide, lady. In fact, it proves that it was an accident. Somebody has to open a window before someone else can accidentally fall out of it, don't they?' He made her theory sound so ridiculous that Rebecca frowned, her conviction quavering for a moment.

O'Hara thought of something else. 'These shots are of a waiter. See, he's wearing one of those short white jackets like the caterers always wear. The guy was probably only doin' his job. I'd say

41

someone asked him to open a window. That don't make him a killer.'

Rebecca sat forward, her mouth set in a stubborn line. 'Sir Edward had on the air-conditioning in his apartment. I know that, because when the party started I heard him remark that he thought it ought to be turned up. So why would a waiter open a window?' She paused reflectively. 'The rooms weren't too hot either.'

Detective Tom O'Hara sighed loudly and deeply. 'Lady, I don't know why you think there was a homicide when we know it was an accident, but if it'll make you any happier I'll show these pictures and the other ones you took to my superior. If we think we should take the matter further, we will do so.' He rose pointedly, eyeing the door. Rebecca could take a hint. Reluctantly, she rose also, slinging her camera bag over her shoulder.

'Thank you,' she said quietly, 'but I'll tell you one thing, Sergeant. That girl, Marissa Montclare, didn't fall, and she didn't jump. I'm convinced she was pushed.

'I told you she was pleading with Sir Edward about something, minutes before it happened, and I think when he ignored her pleas her murderer somehow got her into the library, and managed to push her out.'

O'Hara raised his bushy eyebrows and spoke positively. 'You're wrong there, lady. We got evidence she slipped on the polished floor and fell. One of the guests saw her.' He walked briskly to the door and opened it for her.

'Who?' Rebecca asked, taken aback. 'Who actually saw her fall? I was there, and no one seemed to have seen what happened.'

'We got a witness.' There was a finality in his tone that put paid to further questions.

Outside on the sidewalk, Rebecca walked quickly, deep in thought. Someone was going to a lot of trouble to make Marissa's death look like an accident. She was certain it was Brian Norris. The question she kept asking herself was: whether Brian was covering up because the scandal would be bad for the Tollemache Trust, or if he was somehow involved.

The Hertfelder Photographic Agency was only a short distance away. Rebecca quickened her pace, anxious to get there as soon as possible. The city was quiet and seemingly deserted on New Year's day. Shops were closed, but Stirling Hertfelder would be working and she couldn't wait to see him. He'd spent the night with his parents in Connecticut, to celebrate the New Year, but she knew he was coming back today and for him it was business as usual.

42

Tomorrow's newspapers would need pictures, just like any other day, and Stirling was not a person who missed an opportunity. That was something she'd discovered when she'd first met him.

Four years before, the picture editor of the *New York Herald* had told Rebecca she should take an agent. 'You need someone to represent you,' he'd said. 'Your time should be spent taking pictures, not running around trying to place them. A good agent will also set up assignments for you.'

'What percentage do they take?' She actually enjoyed the business side, but on the other hand she was beginning to realize that it was time-consuming.

'Ten percent, plus the cost of developing and printing your film. I'll introduce you to the best in town. His name is Stirling Hertfelder and he's got one of the most successful agencies in the business.'

'Stirling? What a strange name.'

'It's his Scottish mother's maiden name.'

'Do you think he'll take me on?'

Rebecca had been assured that not only would the Hertfelder Agency take her on, she was just the type of young photographer with talent, energy and ambition that they could really build.

She liked Stirling the moment she met him. Thirty years old and a native New Yorker, he had intelligent and humorous brown eyes, and a beautifully shaped mouth that tilted up at the corners, as if he were permanently amused. He'd flipped through her portfolio of photographs while she sat, heart pounding, hoping he'd take her on.

'What sort of equipment have you got?' he'd asked, pausing to study a shot she'd taken of two little boys watching a baseball game with spellbound expressions.

'Two Leicas and two Rolleiflexes, so that I can have colour and black and white film in each, and a Hasselblad.'

Stirling's eyebrows shot up. 'Expensive gear – the Rolls-Royce of cameras!'

Rebecca grinned. 'It's taken every penny I've ever had, and my parents have given me all my birthday and Christmas presents for the next ten years in the form of cameras. That's why I look this way. I have no money for clothes,' she added jokily.

Rebecca remembered how Stirling's eyes had swept over her, taking in her army surplus cotton trousers and shirt which she always wore when she was working in the days before she could afford designer jackets and trousers.

'Then it's a pity more girls can't afford expensive clothes!' he commented, with his slow sexy smile.

That was the nearest he got to flirting for a long time, Rebecca reflected. It was nearly a year before he asked her for a date. Meanwhile he agreed to handle her work. Soon he'd sold several of her photo-features to leading magazines. Within six months hardly a day passed without one of her pictures appearing in some newspaper or magazine. His manner was utterly professional during those first twelve months, praising her work when it was good, but not pulling his punches if it was not up to standard.

Early on Rebecca realized she'd fallen in love with him but she, too, avoided showing her feelings – perhaps in some unspoken way, she thought, they both knew that letting their relationship become personal might jeopardize their working association. When finally they could resist each other no longer, it was like the touching of two live wires; they sparked and fizzed, igniting each other with the heat of their passion. It was the most exciting time of Rebecca's life as, with Stirling, she explored the limits of her sexuality.

That had been three years ago, and although their love still burned fiercely there had been a shift in their respective feelings. Stirling, who'd had no thought of settling down when they met, now longed to marry Rebecca, or at least live with her. She, on the other hand, who had started out dreaming of drifting white wedding dresses and honeymoons in the Caribbean, now clung more and more to her independence. Success had brought her freedom of a kind she'd never known existed; she was now in complete control of her life and that was something she was scared of losing.

Rebecca looked up and saw she was outside the agency. Hurrying into the building she took the elevator to the second floor.

Stirling was seated at his desk, surrounded by the usual clutter of photographs, negatives, stacks of newspapers and magazines, and an intricate looking telephone system. In the adjoining offices, Rebecca could hear typewriters, fax and telex machines, and telephones ringing. Most of New York might be having a day of rest but for the Hertfelder Agency it was business as usual.

Stirling jumped to his feet as soon as she appeared.

'Hi, sweetheart!' Coming around the desk he took her in his arms and held her close. Although she was tall, he was taller. Long limbed and narrow hipped, he moved with a gangling rangy grace that she always found deeply attractive. Untidy dark hair framed his olive-skinned face, and when he smiled there was something charmingly wicked about his expression. It reminded her of a mischievous little boy, wondering how much he could get away with.

'I was going to call you,' he continued, as he buried his face in the curve of her neck, 'but I thought you'd be sleeping late. How did the Wenlake party go?'

Rebecca hugged him back, suddenly leaning against him as if she needed his support. 'Oh, Stirling, am I glad to see you!'

'Is anything wrong?' He looked anxiously into her face. 'You look done in, sweetheart. What's happened?'

'D'you mind if I sit down? I haven't been to bed yet.' She groped in her capacious bag. 'Here are last night's batch – eight rolls and the sheets of contacts.'

'You've processed them?' He looked surprised.

Rebecca nodded. 'It's a long story. Could I have something to eat before I tell you? I've just realized I haven't had anything since lunchtime yesterday. There were just the usual nibbles at the party . . . and I've only had coffee since.' She also realized she was, unaccountably, close to tears.

'God, Rebecca, what the hell's wrong?' He cleared a space on his office sofa and gently forced her to sit down. 'Wait, I'll get someone to order us food first.' He left his office, yelling instructions to his secretary to go to the local delicatessen. In a moment he was back, holding her hand and looking at her anxiously.

'So tell me, sweetheart. What happened?'

Rebecca told him everything, from the moment she'd arrived at Sir Edward's apartment to her visit to police headquarters an hour before.

Stirling listened intently, his face serious for once, dark eyes gently probing. 'So you're convinced Marissa Montclare was murdered?' he said at last. Marissa was the talk of the town. He'd been about to get Rebecca to do a feature on her 'at home' in her Trump Tower apartment. It would have been a nice follow-up to the feature on Sir Edward Wenlake as the two had been so publicly linked.

'Yes, I'm sure.' Rebecca sounded positive. 'I saw her moments before she died, and she was scared of something . . . or someone. There was no mistaking the fear in her face. I'm also sure that the man in my pictures, opening the window, is her killer.'

Stirling let out a low whistle. 'But the police say she fell accidentally?'

'Yes. They even say there is a witness who *saw* her slip and fall.'

'Then surely that wraps it up, doesn't it? I mean, these photographs of yours aren't proof she was murdered, are they? They just show a waiter doing his job by opening a window in a hot stuffy room.' Stirling spoke sympathetically, seeing that Rebecca was near breaking point from exhaustion and shock. Privately he was convinced she was mistaken.

She shook her head slowly. 'You're right . . . but I'm still sure she was killed. It's a feeling I have, I can't explain it. Perhaps because the Vice-Chairman of the Tollemache Trust, Brian Norris, was so damned eager to describe it as an accident. He spent all his time before the police arrived persuading everyone else to back him up . . . like he was organizing a cover-up.'

'So what are you doing to do now?'

'What can I do? The police aren't interested.'

Stirling made a suggestion. 'What about Sir Edward?'

'I wouldn't want to bother him. He was so upset last night that he locked himself in his bedroom. I've finished the feature on him too, so I don't have any excuse to contact him again.' She rose and walked to the window, gazing down at the street below. When she turned back, her face was deathly pale and she was sweating.

'Stirling, do you suppose she knew anything? I mean . . . well, would she be aware what was happening before she hit the ground?'

He jumped up and went over to her, putting his arms around her and holding her close. 'Hey,' he said softly, 'try not to think about it.'

Rebecca's eyes filled with tears. 'I can't help it! That scream! She sounded so frightened. She must have known, at that instant, that she was going to die.' She covered her face with her hands, her mind reeling with horror as she imagined what Marissa must have suffered. Those final one, two, three, four, five . . . how many seconds did it take to fall fourteen floors? In those seconds, had Marissa felt the cold night air rush past her as she plummeted down to the hard ground? Had she been filled with panic and terror? Had there been a final second of consciousness before the world blacked out forever?

Rebecca found that Stirling was stroking her long hair, pressing his cheek to hers as the tears streamed down her face.

'Come and sit down, sweetheart. You're exhausted and you're in shock.' He guided her back to the sofa, but she was too overwhelmed by what had happened and continued to sob for several minutes. Then she blew her nose on the large handkerchief he'd handed her and managed a wobbly smile.

'God, I'm sorry. I haven't done that since I was a child.'

He smiled tenderly. 'You needed to let it out. Last night must have been traumatic for you. You should go home to bed now, and get some sleep. The food will be arriving in a second and then I'll put you in a cab. You need to rest.'

'I will, but what upsets me is that nobody, apart from Sir Edward, seemed to care about Marissa last night. All the guests wanted was to get away, so they wouldn't be involved, and Brian Norris was determined to sweep it all under the carpet. It was as if her death was no more than an awful inconvenience.'

'People react to tragedy in different ways. It doesn't necessarily mean they don't care. Anyway, I'll have prints made of your shots of Marissa and we'll do a world-wide syndication. She'll make the front page now, especially as they were taken at the party. By tomorrow, when the story's really broken, the likes of Brian Norris won't be able to sweep the whole thing under the carpet.'

A couple of years ago, Rebecca would have felt bad about making money from such a situation, but becoming professional had changed that. It was her job to record events – and sometimes, through her pictures, expose wrongdoing. It was not, she knew, merely a case of making capital out of other people's disasters.

'I'll come over to see you this evening,' Stirling promised later as he saw her into the cab, 'and I'll bring a carry out. You hardly ate anything just now, although you'd said you were hungry.'

Rebecca's eyes widened in appreciation. 'You can be quite special sometimes, can't you?' she said teasingly. 'I sometimes think I could get to like being spoiled.'

His expression softened. 'I wish you'd let me spoil you more. Girls shouldn't be as independent as you,' he said, and she knew he wasn't entirely joking.

The newspapers were delivered to Pinkney House at eight-thirty every morning by a boy on a bicycle who flung them unceremoniously on to the front stone steps as he took the drive in one sweeping non-stop curve. Peters retrieved them immediately, clucking with annoyance at the paper boy's lack of care. Then he hurried to the pantry where an old blanket lay folded on a side-table and an iron stood already heated. Spreading out the *Times* first, he pressed it meticulously until its pages lay once more pristine and smooth. Then he repeated the process with the *Telegraph* and *Daily Mail*, making sure not to smudge the print. With the morning ritual completed, he then placed the newspapers on the hall table with Lady Wenlake's letters.

Angela was the first down on the morning of 2 January, still feeling angry with herself for having overslept the previous day. The first thing that caught her eye was the bold black headline of the *Daily Mail*. Sinking on to one of the carved hall chairs, she read the front page with growing horror. A moment later Simon came lumbering down the stairs. His ideas on running the estate being strictly those of a gentleman farmer, he employed others to get up at five-thirty in the morning to milk the cows. He glanced at what his mother was reading, grabbed the *Telegraph* and slumped on to another chair.

Jenny, coming last down the stairs with her suitcase, was just in time to hear their exclamations.

'Oh, my God!'

'Jesus Christ, what the . . . ? Oh, shit!' Simon expostulated.

'This is dreadful!' Angela cried, appalled.

Jenny looked from one to the other. 'What's the matter?'

'Read this.' Her mother held out the *Daily Mail* with shaking hands.

'He's really done it now,' Simon said hollowly.

Jenny grabbed the newspaper. 'What? Who? What are you talking about?'

BARONET'S GIRLFRIEND PLUNGES TO DEATH, screamed the headline. In smaller print was an account of what had happened, written in sensationally colourful journalese: 'Tragedy at midnight . . . twenty year old falls from skyscraper . . . Sir Edward Wenlake distraught.' And then the final paragraph: 'New York gossip columns described them as "an item". '

Jenny sat down heavily, her mind in a turmoil. Nothing her father had said on the phone the previous evening had suggested it was his girlfriend who had died. Feeling slightly sick, she glanced at the *Times*, which had a much less sensational account of what had happened but nevertheless referred to "Marissa Montclare, constant companion of Sir Edward Wenlake, Chairman of the Tollemache Trust, who met her death when she fell from his fourteenth-floor apartment window."

'You can't possibly go to New York now,' said Angela. 'This is going to bring disgrace on us all. It's not as if Wenlake were a common name . . . everyone will know he's my ex-husband and your father.'

Jenny spun angrily on her. 'It's because of what's happened that I must go! Daddy will need me.'

Angela and Simon looked at her as if she'd betrayed them.

'You knew? You mean last night . . . when you said you were flying to see your father . . . you *knew* what had happened?' Angela asked.

Jenny hung her head for a moment, then levelled her gaze at her mother. 'I knew there'd been an accident, that someone had died. Daddy told me it was a friend of his. These newspapers are just out to sensationalize the whole thing because Daddy's a prominent person.'

Angela dropped her head into her hands and groaned. 'Oh, my God, how can you be so naive?'

'Yes, how can you be so naive!' echoed Simon. 'It's the story of the old man's life, but really . . . a twenty year old! It's too much. We'll have to disown him now.'

'You can't disown your own father,' said Jenny coldly. 'I don't care what's happened, I'm still flying to the States. Whether this girl . . . this Marissa Montclare . . . was a close friend or not, doesn't matter. Daddy sounded very shocked and upset.'

Simon raised his eyebrows mockingly. 'I'm not surprised. I'd be pretty upset too if a girlfriend of mine took a header from my upstairs window. But that doesn't mean you've got to get yourself involved. Steer clear, that's my advice.'

Jenny looked at him contemptuously. 'It would be!' she retorted. Then she turned and ran up the stairs to get the rest of her luggage. Fifteen minutes later she was in her car, making the seventy-mile trip from the village of Pinkney to Heathrow airport.

Chapter Four

'It's good to see you, sweetheart. You certainly lost no time in getting here.' Sir Edward hugged Jenny. As she glanced up at him she thought how tired and drawn he looked. He'd sent his car to the airport to meet her, but had warned her he wouldn't be there himself because of all the media attention. Now, in his apartment, she removed her bulky winter coat and let herself be fussed over.

'Are you all right, Daddy?' she asked, sitting down on the sofa beside him.

'I'm fine. Would you like a drink?' In the past couple of days, Sir Edward had asked Scott to leave a tray of drinks permanently in the drawing-room. It was easier than perpetually ringing the bell, and also he thought made his heavy consumption of alcohol less obvious.

'May I have a Perrier, please?'

'Is that all?' Sir Edward sounded startled. 'Wouldn't you like something stronger?'

Jenny smiled. Her father always tried to get her to drink, although she never did. 'Mineral water will be fine.'

When he'd poured the drinks, giving himself an almost neat whisky, he came and sat down again, placing their glasses on the low coffee table in front of them.

'I suppose you've seen all the papers?' There hadn't been much in the tabloids on New Year's Day because there hadn't been time, but today he and Marissa had become front page news in all the New York newspapers. Rebecca's photographs had been reproduced in all of them, and at the sight of Marissa's smiling face Sir Edward felt a terrible constriction in his throat.

'Yes, I saw the English papers this morning, before I left Pinkney,' Jenny replied in a quiet voice. Was it only this morning? The time difference accounted for five hours, but nevertheless it seemed like an age since she'd stormed out of the house, leaving her furious mother and brother.

'The English papers, too, eh?' He was silent for a moment and then remarked: 'I bet your mother had a lot to say about that!'

'I'm afraid she did. So did Simon.'

'Oh, God,' Sir Edward groaned.

Jenny looked across at him. 'Is it true?' she asked in a small voice.

'Yes, it's true all right. Marissa did fall, though God knows how.' He took a swift gulp of whisky.

'No, I mean . . . well, I know she fell. What I meant was, was she your girlfriend . . . as the newspapers said?'

He'd never lied to his children and now he looked directly at Jenny and answered without hesitation: 'Yes, she was. I was very much in love with her, although you may find that difficult to understand . . . seeing how much younger than me she was.' His voice grated painfully as he spoke, and Jenny was filled by a wave of compassion. 'What was so wonderful,' he continued, 'is that I knew without a shadow of doubt that it was me she cared for. Not my money. Not my position. She didn't need them. She was a girl who had everything. That's why this is such a terrible tragedy . . . such a senseless thing to happen, and such an appalling waste!'

'Oh, Daddy, I'm so sorry. How did it happen?'

He shrugged, spreading his hands in gesture of helplessness. 'God knows. I'm told she slipped on the polished floor . . . but it hardly seems to matter now. The thing is, she's gone, and nothing is going to bring her back. There'll be an autopsy and an inquest, of course, but it all seems such a futile waste of time.' He drained his glass and rose to refill it again.

Jenny watched him, worried by the change in him. Normally her father was bright and breezy, full of energy and life, looking much younger than his sixty-two years. Now he looked like a weary old man.

'Are you sure you won't have a proper drink?' he asked, glancing at her over his shoulder, the heavy crystal decanter in his hand.

'No, thanks. Honestly.'

'Well, I'm going to,' he admitted unashamedly. 'It's the only thing that's keeping me going at the moment. I haven't slept for two nights.'

'Well, I'm here to look after you now,' she said reassuringly.

'I must look like an old fool to you.'

Jenny sounded quite indignant. 'Of course you don't. It's up to you whom you have in your life.'

Silence hung between them like a gossamer curtain, through which they could partly see each other but yet keep something back, private and hidden.

'Have you got a boyfriend at the moment, Jenny?' he asked at last.

'I was going out with someone but it sort of fizzled out. There's no one at the moment.'

'You'll find someone,' he said comfortingly. 'Every woman needs to be loved.'

Jenny thought about her mother, fussing around Pinkney, as cold as her collection of diamonds; an upright, unloved figure who slept alone in a large ornate bed. She didn't want to end up like that.

'I hope there's someone out there who'll have me,' she joked.

They dined quietly at home that evening, waited on by Scott.

'I hope you don't mind, sweetheart, but I daren't go to restaurants because of the photographers.'

'So what's wrong with dining at home? Daddy, I didn't come to New York to hit the high spots, you know. I came to be with you. I don't care if we dine at home every evening for the next two weeks.'

'You're a good girl, Jenny.'

'I like being with you,' she replied simply.

They both went to bed early that night and Jenny fell asleep almost immediately. She knew no more until she awoke with a start, wondering for a moment where she was and what was happening. Turning on the bedside light she peered at her watch. It was only two o'clock in the morning. What had awakened her? Puzzled, she climbed out of bed and went to the door. And then she heard it. A bellowing noise, like an animal in pain, and a moment later a crashing sound.

Slipping on her dressing-gown, Jenny quietly opened the door of her room and began creeping on tiptoe, down the corridor. At that moment another howl filled the air, making her jump. The unearthly sound seemed to be coming from the library. Alarmed now, she wrapped her robe tighter round her and edged forward stealthily until she drew level with the door which was ajar. She peered round it and then stepped back in dismay, almost with a sense of shame. Somehow it seemed wrong to see her father weeping as if his heart would break, great sobs tearing at his throat, fists rubbing his eyes. Scott was with him, helping him to his feet as he swayed drunkenly, talking to him gently and reassuringly; but Sir Edward's grief was terrible to watch, and Jenny slipped away, knowing he would hate her to see him like this.

In a small semi-detached bungalow overlooking the sea, on the south-east coast of England, an elderly couple sat in stunned silence, broken only by the occasional sobbing of the woman. They

53

sat huddled by the electric fire. The orange-coloured light bulb which was cunningly concealed under the glowing fake coals flickered with maddening monotony as the little middle disc whirled round and round. In the corner of the room a television screen, mauve-hued and with the sound turned down, showed scenes from an Australian soap opera.

The man sat with a newspaper on his knee. From time to time he smoothed the paper with his fingers, like a blind person reading Braille, then he would glance down at the photographs of the girl whose broad smile and long shapely legs covered most of the front page. The banner headline was much the same as in the more upmarket newspapers, only more lurid. The general impression it gave was that Marissa Montclare, cabaret dancer and hooker, had met her death at a ''drug orgy in a glamorous Manhattan penthouse belonging to millionaire Sir Edward Wenlake, 62'.

To Mavis and Bert Handford, her parents, that was news. But then they hadn't heard from their Tracy for nearly three years, not since she'd left home at the age of seventeen to go with a dance troupe to America where she'd been determined to seek fame and fortune. Fancy calling herself Marissa Montclare! That hurt them at this moment, almost as much as the news of her death. It showed how ashamed she must have been of her background; how she must have longed to escape the life she'd been born into. The pain of rejection by her only child ripped through Mavis, causing a fresh wave of grief. Why couldn't she have written? Her body was in a morgue, awaiting an autopsy, the newspaper said. How strange, how unreal, reading of her death like this when they hadn't even known where she'd been living.

After a while, Mavis spoke. 'D'you think we should ring up the papers and tell them who she really is?' she asked, as if revealing Tracy's true identity would make a difference.

Bert pondered the question for a long moment. 'I think we should. How else will they know what to put on her . . . grave.' His voice broke and he averted his head quickly, looking out of the window to the small square patch of grass at the back of the house that was their garden; the garden Tracy had danced in as a child, skipping with youthful limbs and even then, a head full of dreams. Bert could see her now – his little princess with silvery gold hair and a laughing face.

'They must be told who she is,' he said firmly.

Mavis nodded. All that work. All those cleaning jobs she'd taken to pay for Tracy's dancing lessons, and ballet clothes and shoes . . . Marissa Montclare, what a name! What had been wrong with Tracy Handford?

'Yes, you tell them,' she whispered. 'It's our Tracy they're talk-ing about. It's our Tracy that's gone.' And then she paused, ruminating, her thoughts far away. 'I wonder what this 'ere Sir Edward's like?'

'Well, I don't suppose he'd be interested in the likes of us,' said Bert, 'but he must have thought our Tracy was a real lady, to have invited her to his home.'

Rebecca awoke early the next morning, refreshed and full of energy. Stirling had brought round a picnic-style supper with ham and cheese, fruit and salad, and her favourite sesame bread; but after she'd eaten she'd been so tired she'd gone straight back to bed and to sleep, and he had cleaned up and gone home. In the early days of sharing an apartment with Karen, they'd promised each other never to have a boyfriend stay overnight.

'Think how awful it would be in the mornings,' Rebecca had said, 'bumping into each other's men as we line up to use the bathroom.' Later, in view of the rapid turnover of Karen's guys, she'd been glad they had made the arrangement, even though it meant Stirling couldn't stay. She also liked to be alone first thing, in the morning, using the time to plan her day without interruption while she enjoyed her first cup of coffee. This morning, however, she jumped out of bed, put on some jeans and a warm sweater and, grabbing her purse, ran out to get the morning papers. Even after years in the business it never failed to give her a kick when she saw her pictures reproduced above the now famous by-line: Photo by Rebecca Kendall.

When she got back to her apartment, she spread out the *New York Times*, the *Daily News*, *USA Today* and the *New York Post*. There in all of them, were her pictures of Marissa. Stirling had done a good job. Within a few hours everyone in the city would be looking at her pictures of the beautiful twenty year old who had died so tragically. The story, Rebecca had to admit, had all the right ingredients for a sensational scandal: wealth, sex, beauty, a power-ful company and an English title. The media would go on milking the situation for days, and as the copyright on the pictures was hers alone, to sell as she liked, she stood to make several thousand dollars. Another Rebecca Kendall scoop.

After a quick cup of coffee and the remains of last night's sesame bread, she loaded up her camera bag with fresh film, made sure she had all the necessary gear, and set off on an assignment Stirling had fixed for her some time before – a commission by *Vogue*, no less. She'd been asked to take pictures of six society women in their homes, each dressed for the occasion by a famous couturier. So far she'd done Mrs Elworth Sumner II, Mrs Dolly Wojtas, and Mrs Mark Zimmerman. Today it was to be Nancy, the wife of Larry Greenfield, President of PPT Chemicals. Nancy and Larry Greenfield had a house in Beekman Place, were worth sixty million dollars, and had joined every benefit committee they could as a means of social climbing.

When Rebecca arrived, a manservant opened the door and showed her into a drawing-room of immense size and opulence. It was decorated in pale blue, with pale blue and white watered silk upholstery and curtains that seemed to be reflected into infinity by large mirrors at either end of the room. Huge white ceramic tubs of greenery and orchids were strategically placed and dramatically lit. Above the marble fireplace hung a portrait of Nancy, done in colours so vivid they jarred with the delicate softness of the room.

Nancy Greenfield appeared almost immediately, in a whirl of scarlet chiffon, set off with rubies and diamonds. According to Rebecca's information, she'd been outfitted by Adolfo and Harry Winston. Guillaume had arranged her hair at dawn, and there was also a make-up artist from Elizabeth Arden hovering in the background. This was lateral advertising at its most chic.

'What a bore this is – getting all dressed up in the morning!' observed Nancy, in a voice that showed clearly she was anything but bored. 'Do you want me to sit or stand? And haven't you got any lights?'

'These are going to be black and white shots using natural light,' Rebecca explained. 'In the style of Lord Snowdon's photographs,' she added, knowing that would mollify Nancy Greenfield. It did not, however, stop her face from falling into unbecoming lines of disappointment.

'Oh!' There was a pause. 'I thought they were going to be coloured photographs, like in *Town and Country*.'

'Not today, I am afraid,' said Rebecca breezily. 'Now, I'd like you to stand by this table in the window. If we can move this tub of orchids a bit to the left . . .'

'The butler will do it,' Nancy interjected rather sharply.

Rebecca pulled out the legs of the tripod, screwed them into position, and then with almost loving care attached her Swedish-made Hasselblad camera on to the top. The camera had cost her a small fortune and was her most prized possession. Being hand-made it was the world's de luxe camera and she never let anyone else touch it.

'Can you turn slightly to your right and look back over your shoulder at me?' she suggested, peering into the viewfinder and focusing.

Nancy did as she was told but looked unhappy. 'You won't be able to see the ruby and diamond necklace if I do that . . . or the ring on my right hand.'

Rebecca sighed inwardly, took a few shots and decided to get Nancy seated in an upright chair. She arranged her skirts around her and then sat facing the camera, hands on her crossed knees so that all her rings and both bracelets could be seen, as well as the necklace and earrings. Rebecca clicked away furiously. The woman looked quite ridiculous, but it was deliciously characteristic of her; she'd have worn six sets of jewellery if she could have found a place to put them all. *Vogue* might not like these particular shots, but to Rebecca they were classics.

'I saw your pictures of that little tramp in the papers this morning,' Nancy Greenfield suddenly observed, raising her face so her double chins would not show.

Rebecca looked up and saw the older woman's spiteful expression. 'Do you mean Marissa Montclare?' she asked coolly.

'Of course that's who I mean! She was drunk, I suppose?'

'No, she wasn't drunk. She was murdered,' replied Rebecca shortly.

'Murdered? That's not what the newspapers say.' Nancy sounded argumentative.

'Well, you know the old saying: "You can't believe everything you read in the newspapers".'

Rebecca unclipped the back section of the Hasselblad where the film was housed, and clipped on a freshly loaded one.

'You don't mean . . . you can't mean that Sir Edward Wenlake had anything to do with it?'

Rebecca compressed her lips tightly to stop herself from saying something rude. Nancy Greenfield was one of the most stupid and nosey women she'd ever come across. She was also a gossip.

'Of course Sir Edward didn't have anything to do with it,' Rebecca retorted crossly. 'Now, can you face the camera again, hands on your knee as before . . . Great! Wonderful. Hold it just like that.'

Rebecca clicked away without the slightest pang of guilt. It would serve the bitch right to be portrayed exactly as she was.

The session over, she packed her gear and left. She wanted to do some grocery shopping and stop back at her apartment before going on to photograph another society woman in the afternoon.

When the cab dropped her outside her building she hurried up the three flights of stairs, her feet in their black leather boots echoing noisily on the uncarpeted surface. During the day, the building was deserted. Karen left for work early every morning, and the other tenants, a choreographer on the first floor, a designer on the second, and the couple who lived at the top, also went out to work. Getting the key out of her pocket, Rebecca climbed the last flight, her camera bag slung from her shoulder, her arms full of groceries. On the landing that led to her door she paused suddenly, an unaccountable wave of uneasiness sweeping over her. Something was wrong. She could feel it instinctively. She knew it even before she realized the door to her apartment was ajar.

'Karen?' she called out, a prickling sensation of fear giving a sharp edge to her voice. The silence was heavy and oppressive. She could see that both locks had been wrenched and the door had been forced open. Nudging it with her shoulder, her heart hammering, she waited until it swung wide open before reaching into the dimness of her tiny hallway to turn on the light. Then she gasped with disbelief.

All the doors inside the apartment had been flung open and every room had been ransacked. Clothes and shoes lay scattered in both bedrooms; in the living-room, books and ornaments and lamps were strewn over the floor and a vase lay broken, flowers thrown about, water soaking a dark stain into the carpet. The kitchen was as bad: everything had been pulled out of the cupboards, and the contents spilled so that cereals and sugar and coffee lay in a congealed mess of honey and olive oil and ketchup. Even the refrigerator had been plundered.

With a groan of disgust, Rebecca turned away and noticed immediately that the door to the darkroom was shut. For a moment she hesitated as she realized how vulnerable she was. If anyone was hiding in there and they decided to attack her, there'd be no one to come to her rescue. For a moment she thought of running back down the stairs and out into the street where she could get to a phone and call the police; but suddenly, she felt a surge of rage. How dare anyone break into her home and destroy her possessions? It was the ultimate in offensiveness, a gross act of intrusion, and from the looks of it a gesture of wanton destruction.

The sweat was running down her back now and her throat had gone dry. Wildly she looked round for a weapon with which to defend herself. All she could see was a large striped umbrella one of Karen's boyfriends had left behind. Grabbing it, she kicked open the door to the darkroom and flicked on the light.

Before her lay a scene of devastation. Tanks full of chemicals had

58

been knocked over, soaking everything and filling the air with the suffocating stench of formaldehyde. With stinging eyes and a sense of despair Rebecca surveyed the damage. Thousands of dollars worth of lenses, the enlarger, printing paper, thermometers, filters and light meters, things she'd worked hard to save up for, lay smashed and destroyed in a stinking chaotic mess of stainless steel and glass. Everything had been turned over and tossed aside in what looked like a frenzied effort to find something specific. The TV set and the video recorder and stereo equipment in the living-room hadn't been taken, nor had the string of pearls her grandmother had left her, for she'd seen them a moment before on the bedroom floor. Then the explanation dawned on her with frightening clarity.

Whoever had broken into her apartment had been looking for something specific and she had no doubt what it was.

Bert Handford opened the dilapidated photograph album and pointed to a snapshot of a young girl in a tutu posing self-consciously on the top of a low brick wall, her head held coyly to one side. 'That's our Tracy,' he said, his voice filled with pride.

The reporter from the *Margate Echo* scrutinized the picture, his brows furrowed. It was out of focus as were so many in the album, taken by Bert himself, he was told. It was hard to tell if the little girl, looking archly over her shoulder into the lens, bore any likeness to the boldly smiling dancer on the front page of the national tabloids.

'Always dancing, she was,' said Mavis, in a voice hoarse from weeping.

'You see,' Bert explained painfully, 'we thought we ought to say that this Marissa Montclare is really our Tracy. It needs to be sorted out, like, so that people know. Would you be able to do that for us? Put in the papers who she really was?' He'd called up the *Margate Echo* because it was the only newspaper whose telephone number he had. He and Mavis had put in a small ad a couple of years back, when they'd wanted to sell the sideboard his mother had left him. He recalled that the *Echo* had been very helpful then.

Bert looked hopefully at the reporter and thought that they gave responsible jobs to very young men these days. Lads, really. Just boys.'Would you be able to get it into the newspapers?' he repeated. 'Nobody's told us nothing. They can't know who she really is, you see. I'd get on to this lord . . . this whoever . . .'

'Sir Edward Wenlake,' interjected the journalist.

'Right. But I don't know where he lives in America.'

'In New York. It shouldn't be difficult to find out.'

'Right. Tracy must have had other friends. What we don't

understand is, it says she was a rich girl. Last we heard, she wasn't earning much at that club where she danced.'

'In Las Vegas,' said Mavis Handford.

'That's right,' said Bert.

The journalist scribbled in his pad, doubt written all over his face. As far as he could see there wasn't the faintest resemblance between Tracy Handford, perched on the garden wall in her tutu, and Marissa Montclare, with her mile-long legs and deep cleavage. He supposed it was the money this couple were after. Greed could drive people to any lengths. The tabloids had said "Marissa was worth in excess of two million dollars". Of course all newspapers exaggerated, but even so . . . coming from a home like this? He looked around at the shabby furnishings and at the ordinary couple, and was sure it was a case of mistaken identity. Nevertheless, he'd been trained to follow up every story he was given so, sighing inwardly, he pressed on.

'Could I borrow this picture?'

Bert and Mavis looked anxiously at each other. The album was all they had left of their beloved child. 'If you let us have it back,' Bert said reluctantly.

'We'll have a copy made and I'll see you get the original back by the end of the week.'

Half an hour later he was back in the small offices of the *Margate Echo*.

'Couple of old cranks, if you ask me,' he remarked, after he'd told his boss what had happened.

'Better check it out,' said the Editor. 'You never know.'

'The damned fool!' claimed Angela Wenlake, throwing down yet another newspaper in which her ex-husband was featured. The notoriety she was suffering in the village as a result of the scandal was infuriating and highly unfair. After all, as she told Simon, she and Edward had been divorced eleven years ago. Why should she be constantly linked with him now? Yet all the papers, especially the tabloids, were desperate to dredge up every bit of 'background interest', as they called it, and the whole family history was being laid out for everyone to read. Not that 'descended from George II' or 'related to the first Duke of Saxmundham' cut much ice in Pinkney these days. Half the village seemed to be Labour supporters and the other half were yuppies from London who were only interested in making money and had no taste when it came to spending it. Angela most resented being referred to as "the ex-Lady Wenlake whom Sir Edward deserted", or worse, "the woman he left behind".

'I don't know what he could have been thinking of,' Simon agreed.

'A girl of twenty, I ask you! Any fool would have known it would end in trouble.'

'It's going to be very embarrassing, facing everyone at the Hunt Ball, and what am I going to say to the Lancasters and Freddie? They arrive at the end of the week.' Absently, Angela Wenlake stroked the King Charles spaniel on her knee. He was called Boffin and hardly ever left her side.

'Nobody can blame you, Mother,' protested Simon. 'At least he lives in America and not here. You'll just have to wash your hands of him completely – say you haven't talked for years, that sort of thing. And it's true, isn't it? I mean, Jenny may insist on seeing him, but you and I haven't.'

'It's still a disgrace in the family,' Angela said severely. 'We keep getting mentioned in the press, which of course wouldn't happen if we were ordinary people, but once one has a title . . .' Her voice drifted off, as if the burden of having noble blood was too much for her to bear.

'It'll blow over soon though, won't it?' Simon's pink face looked hopeful. 'I mean, these things do get forgotten fairly quickly. All we need is another bit of scandal happening to someone else and we'll be in the clear.'

Angela sighed. 'Yes, you're right. I suppose it could have been much worse. I mean, suppose the girl had jumped . . . think what an uproar that would have caused! My God, how would I have explained that to the Lancasters? At least she only slipped and fell. Drunk probably. But it's all a most unfortunate embarrassment for us.'

Simon nodded sagely, his twenty-five years seeming like a lifetime of experience to him. One day he'd inherit the title and become Sir Simon Wenlake. Meanwhile, he knew he'd never behave as foolishly as his father.

The Earl and Countess of Lancaster arrived on the Thursday morning, driven in their old Daimler by their son, the Honourable Frederick Wareham. Angela Wenlake came out to greet them as soon as she heard the crunch of the tyres on the gravel driveway. After they all touched cheeks and kissed air and exclaimed how lovely it was to see each other again and how marvellous they all looked and weren't they lucky with the weather? Angela led them into the house, while Peters hovered, ready to unload their luggage and take it up to their rooms.

'My dear, where's Jenny?' asked Lady Lancaster, as they sat having afternoon tea in the drawing-room a little while later.

Angela Wenlake cleared her throat and looked over at Freddie, but he appeared to be absorbed in a conversation about shooting with Simon.

'She's away,' said Angela in a low voice. 'You know, this dreadful business . . .' She moved closer as if to confide. 'She's such a kind-hearted girl, she insisted on flying over to see Edward. Of course I expect her back at any moment. I mean Edward must have gone mad. A girl that age! The male menopause of course, my dear. Don't let anyone tell you it doesn't exist.'

Lady Lancaster looked across at her elderly husband who was on the point of dozing off on the sofa.

'I don't think I need worry about that with him,' she observed with a smile. Then she added, 'I do think it's sweet of Jenny to have gone to visit her father. She's always been devoted to him, hasn't she? A real "father's girl".'

Angela's smile froze as she offered the cucumber sandwiches. It was true about Jenny and Edward, and for some reason it always pained her.

The Hunt Ball, held at nearby Haversham Hall, was the following night. Simon had invited Charlotte Cowan to partner Freddie, much to Angela's fury, while he himself was escorting a pretty debutante called Rosemary Burgess whom he'd met earlier in the year.

'Can't you push Rosemary on to Freddie and take Charlotte yourself?' demanded his mother.

Simon gazed at her with eyes as clear and untroubled as a summer's sky. 'Why should I? I like Rosemary, and last time he was here Freddie rather liked Charlotte.'

'God, you're so stupid,' cried Angela. 'That's the whole point, he *did* like Charlotte! What about Jenny? I know it's her fault that she's not here, but we don't have to throw the opposition into Freddie's arms, do we?'

Simon shrugged. 'I never did think he was interested in Jenny, except as a friend. He'd have asked her to marry him by now if he was going to.'

Angela Wenlake refused to be defeated. 'Rubbish! He's been stationed in Germany. He'll wait until his army career is more established before he settles down.' She made a note to readjust the seating plan for dinner, so that Charlotte Cowan ended up at the farthest end of the table from Freddie Wareham.

The next morning, Angela was so busy that she didn't have time even to glance at the newspapers which Peters had as usual laid on the hall table. Eighteen guests were expected for dinner that evening before they all went on to the ball, and she wanted all the arrangements to be perfect. Heather the cook and Ruby the kitchenmaid were already hard at work, helped by some of the women from the village who were glad to earn a few extra pounds. On the large scrubbed kitchen table lay a side of venison, which had been shot by Angela's brother when he'd stalked in Scotland with the Queen recently, and beside it were a mound of vegetables and fruit which Harrods had delivered from London the previous afternoon. Eggs for meringues and jugs of thick whipping cream stood on the side with a whole Stilton cheese which had a section scooped out and filled with port. A whole smoked salmon lay resplendent on the draining-board, waiting to be sliced.

After Angela had said a few encouraging words to everyone in the kitchen, she put her head round the door of the flower room. Here buckets of water stood on the stone floor, filled with masses of yellow lilies which had also been delivered by Harrods. A marvellous little woman from the village, who always did the church flowers, was coming to arrange them later. That just left Peters, in the butler's pantry. He was polishing the silver candlesticks as if his life depended on it. Angela had an encouraging word with him too, ticking off her lists as she went through everything; wine still had to be brought up from the cellar, champagne put on ice, and of course Jones the gardener must be told to bring in several baskets of logs for the fires.

It wasn't until she paused to have morning coffee in the library with the Lancasters and Freddie that Lord Lancaster remarked on what he'd been reading in the morning's newspapers.

'Her real name's Tracy Handford,' he announced.

'Whose real name?' asked Angela, although somehow she knew, had guessed with a sinking heart what he was talking about.

'That girl. You know, the one who fell from Eddie's window,' he mumbled through his bristling white moustache.

'Tracy Handford,' Angela repeated in a flat voice.

'I didn't think it could really be Marissa Montclare,' Lady Lancaster observed calmly, 'it's too fancy a name.'

'It seems,' continued Lord Lancaster, 'that she was a chorus girl at one of the casinos in Las Vegas, The Golden Palm. She was a cabaret dancer. When she went to New York she changed her name, told everyone she came from Houston and was the heiress to a railroad fortune.'

Angela sat down, her legs suddenly weak. 'A cabaret dancer!'

Lord Lancaster nodded with relish. In his opinion old Eddie should be congratulated on getting himself such a gorgeous bit of crackling in the first place. 'Apparently she was English, from a very ordinary background. Her parents live in Margate.'

'Margate,' echoed Angela faintly.

'She went to America when she was seventeen. Got herself a job with a troupe of dancers and they performed in cabaret in one of those casinos in Las Vegas. This is extraordinary though!' He stopped and read a paragraph a second time.

'What is it?' Angela wasn't sure how much more she could take.

Lord Lancaster looked up, his blue eyes quizzical, his bushy white eyebrows puckered together. 'It says here that she was a very wealthy young woman. Worth at least two million!'

'How can that be?' exclaimed Lady Lancaster. 'I didn't think dancers made a lot of money.'

Angela's voice was strained. 'They don't. Either Edward must have been giving her some, or she was a prostitute.'

The old earl looked startled. 'That doesn't sound like old Eddie to me. Taking up with a Lady of the Night? Never!' They'd been to Eton together and there were some things a gentleman didn't do. Going with prostitutes, in his opinion, was one of them.

'Have you spoken to Jenny?' asked Lady Lancaster. 'She must know what's going on.'

'No, I haven't spoken to her since she left.' Angela sounded cool. 'I don't suppose Edward has dared tell her everything, in any case. Oh God, I suppose everyone at the ball tonight will have read the newspapers! How could Edward do this to us all?' she added angrily.

'It's hardly his fault,' protested Lord Lancaster. 'I mean, it was an accident. Accidents happen all the time. On the hunting-field, out shooting. You can't blame him because there was an accident, Angela.'

'I'm not blaming him for the accident, John,' Angela said bitterly, 'I'm blaming him for letting it happen to such an undesirable person!'

The police sergeant, who had come in answer to Rebecca's emergency call looked at her curiously. He'd examined the damage, made a few notes, and called for a finger-print expert. Now, as he sat taking her statement, he probed more deeply with his questions.

'Why do you think someone broke in to steal your film?'

'Because I'm sure I have some pictures of the man who killed Marissa Montclare,' Rebecca replied, having already explained her theory. 'Whatever Detective O'Hara says, I'm convinced she was murdered and I'm convinced I've got the murderer on film. It so happens my agent has the film now, but whoever broke in here couldn't have known that. It could easily have been in my darkroom.'

'Well, I can't comment on what Detective O'Hara says – he's in a different precinct to mine – but in view of what you say I will inform him of what's happened and tell him you think the intruder was after your films.'

Rebecca looked at the serious well-spoken young cop and wished he were involved in Marissa's case instead of O'Hara. He seemed an altogether more intelligent person, prepared to listen and sympathetic to the shock she'd received.

'Thank you. To me it seems obvious. Why else would anyone ransack the apartment and practically demolish the darkroom and then not take anything? I'm sure they were looking for those pictures, and I think they were as mad as hell when they couldn't find them.'

'Did you tell anyone you were going to show them to Detective O'Hara?'

Rebecca shook her head. 'After I'd been to the precinct, I told my boyfriend – agent, that is – but no one else know, except of course for my roommate, Karen.'

'Then we must suppose that whoever murdered the young lady knew you'd taken lots of pictures, and they weren't taking any chances in case you'd got an identifiable shot of them.'

'Exactly.' Rebecca felt a wonderful sense of relief that he believed her. After her interview with O'Hara, she'd begun to doubt herself.

Karen returned home at six in the evening to find Rebecca trying to clean up the place. The finger-print expert had brushed silver powder on various surfaces and it wasn't easy to get off.

'What the hell?' Karen stood in the middle of the living-room, her legs in bright pink leg-warmers planted wide, one hand ruffling her mane of curly blonde hair. 'What's happened, for Chrissakes?'

Rebecca explained as briefly as she could. 'I'm sorry about this, Karen. At least I don't think any of your things has been stolen.'

Karen charged into her bedroom and surveyed the mess. 'Now I'll *have* to clean it, I suppose. What a drag! Isn't it gross to think of someone going through all your stuff!' She picked up a pair of very brief blue lace underpants. 'They've even been through my panty drawer! And they must have found my picture of Tony. I threw it in there the other night when I was so pissed off with him.'

'Do pictures of your discarded boyfriends always end up in your panty drawer?' asked Rebecca, glad to have her roommate home. Karen always made her laugh, and right now she felt in need of cheering up.

'Always,' replied Karen. 'Face down if I never want to speak to them again, face up if I just might.' She turned and wandered back into the hall. 'How are we going to get rid of this smell? It's stifling.'

'I'll have to unlock the darkroom window and leave the place to air for several days. That will help dry it out too.' As she spoke she went into the darkroom and unscrewed a sheet of black-painted plywood that she had fixed tightly across the window to make the room light-proof. 'I could kill whoever did this!'

'I suppose you're insured?'

'Yes, but it's a real hassle! It'll take ages to replace all my gear. Thank God Stirling keeps all my negatives in his office or I'd have lost everything – every picture I've ever taken.'

'I'm scared,' Karen said suddenly. 'What if they come back?'

Rebecca shrugged. 'I don't think they'll do that. They know I don't have what they're looking for. Stirling is going to take extra precautions at the agency, though, in case they try there. He's putting the films in a safety deposit box in the bank.'

Karen didn't look convinced. 'I still feel nervous! Damn! I wish I hadn't had that fight with Tony. I could have gone to stay with him. I don't feel like staying here at the moment.'

'You could go to your sister.'

'I might just do that. What about you? You're not going to spend the night, are you?'

'I don't see why not. I don't believe they'll be back. I've had new locks put on the door. I'm really not worried.'

'Jesus, you're brave!' Karen looked at her with a mixture of amazement and admiration. At that moment the phone rang and she jumped.

'It's all right,' said Rebecca calmly, 'it's probably Stirling. We're going out to dinner and maybe he's running late.' She picked up the receiver. 'Hello?'

'Rebecca?'

The voice was familiar, but she couldn't quite place it.

'Yes,' she replied cautiously.

'Hi, this is Jerry. Jerry Ribis. I dropped you off on New Year's Eve after . . .'

'Of course, I remember. How are you?'

'Fine.' His voice was warm and attractive, and she remembered his boyish face and eager expression. 'I've seen your pictures of Marissa Montclare in all the papers. You're a marvellous photographer.'

Rebecca smiled, touched by his admiration. 'I don't know about that,' she replied modestly.

'I was wondering . . . I'm sure you're busy . . . but I wondered if you'd be free for dinner one night?' The invitation came out in a rush, and Rebecca could just imagine him blushing on the other end of the line.

'Who is it?' Karen was asking behind her.

Rebecca cupped the mouthpiece with her hand. 'A sweet young lawyer I met.'

Karen was instantly riveted. 'Ask him up,' she mouthed.

Amused, Rebecca turned her back on her friend and tried to keep the laughter out of her voice. 'I'm afraid I'm rather tied up, Jerry.'

'Oh.' He sounded very disappointed. 'Perhaps lunch one day? Or a drink even?'

Rebecca had been going out with Stirling for such a long time she'd almost forgotten what it was like to fend off admirers. 'I really am very busy,' she said gently. 'It's sweet of you to ask me out, but my time is fully committed.'

There was a pause, and then he said slowly: 'Gee, that's a shame. Well, can I call you again anyway?'

Rebecca smiled. 'Sure, but I can't guarantee I'll be free. Thanks all the same.'

'Well . . . goodbye then. I'll hope to see you some time.' He sounded awkward, embarrassed, as if he weren't used to being rejected.

'Goodbye, Jerry.' Rebecca replaced the receiver and swung round to look at Karen who'd been listening avidly. 'How about that?' she asked, amused.

'Why didn't you ask him to come up for a drink?' demanded Karen. 'You might not want him, but you might give your best friend the chance to be taken out to dinner! What's he like? Where did you meet him?'

By the time Rebecca had finished explaining, Stirling had arrived. He took one look at the mess in the darkroom and gave a long low whistle.

'My God, they sure knocked hell out of the place! What a bum wrap!' he exclaimed. 'You can't stay here tonight, Rebecca.'

'That's what I said,' Karen interjected. 'I'm going to my sister's place. Nothing would induce me to stay,' she shuddered. 'The place gives me the creeps.'

Rebecca looked distressed. 'But this is my home. Of course I'm going to stay. It would be stupid to run away now – they're not going to bother coming back knowing there's nothing here for them.'

'Becky, honey.' Stirling came and stood close to her, looking down into her face. Then he raised his hands and touched the long silky hair that fell about her shoulders. 'I don't know about you, but I won't be able to sleep thinking of you alone in this place after what's happened. I want you to come back with me.'

'That's right,' said Karen.

'But I feel perfectly safe here . . .' Rebecca began. Stirling interrupted her, his voice unusually stern.

'Listen, if you're right about this whole thing, and I think you probably are, you're dealing with killers. They got rid of Marissa Montclare for some reason . . . what's to stop them from getting rid of you just because they're afraid you know too much? For God's sake, Rebecca, you must take this thing seriously. You're coming with me, and you're going to stay with me until this whole affair has been cleared up.'

Rebecca's eyes sparked with annoyance. 'This is my life, Stirling, and I won't be told what to do,' she retorted, extricating herself from his arms. 'I have no intention of leaving here. And if whoever-it-is wants to kill me, they'll try it anyway: in the street, in the subway, wherever!'

Karen looked shocked. 'Rebecca, how can you be so cool?'

'She's being crazy and stubborn,' Stirling said angrily.

'Well, I'm staying here, in my own apartment and that's that,' Rebecca said firmly. 'Now, are we going out to eat or not? Because I'm starving.'

Stirling shook his head in frustration. 'Oh, Christ, why are you so obstinate!'

Rebecca picked up her purse. 'Are you coming?' she asked airily. He followed her slowly.

'I'll be gone by the time you get back,' Karen called after them. 'I just wish *I* had a gorgeous boyfriend to go and stay with!'

'Don't forget to lock the door . . .' Rebecca began, and then she broke off, laughing '. . . even if the horse has bolted.'

The guests began arriving at eight o'clock, the women like a flock of chattering birds in gauzy diamond-encrusted finery, the men strutting like well-groomed penguins. Peters served champagne cocktails in the drawing-room. Angela had taken down the Christmas tree and the florist from the village had arranged large vases of lilies mixed with greenery from the garden. Quails' eggs served with celery salt were passed around in crested silver dishes, and on a little round Georgian table in the centre of the room a dish of fresh crisp crudités was arranged on a bowl of crushed ice.

To Angela's relief, no one seemed to be mentioning the débâcle of Edward and the Dancing Girl. In fact, all the guests seemed to be pointedly keeping off the topic as she moved among them, making introductions, having little chats, complimenting some of the women on their dresses, asking the men how the hunting season was going. Gracious in black lace and a blaze of emeralds and pearls, she epitomized the perfect hostess, seeing that all her guests were looked after and their glasses constantly refilled.

'Jolly good show tonight, m'dear,' remarked Lord Lancaster as she came up to him. 'This is a perfect send-off for the ball. Nothing like a good dinner to set one up!'

Angela smiled gratefully, her sharp-featured face and grey eyes softening for a moment. 'Thank you, John. I think it's going very well, don't you? Dinner will be announced in about five minutes and thank God . . .' she leaned forward and whispered in his ear '. . . so far, no one has mentioned you-know-what!'

Lancaster nodded, understanding. 'Good! Personally I think you'll find the whole thing will soon be forgotten. People have very short memories.'

'Yes, I'm sure you're right.' Angela felt comforted. Soon there would be a new scandal to galvanize the media, and the story of Edward and the Dancing Girl would quickly be forgotten.

At that moment she heard sounds of a commotion coming from the hall. It sounded as if Peters was arguing with someone. As the voices grew louder several of the guests stopped talking and turned their heads to listen.

'I've got to put a stop to this,' Angela muttered under her breath, but at that moment the drawing-room door flew open and a small thin man came hurtling into the room, almost skidding to a halt as he rushed up to Angela. Seedy-looking in a raincoat buttoned up to the neck and with long strands of dark hair draped over his bald crown, his eyes flashed suspiciously round the room. He looked startled as his gaze fell upon the elegantly dressed guests.

Flustered and red in the face, Peters came rushing in and grabbed the man's arm trying to drag him away.

'Get off!' the man snapped, turning on the butler like an angry terrier. The dinner guests clustered closer, intrigued.

'What is the meaning of this?' Angela demanded icily.

'M'lady, I'm sorry—!' Peters got no further. The man stepped forward and spoke in a high piping voice.

'You're Lady Wenlake then? It's Lady Wenlake I want to see.'

Peters tried to intervene. 'I'm very sorry, m'lady. I did my best to—'

'My name is Mike Wilson, from Lawson, Martin & Grant, Gene-alogists and International Probate Researchers,' he declared.

At that moment Angela Wenlake knew with a sense of doom that this dreadful little man was there because of Edward and the Dancing Girl.

'I am here representing Mr and Mrs Bert Handford, the parents of Miss Tracy Handford, better known as Marissa Montclare of New York City,' Mike Wilson announced pompously. In the electrifying silence that followed, Angela stood and prayed that a hole would appear in the floor into which she could disappear.

'Mr and Mrs Handford,' he continued relentlessly, 'have appointed us to recover the fortune left by their daughter, Tracy Handford, which is being held in America following her demise. In the absence of Sir Edward Wenlake, they are looking to you, Lady Wenlake, to assist them in this matter.'

Mavis and Bert Handford had never really wanted to make a fuss, only to set the record straight; but when all the newspapers came out with the truth about their Tracy being the girl who had died at Sir Edward's party, they were pursued by a firm called Lawson, Martin & Grant who had assured them they would suffer 'unfair deprivation' by the upper classes unless they put up a fight to inherit what was rightfully theirs.

Bert and Mavis had sat bemused that first evening when Mike Wilson called at their house, because they weren't sure what 'rights' they were supposed to have.

'Your daughter was worth a bit,' Mike assured them. 'That money is now rightfully yours. Mark my words, those people she was mixing with at the end, like Sir Edward Wenlake, they won't care what happens. They'll just want to sweep the whole thing under the carpet because it is an embarrassment to them. Gawd knows what'll happen to all her money if you don't get a claim in, quick like!' His beady eyes darted to and fro, so that they could almost see the workings of his mind.

Bert and Mavis looked at one another and said nothing. Their grief was still too new, their pain too deep, to think about things like their Tracy's money.

'Now don't get me wrong!' Mike continued, raising both hands in a gesture of surrender although they showed no sign of opposing him. 'There are a lot of sharks around these days and I'm here to protect you.' On his knee was a cheap blue cardboard folder marked 'Marissa Montclare/Tracy Handford.'

'So what do we have to do?' Bert asked at last.

70

Mike raised his right hand again, and they saw his nails were bitten down to the quick. 'Leave it to me. I'm doing you a favour, really. I don't like to see a case like this, where hard-working parents are done out of what is rightfully theirs because there is no one to look after their interests.'

Mavis turned her gold wedding band around and round on her plump finger, finding it hard to hold back the tears. No money in the world was going to give her back her lovely girl. Rights, whatever they might be, meant nothing to her at this moment.

Bert shuffled his feet in their beige bedroom slippers and knew he was no match for this fast-talking man who had fast-talked his way into their house.

Mike Wilson was now in full flow. 'I will set out to collect Marissa's . . . I mean Tracy's . . . money, saving you a lot of worry and trouble.' With a flourish he withdrew his fake gold pen from his inner pocket and opened the blue file. 'Now, if you can tell me . . .'

'But what's in it for you?' Bert asked bluntly. He might not be too bright but he knew nobody does anything for nothing.

Mike's breezy manner didn't falter. 'I take a small percentage.' Then he continued smoothly, 'I will be flying to America, finding out if she left a will, finding out if her money is in a bank or in shares or stock or whatever. Then there will be your claim as her next-of-kin to put forward and establish . . . there is a lot to be done, I assure you, but it won't cost you a penny. After all . . .' here his voice took on a sanctimonious tone '. . . you've both worked very hard all your lives, and you must have spent a lot of money on . . . on . . .' Here he stumbled for a moment, unable to remember either of their daughter's names '. . . your little girl when she was small. You had to pay for dancing classes, I expect? And ballet shoes? Yes? Well then, I'm sure she'd have liked you to have whatever she left, isn't that right?'

They could see from his flushed face how he relished the pursuit of money, even if it wasn't his own. Lawson, Martin & Grant, established in 1930, had once been a highly respected company whose job it was to trace beneficiaries of wills, identify heirs, and carry out research for relevant certificates and documents. After World War II, however, it had changed hands and become a rundown concern with not a Lawson or a Martin or a Grant anywhere in sight. Mike Wilson, a would-be lawyer who had failed to qualify, had joined during the seventies, and since then had ferreted out fortunes for other people from which he deducted a hefty percentage. Keeping an eye on the newspapers for likely clients, he pursued his quarry with dedication, tracing missing relatives and unlikely heirs as far away as Australia and as near as the next town. His success rate was high.

Bert and Mavis sat in silent acquiescence while Mike did the talking. They'd loved their only child with all their hearts, and they'd been proud of her. To them, scrimping and saving so that she could have everything she wanted had been a privilege not a hardship. It had been a joy to make her happy.

Mike Wilson's tone was still coaxing. 'Now, I'm going to need your help if I'm to recover all the money for you. Tell me, what do you know about her life for the past two or three years? Who were her friends? Do you know where we can contact Sir Edward Wenlake, or failing that Lady Wenlake? We might just be able to get them to advance some of Tracy's money to you . . . seeing as she was with Sir Edward at the end.'

Sir Edward lay in the voluptuous darkness of his brown velvet and satin bedroom, unable to sleep. His mind was in a turmoil, trying to grapple with the new-found knowledge that Marissa Montclare hadn't been Marissa Montclare at all. She'd been someone called Tracy Handford who came from the English seaside resort of Margate, where day trippers from London ate candy-floss and winkles on the pier and wore funny hats with slogans like 'Kiss me Quick' printed on the front. This background of coachloads of working-class people out for a day by the sea, dragging their small children along in the wake of an aroma of fish and chips, was so removed from the picture he'd built up in his mind of Marissa's childhood that the two could not be reconciled. For three months now, until he'd read the latest newspaper scoop, he'd imagined her growing up in the rich comfort of her parents' home in Houston, while her father made a fortune manufacturing railroad equipment. This new revelation staggered him. All these months, furnished by her descriptions, he'd had these pictures in his mind of the poor-little-rich-girl, losing her mother from cancer when she was seven, and then her father from a stroke the previous year. And he'd thought how brave she'd been, at just twenty, to come to New York all by herself in order to make a new life and a fresh start.

Now, Sir Edward felt cheated out of his fantasy of Marissa as the lonely heiress in Trump Tower, and of himself as the older wiser knight in shining armour, ready to love and protect her from the evils of the world. All the time, he kept repeating to himself, she'd been someone entirely different.

He climbed out of bed, pulled on his monogrammed silk dressing-gown and padded barefoot into the drawing-room. From the side-table he poured himself a large whisky, knowing he was drinking too much but unable to resist the temporarily calming effect of the liquor. Then he went back to his bedroom. Maybe, in a while, he'd get some asleep.

An hour later he was still awake, his mind tormented by the two pictures of Marissa that would not fit together. He remembered her accent, a mid-Atlantic American he'd been unable to place. Her natural accent had probably been cockney he thought with shock. Nothing he had known about her had been real. Her background, her dead parents, even her accent – all of it had been a lie. Had her fortune been a lie too?

Judging from the newspapers her real parents, Bert and Mavis Handford, had no money at all, and yet he'd been to Marissa's apartment, seen the lavish furnishings, paintings, cupboards full of clothes from Chanel and Bill Blass and Giorgio Armani, witnessed her opening a jewel case full of Cartier, Tiffany and Van Cleef and Arpels pieces. How had she come to be so rich . . . unless of course she was a high-class hooker?

Sir Edward closed his eyes in a paroxysm of pain, unable to bear the thought. One of her lovers must have been at least an Arab oil magnate . . . and yet he was convinced she wasn't that experienced. Then he was struck by another thought. Why hadn't she charged *him* if she'd been a call girl? Could it have been because . . .

He thought back to the evening they'd met at a gala cocktail party for charity. Marissa had been introduced to him by the wife of a Wall Street broker he'd known for some time. They'd gone to bed three nights later because he'd fallen in love with her from the moment he'd set eyes on her. He'd thought then that Marissa had fallen in love with him too. Their desire seemed mutual. It was the most wonderful thing that had happened to him, and the reason he was sure their relationship was going to work was because Marissa had money of her own. He would never have to wonder if she was really after his money, and that had made him feel good. She'd even taken an interest in his business, listening sympathetically when things were going badly or congratulating him when he'd closed a good deal. He remembered now that he'd even thought of marrying her in time.

But that had been Marissa Montclare. Who in hell's name was Tracy Handford, and what had *she* wanted? And what had she said to him minutes before she died? He racked his brains, trying to remember. Like someone peering over the rim of consciousness, he nearly grasped the truth at one point then it slid away again, lost in the alcoholic daze of that night. What was it she'd said? Suddenly, like a narrow shaft of light in the blackness, something came back to him. A spy . . . that was it. That's why Marissa had died! The word went zinging through his head in a wave of momentary clarity. She'd said something about 'a spy' . . . but what? He leaned back against the pillows again, frowning deeply in an effort to concentrate. He could see her face in his mind's eye, her eyes wide and alarmed and her manner agitated . . . but what in God's name had she actually been saying about a spy?

Oh Christ, why hadn't he listened? Why hadn't he paid more attention? Remorse and grief mingled as he cursed himself for having drunk so much that night. Never again, he swore. It horrified him to think that if he'd been sober Marissa might still be alive . . . and so would this stranger called Tracy Handford, about whom he knew nothing.

Angela Wenlake hustled Mike Wilson out of the drawing-room, away from her curious dinner guests. Whispering to Peters to offer more champagne and so delay dinner for ten minutes, she led the way hurriedly to the library.

Not once did Mike pause in his loquaciousness. Like a machine that had been tightly wound, he poured out his reasons for being there.

'. . . I wouldn't be troubling you, Lady Wenlake, if only Sir Edward Wenlake were in England, but as he is the only person who will know anything about Tracy Handford's money her parents are most anxious . . .'

Angela raised her hand in a gesture of irritation. *'Please,'* she commanded, her eyes blazing with anger, 'please will you listen to me? In the first place, you have no right to come barging in here when . . .'

'But I ask you, Lady Wenlake, what else am I supposed to do? Where else can I start but here when your husband is abroad? It has become a matter of urgency as her parents . . .'

'Ex-husband,' Angela said sharply.

'Very well, your ex-husband. They are in need of money; they've already suffered enough as it is. A great tragedy, losing their only child. They're not being greedy, I assure you, but they have a right to what is theirs, haven't they?'

Angela protested, 'This has nothing to do with me. I don't know anything about this wretched girl.'

Mike Wilson's face took on an expression of deep hurt. Dropping his voice to a whisper he continued: 'That's not very nice, Lady Wenlake. Not very nice at all. How would *you* feel if your daughter had died?'

'I wouldn't employ you in the first place,' she retorted.

'What d'you mean by that?' he asked, offended. 'I'm only doing my job! It's natural the parents want to recover what is due to them. They invested a lot in their daughter.' Mike Wilson paused to look around the book-lined library as if appraising the value of its contents. 'Nice place you've got here.'

Angela Wenlake's cheeks flamed. She strode to the carved pine fireplace and pressed the bell in the wall, long and hard.

'You will leave at once,' she said. 'You had no right to come here in the first place. I am divorced from Sir Edward and therefore cannot be held responsible for anything he might be involved in.'

Mike rubbed his hands together in a gesture of appeasement. 'But you could make Sir Edward aware of the situation, couldn't you? I have to contact him in New York . . . perhaps you could tell him I'm coming? And then there is the American legal system to deal with . . . well, it will take a long time, won't it? I'd hoped that if we could ascertain the amount Tracy Handford had left, you or Sir Edward could at least give an advance to her poor parents.'

'I have nothing further to say to you.' Angela Wenlake walked towards the library door. At that moment Peters entered the room in response to the bell.

'Show this person out,' commanded Angela. 'And then you may announce dinner.'

Mike Wilson started to protest, loudly and whingeingly, but Angela swept past him, her face a mask of suppressed fury. Edward would pay for this, she swore to herself. How dare he bring disgrace on them all! Jenny must fly home tomorrow, too. The sooner they all disassociated themselves from this scandal, the better.

Rebecca was in the bath when she heard the doorbell ring, loudly and persistently. Cursing, she wrapped herself in a white terry bath sheet and peeped through the spy-hole in her apartment door to see who it was. A moment later she was letting in the young cop who had come in response to the report of her burglary.

'I'm sorry to disturb you,' he said, as she dripped water on the rug.

'That's all right.' Rebecca clutched the towel tighter and showed him into the living-room. 'Have you caught the robber?'

'No, and I'm afraid I think it's unlikely that we will. There were no prints and nothing was taken that we could put a trace on.'

'I see. So what happens next?'

'We contacted Detective O'Hara, and reported your suggestion that the robbery might have been linked to the photographs you took at Sir Edward Wenlake's party.' He withdrew a small notebook from his back pocket, and flipped through the pages until he came to one in particular. 'Here we are. These are the details.' He frowned, studying the page.

'What did he say?' Rebecca inquired, hitching the towel higher.

The police sergeant snapped the notebook shut and looked at her, making her conscious of her bare shoulders and arms.

'Detective O'Hara said there was no reason to connect the robbery in your apartment with anything that happened at Sir Edward Wenlake's New Year's Eve Party. Apparently there were witnesses able to state that Marissa Montclare died by accident. So I'm afraid that's as far as I can go, Miss Kendall. The two events don't seem to be linked in any way.'

Rebecca stared back at him, her dark eyes filled with doubt. 'I don't believe that,' she said flatly. 'I simply don't believe it. Why was nothing taken then?'

He shook his head. 'Beats me, but that's what I came to tell you.'

'It doesn't make sense. Marissa's death was no accident, and my burglary was not a random break-in.'

'I'm afraid there's nothing else I can do. If we find out who broke into the apartment, we'll let you know.'

'Thanks.'

She held open the apartment door for him.

He left, shoes clattering down the cement steps. When he'd gone, Rebecca turned the hot tap on full and climbed back into the bath, more determined than ever to find out what the hell was going on.

Chapter Five

The name of the company was engraved on a brass plaque by the entrance: De Vere's Catering. Below in smaller lettering were the words: 'Receptions, Weddings, Banquets'.

Rebecca pushed open the glossily painted dark blue and white door, and found herself in an elegant office furnished like an expensive hotel lobby. Grey walls and carpets and pedestals displaying arrangements of pink and white flowers gave it a feminine touch. Brilliantly lit display cabinets showed examples of silver cutlery and entrée dishes, a variety of candlesticks and a dazzling arrangement of cut crystal glasses in different shapes and sizes.

So this is where Sir Edward comes when he wants a party arranged, thought Rebecca, shuddering at how much it must cost. The superior-looking young man sitting behind the antique gilt-embossed desk looked up, swept his eyes over her and went back to talking on the phone. Rebecca smiled inwardly. In her dark pants and warm leather jacket, her camera bag slung from one shoulder, she was obviously not his image of how a prospective hostess would look.

Seating herself on a little gilt and grey chair, by a little gilt table, she flicked through beautifully bound leather folders, one embossed Menus, the other Wines. Her eyes widened as she glanced at 'Suggested Menu for an Informal Dinner for Eight'. Stuffed quail . . . lobster cooked in champagne and served with foie gras and artichoke in ratafia jelly . . . bitter chocolate tier with cinnamon ice-cream and compôte of cherries . . .

Rebbeca's mouth began to water and she wished she'd had more than a cup of coffee for breakfast.

At last the young man finished his call and turned enquiring eyes towards her.

'Can I help you, ma'am?' he asked, in a tone of voice that suggested it was unlikely.

Rebecca came directly to the point. 'I believe you did the catering for Sir Edward Wenlake's New Year's Eve party?'

The young man sprang back, his expression now positively hostile. 'Did Sir Edward inform you of that?'

'No, I saw your vans outside when I arrived,' she replied bluntly. 'I was there, taking photographs.'

'I see.'

'Don't worry, no one had food poisoning,' Rebecca said lightly, taking a large buff envelope out of her case. 'I just wanted to know if this man in the photographs is one of your regular waiters?' She laid one of her pictures on his desk.

'All our staff who were working at that party have already made statements to the police,' the young man replied pointedly, without looking at the picture.

'I'm sure they have, but what I really want to know is if this man is one of your regulars? You see he's not wearing exactly the same white coat as the rest of your staff.'

Rebecca whipped out another photograph which showed a regular waiter offering a glass of champagne to Sir Edward. She placed it on the desk beside the first one. 'Your waiters have a logo on their breast pocket, don't they?' She pointed to the entwined D.V. in dark blue silk embroidery. 'But *this* waiter,' she continued, picking up the first print, 'has a plain white top. The mandarin collar is a slightly different shape too.'

For the first time the young man's composure seemed shaken. He compared the two photographs. 'That certainly isn't one of our waiters, nor is he in one of our jackets,' he said slowly. 'Who is this man?'

'That's what I'm trying to find out. Are you absolutely sure he's not one of yours? After all, when you're busy you surely hire extra help from an agency, don't you? Couldn't this be one of them, whom you've never happened to have used before?'

The young man shook his head. 'We never hire from an agency. Every maid and every waiter is known to us personally. They have to be. How could we send unknown people into private houses? The security risk would be enormous.'

Rebecca nodded, understanding. 'Yes, I see.'

'Why do you want to know where this man comes from?'

'Because someone let him roam around freely at Sir Edward Wenlake's party that night, and I'm convinced he's the man who pushed Marissa Montclare out of the window.'

The young man looked shocked. 'I'm sorry I can't help you – he's definitely not one of ours.'

Scott the butler regarded Rebecca with small serious eyes. 'I'm afraid Sir Edward isn't in, madam,' he said, remembering her from the party.

'Is he at his office?' The headquarters of the Tollemache Trust were also on Park Avenue, but down by Forty-Ninth Street, in a new glass and chrome skyscraper near the Union Carbide Building. Rebecca had been there once, to photograph Sir Edward sitting at his rosewood desk in a large pale green office, with windows from floor to ceiling overlooking the Pan Am building. The aura of power surrounding him was inhibiting.

This is the man, she'd told herself as she set up her tripod, who has fifteen billion dollars 'spending' money for the company, and it was his decision whether that money should be invested in a chocolate manufacturer or an airline, a chain of hotels or a chemical plant. Sir Edward was said to be able to read a balance sheet in the time it took most people to turn a page, and his business acumen, which often relied on gut instinct, had brought about a growth in the company that had given him an international reputation as a financial wizard from Tokyo to Zurich and from London to New York. The Tollemache Trust's profit before tax was in the region of one hundred and forty-six million dollars.

'That's right, madam,' Scott was saying. 'Sir Edward won't be back until later.'

At that moment a young woman with soft fair hair and languid blue eyes came into the hall. She was dressed in a typically English fashion, wearing a navy blue pleated skirt and cashmere cardigan with a plain white blouse. She resembled an overgrown schoolgirl, thought Rebecca.

'Can I help you?' the girl asked pleasantly. 'I'm Jenny Wenlake.'

Rebecca smiled involuntarily at the obvious likeness between father and daughter. 'I thought you must be. You have your father's eyes. I'm Rebecca Kendall.' They shook hands and Rebecca noticed that Jenny's handshake was limp, something she always associated with insipidness. 'I've got some photographs I want to show your father.'

'Won't you come in? Daddy shouldn't be long,' she said, leading the way into the drawing-room. 'Would you like some tea?' She smiled and Rebecca thought how much prettier she'd be if she wore a little make-up.

'Could I have coffee, please?' Rebecca followed her into the room, which was dazzlingly pretty by daylight.

Jenny laughed. 'Of course! I always forget that most Americans prefer coffee. We'll both have coffee please, Scott, and some biscuits.'

'Certainly, Miss Jenny.'

Rebecca noticed the easy way that Jenny gave orders to the butler. She was obviously used to dealing with servants.

The two girls seated themselves on either side of the fireplace in which apple wood logs burned. Jenny was the first to speak.

'What are these photographs you want Daddy to see?'

Rebecca hesitated, wondering how much Jenny Wenlake knew about the New Year's Eve party and Marissa's death. From the way she spoke, she sounded young for her age and there was a certain innocence about her face that seemed strange in the daughter of such a sophisticated man. Then Rebecca remembered that both Jenny and her brother had been brought up by their mother in England. Perhaps that accounted for Jenny's seeming immaturity.

'It's all right,' Jenny was saying, as if she'd read Rebecca's thoughts, 'I know what happened. Daddy told me everything. I've flown from England to be with him.'

Rebecca took the Kodak box full of prints out of her capacious bag. 'These are some of the pictures I took that night,' she said. 'I was going to ask your father if he knew one particular person.' She placed the print of the waiter on the low petit point-covered seat that stood between them. Stacked with books and magazines, it obviously doubled as a table.

Jenny picked up the picture and studied it. 'It's one of the hired waiters, isn't it?' she asked, surprised.

'That's right, but the catering company your father used that night has no idea who he is. He's not on their staff.'

Jenny bit on her lower lip. 'And what do you think he's got to do with the accident?'

'Accident?'

'Yes, the accident.' Bland blue eyes gazed innocently into Rebecca's.

'I don't think it was an accident,' she said in measured tones. 'I think Marissa was murdered and I think this man, posing as a waiter, was her killer.'

Jenny turned pale and there was a stunned silence in the room, broken only by the soft crackling and hissing of the blazing fire. 'I don't think that can be right. Daddy said it was an accident,' she said at last. She sounded like a little girl at that moment, a child who takes Daddy's word as gospel.

'That is the general opinion,' Rebecca agreed, 'but I was here and I remember what happened just before she fell from the window. She was very scared of something . . . or someone, but no one paid

80

any attention to what she was saying,' she continued, choosing her words with care. 'A minute later she was dead.'

Jenny's slim hand, with its smaller version of Sir Edward's crested signet ring on the little finger, flew up to her mouth in a gesture of horror.

'My God! Does Daddy know this?'

At that moment Scott entered the room with the coffee set out on an ornate silver tray, the cream and sugar in a little silver jug and matching bowl.

'Scott,' asked Jenny, looking up at him, 'do you know this waiter? Apparently he was at the party here on New Year's Eve but the caterers say he's not one of theirs. Did my father get in any other outside help that night?'

Scott scrutinized the photograph. 'No, Miss Jenny. No extra staff were hired that night. I can't understand De Vere's saying he's not one of theirs. All the waiters and maids came from them.'

'Don't worry,' said Jenny, 'we'll ask my father when he returns.'

When they were alone again, she went through all the photographs in the Kodak box – pausing, Rebecca noticed, when she got to the ones of Marissa which she studied with an intensity that Rebecca found interesting and disturbing. She seemed fascinated by the showgirl, and Rebecca supposed she was trying to discover the reason for her father's infatuation.

'Are you sure it wasn't an accident?' Jenny asked at last. 'This looks like such a happy . . . well, normal sort of party. If it isn't a rude question, why were you taking pictures? Daddy doesn't usually have the press.'

Quickly, Rebecca explained who she was and why she'd been at the party. She also described the robbery in her apartment. 'Now that I've become involved, through no wish of my own, I feel bound to find out what happened,' she concluded. 'I mean, the whole thing becomes more mysterious every day. We read in the newspapers only yesterday that Marissa's real name was Tracy Handford, and that she was English when we all thought she was American. That must have come as quite a shock to your father. And now we find that the catering company didn't send this waiter, which strengthens my belief that he is the killer.'

Jenny looked down at her hands and twisted her signet ring, but she remained silent as if deep in thought.

Rebecca sipped her coffee and decided to change the subject until Sir Edward returned. His daughter was obviously fiercely loyal to him and was not going to be drawn into any speculations.

'So,' asked Rebecca pleasantly, 'how long are you here for? Do you often come to New York?'

Jenny seemed to relax as she talked about her trips. 'I'd like to live over here for a while,' she admitted at last, 'but my mother won't hear of it. She's scared I won't get to meet any eligible young men.'

Rebecca laughed. 'When I left home my mother was afraid I'd meet too *many* eligible young men. She was scared I'd want to marry right away, before I got my career off the ground or knew what life was all about.'

'Really?' Jenny sounded deeply surprised. '*My* mother can't wait for me to marry . . . providing she considers the person I choose to be suitable.'

'What do you do?'

'I'm a kindergarten teacher at a private school in London,' said Jenny. 'I love children so it's good fun, but I'd like to do something else for a change. Get a job here perhaps. Daddy says he can always find me something to do in the Tollemache Trust.'

Rebecca, who disapproved of parents pulling strings to help their children, was saved from replying by the arrival of Sir Edward. He came hurrying into the room and she noticed how he'd aged in the last few days. Puffy bags hung under his eyes, and his skin was a sickly shade of greyish yellow. He came forward to greet Rebecca with his accustomed graciousness and charm, but she found something heartbreaking about the look in his eyes and the slight quaver in his voice.

'Daddy, how lovely you're back so early,' said Jenny, jumping up to kiss him.

He patted her shoulder but almost immediately his eyes swung around the room until they came to rest on a tray of drinks in the corner.

'Can I get you something, darling?' he asked Rebecca, and she knew once again he'd forgotten her name.

'No thanks.'

'I don't suppose you will, Jenny?' he remarked, filling a glass with whisky for himself.

Jenny eyed the glass dubiously. 'No thanks. It's a bit early.'

As Sir Edward came to sit down beside them Rebecca could see he was exhausted.

'I'm sorry,' she began, 'this must be an awful time for you and I hate to bother you, but I think this is important.' She reached for the photographs.

'What is it?'

'Daddy,' interjected Jenny looking troubled, 'Rebecca seems to think your friend, Marissa . . . that is, Tracy . . . was murdered.'

Sir Edward's expression changed to one of deep distress and he hesitated before he spoke. 'I don't *think* she was killed,' he said at last, but there was little conviction in his voice.

'Aren't you sure?' Jenny gasped.

'I wasn't in the room where it happened . . . What have you brought me, darling?' He turned fretfully to Rebecca.

She handed him the relevant picture. 'I just wondered if you knew this man at all? Did you ask him to help at the party perhaps? Have you ever seen him before?'

Sir Edward shook his head. 'I've no idea who he is. Why?'

Once more Rebecca explained the purpose of her inquiries and told him about the break-in at her apartment. 'I think whoever killed Marissa knew I had him on film, and that was why he broke into my place, to try and recover the film.'

'I see.' Sir Edward nodded slowly, his forefinger rubbing his bottom lip in an absent-minded gesture.

Rebecca turned to look him full in the face. 'What was Marissa asking you, just before it happened?'

He turned tortured eyes on her. 'I don't know . . . except . . . except . . .'

'Yes?'

'I've been wondering, in the past couple of days, if she could have been . . . a spy.'

Rebecca and Jenny looked at him in astonishment.

'A spy!' cried Jenny.

'What makes you think that?' Rebecca asked.

'Because I'm sure she said something about "a spy". It was either "a spy's here" . . . or . . . Oh, Christ, I don't know! I'd give anything to remember what she said.' Sir Edward drained his glass and rose to get a refill.

'A spy who knew too much?' Rebecca suggested quietly.

Jenny looked bewildered. 'Why has everybody been saying it was an accident if it wasn't? Even the newspapers say she slipped and fell, and according to Rebecca the police say it was an accident too.'

Rebecca nodded in agreement. 'Things aren't adding up, in my opinion.'

Sir Edward looked embarrassed as he sat down again, a fresh drink in his hand.

'Brian Norris took charge of everything that night. I was too shocked to take in what had happened and he felt, for the sake of the company you understand, that there would be less of a scandal if it appeared to be an accident.'

Rebecca looked deeply shocked. She'd known all along that that was what Brian Norris had been up to, but to find that Sir Edward was also actively involved in the cover-up horrified her.

'But there already *is* a scandal,' she pointed out.

'I know, but think how much worse it would be if it were thought either that she was murdered or that it had been suicide!'

'But what about her killer? Is he to get away with it just because it's more convenient to look the other way?' Rebecca couldn't keep the irony out of her voice.

'What can I do? Without any real evidence that it was murder there's no point in putting forward a lot of theories. The main thing is the police are satisfied it was an accident, and I think we're going to have to leave it at that,' he said with finality. He finished his drink and stared into the empty glass. 'After all, nothing is going to bring Marissa back, is it?'

As Rebecca was leaving his apartment a few minutes later a realization struck her with such blinding force that her senses reeled. *Why* hadn't the police taken her more seriously? *Why* wouldn't they even consider her theory? Because, she was now sure, someone had bribed them to ignore the facts and that person had to be either Brian Norris or Sir Edward himself.

Stirling regarded Rebecca over the rim of his glass of red wine. 'What shall we call you now – Sherlock Holmes?' he teased.

Rebecca laughed as she curled up on the soft beige suede sofa that dominated his living-room. The deep ochre lampshades threw warm lights on her brown hair and the jade green of her sweater. Stirling leaned forward and kissed her gently on the mouth. He thought he'd never seen her look more desirable.

'I've got to find out what happened,' she remonstrated gently. 'Sir Edward's taken the soft option by going along with the accident story but I'm not going to.'

'You're right of course,' Stirling agreed. 'But I still wish you'd move in here with me, at least for the time being.'

Long slim fingers with pink-painted nails gently sealed his lips. 'You know I'm not going to do that,' Rebecca said softly. 'It would be like running away. Going into hiding. You forget I'm a liberated independent woman who can look after herself.'

Stirling grinned. 'More's the pity!' He kissed her again, lifting her hair on either side of her face.

Sensuously, she uncoiled her long slim legs, so that she lay along the sofa, her arms around his neck. 'You could persuade me to do one thing, though,' she whispered with a wicked smile.

'And what would that be?'

'I'll stay just for tonight, if you like?'

For an answer he held her tight and kissed her again. Then she rolled over so that she lay on top of him, and he held her, imprisoned, his arms and legs binding hers.

'You can't get away now,' he grinned. 'You're all mine, to do what I like with!'

Rebecca let herself go limp, resting her full weight on him. 'Suits me fine,' she quipped, 'but you'll have to do all the work!'

'What . . . like this?' he demanded, rolling over and taking her with him, pinning her beneath his weight now.

'Like any way you want,' she said dreamily.

Slowly Stirling started to undress her, exposing her creamy shoulders and pink-tipped breasts, kissing her inch by inch as he did so, until she stirred beneath him, responding to his touch and running her hands through the dark waves of his hair.

'I want you,' she whispered as he removed the rest of her clothes and then took off his own. The room was warm and the mellow light cast an amber glow on their bodies as they moved, entwined, in the languorous moments of foreplay before the ever-glowing fire between them burst into flames. Then, with a rush of longing, Stirling pressed himself hard against her, holding her so close she could hardly breathe.

'God, I love you,' he whispered.

'Stirling.' She said his name lingeringly, and her eyes were dark and dazed. 'Oh, Stirling, I love you too.' She clung to his neck as he entered her and, as if they could never bear to be unlinked again they held on to each other as their movements became faster and more urgent. Only then did he seem to pierce her soul, impale her on a point of fire and keep her there until at last, with a final thrust, she climaxed, crying out his name again as she did so.

Dawn was still breaking over Manhattan as Sir Edward left for his office the next morning. Ever since 'it' had happened – and his mind shied away from forming words that described 'it', as the pain was still too sharp to bear with equanimity – he'd gone to work early because that was the only way he knew of dealing with his emotions. Throughout his life, work had been the antidote to everything: his divorce, his separation from his children, even his home-sickness, for he'd been forced to transfer the Tollemache Trust to New York during the famous 'Winter of Discontent' in England, ten years

85

before, when the Labour government had driven the country into a financial slump. He still missed the delicate greenness of an English spring, when the woods were carpeted with bluebells and the hedgerows thick with yellow primroses.

Harvey, his chauffeur, was waiting for him on the sidewalk beside the Lincoln Continental. With a quick glance to left and right, to make sure no reporters or photographers were lurking in the cold grey shadows, Sir Edward hurried forward and slipped into the car, unobserved. A moment later it swung away from the kerb and was swallowed up in the stream of traffic already rumbling down Park Avenue.

Ahead of him lay a day of discussions and meetings. He tried, as he looked out of the window at the bleak streets already filled with strained-looking people hurrying to work, to concentrate on the decision that had to be made. Falcon Machine Tools, one of the seventeen industrial companies they owned in the United States, was showing heavy losses. Forever Batteries Inc. needed to be expanded. Coronet Cement was under-capitalized . . . and Marissa lay dead, smashed on the sidewalk below his window.

The building was deserted when Sir Edward arrived, except for the security guards. Taking the executive elevator, which was lined in sapphire blue suede, to the tenth floor, he went straight to his office. Elsbeth, his secretary, would not be in yet, but he could go through the various reports that had to be read and he could study them before the hubbub of the day began.

Seating himself at his desk, he glanced through the documents before him. There were reports from the construction section of the company; there was also a feasibility study about a chemical plant in Ohio, and plans for a new car factory near Philadelphia; there were financial forecasts and a projected growth index and the sales turnover figures . . . and there was Marissa's sweet face looking up at him when he made love to her.

With a muttered oath, he pushed himself away from his desk and, rising, went over to a cabinet in the corner of his office. Taking out a bottle of whisky normally kept for visitors, he poured some into a tumbler and drank it quickly with his eye on the door. Then he glanced at his watch. It was 8 a.m. He was turning into an alcoholic and there wasn't a damn thing he could do about it. It was the only way he could keep going. Marissa's face, her voice, the adorable way she did things, haunted him night and day. He could smell her in the air and see her in the shadows; she filled his thoughts and turned his dreams into nightmares. He said her name in silent anguish as he sat once again slumped at his desk.

86

Marissa – why did you have to die and deprive me of the greatest happiness I've ever known? Marissa – what took you away from me just when I'd found you? He sat in wretched contemplation until the whisky took effect.

When Elsbeth arrived for work she found Sir Edward briskly dictating letters into a dictaphone. He'd already got through a lot of work, and she remarked to her assistant that he seemed to be bearing up remarkably well.

When he entered the boardroom at ten o'clock, he greeted the eleven directors and associate directors and the eight executive officers with his usual breezy charm. They responded with warm politeness. He'd always been a popular chairman, but now their friendliness was tinged with curiosity as they wondered what it must feel like to be at the centre of such a scandal.

'Shall we start?' Sir Edward suggested, taking his place at the head of the long polished table on which were placed leatherbound blotters in front of every seat, and clusters of bottled water and glasses on silver trays. Brian Norris always sat on his right. Today the little man seemed to be oozing self-confidence. He felt he'd handled the whole ghastly incident with brilliant understatement, and in particular retained his boss's public image with near genius. Sir Edward had come out of it all with his dignity intact. Tragic accidents did happen from time to time. They were all part of life's rich pattern, Brian maintained. Most important of all, stock in the Tollemache Trust was holding steady. There had been a little lurch – a mere couple of points down – twenty-four hours after the stories had hit the press, but it was back up again and Brian felt the worst was over.

'There's nothing more that *can* come out,' he'd told his wife the night before. 'We've had Marissa's death, and we've had the revelation that she was really a dancer called Tracy Handford. That should be the end of it.'

'I fucking well hope so,' Christine said sharply.

'Language, Chrissie,' he reminded her.

Now, as the board meeting progressed, Brian's gimlet eyes and fast mind concentrated on the agenda with total dedication. He hadn't got as far as this, he reckoned, to let anything distract him now from his true purpose; and that purpose was to end up exceedingly rich and powerful, and possibly in Edward's shoes.

'Chairman,' he said as the meeting came to an end and Edward was asking everyone if there was Any Other Business, 'the directors have asked me to enquire what assets in the form of other companies you are contemplating bidding for?'

'None at the present time.'

Brian raised his eyebrows. 'How do you mean . . . none?'

'I mean exactly that,' Sir Edward replied evenly. 'I know we have made it our business to buy up other companies but this is not the right time. In my opinion, the situation has changed dramatically since Black Monday last October. The prices are unrealistically high and the banks are lending far too much for all the leveraged buy-outs that are happening. Companies are going bankrupt all over the place and that has a disastrous knock-on effect. No, for the moment Tollemache must sit tight and consolidate our profits of all the companies we do own, both here and in the United Kingdom.'

'I don't entirely agree,' protested Brian, and several of the directors murmured in agreement. 'We've made our name and increased the value of our stock by buying up other companies. Admittedly, there are times when we've gone into a situation in order to strip the assets, but on the whole, with our investment, companies have flourished under our management.'

'Of course they have, but there's no point in buying just for the sake of buying,' Sir Edward retorted testily.

The meeting adjourned, he hurried back to his office with a feeling of annoyance. What the hell was Brian playing at? He knew their policy of 'when in doubt, don't', and yet he had challenged Edward's business acumen in front of the Board. He also seemed to have got the backing of several of the other directors too. Perhaps, Edward concluded, Brian had seen a chink in the Chairman's armour which he thought he'd try and slip through? Certainly the little man's ambition should not be underestimated.

At that moment, Elsbeth came into his office, looking flustered. 'I'm sorry, Sir Edward, but I have a man in my office who refuses to leave! He's insisting he wants to see you on private business, and although I've told him you're unavailable he says it's urgent. I've tried to get him to make an appointment, but he says he must see you now.' She glanced nervously over her shoulder as if expecting the man to appear.

'Who is he?'

She glanced down at the card she was holding. 'A Mr Mike Wilson,' she read, 'from a company called Lawson, Martin & Grant, Genealogists and International Probate Researchers. What shall I tell him, Sir Edward? He says he's flown from England to see you.'

If Sir Edward had a faint inkling, even the shadow of a premonition, he didn't show it, although all his instincts told him it had something to do with Marissa.

'You'd better show him in, Elsbeth.'

A minute later a small thin man, with a long hank of hair droop-
ing over his bald head, and an ingratiating smile, came bounding
across the ocean of pale green carpeting, his nicotine-stained
fingers extended.

'Pleased to meet you.' Mike Wilson's tone was smarmy.

Sir Edward observed the cheap blue suit and polyester shirt, and
then he glanced down at the business card the visitor was proffer-
ring. Sir Edward hadn't been away from England long enough to
forget that a person's address, whether business or private, told
you more about them than anything else. He read that the offices
of Lawson, Martin & Grant were in Hackney, East London. Snob-
bishly he sniffed slightly, knowing he'd have been prepared to give
Wilson more attention if his company had been situated in Mayfair
or Belgravia.

'Good morning,' he said, with an exaggerated cordiality that
bordered almost on rudeness, 'and what can I do for you?'

Uninvited Mike Wilson seated himself in one of the leather chairs
and opened his briefcase.

'I represent Mr and Mrs Handford, the parents of poor Tracy
Handford who, of course, you knew.' There was an insolent inti-
macy in the way he said it, as if they shared a secret or were close
confidants.

Sir Edward looked at him coldly.

'Obviously they're very upset . . . she was their only child . . . it
came as a great shock . . . nobody's told them anything . . .' Mike
rattled on, as if he was setting the scene for what was to follow.
'They're quite elderly, you know, and they've worked hard all their
lives.'

Sir Edward continued to sit in icy silence, unnerving Mike whose
manner usually evoked some kind of response from other people.

'I've come to find out if you know where all Tracy's money is,' he
concluded.

'I have no idea. Why should I?' Sir Edward spoke stiffly. 'Her
money was her own. I wasn't her keeper, you know.'

Mike looked abashed and momentarily out of his depth. Then he
rallied at the thought of his handsome percentage. 'I know it was
her money, but you must know where she banked! Do you know if
she left a will? Did she have any bonds or stocks and shares? Did
she—'

'I will not stand for this impertinence,' Sir Edward cut in. 'Get
out of my office, at once! How dare you come here—'

Mike wrung his hands in a contortion of appeasement. 'But, Sir
Edward, if you would just be good enough to hear me out. I don't

come on my own behalf, I've been sent, indeed instructed, by the poor unfortunate girl's family. Would you have me deny them what is rightfully theirs? I came straight to you for help because you knew Tracy. She has no next-of-kin in the United States. Her money and assets have probably been frozen, but the question is, where?'

'I'm afraid I can't help you.' Sir Edward rose dismissively. 'Marissa's . . . er . . . Tracy's private affairs were her own. Now, if you'll kindly leave?'

'Wait a minute!' Mike looked enraged and insulted. 'I haven't come all this way to be given the bum's rush. What am I going to say to her parents? I think you should at least recompense them for the loss of their daughter. Give them an advance or something while we trace what she's done with her money.'

Sir Edward's voice was quiet, but his pale eyes blazed. 'Get out! And don't ever come back here. Marissa was not my responsibility and I was not privy to her financial arrangements. Go, before I call the police and have you charged with harassment.'

Mike backed off, knowing he was temporarily beaten. Desperation drove him to change his tactics. 'Look, Sir Edward, I'm only doing my job. The sooner I know the state of her financial affairs, the sooner I'll be on a plane back to London. She must have told you something?'

Sir Edward, ignoring him, strode out of his office and into the adjoining one.

'Elsbeth,' he called, 'will you phone for security?'

'OK, OK, I'm going.' Mike struggled to his feet, trying to shut his briefcase at the same time. A strand of hair fell further forward, partially covering one eye. Then he spun round, his tone venomous.

'Tracy's parents will have to sue you for negligence and damages, you know. Having an open window that someone can fall out of amounts to gross negligence. You'll be hearing from us, mark my words!'

Stirling was up early, creeping out of bed so as not to disturb Rebecca. He showered, made french toast and coffee, and was carrying it into the bedroom when she stirred and opened her eyes.

'Hiya, sweetheart,' he said softly. 'Ready for breakfast?'

Rebecca rolled over, an expression of delight crossing her face when she saw the tray. 'Wow! Do you always give five-star service to your guests?'

He placed the tray on the bed, and climbed in beside her. 'Only to very special ones.' His lips skimmed her bare shoulder and then he planted a kiss at the base of her throat.

Rebecca nuzzled his back. 'You're spoiling me again . . . and I love it!'

'What are you doing today?'

She lay back munching the french toast. 'At eleven o'clock I'm taking pictures of the Japanese President of Yama-Moto for the cover of *Newsweek*.'

Stirling slapped his forehead. 'Shit, I'd forgotten! Be sure and take black and white shots as well as colour. Once *Newsweek* has taken it's pick there'll be quite a demand for the others.'

'OK.'

'I've got to get into the office early because we're short staffed today. Will you be all right, here?'

She looked at him with mock defiance. 'What d'you mean – will I be all right? Of course I'll be all right! I'll drop the film off at your office at lunchtime and then I thought I'd go shopping and buy something we can have for dinner tonight at my place.'

'You – cook?' Stirling eyed her in amazement. Most evenings they ate a carry out or went to some little nearby bistro or restaurant. Cooking was definitely not one of Rebecca's talents. 'What are you going to buy?' he asked, intrigued.

She shrugged. 'A chicken, steaks, some vegetables – I don't know. Things I can broil. And we could have some fruit and cheese.'

Stirling grinned. 'Great! Hardly what I'd call *cordon bleu* though.'

Rebecca pretended to look indignant. 'My roast chicken is fabulous. So are my baked potatoes with soured cream and chives.'

Laughing, Stirling put his arm round her and pulled her close. 'That's not cooking,' he teased, 'that's turning on the cooker and assembling everything. Remember the night you . . .' He started to chuckle, '. . . the night you tried to heat up a frozen lasagne and got the timing wrong? It was still a block of solid ice in the centre.'

She looked offended. 'How was I to know it had just come out of the freezer?'

He kissed the tip of her nose. 'Who wants a woman with a degree in domestic science anyway! You buy the food . . . and I'll provide the alka-seltzer.'

'Well, I'm an artist,' she said gaily. There was a pause and then she added: 'Perhaps we'd better have a carry out after all.'

'We'll eat at Costello's,' said Stirling firmly. 'And now I must get going or I'll be late.' He turned to kiss her on the lips, first softly and then hungrily. 'Jesus, I'd like to stay,' he said longingly.

Rebecca eased herself gently away. 'Not this morning, Josephine,' she said. 'Maybe tonight!'

He kissed her again. 'I can hardly wait.'

When he had left, Rebecca bathed leisurely, checked that she had enough film, and was just about to leave when the phone rang. She crossed the living-room, which was flooded with winter sunshine, and picked up the receiver.

'Hi!' she answered flippantly. 'Don't tell me you've decided you want me to cook dinner after all?'

A moment later she'd dropped her camera bag and was clutching the telephone receiver, her face drained of all colour.

'I want those negatives.' The voice sounded metallic. It reminded her of the sort of voice used for robots in children's television movies. 'You'd better make sure you do as I say or you might end up like Marissa Montclare.'

'Who is this?' she cried. 'Who are you?'

'Get those negatives you took at the party and I'll tell you where to send them.' There was a click and the line went dead.

Rebecca stood by the phone for several minutes as the full implications of the call sank in. What alarmed her most of all was that whoever had made it must be following her movements, or how else did he know she'd spent the night at Stirling's apartment? In spite of what O'Hara said, she'd been right about the burglary too. This proved it. There must be incriminating evidence on her film and they'd been prepared to take her place apart to find it. She took a deep breath and looked at her watch. As soon as she'd finished photographing Mr Watanabe she'd go back to the police station and tell them about the call. She'd have to make them believe her now, because it was obvious her life was in danger.

Mr Watanabe was small and thin with teeth like a row of ivory piano keys. He squinted implacably at Rebecca through thick steel-rimmed spectacles as one of his many minions showed her into his suite at the Waldorf Astoria. Then he bowed deeply. Rebecca bowed back, remembering it was the custom in Japan rather than shaking hands.

'Velly pleased to see you,' said Yuki Watanabe, beaming.

Rebecca set up her tripod near the window. Then asking Mr Watanabe to sit in an upright chair she started working swiftly and surely, forcing herself to put the threatening call to the back of her mind. The sunlight, diffused by the thick white muslin curtains that hung from the large window, was an ideal form of illumination, soft and flattering. She slowed the shutter speed of her Hasselblad, and then started clicking away, getting Mr Watanabe warmed up, knowing the first few shots were always useless. It could take a couple of rolls of film to get a sitter to relax.

'Can you look this way, please?' she suggested, watching him closely. Everyone had one side of their face that was better than the other, a side that was the most photogenic. With the eye of an artist, Rebecca angled Mr Watanabe until she found the position for him, and then she clicked away, taking a couple of dozen shots before having to re-load the camera.

Usually she chattered as she worked, keeping her sitter alert and interested, otherwise the eyes were inclined to go 'dead'; but today her thoughts were in such a turmoil, and her head was so filled with the sinister phone call, that small-talk was impossible. The knowledge that a killer was roaming at large in the city, following her movements, disturbed her deeply. Stirling had placed the eight films in a bank vault. Everyone in the agency knew it.

Perhaps the killer knows it too now, thought Rebecca. Perhaps he's watching all the time . . . seeing what I do and where I go . . . observing Stirling at work and what's going on there. Most importantly, she asked herself, what do I do when he calls again? For call again he would, she was sure of that.

'How was Yuki Watanabe?' Stirling asked when she arrived at the agency a couple of hours later. 'Was the session OK?'

'The session was fine,' Rebecca replied drily, dumping the films for processing on his desk.

'What's wrong?'

When she'd finished telling him about the call and her visit to the police station after she'd finished her assignment, Stirling looked grave.

'What did they say?'

'They couldn't care less. They said it was probably a crank or someone playing a practical joke,' she added grimly. 'I saw O'Hara's sidekick and he'd obviously been given his boss's version of events.'

'If this man calls again . . .'

'*When* this man calls again,' she corrected him.

'OK. When this man calls again, tell him the negatives are locked away where he'll never find them. And bluff like hell: say the police are taking a very serious view of all this.'

Rebecca nodded but looked unconvinced. 'I wish it were true, but each time I've reported anything - first the burglary, and now this call - I haven't been taken seriously. Do you think they could have been got at?'

Stirling regarded her closely, not wanting to alarm her more than was necessary.

'If O'Hara's been bribed,' he said as if weighing his words, 'then it's either by Marissa's killers, for obvious reasons, or Sir Edward was right when he said she was a spy and this is the work of Intelligence. Or . . .'

'Yes?' She looked at him intently.

'. . . Sir Edward himself may be pulling the strings. It fits, doesn't it? Tollemache Trust Stock would drop right off the Dow Jones Index if the company were involved in a major scandal.'

Chapter Six

Jenny was beginning to wish she hadn't come to New York this time. Her father seemed to be almost oblivious of her presence and she found herself pottering around his opulent apartment most days looking for something to do. She'd like to have ventured farther afield than Park and Fifth Avenue, but she didn't dare. Tales of muggings and stabbings and crack-crazed attacks kept her to the places she thought to be safe, like Bloomingdale's or Bergdorf Goodman or Doubleday's, and so she did a little shopping each morning, read or watched television in the afternoons and spent the evenings looking forward to her father's return.

Not that the evenings were wonderful. When he did appear she could tell he'd been drinking, and although he wasn't actually drunk, he was remote and glassy-eyed, as if part of him had absented himself and said, 'I'm not really here. I'm not a part of what's happening.'

Jenny would retire to her room as soon as Scott had served dinner, feeling hurt and rejected and, worse, deeply disappointed. Always in the past, ever since her parents had divorced, Sir Edward had made a special fuss over her as if perhaps he felt a certain guilt at having left her mother. Whenever she'd visited him in the States he'd taken her everywhere with him, making sure she was never bored or lonely, providing for her amusement even when he was working hard at the office. The chauffeur had always been at her disposal to take her anywhere she wanted to go, and of course she had acted as hostess for him when he gave dinner parties.

Now all that had changed and Jenny knew it was because of Marissa. Her father had been utterly besotted by her in life, and he was still besotted by her in death. Overwhelmed by memories and tortured by regrets, there was no place in his life for anyone else right now and it came to Jenny, with a realization that was like a bitter ache, that she didn't come first with anyone any more.

Her mother had always preferred Simon and made no secret of it. So far there was no lover to fill Jenny's lonely hours either. No young man had ever seemed as clever and amusing and charming as her father, and so she grew quickly bored by them, wearied by their naivety, finding their lack of worldliness and polish tedious. She was used to the stylishness of an older man and found her own generation awkward and juvenile by comparison.

Up until now, spending all her holidays with her father had been compensation enough for not having boyfriends of her own; but it came to her now, in a wave of jealousy, that she resented his love for Marissa even though the girl was dead. Passing lady friends she'd been able to accept, because she'd always known her father's feelings had not been serious and the relationships would not last; but this was different. He'd probably have married Marissa if she'd lived – a girl three years younger than herself. Jenny knew she'd have hated that, and she also knew now that she was unable to accept a deep love in her father's life. The thought distressed her, but there was nothing she could do to change her feelings or her dependency on him for her happiness. She couldn't even find a lover of her own.

When Angela phoned, demanding she return to England, Jenny was, however, loyal to Sir Edward.

'Daddy needs me,' she said firmly. 'We're staying quietly in the apartment, and in spite of everything I'm having a very nice time. I'll be back at the end of next week for the start of the new term, but I don't want to leave here before then.'

Angela Wenlake was not impressed. 'I hope the school keeps you on,' she snorted. 'Everyone in Britain has heard, or read, about the scandal. I'm embarrassed to show my face in the village. I'll never forgive your father for making a public spectacle of us all!'

'It wasn't his fault,' Jenny protested.

'Of course it was his fault! I always knew his womanizing would land him in trouble, and now he's dragged the whole family down with this latest debacle. I don't see what good your staying in New York will do. What sort of people are you meeting, for God's sake?'

Jenny thought quickly. 'As I said, we're staying quietly in the apartment. We haven't been socializing.'

'That doesn't sound like Edward,' Angela retorted. 'Have it your own way, then, but don't be late getting back for school, and for goodness' sake tell your father to be more discreet! I've even had my Hunt Ball dinner-party wrecked by some terrible little man who was after money!'

'Really?'

'Yes. He said the wretched girl had been very rich.' The tone of Angela's voice made Jenny wince. It was as if her mother found it highly surprising that a girl from Marissa's background *could* have money. 'Apparently her family are out to claim it. I mean, really! Then he had the audacity to ask me – *me* – to advance some cash to them. Have you ever heard anything so iniquitous?'

Reluctantly Jenny agreed that she hadn't.

'Don't let him near you if he turns up in New York,' commanded Angela. 'He's a sleazy little man who calls himself a genealogical researcher. He's a con man, of course! No doubt about it. He'll take your father for a ride, though I don't suppose it'll do any good warning him first.'

'I'll mention it to Daddy.'

Mother and daughter hung up a moment later. They had nothing more to say to each other. Jenny went back to the book she was reading, and wondered if her father would be home late again tonight.

He came up from behind with a suddenness that made Rebecca catch her breath. His large powerful hands gripped her around the waist and she could feel his hot breath on the back of her neck. Grabbing the little fingers on each of his hands, she tried to bend them back but he was too strong and his grip remained vice-like, holding her against his body so that she could not turn either way.

With an effort Rebecca managed to kick him in the shin, aiming with as much accuracy as she could, trying to take him unawares, and then she dropped down on to one knee and, bending forward, wrenched with all her might at the sleeve of his jacket. Miraculously she felt him tipping slowly forward, head first, over her shoulder. Then, using all her strength, she heaved and pulled until for a moment she thought her back would break and her kneeling leg give way under her, but she gave a final powerful tug and he toppled, crashing on to the ground before her.

Quickly, before he could recover himself, she applied an arm-lock, pinioning him so he was unable to move. The effort left her breathless and exhausted, and for a second she loosened her grasp.

'Break! Good. That was excellent, Rebecca.'

She rolled away, and sat grinning as she looked up at John, her self-defence instructor.

'You're so heavy,' she complained. 'I hope if I'm ever attacked it will be by a slim little man who weighs about a hundred and fifty pounds! What d'you weigh? A hundred and ninety?'

'About that,' he smiled back at her. His name was John Golden, and he ran evening classes in self-defence for women two nights a week at the Hydra Gymnasium on Thirty-Ninth Street and Madison. Rebecca had enrolled after she'd received the threatening telephone call, and already she felt more confident as she went about her business.

'Let's do it again,' said John.

They repeated the moves, and then he got Rebecca, and the twelve other women in the class, to practise defence from strangleholds, from being attacked from the front, held by the wrists, and grabbed by the hair.

'Use your hands and every part of your body when defending yourselves,' he said, 'and don't be afraid of hurting your attacker!'

There was a muffled giggle from the back of the class.

'I'm serious,' John chided. 'Some women are scared of hurting another person. Don't think about it! Your duty is to yourself. Now, gather round, girls, and we'll run through the basics of self-defence one more time.'

Rebecca sat at the front, absorbing every word. This wasn't something that just might be useful one day, if she should happen to find herself in a dangerous position; this knowledge, newly found and carefully practised, could save her life. Marissa might not be dead now if she'd known a few tricks.

'OK.' John sat facing them, a muscular good-looking young man to whom physical fitness was life itself. 'What's the first rule of the game?'

'Keeping out of trouble,' said Rebecca quickly. 'Keep to well-lit streets if you're out walking; keep away from doorways; walk confidently and walk towards oncoming traffic.'

'Good. Anyone know why?'

'To avoid kerb-crawlers,' said one of the women.

'Right. What else?' John looked round the class expectantly.

'Avoid deserted places?' someone suggested.

'Yes. Avoid empty subways, carriages, car-parks, streets, and anywhere that's isolated. What do you do if you are attacked?'

'Scream,' said Rebecca. 'Yell. Shout "NO"!'

'OK,' John nodded, raising his hands so his arms, brown and muscular, flexed at the elbow. 'But suppose you've done that and your attacker is still coming at you. What else do you do?'

'Go for his face or his balls!' said a voice from the back.

'That's right. Grab him by the balls and twist . . . or stick two fingers up his nose, in his eyes, or you can pinch his ears, nose, cheeks. Another place it hurts to be pinched is here.' John indicated the skin just above his waist, at either side of his body.

One or two of the women grimaced with distaste but Rebecca leaned forward, her expression questioning. 'I'm not sure I'd have the strength to twist my hands out of someone's grip if I were caught by the wrists,' she said.

'There's a trick to get out of that one: open your hands quickly outwards, and you'll break the grip,' John replied. 'Now, can anyone tell me what else you can do to help yourselves?'

'Always wear shoes you can run in.'

'Have a shoulder bag and hold it close to the body.'

'Don't wear a lot of jewellery.'

'Don't wear tight skirts.'

The answers came in from all over the room, and then Rebecca raised her hand to ask a question.

'Is there anything we can carry as a means of self-defence?'

John made a face and answered hesitantly. 'That's a tricky one. Obviously no one is allowed to carry knives or a gun or anything that could be described as an offensive weapon. That includes scissors, an aerosol that could blind . . . that sort of thing. Permissible are umbrellas, car keys, walking-sticks. You can use them quite legally.'

'What about a lit cigarette?' Rebecca asked. 'I don't smoke but I've often thought a lit cigarette could be a deterrent, especially if you aimed it at someone's face.'

John nodded. 'Good point! Now, girls, that just about winds it up for tonight, but remember all we've discussed and help yourselves by keeping out of trouble if you can, and keeping fit.'

There were murmurs of thanks as the class broke up. Rebecca slipped on her thick red winter coat over the track suit she'd worn for the class.

'Thanks, John,' she called out as she left. 'See you next Tuesday.'

'OK! See you.'

Outside it was dark but incredibly mild for January. She caught a cab and gave the driver her address. It was nine o'clock and she knew Stirling was playing squash this evening, so as soon as she got home she'd get through all the boring chores, like cleaning the apartment and washing her hair, and then she'd go to bed early. Tomorrow she was taking pictures at an anti-abortion rally that was scheduled to take place at the New York Women's Health Centre. A lot of action was expected and she knew the police were standing by, anticipating they'd have to make arrests. She'd get some lively pictures, so a quiet evening would suit her perfectly.

When she got out of the cab, she could hear loud music coming from the choreographer's apartment on the first floor. He was playing the Tchaikovsky overture from *Romeo and Juliet* and she paused to listen for a moment, relishing the beautiful music as it came floating through the half open windows. Then she hurried up to her apartment, remembering the TV movie she wanted to see that evening.

The first thing she noticed was that the amber light on her answering machine was lit, showing there were messages for Karen and herself. Absently, she flicked the switch while she turned on lamps and drew the curtains, making the place instantly more cosy.

'Hi, sweetheart.' It was Stirling's customary greeting. 'Have you remembered I'm playing squash tonight? I'll call you later, when I get home. By the way, your pictures of Elizabeth Taylor arriving at the Plaza have sold very well. Talk to you later. 'Bye, darling.'

There was a click, a buzz and then the familiar voice of Karen came on the line.

'This is me,' she began. 'I stopped by earlier today to pick up some clothes, so don't worry if things looked disturbed in my room. I'm getting a bit bored staying at my sister's so I might move back at the weekend. Talk to you later.'

Rebecca hung up her coat, thinking it would be nice to have Karen around again. She was fun to be with in a zany sort of way, and it was amusing to have someone to gossip with.

The next message was another call from Stirling.

'It's me again, sweetheart. Hold on to your hat because I think I've got an amazing assignment for you! How would you like to fly to London to cover a gala ball that Prince Charles and Princess Diana are attending? I'll tell you more when I see you!' There was a click and the line went silent again.

Rebecca clapped her hands together in delight. She'd been to London before, but never to photograph royalty! If she could get even one perfect shot of the princess it could make magazine covers around the world. For Stirling to have arranged this for her, when there were so many photographers who would give their right arm for the chance, was a tremendous coup. Her thoughts were interrupted by the click and buzz of another message on the machine.

'How did you enjoy your class tonight?' asked a metallic voice. Rebecca froze, recognizing the strange, almost mechanical tones of the man who had called before. 'I hope you have your films ready for me.' There was something about the voice that was detached, disembodied, and more than anything else, cold and pitiless. 'At noon tomorrow, I want you to put the films in a brown paper bag and leave them at the Post Office on Thirty-First Street and Eighth

100

Avenue. Put them on a counter on the right as you enter, and then walk straight out of the building again. No tricks! Tell anyone, and you're dead.' There was a click and silence.

Rebecca sank slowly on to a chair, her legs shaking. She felt exposed, vulnerable, as if the walls had eyes and ears and she was being observed all the time. Whoever it was knew she'd been to a class tonight and must have left the message on her machine whilst she was on her way home. Presumably they also knew the negatives were in a safety deposit box. That meant she'd have to appear to get them out of the bank in the morning, even though she had no intention of giving him the actual films. Any 35mm negatives of party scenes would do for the time being.

'I don't like it,' Stirling told her when she phoned him later. 'Let me go and do the drop for you.'

'No, I'll do it,' she said. 'I just want you to let me have eight films that don't matter to leave in place of the ones they want. Can I pick them up from your office on my way to the bank?'

'I'm coming to the bank with you,' he said firmly, 'and I'm coming to the Post Office too. We needn't appear to be together, but I want to get a look at whoever it is who does the pick-up.'

'Are you crazy? If they know all my movements they'll certainly know what you look like. Whoever I ask to act as a look-out must be unknown to them, and it's got to be someone I trust . . . I know who! Stirling, I've got to make a call. I'll call you back later.'

'Wait! Rebecca, not so fast! Who are you going to . . . ?'

'Leave it to me,' she said ambiguously. 'I'll let you know if I'm successful.'

Karen had been doubtful at first.

'There's nothing to it, honestly,' Rebecca assured her.

'But these people sound dangerous,' Karen protested. 'I'm not going to move back to the apartment if they're still threatening you. This man sounds scary . . . and he's probably the killer!'

'All you have to do is watch,' Rebecca persisted. 'Nobody's going to know you're there.'

'Even so,' said Karen. Then she added: 'I've got this new guy. His name's Dick. If I can get him to come along with me, will that be OK?'

Rebecca's sigh bordered on the impatient. 'I'd rather nobody else knew what was going on. For heaven's sake, Karen, I'm only asking you to stand in line and buy some postage stamps while you keep your eye on a small brown bag to see who picks it up. I'm not asking you to commit some dangerous act of espionage or steal nuclear secrets from the State Department!'

101

'OK, OK, but I'd still like to have Dick with me. He doesn't have to know what I'm doing. I don't have to tell him I'm watching out for anything. Noon did you say? Fine. I'll tell Dick I have to go and buy some stamps in my lunch hour.' Karen sounded determined.

Rebecca, on the other end of the line, shrugged. Trying to prise Karen away from the current man in her life always had been impossible.

'OK, but for God's sake act naturally. Don't look like you're watching.'

'I know how to be subtle,' Karen protested. 'Where shall we meet afterwards so I can tell you what the pick-up looked like?'

'What about just inside Penn Station, where they sell newspapers? It's opposite the Post Office.'

'I'll be there.' Now she was used to the idea, Karen sounded quite excited. She'd always complained that her job was dull compared to Rebecca's; now she was getting to see some of the action.

The next day it was raining heavily, and when Karen came out of her office near the Rockerfeller Center she knew at once she'd have trouble finding a cab to take her across town.

Traffic was bumper to bumper honking, hooting, swishing up small waves of muddy spray. The never-ending tide of metal thundered steadily past as Karen stood there, clutching an umbrella and worrying about her good shoes getting ruined.

Her eyes strained to watch the oncoming traffic, praying for an empty cab. Her head began to ache. What would Rebecca say if she failed to turn up? She cursed Dick for being too busy to take a lunch-break. He was always good at finding cabs. Karen glanced at her watch. It was twenty to twelve. Even if she started walking now, she'd never make it to the Post Office by noon.

Rebecca had met Stirling at the Citibank on Lexington shortly after ten o'clock. They'd made it look as if they were really removing the films from the safety deposit box. When they walked out of the building ten minutes later, she was carrying a brown paper bag, rolled over at the top and full of the film Stirling had brought with him in his pockets. They were of another party and at a glance even he'd have found them hard to distinguish from the relevant ones. With negatives no bigger than a large postage stamp, the images were so tiny it would need a magnifying glass to identify them.

'What happens when he discovers we've tricked him?' Rebecca asked, as she and Stirling walked briskly through the rain, back to the agency. 'He's going to be mad as hell.'

'That's why I want you to fly to England as soon as possible, so you're out of the way. I know this event with Princess Diana isn't for another ten days, but I'd feel happier if you were in Europe. I'm trying to get you some other assignments, maybe in Paris, which I'm hoping will have the effect of drawing the heat off you.'

Rebecca looked thoughtful. 'I wonder what his next move will be?'

Stirling shrugged. 'God knows, but you're not hanging around to find out. I want you to move in with me tonight. No, Rebecca!' He raised his hand as he saw her starting to protest. 'I'm not going to let you go back to your apartment. Once they discover we've given them the wrong films, they might do anything.' He spoke with finality and his dark eyes looked at her almost angrily. 'It's crazy staying alone in your apartment with all this going on. I don't know what the hell you're trying to prove.'

She looked stubborn. 'Would *you* move out of *your* apartment under the same circumstances?' she demanded.

'That's different. I can look after myself.' Stirling protested.

'Well, so can I, and you'd better believe it,' Rebecca retorted. 'I'm willing to go to Europe, because that's to work, but I refuse to run away because—'

'—because there's a killer on the loose, and he's soon going to be after your blood!'

Rebecca flinched slightly. 'Don't exaggerate, Stirling,' she said, trying to keep her voice light.

'I'm not exaggerating, sweetheart. You've got a photograph of the man who killed Marissa Montclare, at the scene of the crime, and if only the police would believe you, that photo could be circulated and he'd get picked up in no time at all. Do you wonder he wants that film back? In my opinion, he'll stop at nothing to get it back, or to eliminate the person who can identify him.'

Rebecca was silent. It was stupid of Stirling to say it was unsafe for her to stay in her apartment. If the man who had killed Marissa was as determined as all that, she wasn't safe anywhere.

When the yellow cab swerved towards the kerb, sending up a spray of rainwater that threatened to soak Karen up to the knees, she couldn't have cared less. The fact that she'd found an empty cab at all, and that it was only fifteen minutes to twelve, meant she still had a chance of getting to the Post Office on time.

'Thirty-First and Eighth,' she told the driver, as she jumped into the back, raincoat soaking, closed-up umbrella dripping water that seeped into the carpet at her feet. 'I'm in a hurry.'

The Hispanic driver flung up his hands angrily. 'How can I

fuckin' hurry in all this traffic! It's a terrible day. The traffic's bad. How am I supposed to hurry? Eh?'

'I've got to get to the Post Office before twelve,' begged Karen. 'Aren't there any short cuts you can take?'

Impatiently he crashed the gears and the cab jerked forward. 'I've been out in this fuckin' rain since early this morning!' he shouted. 'And all I've had is people tellin' me to fuckin' hurry! Whatsa good of that? Eh?'

Without answering Karen looked through the windows and saw the crowds charging along, heads bent against the wind and rain, clothes dripping, feet sloshing in puddles and expressions of acute discomfort on their faces.

'I worka days and nights!' the driver continued, taking both hands off the steering wheel in a gesture of disgust. 'I worka all the time! People! They're never satisfied. I'm fuckin' sick of people tellin' me to go here, go there, and always wantin' to hurry!' He made a noise in his throat that Karen thought was going to herald a spit. Instead he let out a groan that was heartfelt. 'Some of the rides I get are so short I'm *losing* money! Why should I worka my arse off for a few lousy cents, eh? I'm asking you? How am I supposed to make a livin' like that?'

If she hadn't been so desperate to get to the Post Office on time, she'd have told him what he could do with his cab, but to say anything would only bring forth a further volley of rage and then she'd never get there. He mistook her silence for dissent. Putting his foot down hard on the accelerator, the cab shot forward into a gap in the traffic throwing her back against the leopardskin-patterned plastic seat covering.

'Whatsa guy supposed to do?' he roared. 'You tell me that! It's the same all over this fuckin' city. Too many cars! They should forbid cars in the middle of New York. How'm I supposed to get around? And you tells me to hurry!' He crashed his hands down on the steering wheel and wrenched it to the right as they shot up Forty-Eighth Street.

Karen glanced at her watch. It was ten minutes to twelve. They still had to cross Sixth Avenue before they could head downtown. Would they make it in under ten minutes? Cursing herself for not having organized things better, she sat silent and watchful, listening to the manic flow of grumbles from the driver as he dodged and braked, speeded and halted.

Rebecca was going to be furious if she wasn't there on time, and Karen could understand why. This might be the one chance of identifying the guy who'd killed Marissa.

Rebecca had taken the precaution of booking a cab from Express Limousines, with whom the Hertfelder Agency had an account. It picked her up from Stirling's office at eleven-fifteen, and it was at that moment that she wondered how Karen was going to get around on such a terrible day. Knowing Karen, she wouldn't think to call a car in advance, even though the rain had been coming down in a steady curtain all morning, and she'd never cope with the subway.

Karen wasn't very good at coping at all because she'd always depended on some boyfriend or other to take her everywhere and look after her. Rebecca bit her lip with anxiety. Maybe she'd been silly to ask her roommate to act as a spy for her today. She'd done it because she could at least trust Karen to keep her mouth shut, and she thought it unlikely the killer would know what she looked like; but Karen was scatty. She might be so busy thinking about her new boyfriend that she'd forget to go to the Post Office at all!

The car crawled down Seventh Avenue with Rebecca in the back, clutching the brown paper bag. Her stomach muscles were tense, knowing that the man with the unearthly metallic voice would soon be holding this very parcel . . . and soon also discovering he'd been given the wrong film.

She leaned forward to speak to the driver. 'Will you wait for me outside the Post Office? I'll only be a moment.'

He shook his head. 'I won't be able to wait. There're always cops around Penn Station. You're not allowed to wait.'

'Could you drive round the block and come back for me then? I promise you I'll be very quick.'

The driver looked doubtful. There were usually long lines at the Post Office; the young lady was optimistic if she thought she'd be out in 'a moment'.

'OK,' he said reluctantly. 'I'll go round the block. Then where to?'

Rebecca thought for a moment. 'Hell!' she exclaimed aloud. She and Karen had not reckoned on the rain and the traffic jams that were snarling up the city today and she'd arranged to meet her flatmate just outside Penn Station. Then she decided that if she dashed across the street to the Station when she left the Post Office, she could wait for Karen and they could get into the car together, providing the driver had gone round the block several times.

'I'm sorry,' she said apologetically, 'my plans are a bit complicated. I shall certainly want to go back to the Hertfelder Agency. I might also want to stop at Rockerfeller Center on the way.'

At last the Post Office came into sight, a vast imposing

municipal-looking building at the top of steep stone steps which ran from one end of the frontage to the other. In the rain it was deserted except for an old woman struggling up the steps, battling against the wind, and a black mother with two small children, emerging through the grand portals. But any minute now, thought Rebecca, whoever killed Marissa will be coming through those doors, if he isn't already inside, watching for me to arrive.

Karen headed up the steep steps of the Post Office, her head bent and her raincoat clutched tight round her. She was soaked, her feet squelched as she walked and her good shoes were ruined, but at least, she thought triumphantly, she was here. There was no point in opening the umbrella. The wind was so strong it would blow it inside out, and anyway her hair was already clinging to her face in dripping tendrils. As she glanced up she saw with relief that she was still in time. Rebecca was ahead of her, nearing the top of the steps. As Karen hurried she saw her disappear into the cavernous building. She glanced around nervously but there was no sign of anyone watching, and even if there had been, there was nothing to connect the two women.

Karen entered the bleak high-vaulted chamber, with its grey walls and counter running down the whole length of one side. Only two of the windows were manned, and there was a long line of rain-soaked people waiting dispiritedly to be served. At either end were counters one could lean on to write, and she saw Rebecca walk straight to the counter on the right. Then, as Karen joined the end of one of the lines, she watched Rebecca turn and leave without glancing either to left or right. Lying on the counter, was a brown paper bag that to the casual observer looked as if it contained a few small groceries.

The queue shuffled forward and Karen watched cautiously. At any moment . . . A young woman approached the counter, stopped to write something down, and then turned away again. The brown bag was still there. Then two teenage boys sauntered over and, leaning on the counter inches away from the package, entered into a deep discussion. One of them took a piece of paper out of his pocket and consulted it. Then the second one scooped some change out of his back pocket and appeared to be counting it. Suddenly they both laughed and joined the back of the line Karen was in. The package was still there.

With mounting tension, she kept her eyes fixed on it as she edged forward, the musty smell of damp clothes and sweat permeating the air around her. She was nearly at the head of the queue now. She

hoped the two people in front of her would have complicated transactions, so that she could go on standing there . . . watching . . .

An elderly man shuffled in, with rain streaming from his shabby
coat and his boots leaving little pools of water where he stood. He
moved over to the counter and stood just by the package for a long
moment, as if pondering. Karen stood watching openly now, an
expression of astonishment on her face. This can't be the right one,
she thought, straining forward. This tramp . . . this vagrant . . .
surely he wasn't mixed up in Marissa Montclare's death? Unless of
course he'd been sent as a decoy, someone to put everyone off the
scent of the real killer.

The old man tottered towards the counter where the package lay,
seemed to sway, and then he turned away and shambled slowly out
of the building. The package was still there.

Karen was first in line now. 'Yeah?' asked the clerk, from behind
the bronze grille. She looked tired and harassed and her fingers
were dirty from handling coins.

'Oh!' Karen paused, confused. 'Can I have . . . er . . . can I have
ten twenty-five-cent stamps, please?' For a second she dragged her
eyes away from the package, to glance swiftly down into her purse
to get out a five dollar bill. She slid it across the counter under the
grille, and as she did so she looked back to where the package lay. It
had gone.

'I don't know *how* it happened,' said Karen fretfully. 'I didn't take
my eyes off it for more than three seconds and when I looked up
again it was gone! I couldn't believe it! I looked all around to see if I
could see anyone leaving the place with it, but it had vanished.
Utterly and totally vanished. I didn't even see anyone who was
likely looking! Oh, I'm sorry, Rebecca. If you knew what a hard
time I had getting there – and I really thought I'd catch the person
red-handed. I could kick myself.'

They were in Rebecca's cab, which had been cruising around and
around the block, waiting for her to emerge. When she shot out of
Penn Station, dragging Karen with her, the driver had looked as
annoyed as if she'd tricked him in some way. Now they were crawling, bumper to bumper, up Eighth Avenue on their way to drop
Karen off at her office.

'I think it confirms one thing,' Rebecca thoughtfully observed,
'whoever took it was aware he was being watched.'

'Oh, my God.' Karen's feelings were mixed. If that was true it
meant it wasn't entirely her fault, but on the other hand it meant the
killer knew who she was.

'Whoever took the package must have been damned quick,' Rebecca continued, trying to keep the disappointment out of her voice. They'd been so near . . . and if only the police had listened to her in the first place, none of this would have happened. They could have had the whole Post Office surrounded, a closed-circuit television camera set up to observe the counter where she'd left the films. They could have picked up whoever it was in seconds. Frustration made her give a deep sigh.

'I'm sorry,' Karen repeated, contritely.

'Oh, it's not your fault. It's just that I feel so defeated. I'd really hoped to get something definite to go on before I fly to Europe.'

Karen's round grey eyes looked at her in surprise. 'Flying to Europe . . . when? You never told me! Why are you flying to Europe? What are you doing about the apartment? I'm not going back there if you're going to be away!'

Rebecca grinned. 'Hang on there, Karen.' When she told her the arrangements Stirling had made, Karen's eyes grew larger and rounder.

'Photographing Princess Diana!' she gasped. 'Rebecca, you're made!'

'There will be other photographers there, too,' Rebecca interjected, 'it's not an exclusive, you know.'

'But think of it . . . you must tell me exactly what she's like. Wow! Can I tell Dick? He'll be very impressed.'

'Better not,' Rebecca warned. 'I don't want any of my rivals trying to get in on the act. Let's wait until Stirling has sold all my pics, and then you can shout it from the rooftops!'

Rebecca awakened the next morning to find Stirling kissing her neck just by her ear, where she was particularly sensitive. It sent the blood tingling through her veins as she stretched luxuriously, arching her back and raising her arms above her head. Then Stirling's mouth slid down to her breasts and his lips, strong and moist, took one of her nipples into his mouth. A stab of desire, hot and urgent, caught her unexpectedly, sending her pulses racing. She arched her back even more, almost inducing an orgasm before his hand had slid between her legs.

'Oh . . . Stirling!' Rebecca gave an involuntary gasp, squeezing her thighs on his hand, pressing down hard as she felt the first surge of a climax begin. It seemed as if she couldn't breathe, so strong were the waves of pleasure that swept through her again and again. Skilfully, he slipped his fingers inside her, pressing deeply and gently, so that she cried out and clung to him as if she would never be satisfied.

'OK?' he whispered at last, as she lay still and flushed in his arms.

'Fantastic!' Her voice was husky, still breathless. 'I'm sorry I couldn't wait. It just happened. I think I was wanting you before I even woke up.' She kissed his cheek and his temple and the corner of his mouth, soft little kisses that were deeply affectionate. 'You're a wonderful lover.'

'So are you.' He started to stroke her again, and she could feel his erection pressed hard against her thigh. Putting her arms around him she kissed him fully on the mouth, her tongue darting in and out, and then she rolled him on to his back so she could sit astride him.

'It's your turn now,' she murmured, her voice still husky.

'I want you,' he whispered and she knew his need was urgent. Whenever they made love in the mornings, which wasn't often because she usually went back to her own apartment at night, Stirling was wonderfully ardent, his long lean body eager and insatiable. How well she knew him, she thought as she lowered herself, taking him inside her so that he groaned with pleasure, grasping her hips to hold her down. He pushed himself upwards, wanting to bury all of himself in her exciting wetness, pressing hard up inside her so that she, too, groaned. Then, holding him tight with her strong slim thighs, she rotated her hips, lifting herself tantalisingly so that he grasped her tighter.

'Keep me inside you . . . for God's sake!' His voice caught. Then he pumped frantically, craving for release. But teasingly, determined to prolong the delicious torment a little longer, Rebecca lifted herself up again, leaving him for a moment, curbing his climax so that it would be all the better when it came.

'Rebecca . . .' She lowered herself again and matched her rhythm to his, riding him until he roared with pleasure, moving her hips from side to side until, eyes squeezed tight shut, he crested the final peak and lay, throbbing and spent, beneath her.

'I love you,' he whispered, breathing hard.

'I love you too,' Rebecca whispered softly, knowing it was true but wishing it was more. She did love Stirling with all her heart . . . but not enough to give up her own apartment as he would have liked. Not enough to make that final commitment he wanted.

They lay together a little longer, and then Stirling opened his eyes again and smiled.

'Quite a way to start the day, eh?'

Rebecca nodded. 'A beautiful way to start the day.'

He grinned ingenuously. 'It could be like this every morning, you know.'

Her eyes flew open, knowing she'd stepped right in to his little trap.

'Ah, but would it be so special if it did?' she countered.

'I don't see why not. Listen, Becky sweetheart . . . why don't we give it a real try? Instead of just spending evenings with me, why don't you move in? And I don't just mean staying here while you're being threatened. I mean for real. Forever!' Stirling's expression was so eager, Rebecca hated to hurt him.

'It *is* great at the moment,' she replied slowly, 'but is that because we both know it's not permanent? What's that joke? "I can only maintain a relationship when I know it's not going to last." Stirling, how much of what we have is because we're not living together and taking each other for granted?'

He looked sombre. 'You mean you're only happy with me because you don't think we'll be together forever? Is that it?'

Rebecca hesitated. 'No, not exactly,' she said at last. 'But from my observation the best affairs last because the couple never become complacent or take each other for granted. That can happen so easily when people live together.'

'That's rubbish! My parents have been married for over forty years and they're absolutely devoted. So are yours, aren't they?'

'Yes, but our parents' generation were different. They didn't have the expectations of our generation. We want it all, Stirling, careers, children and happy-ever-after too. It's unrealistic.'

He sucked in his under-lip thoughtfully. 'It's going to happen to us one day, you know; being settled, having kids, even being married. So why not sooner rather than later?'

Rebecca shot him a horrified look. 'Oh, my God, this is getting too heavy for me!' She climbed out of bed and reached for his dark blue towelling robe. 'I don't know whether I want any of that, Stirling. All I want is my career, which I love, and to have you in my life . . . And to have the *best* of you in my life, and for you to have the *best* of me in yours.'

'They always say there's no such thing as a free lunch.'

'What d'you mean by that?'

'Think about it, sweetheart. Nothing is for nothing, and you can never avoid the so-called bad or boring times by only wanting to settle for the good ones.'

Rebecca looked disconcerted. 'I'm sorry if I'm raining on your parade and I'm not just going for the "good times",' she protested, 'but I do believe familiarity breeds contempt and that would be a tragedy in our case.' She sat down on the edge of the bed, the robe hugged around her and her slim legs crossed. 'Things are perfect the way they are, honey,' she said. 'Why don't we leave it at that?'

Stirling raised his tanned hands in mock surrender. 'OK! OK!' He sounded surprisingly good-tempered. 'It was only a suggestion. We'll play it your way if the idea of living together throws you into a decline. Now, will you make some coffee or shall I?'

Rebecca leaned forward and kissed him on the cheek. 'I'll make it, and I might fry you an egg too.'

Stirling flung himself back against the pillows, pretending to be shocked. 'She says she'll cook me an egg! Greater love hath no woman than this, that she shall cook an egg for her man.'

The moment of discord had been averted, but it had cast a shadow over both of them and made Rebecca feel strangely disquieted for the rest of the day.

Chapter Seven

'I'm afraid it hasn't been much fun for you this time, darling.' Sir Edward sat facing Jenny, nursing his whisky and soda. It was early evening and she was flying back to England first thing the next morning. Scott had drawn the oyster brocade curtains, shutting out the spangled darkness of the Manhattan skyline, and the room was bathed in the soft glow of the peach silk-shaded lamps.

'I haven't been able to take you anywhere,' he continued, his pale blue eyes sad. 'I hope it hasn't been too dull. You must have been awfully bored?'

'No, not at all,' Jenny lied, smiling. She hated the thought of leaving him and going back to London and her little shared flat and her job at the kindergarten. Usually on their last night together her father took her to dinner somewhere special, but tonight she knew Scott had been given instructions to serve dinner in the apartment. 'It's been a terrible time for you,' she added sympathetically.

He didn't reply but gazed into the depths of his glass, silent and morose. Then he seemed to remember his duty as a father and a host, for he remarked politely: 'Perhaps you can come over at Easter?'

'I'd like that.' She felt rather childish at accepting his casually spoken invitation with such eagerness, but it would be wonderful to come back and she knew it would give her something to look forward to through the dreary winter months ahead. 'I have nearly four weeks.'

He raised his eyebrows and looked at her blankly. 'Four weeks?'

'Four weeks' school holidays. Of course I wouldn't expect you to have me to stay for the whole four weeks.'

'Oh, I'd like you to stay, Jenny. It's a great comfort having you here.'

'Is it really?' She leaned forward, her pale skin flushed with pleasure. 'I wish I could have done more to . . . er, well . . . to cheer you up.'

Sir Edward averted his gaze and his bottom lip seemed to tremble for a second. 'That will take time,' he said gruffly.

Jenny felt embarrassed. She remembered seeing him drunk and crying shortly after she'd arrived, and now she feared he might start crying again. She'd been a fool to mention cheering him up. It sounded schoolgirlish and banal.

'Yes, of course,' she said hurriedly.

A heavy silence fell. They could both hear the chink of silver and crystal as Scott set the dining-table for them in the next room. Jenny wished her father had invited a couple of his close friends to supper, to lighten the atmosphere.

'Are you packed?' he asked.

'Yes. All packed.'

'The car will take you to the airport in the morning. I'm sorry I can't see you off but I've got an early meeting.'

'That's all right, Daddy.'

'Is your mother or Simon meeting you at the other end?'

'I left my car at the airport.'

'Ah, yes. I see.'

Another silence followed then, rising, Sir Edward took her glass out of her hand. 'You'll have another drink,' he said, 'another boring mineral water, I suppose?'

'I'm having tomato juice with Worcester sauce, Daddy.'

'Ah, yes. Of course.' Sir Edward went over to the drinks tray. When he came back and sat down he seemed to be angry about something. 'You ought to live a bit more, Jenny,' he said, suddenly and irritably.

She looked startled, glass midway to her mouth. 'How d'you mean?'

'Live a bit more! Enjoy yourself! Your mother seems to have made you afraid of having a good time.'

Jenny gulped, taken aback. 'I do have a good time . . . usually.'

'My dear child, you don't know the meaning of what it is to have a good time.'

'Yes, I do, Daddy. I have a good time when I come to New York, and I go to quite a few enjoyable things in London, you know.'

Sir Edward looked at her severely. 'Do you know what it is to drink champagne all night and dance in the arms of a young man you're in love with? Do you know what it is to go on a boat on the river at dawn, just as the sun is coming up? And then to go somewhere for eggs and bacon and more champagne? Do you know what it is to spend long balmy afternoons making love and then to go swimming together, naked? Have you ever once in your life done anything that was mad and wonderful and reckless and exciting?'

114

Jenny looked crestfallen. 'Well, no. You may have done all those things, but it's different for a girl.'

'Rubbish! That's just an excuse!'

'I don't think it is.' Jenny tried not to sound hurt. Her father was making her feel she must be dreadfully dull and boring.

'Of course it's an excuse! Why haven't you got a boyfriend?'

'Because . . . well, I haven't met anyone I particularly like.'

'It seems to me you haven't given anyone a chance. Next time you come to New York I'll have some nice young men lined up for you to meet, and I'll make sure they're fun-loving young men. Take you to clubs and out dining. Drives to the shore for midnight bathing. All that sort of thing. You shouldn't be stuck with an old man like me.'

Jenny looked at him earnestly. 'But I prefer being with you, Daddy. Most young men are awfully silly and immature.'

'Well, for God's sake get yourself an older man, but for heaven's sake, get yourself someone! You need the experience. You haven't learned to live yet, Jenny. Life's too short to spend it reading books and staying indoors at your age.'

'New York is hardly the place to go running around,' Jenny protested. 'It wouldn't be safe.'

'Marissa managed,' he said hollowly. 'She had guts and she knew how to enjoy every moment.' His mouth quivered slightly.

'I'm not Marissa,' said Jenny quietly, suddenly understanding what had caused his outburst.

'It's not that, darling,' Sir Edward suddenly sounded contrite, 'I wasn't trying to compare you. It's just that Marissa was so young when she died and yet she'd enjoyed every minute of her life! She wasn't afraid of anything. She was someone who dared . . . and now I thank God, for her sake, that she did. Marissa really lived life to the full.

'I want you to dare to do things, Jenny. Stop worrying about what people might think. Above all, stop worrying what your mother will say. I know she wants you to marry some eligible young man with a title, but for heaven's sake live a bit before you do all that. Sow your wild oats! Have yourself a ball, as they say over here.' He took another gulp of his drink and looked at her with blue eyes turned fierce.

'I'm not sure I'm the type,' said Jenny miserably. Her father's undisguised criticism had cut deeply, and although he'd assured her he wasn't comparing her to Marissa, she knew the girl had been someone he'd admired as well as loved. Jenny knew she could never be like that.

'Anyone's the type to have some fun,' he said. 'You've just got to learn to let yourself go.'

'Yes, Daddy.'

'Get drunk occasionally. Have a bit of a sex life. After all, you are twenty-two, aren't you?'

'Twenty-three.' She said it so softly he could hardly hear her.

He looked shaken. 'Twenty-three,' he repeated. Marissa had only been twenty. Of course Jenny was right in a sense; she wasn't like Marissa. Jenny hadn't the same zest for life, the same desire to catch the moment and enjoy it to the full. But then Jenny hadn't had to struggle from a working-class background to make something of herself, either. She'd been protected by going to good private schools, always having enough money, and of course aristocratic parentage. She'd also been dominated by an ambitious mother who had made her conform in all things, lest she acquired a reputation that might deter young men of good birth.

Who was to be pitied the most, wondered Sir Edward, as he sat slumped in depression, Marissa or Jenny? Marissa's brave struggle, first as a dancer and then as a socialite, had been an impressive grab at fulfilling her dreams and fantasies even though it had ended in tragedy. What lay behind the fact that she was really a girl called Tracy Handford, and how she'd acquired her seemingly enormous wealth, were other matters. The point was that for all Jenny's privileged upbringing and advantages she was still an inexperienced girl, living the life of a lonely dull middle-aged woman. Unless she did something drastic she might never have the chance to enjoy herself as Marissa had, even in her brief life.

' "One crowded hour of glorious life is worth an age without a name" ,' Sir Edward quoted to himself, forgetting Jenny's presence in the room.

She looked down at her hands with their short unvarnished nails, and thought of the pictures of Marissa which Rebecca had shown her. Marissa with her long red nails and fingers adorned with sparkling jewels; Marissa with hair that had been like burnished silver; Marissa, who had been tall and slim with legs a mile long, and with what people called 'charisma'. Jenny knew she was only of medium height and build, with dull fair hair and an ordinary face. She also knew she could enter a room twice and still not be noticed. Up until today she'd been quite happy with the way she was because her father seemed to approve of her, but now his attitude had changed and she was filled with aching self-doubt.

'What do you think I should do, Daddy?' she asked wretchedly.

Sir Edward glanced up from his glass and saw a pleasant-looking girl gazing back at him with an air of hopelessness. Briefly he wondered what it took to ignite an unkindled fire. All the women he'd ever known, even Angela, had simmered with passion in their time, been hot with desire and feverish to extract every ounce of fun from their existence. What did you do with a girl through whose veins milk and water flowed . . . who hung on your words like a young adolescent?

'Fall in love, I suppose,' he said in desperation. 'Have an affair . . . I don't know, Jenny. Perhaps if you had some more fun-loving girlfriends they'd show you the way. Why didn't you get friendly with that nice young photographer . . . er . . . what's her name?' He snapped his finger.

'Rebecca Kendall,' said Jenny.

'That's it! Rebecca. Very go-ahead girl, not scared of anything. Next time you're over, you should invite her for lunch.'

Jenny wrinkled her nose. 'I thought she was rather formidable actually. Not that I didn't like her,' she added quickly, 'but she seemed so high-powered.'

Sir Edward shrugged. 'She does a good job,' he said briefly.

Dinner that night was a silent affair. Jenny felt too hurt to say much and her father had drunk himself into a state of glassy-eyed unawareness. When it was over, she excused herself and went to bed. Her trip had been a disaster. She should never have come. Tomorrow it would be almost a relief to slip back to London, where she needn't make an effort to be fascinating and where the little children in the kindergarten would think her marvellous however she looked or acted.

Stirling insisted Rebecca spend the next night with him as well. She was catching the first flight to London from JFK airport the following morning, and apart from anything else, he was expecting repercussions when it was discovered she'd left the wrong films at the Post Office.

'It really is too damned dangerous for you to stay at your apartment until this whole thing has been cleared up,' he stressed as they dined on her last night at one of her favourite restaurants, El Charro in Greenwich Village. Sitting at one of the dark oak tables, she sipped a Tequila Sunrise while Stirling had some of their Tecate beer, served traditionally with salt and a slice of lemon.

'Suppose it's never cleared up?' she questioned him. 'If O'Hara and the rest of the cops continue to insist it was an accident, and Sir Edward is happy to go along with that for business reasons, it means there's only you and me and Karen who are convinced it wasn't. I wish I knew what to do next.'

'You don't have to do anything, sweetheart, except fly to London tomorrow, spend two weeks doing your work and not worrying about anything,' replied Stirling, signalling to one of the Hispanic waiters. 'Let's order, then we can talk in peace. What are you going to have?'

Rebecca consulted the menu. 'I'd like to start with sweetcorn and pepper soup – the *sopa de elote con rajas* – and then I'll have spare ribs, but instead of chilli and cream sauce I'd rather have the smoked *jalapeno* sauce.'

'OK. I feel like fish tonight so I think I'll have red snapper cooked with capers, olives and oranges . . . and *quesadillas de chorizo y papa* to start with.'

Rebecca looked intrigued. 'That's a new one on me – what is it?'

'Tortilla . . . probably made with wheat rather than corn, and filled with spicy pork sausage and potato and cheese and onion and . . .'

'Stop! Stop, I can't bear it! I'm so hungry, Stirling, I could eat a whole cow! D'you realize I haven't eaten at all today? I missed out on lunch because I had to buy some clothes for the trip, and the whole afternoon has been taken up with finalizing all my assignments for Europe.' Rebecca's eyes sparkled with excitement. She looked vital and full of energy.

Stirling nodded. 'I know, but I think it's all buttoned up now, don't you? You've got the special pass to photograph Princess Diana at the gala ball, and I've got you into 10, Downing Street, to get pictures of Mrs Thatcher "at home". You're flying to Paris to photograph some of the top designers, and although it's the wrong time of year, try and get some American ladies choosing their clothes. *W. W.* loves that sort of thing!'

'I know.' Rebecca smiled, knowing exactly what he meant, understanding all that she had to do. She also hoped that she might pick up a few more scoops along the way, but she wasn't going to mention what she had in mind now. It would be more fun to surprise Stirling and show him what she could really do when she had the chance.

'When you get back,' he was saying as he reached out to take her hand, 'I'm really being serious when I say I want you to move in with me, sweetheart.' He grinned, his tanned face breaking into attractive lines, dark eyes twinkling. 'I never thought I'd have to take advantage of death threats to get you to live with me, but if that's what it takes . . . !' His eyes bored into Rebecca's, making her heart thump.

'I'll stay with you until the heat's off, anyway,' she promised

118

gently. She didn't want a repeat of this morning's argument but she couldn't commit herself either. In fact, she realized that Stirling would be deeply hurt if he knew how she was longing to get back to her own apartment, and to listening to Karen's endless talk about her different boyfriends, and to spending happy hours pottering about in her darkroom which still had to be cleaned up and re-equipped.

He was squeezing her hand tighter. 'I'll miss you, but I think this trip will be wonderful for your career.'

'And I think you're very clever to have fixed it,' she said with genuine gratitude.

'Goodbye, darling. Have a good journey, and don't forget you're coming over again for Easter.' Sir Edward kissed Jenny on both cheeks as he got ready, the next morning, to leave the apartment before her. In spite of his heavy drinking the previous evening, he looked ruddily healthy and his pale blue eyes were clear. He also seemed to be much more cheerful.

'Goodbye, Daddy. Take care of yourself.' Jenny clung to him for a moment, always emotional when they had to part.

He patted her shoulder. 'You too, my sweet. Next time we'll have some fun too. Go to a few Broadway shows, eh? Dine in some good restaurants? What d'you say?'

Sir Edward seemed to have forgotten his tirade of the previous evening and he was once again the father of her childhood, brimming with charm and bonhomie, promising her the earth; and she was once again his little pet.

'That would be lovely,' Jenny reached up to give him another kiss.

Then, in a flurry of goodbyes, Scott was helping him on with his vicuña coat and handing him his briefcase while Sir Edward rattled out last-minute domestic instructions before dashing to the elevator, saying he couldn't keep the chauffeur waiting in case there were still some of the press lurking about outside the building. A moment later, with a final wave of his hand, he was gone and Jenny was left standing, feeling as she always did at his departure – alone, and with an aching emptiness inside her. It was always the same. She could remember right back to her childhood when he used to go up to London from Pinkney, the awful feeling of deflation that used to swamp her as she stood in the drive. It was as if all the fun had gone from the world, leaving it a colder sadder place.

Slowly, she went back to the dining-room where only minutes before the air had been filled with Sir Edward's lighthearted chatter. She poured herself another cup of coffee. The room was so quiet now she could hear the roar of the traffic fourteen floors below, although the windows were closed. The ticking of the clock in the hall seemed to reverberate throughout the apartment. Even Scott had vanished into the kitchen. He and the cook must be talking in whispers, she thought, for there wasn't a sound from either of them.

At last the hired limousine arrived to take her to the airport to catch the ten o'clock flight. With a feeling almost of relief Jenny quickly put on her tweed coat and woollen gloves and hurried to the elevator, followed by Scott carrying her suitcases. She wanted to shake off the gloom brought on by her father's departure and the quickest way she knew was to get involved in the hustle and bustle of departure herself.

She also wanted to try and forget his words of criticism last night. It wasn't her fault, she told herself, if she was dull and boring and didn't have the capacity to enjoy life as Marissa had done. If Marissa had sparkled and shone and filled her father's life with joy and laughter, so that now she was gone his heart was broken, then Jenny couldn't compete. She wouldn't try, either. She would creep back to England like the little grey mouse she was, and get on with the quiet life she seemed to have chosen for herself.

Rebecca strode into the first-class lounge at JFK, helped herself to a glass of fresh orange juice and a croissant from the buffet, and then settled down with the *New York Times* while she waited for her flight to be called. Travelling first or club class was one of the perks she allowed herself now that she was successful, and in her opinion the extra cost was worth it. For one thing she could avoid the crowds in the departure lounge, but best of all, first-class and club-class passengers were always allowed off the plane first, and their luggage always appeared first on the carousel.

Wearing black pants and a maroon leather jacket, she looked relaxed as she ate her breakfast and scanned the newspaper to see if any of her recent photographs had been reproduced. Things happened so quickly in the media that Stirling didn't always have time to let her know when a picture editor requested one of her shots.

Finding nothing she started to read the news, always on the lookout for a situation to photograph. She was so engrossed in a piece about an archaeological find in the centre of London, that had turned out to be the original foundations of the theatre where Shakespeare staged his plays, that she wasn't at first aware she was being watched. As she read that dozens of leading actors were

120

petitioning to prevent an office building from being built on the site, demolishing the fragile remains forever, and she was thinking what a great feature she could make out of it – especially if she could get some of the Knights and Dames of the British theatre to pose among the ruins – she was unaware that someone was approaching, slowly, across the half empty lounge.

Suddenly Rebecca was conscious of a shadow falling across the page she held. Freezing, she held her breath while trying to remember in those seconds who had been in the lounge when she'd entered. There were four Japanese businessmen, huddled in whispered conversation, their heads close together; there was what looked like an Englishman in a handmade Savile Row suit, carrying a briefcase; and there were a couple of young women in crisp executive suits, exuding briskness and efficiency. For a moment she felt a surge of panic, then he spoke.

'It is Rebecca, isn't it?' There was a hint of laughter in his tone.

Her head shot up, and then a flush spread over her face. 'Good heavens! Fancy seeing you again!' It was Jerry Ribis.

'How are you?' He shook her hand warmly and sat down beside her.

'I'm fine!' Her heart was still pounding and she felt foolish in her relief. Fancy imagining Marissa's killer was pursuing her at every turn! She took a deep breath and chided herself for being paranoid. 'Where are you off to?' she asked, trying to steady her voice.

'Rome. Just for a week. I've got a short vacation due to me, so I'm flying over to see my sister,' replied Jerry.

'That's nice. Have you been to Italy before?'

Jerry shook his head, grinning. 'Nope. This is the first time. Where are you going?'

'London – then on to Paris. All work, I'm afraid, but it should be interesting.'

'Will you be away long?'

'A couple of weeks.'

Jerry moved closer. 'Perhaps we could meet when you get back? I'd really like to take you out to dinner one evening.'

Rebecca smiled, remembering Karen's eagerness to meet him. 'I'm a bit tied up, you know,' she said pointedly, 'but why don't you come round to my apartment for a drink? I could get a few friends . . .'

'I'd like that.' His smile deepened, and she thought that he looked quite attractive with his hazel eyes and curling brown hair. 'I'll call you when you get back,' he promised, rising. 'I'd better go now, I heard my flight being called a minute ago. Have a great time! Take care of yourself!'

'I will.' Rebecca almost wished he were going to London too. He'd have been amusing company on the flight. She watched as he strode out of the lounge, weaving his way round tables of magazines and flowers and arrangements of blue armchairs and sofas. She glanced at her watch; they would be calling her flight any moment too.

Bending down to get her boarding pass out of her hand luggage, she saw something glinting on the soft pile of the blue carpet by her feet. Looking closer, she saw it was a small bunch of keys, the type that open luggage or jewel boxes. Her eyes flew to the exit. Jerry Ribis had gone and these were obviously his. He'd carried a raincoat over his arm and she remembered it had slid to the ground while he'd been talking to her. The keys must have fallen out of the pocket.

Springing to her feet, she hurried over to the stewardess who was on duty at the reception desk.

'Excuse me,' she said quickly, 'I've just found these keys on the floor. I think they belong to a Mr Jerry Ribis. He's just left here to catch his flight to Rome. Can you get them to him?'

The well-groomed young woman, in her smart navy blue uniform, gave a fleeting smile as she took the keys from Rebecca, and then frowned in puzzlement. 'Did you say Rome, madam?'

Rebecca nodded. 'He's just left . . . only a moment ago.'

The stewardess picked up the phone and talked rapidly to the person on the other end. Rebecca heard her repeat Jerry's name several times, and twice she said: 'Yes, Rome.'

Rebecca looked inquiringly at her. 'Is there a problem?'

'Yes, madam, there is.' Her frown had deepened. She looked down at the bunch of keys in her hand. 'Are you sure the gentleman said he was flying to Rome?'

'Yes. He also said, just before he left, that he'd heard his flight called a moment before. What's wrong?'

'There aren't any flights to Rome this morning, madam, and the steward who was here before I came on duty just now, said nobody by the name of Mr Jerry Ribis had checked in this morning.'

Jenny paused by the display of perfumes in the duty free shop at JFK, and wondered if it would be a good idea to buy some for herself. Usually she only bought a large bottle of gin to share with her flatmates, but now she paused, tempted, trying to decide which scent she should get. Claude Montana's bottle was a sensational shape, but then the smell of Estée Lauder's Beautiful was gorgeous. Of course, there were Dior and Chanel and Yves Saint

Laurent too. Bewildered, she sniffed from the sample bottles, getting more confused by the minute. If she didn't make up her mind soon she'd miss her flight. Finally, she decided on a large and very expensive bottle of Ysatis by Givenchy.

Once bought and paid for, its presence in her hand luggage gave her a lift. Pulling her tweed coat tighter round her, she set off for the departure gate at a quickened pace. Buying little presents for herself always had that effect. Perhaps I should do it more often, she thought.

'Good morning.' The air hostess greeted her smilingly. Jenny, travelling first class at her father's insistence, was among the last passengers to board.

'Good morning.' She looked forward to being pampered for the next few hours. She loved the way they always served chilled champagne before the plane even took off, followed by a delicious breakfast. She'd had only coffee that morning and already she felt hungry. Entering the compartment, with its spacious seats and wide centre aisle, she found it was almost empty. There were only a few businessmen, briefcases already opened as they continued to work as if still in their own offices. The steward settled her in a window-seat and fussed around her with small downy pillows and soft cashmere rugs. Jenny leaned back, luxuriating in the comfort, and then she saw a young woman seated across the aisle, looking out of the window. With a start, Jenny realized it was Rebecca Kendall.

'Hello,' she said shyly, leaning forward.

Rebecca turned her head sharply, her eyes wary. When she saw who it was, her face softened and she smiled.

'Why, Jenny, what a surprise. How amazing you being on this flight. How are you?'

'I'm fine. On my way home. School starts again in two days' time.' Jenny sipped her champagne, wishing she had a more exciting job. If only she could have said to this self-confident and composed-looking young woman something like: 'Parliament reopens after the Christmas recess and I have to get back to the House of Commons', or even: 'We're frightfully busy in the company, and I've a heavy schedule to deal with'. As it was she'd sounded like a schoolgirl, and looking down at herself, in the grey pleated skirt and navy sweater she'd put on that morning, she felt she even looked like one.

Jenny pushed her hair back from her face with a nervous gesture. This was what her father meant, she thought. She hadn't really lived and it showed. It particularly showed when she compared herself to someone like Rebecca Kendall.

'Why are you going to England?' she asked, wishing she felt more confident.

'Work,' Rebecca replied briefly. She seemed to be pondering something, and then she leaned over towards Jenny. 'Say, do you know if anyone's sitting next to you? I thought, if the seat was empty, we could talk.'

Jenny looked around and saw that the stewards were closing the door. 'I don't think there's anyone else getting on board.'

'Great.' Rebecca sprang to her feet, crossed the aisle and slid into the seat next to Jenny. 'That's better,' she remarked, fastening the safety belt. 'We couldn't have shouted all the way to England.'

Jenny gave a polite little laugh and sipped some more of her champagne. A steward hovered with a fresh bottle, leaning forward to refill her glass.

'Some champagne, madam?' he suggested to Rebecca.

'No thanks, but I'd like another glass of mineral water, non-carbonated please.'

'Certainly.' He skimmmed away to get it for her.

'Don't you like champagne?' Jenny asked.

'I love it,' grinned Rebecca, 'but not at nine o'clock in the morning, and certainly not when I'm flying. D'you want to know how to avoid jet-lag?'

Jenny nodded avidly.

'Drink eight pints of liquid on a flight, preferably plain water. That's what they make the crew drink, and it prevents you from getting dehydrated.'

'Really?' Jenny was amazed. She looked longingly at the golden bubbles floating to the top of her glass. 'Oh, well!' She shrugged and gave a little laugh. 'Daddy paid for my ticket so I might as well enjoy every moment of the luxury before I return to the old grindstone.'

'How is your father?' asked Rebecca.

'Up and down,' Jenny replied thoughtfully. 'He hasn't really got over Marissa's death yet. It was more of a shock to him than I'd realized.'

Rebecca nodded understandingly. 'He's probably feeling it more now than he did at the time. I think he was still numb when I saw him the other day. Have you heard anything more from the police? Any more developments?'

'There's been an inquest, you know.'

'And?'

'They brought in a verdict of accidental death.'

'They did? Oh, my God.'

'Don't you think it could have been an accident, Rebecca? Wouldn't there have been lots of inquiries if anyone seriously thought Marissa had been murdered?'

Rebecca looked at Jenny speculatively, wondering if she could trust her. Finding Jerry Ribis was travelling under a false name, if he was travelling at all – and it certainly wasn't to Rome – had made her feel suspicious and uncertain about whom she dared trust, and for a moment she felt a pang of regret at leaving Stirling behind. She didn't scare easily, but the events of the past half hour had shaken her.

'What is it?' asked Jenny, looking at her.

Rebecca took in the blue eyes and pleasant but ordinary face and decided Jenny Wenlake hadn't a deceitful bone in her body. There was a particular honesty about her that was appealing, and whilst she might not be a bright spark, there was a sense of integrity Rebecca liked. She decided to take the girl into her confidence.

'I'll tell you exactly why I think Marissa was murdered . . .' She told Jenny everything, leaving out no detail, while the steward served fragrant coffee and succulent scrambled eggs on toast, croissants and marmalade. As Jenny munched her way through a large breakfast, she listened with growing amazement. When Rebecca got to the part about meeting Jerry Ribis in the VIP lounge, Jenny gave a little gasp.

'Do you think he's following you?' She craned her neck to look around, but a curtain divided the first-class passengers from the rest of the plane. 'What are you going to do?'

'As soon as I get to London I'm going to call Stirling. Maybe he can find out something about this man. Have you ever heard of him? I presumed, when I first met him, that he was a friend of your father's. Now I'm convinced he is somehow tied up with Marissa.'

'I'll ask Daddy,' said Jenny, carefully dabbing the corners of her mouth with the royal blue linen napkin that matched the cabin's upholstery. 'It makes one wonder though, doesn't it?'

'What does?' asked Rebecca.

'Who this Jerry what's-his-name is? Do you think he was a boy-friend of Marissa's? Perhaps he was jealous and that's why he killed her!'

'Then who is the man dressed as a waiter, opening the window in the photograph?' Rebecca shook her head. 'I'd say he was the one who pushed her out. Jerry struck me as very sweet but rather ineffectual. Surely he couldn't have been Marissa's boyfriend? I can't believe he's the one who killed her, either. I wonder why he's interested in me?'

'Perhaps he thinks you know more than you actually do.'

Rebecca looked at Jenny with renewed respect. 'You could be right. Maybe he just wants to get to know me better so he can find out exactly how much I do know. If he isn't flying to Rome today, I wonder where he *is* going?'

'Keep a lookout when we land,' Jenny advised. 'I'll stick close to you and you point him out if you see him.'

'Don't worry, I will!'

'Where are you staying?'

'The Belgravia-Sheraton. It's central and I have a lot of running around to do. You live in Kensington, don't you?'

'Yes. I share a flat with a couple of girlfriends. You must come to supper one evening while you're in England.'

'I'd like that.'

The rest of the journey passed uneventfully as Rebecca and Jenny got better acquainted, growing to like each other as the hours passed. Jenny was inspired by Rebecca and deeply impressed too. For someone who was only a year older than herself, she seemed so poised and self-possessed; her career was also burgeoning, which Jenny found quite depressing. No wonder her father had said she ought to be more like Rebecca. Even the way she dressed expressed sophistication and worldliness.

'Do you have a boyfriend?' she heard Rebecca ask.

'Not at the moment,' Jenny replied, trying to keep her voice light, wishing she were brave enough to lie a bit, invent some gorgeous young man who was crazy about her.

'Well, you're wise not to get tied down too soon,' said Rebecca. 'I adore Stirling, but I don't want to settle down yet. I've got a lot of living to do first.'

'I think I'd want to settle down if I met exactly the right person,' Jenny blurted out honestly. 'The trouble is, I never seem to.' Her voice sounded so doleful that Rebecca burst out laughing.

'It'll happen!' she said cheerfully. 'And when it does you'll know all about it, like I did when I met Stirling.'

'Mummy will be bound to disapprove . . . unless it's a duke or a marquis or at least an earl!'

Rebecca's mouth twitched, trying to picture Sir Edward's ex-wife whom she'd heard about, imagining her to be very snobbish and autocratic. 'I don't suppose you do what your mother says,' she joked.

Jenny shot her a knowing look. 'You're dead right, I don't.'

The plane landed at Heathrow at nine-fifteen in the evening, English time. Jenny and Rebecca disembarked and were swept through Immigration with the other first-class passengers. When they got to the carousel, Jenny agreed to collect their luggage while Rebecca kept a look out for Jerry Ribis in case he was among the tourist-class passengers. There was no sign of him.

'I don't expect he's followed you to England,' said Jenny comfortingly as she pushed their luggage trolley.

'Maybe not. Maybe he just wanted to be sure that I was leaving the States. What is so awful,' Rebecca continued, having a last look round the crowded arrivals hall, 'is that I feel Big Brother is watching me all the time now. I feel that everything I do is being noted and that everywhere I go is being covered.'

Jenny spoke with confidence. 'If you have any problems our British police are wonderful. They'll help you.'

'That's what I used to think about our police back home,' Rebecca laughed ruefully. 'Now I'm convinced they're all crooked. Well, I'm sure O'Hara is.'

'Can I give you a lift into London? I've got my car parked in one of the car-parks here.'

'Thanks. That would be great.'

An hour later Jenny dropped her off at her hotel, which was in the heart of Belgravia, surrounded by large white-porticoed nineteenth century houses that exuded wealth and elegance.

'I'll call you tomorrow and make a date for you to come to supper,' Jenny called as Rebecca waved before disappearing through the revolving door into the luxurious lobby.

As Jenny drove on to the less opulent area of Kensington, she marvelled at Rebecca's assurance, imagining herself in the same position, alone in a strange city with few friends and challenging assignments ahead of her.

I'd be scared shitless, thought Jenny, as she put her foot down hard on the accelerator, longing for the warmth and safety of her bed.

On the hall table of her Kensington flat was a note from Sally, one of her flatmates. It was written on a sheet of their best headed blue writing-paper, and Jenny picked it up, thinking it must be a welcome home note.

Dear Jen,
Please contact your mother immediately. It's urgent.
Love, Sal.

Jenny stood staring at the note, knowing in her bones it couldn't be good news. Summonses from her mother rarely were.

127

*　　*　　*

Angela Wenlake's voice had a harsh edge to it that Jenny had never heard before.

'Simon's injuries are very serious. It could go either way. Clover rolled on him, you see.'

Jenny closed her eyes, visualizing the great roan brute, legs pumping frantically in the air as it struggled to regain its feet; and her brother, crushed into the ground by the solid weight of the highly bred hunter.

'Oh my God!' she said, sitting down suddenly because her legs had gone wobbly. She and Simon weren't close, but she wouldn't have wished this sort of accident on anyone. The thought of being pinned under a massive struggling animal filled her with horror.

'When did it happen, Mummy?' she asked faintly.

'Early this afternoon. I've got hold of your father . . . he's flying over. He'll be here in the morning. I only missed you by moments when I called.' Angela's voice grated, tearless but agonized.

'Oh my God,' said Jenny again.

'Can you come at once?'

'Now?' She already felt as if she'd been travelling for days.

'I'm here on my own, Jenny. The hospital sent me home because there's nothing I can do and Simon's unconscious anyway. They told me to rest, but I can't . . . I can't stop thinking.' There was a pause, and then as if it required enormous effort she said: 'I need you here with me.'

It was the first time Jenny ever remembered her mother saying anything like that to her.

'OK, I'll drive down now.'

In spite of the exhaustion she felt after her early start in Manhattan, the flight over, and finally the drive in to London, she gathered up her suitcases again, not bothering to repack. Then she left a note to tell Sally what had happened.

It was colder than ever, the roads glazed with ice and the air sharp and raw. As Jenny left the suburbs of London behind, heading for the south west, bands of freezing mist enveloped the car. Unblinking, she gripped the steering wheel, fighting her tiredness and praying she wouldn't hit a patch of black ice. The yellow sodium lights of the motorway cast a sulphurous glow on the winding road, turning her skin a jaundiced shade.

What awaited her at Pinkney House she did not dare think. She was no closer to her mother than she was to Simon and the role of comforter would sit uneasily on her shoulders. What was she supposed to do when she arrived? Hug her mother? Put her arms round

128

her and give her a kiss? Jenny flushed in the darkness of her car, embarrassed at the thought, for Angela had never been a tactile mother and now it was too late. Too late for many things, but especially too late to build a bridge from such barren shores. Then Jenny remembered that her father would be joining them in the morning, and felt a wave of thankfulness. It would be the first time the family had been together for eleven years, but if her father were in charge then she'd be able to bear anything.

Chapter Eight

Rebecca was up early the next morning, her misgivings about Jerry Ribis having faded after a good night's sleep. There were a dozen plausible reasons, she told herself, to explain what had happened. Jerry might not have been flying direct to Rome but stopping off someplace else; the airline might have made a mistake about his name not being listed. She had no earthly reason to be suspicious of him and she began to regret having made such an issue of it when she'd been telling Jenny what had been happening. Jerry had been a guest at Sir Edward's party, he'd given her a lift home afterwards, he was slightly attracted to her and that was all there was to it. Chiding herself for being so neurotic, Rebecca loaded her two Rolleiflexes, one with colour film and one with black and white, and set off for her first appointment of the day.

Stirling had arranged for her to photograph the American Ambassador to Great Britain and his wife for *Town and Country* magazine. The Ambassador's residence, Winfield House, had originally been built by Barbara Hutton as a private town house. When Rebecca arrived at the elegant white building in Regents Park, she was welcomed by a private secretary.

'We thought perhaps you'd like to take the pictures in the drawing-room,' he suggested, leading her to a magnificent room furnished with antique furniture and mirrors, overlooking rich parkland which suggested they were in the countryside.

'This would be perfect,' Rebecca agreed, quickly setting up her tripod and cameras. She'd also brought with her a portable flashlight unit with three flashheads. Once plugged into the electric mains, she linked them by wires to the camera shutter.

A few minutes later, the double doors at one end of the room opened and the Ambassador and his wife entered.

'Good morning. I hope we haven't kept you waiting,' the Ambassador greeted her as he came forward, his hand outstretched.

Rebecca felt slightly overawed. He was a regal, handsome-

131

looking man. His pretty wife was exquisitely dressed. This, she imagined, must be what it would be like to photograph royalty.

'Good morning,' she said, thankful she'd put on a smart red suit instead of the trousers she usually wore.

As soon as she started working, though, telling them where to sit or stand, she forgot her shyness. Once in control of a situation she knew well, her confidence flowed back. Concentrating on the lighting, and posing them at their most flattering angles, she chattered away inconsequentially so that they would look relaxed too. In twenty minutes the session was over and she knew she'd got some excellent shots, striking a balance between formality and casualness.

'Thank you very much,' she said, as they all shook hands.

'Thank *you*,' replied the Ambassador, smiling warmly, making Rebecca wonder as the car took her back to her hotel what it must be like to live in such a rarefied atmosphere. In the Diplomatic Corps, she knew, it was necessary to be charming and gracious at all times. It was hard to imagine what it must be like being eternally pleasant to strangers, having to think before you said anything for fear of giving offence or causing an international incident, and eternally smiling because if you didn't people might think you were bored.

When Rebecca got back to the Belgravia-Sheraton she found a message from Jenny saying she'd had to go to the country because her brother had had an accident, but she'd call in a couple of days.

'There was another phone call for you,' said the receptionist. 'It came in just a minute ago.' She handed Rebecca a folded sheet of hotel writing-paper on which she'd written the message.

Rebecca read the note, and suddenly her heart felt constricted in her chest as if it were being squeezed tight. She found it hard to breathe. She could even feel her cheeks going cold and stiff as the blood drained from her face. For the first time she was filled with a real sense of fear.

'Everything all right?' enquired the receptionist anxiously. 'The caller didn't leave a name . . . said you'd understand the message and know who it was from.'

'Oh. Yes. Thanks,' said Rebecca. Then she turned, almost stumbling, towards the elevator, her one idea to get to her room as quickly as possible. She knew who it was from all right, and she could imagine the metallic-sounding voice as it left the message for her . . . such a succinct yet subtle message too. Only she would know what it meant.

Once in her room, she sank on to the bed and read it again.

Pity about the wrong films. Enjoy your trip. It will be
your last as I can't afford to lose you. I'll be waiting for
your return.

Rebecca sat on the bed for a long time, wondering what to do next.
It was a death threat, no doubt about that. He'd discovered she'd
left the wrong films at the Post Office and now he planned to kill
her on her return to the States. But why wait? Why not kill her here
and now, while she was in London? Rebecca reached for the phone
and asked to be put through to reception.

'That second message you took for me,' she said, when she'd
given her name and room number. 'Can you tell me if it was a local
London call or a transatlantic one, please?'

There was a pause, and then she heard the receptionist say: 'We
can't be sure, madam, but we think it was a transatlantic call.'

Rebecca took a deep breath. 'Thanks,' she said briefly and hung
up. Then she tried to think logically although her head was spinning. The killer, whoever he was, was still in the States and
yet – and this was the important part – from the message it seemed
he was going to wait for her to get back before striking. Why? What
was he waiting for? Surely as far as he was concerned, the sooner
she was out of the way, unable to identify him, the better?

The door swung open gently and Sir Edward crept quietly into
Simon's room at the Mount Royal Hospital in Andover, Hampshire.
Angela glanced up from her position at the head of the bed but her
expression remained impassive. Jenny rose swiftly though and
flung her arms around her father's neck.

'Hello, my pet.' He hugged her and she felt the most enormous
sense of relief that he had arrived. It was ten o'clock in the morning
and she and Angela had been at the hospital since seven, sitting in
silent vigil by Simon's bed. They had not talked. There seemed
nothing to say as each sat gripped by their own private doubts and
fears, with Simon lying between them so pale and still he might
already have been dead. Angela was filled with terror that her
beloved son might not recover, while Jenny felt regret because she
could not care more.

'How is he?' whispered Sir Edward, going to look down at the
son who would one day inherit his title and half his wealth.

'There's no change,' Angela replied tightly, and Jenny noticed
they had not even greeted each other. Not that it mattered now, she
reflected.

'What do the doctors say?'

Angela shrugged, helpless for once in her life. 'He's got a ruptured spleen, damaged kidneys and severe spinal injuries. He's also severely concussed; he hasn't regained consciousness since it happened yesterday afternoon.'

Sir Edward looked grave. 'Not so good, eh?'

'Not so good,' repeated Angela. Her claw-like hands, bare of diamond rings for once, lay tightly clenched in her lap and Jenny wondered if, over the years, her mother had ever given way to her emotions. Had she cried when she'd discovered Edward having an affair with their nanny? Had she wept when she'd kicked him out of Pinkney House, demanding a divorce? Had she ever shed tears during the ensuing years as she'd sat in lonely splendour in the grand house, with only her son for company, knowing all the time that Edward was enjoying himself with an endless string of women friends?

'Are you all right, Jenny-Wren?' Sir Edward was asking gently, breaking into her thoughts. He hadn't called her by that pet name since she'd been a child. Jenny could feel Angela bristling with resentment that even at this moment of crisis in their son's life, Edward still seemed to be more fond of Jenny than he was of Simon.

'I'm fine, Daddy.' She gave a wan smile.

'Why don't you go home and rest? Your mother and I will stay with Simon. You look exhausted.'

Jenny looked from one to the other, trying to gauge her mother's reaction, wondering what she'd say if Jenny deserted the favourite's bedside.

'Go on, hop it!' urged Sir Edward, putting his arm round her shoulders and guiding her towards the door. 'There's nothing she can do here, is there, Angela? Go home and have a couple of hours' sleep, and I'll see you later.'

'Are you sure? You must be tired, too,' she whispered.

'I slept on the flight over.'

Jenny hesitated. 'Are you staying at Pinkney?'

Without looking at his ex-wife, Edward answered unhesitatingly, 'Yes, of course.'

Jenny gave a pleased smile, and slipping out of the hospital hurried to the car-park where she'd left her little blue Golf GTi. Nearby she saw a hired limousine parked near the entrance, the chauffeur sitting inside reading a newspaper. So that's how Daddy travelled from the airport, she thought, not doubting for a moment it was his. Her father did everything with style; even hurrying to the bedside of his estranged son.

When she got back to Pinkney, she told Peters that Sir Edward had arrived and would be staying with them.

'Certainly, Miss Jenny,' he replied. 'I'll get Ruby to prepare a room and I'll tell cook there will be one extra for dinner tonight.'

'Thank you, Peters,' said Jenny, leaving it to him to decide which bedroom her father would sleep in.

Mike Wilson, sitting in a run-down cafe on Second Avenue, sipped his cup of lukewarm tea and wondered what the hell to do next. So far he had drawn a complete blank in tracing the reported fortune of Marissa/Tracy and he was beginning to feel desperate. In spite of staying in a cheap and somewhat sleazy downtown hotel, his trip to New York was costing Lawson, Martin & Grant a lot of money and their patience was running out.

In their initial eagerness to make a quick buck, it had at first seemed like an easy and straight-forward matter; a rich girl had died and her parents, being her next-of-kin, were eager to claim what was rightfully theirs. In fact, Mike's boss had been worried by only one thing at the beginning, and that was that they wouldn't be the first firm to persuade Mr and Mrs Bert Handford to let them handle the matter. However, Mike had been able to congratulate himself that he had got to the Handfords before anyone else and had locked them into an agreement while they were still in a vulnerable state after their daughter's death.

He stirred his tea, and gazed absently out of the cafe's dirty windows at the trucks that thundered past on the uneven roadway, shuddering under the weight of their loads. In the beginning, he reflected, when he'd been planning this trip to New York, Tracy Handford had been a person of substance. No matter that she was a corpse in some mortuary on the other side of the Atlantic, she had a mother and a father, a home address and there were people who had known her, and had been to dancing school with her, before she'd left home at seventeen to go to Las Vegas. He'd got a copy of her birth certificate and even her parents' marriage certificate. In other words . . . she was traceable.

To his confusion though, Marissa Montclare by contrast seemed to have left no traces at all! Within hours of arriving in New York he discovered that whereas in England Tracy Handford had been a verifiable flesh and blood person, Marissa Montclare now appeared to have been a myth. A non-existent person whom no one seemed to know . . . at least no one in an official capacity, and that was all Mike was interested in. Had she been . . . *could* she have been . . . a figment of an over-zealous gossip columnist's imagination? he asked himself in desperation. An invention with which to grace the tabloids and titillate readers?

For days now he'd been making inquiries, including doing searches of income tax and social security records, and he could find no trace of her, much less of her money. The police department in the precinct where she'd died were equally unhelpful. Some jerk called Detective Tom O'Hara, thought Mike bitterly, had as good as told him to take a running jump. Said the inquest had returned a verdict of accidental death and the case was closed. No, he didn't know anything about Miss Montclare's financial situation. No, he had no idea where she'd banked. Mike had soon found himself out on the street again.

Next, he visited a couple of the newspapers that had covered the story in all its luridness, but although he got to see the editors they refused to give him any information that he hadn't already read in their pages, saying they must protect their sources of information. For the moment it seemed to Mike that the whole of New York had closed ranks and conspired to swallow up all traces of the rich young woman who had died on New Year's Eve. It was as if people were pulling down an impenetrable blind between himself and Marissa's money, and he didn't know how to get round it.

It hadn't surprised him when the snooty Lady Wenlake had given him the bum's rush, he reflected; he wasn't even so amazed when that arrogant old sod Sir Edward had refused to help. Everyone knew the aristocracy had a great knack for brushing the dirt under the carpet. But when the doorman at Trump Tower said he'd never heard of Marissa Montclare and she'd never had an apartment there, Mike began to feel his head reel and his senses spin. That's when he'd started walking the wet streets of Manhattan in a numbed daze, until he'd come upon this cafe with its faded pale green-painted exterior and broken Coca-Cola sign.

What was he to do next? he asked himself, pulling a handful of press clippings about Tracy/Marissa's death out of his briefcase. He studied them once more, although he knew what they said by heart, and the photographs of her taken at the party were as familiar to him as if he'd taken them himself.

Then something caught his eye, something he'd overlooked. There was someone else who might be able to tell him something, maybe give him a lead. Photo by Rebecca Kendall it said under all the pictures. He'd find out where this Rebecca Kendall hung out and he'd go and see her.

Rising, he paid for his tea and left the cafe in a more cheerful frame of mind. It had also occurred to him that the doormen must work different shifts at Trump Tower and that one of them must have known Marissa Montclare!

'Is everything OK, sweetheart?' Stirling asked Rebecca when she called him later that day.

'Fine,' she lied, having decided it would be pointless to worry him. There was nothing he could do in any case. He was stuck in New York working his butt off, and anyway, she told herself, she felt comparatively safe while she remained in Europe. Whoever had threatened her would not attempt to do anything because a cover-up in another country would be more difficult. But in New York, she was sure Marissa's killer had the protection of the police. The more she thought about Detective O'Hara, with his cunning little eyes and sweaty hands, the more she was sure he was in the pay of whoever had committed the murder, and she was sure too that she herself ran the risk of having a 'fatal accident' when she re-entered that particular precinct. That is, unless she returned the incriminating films.

'How did the session at the Embassy go?' Stirling was asking her. 'Get some good colour shots?'

'Yes, great,' replied Rebecca, with forced cheerfulness. 'They were a charming couple. The film is already on its way to you by Federal Express. You should get them within forty-eight hours.'

'Great! Listen, honey, while you're in London, is there any chance you could get backstage at one of Andrew Lloyd-Webber's productions, to get some shots of the Queen's son, Prince Edward, helping out?'

'I could try,' agreed Rebecca. 'I don't think the Prince actually works backstage. I've heard he's in the production office.'

'Great! Even a shot of him arriving with some props or costumes or something would be of interest,' said Stirling. 'Better still if you could get a quote, of course.'

'I'll see what I can do,' she promised, and then added, 'Everything all right with you, Stirling?'

'I'm OK, sweetheart, but missing you like crazy.'

'I miss you too,' Rebecca said wistfully. 'I wish you were here with me.'

Stirling caught the touch of longing in her voice. 'Are you sure you're all right?' he asked. It wasn't like Rebecca to sound so vulnerable.

'Of course,' she replied stoutly. 'I'm allowed to miss you, aren't I?'

'I hope so,' he joked. 'Now you take care of yourself. At least our

137

mutual friend is quiet, with you away. I wonder if he's discovered he's got the wrong films? Anyway you can forget all about him for the time being, can't you?'

'I sure can.' She managed to sound breezy, wondering if she was doing the right thing by remaining silent, but knowing that if Stirling was aware of the danger facing her on her return, he would get into a panic.

'Have you heard of a man called Sly Capra?' Mike Wilson inquired abruptly.

Stirling, watching the shabby little man through narrowed eyes, paused before answering. In the brief time Mike had been in his office, ostensibly looking for Rebecca whom he had said he wished to talk to, Stirling had come to the conclusion that this was someone he neither liked nor trusted.

'Why do you ask?' he said cautiously.

Mike leaned forward, the long strand of hair falling over his forehead, a greedy glint returning to his grey eyes now that he felt on the brink of success once more. 'Because that is the name of the man Tracy or Marissa, or whatever you call her, was living with in the Trump Tower.' He sat back, pleased with himself for having caused the startled look on Stirling's face.

'I thought she was living on her own. How d'you know this?'

'I'd been trying to find out which apartment she had,' Mike explained. 'The first doorman had never heard of her, but the second one I talked to . . . Well, he knew her because he knew she was living in Sly Capra's apartment. As a matter of fact, I saw him yesterday.'

'Who? Sly Capra?' Stirling asked sharply.

'Yes. The doorman pointed him out to me. He's given up the apartment since Marissa died, but apparently he has another girl-friend who lives in Trump Tower and he was on his way up to visit her. It was pure luck that I chose that moment to ask the doorman about Marissa.'

'Did you get to speak to this man . . . Sly Capra?'

Mike smirked. 'I certainly did! Only briefly. He said he was in a hurry, but I'm hoping to set up a meeting with him. I told him where I was staying and he said he'd be in touch.'

Stirling looked at Mike Wilson speculatively.

'Tell me,' he said with forced casualness, 'what exactly is your interest in Marissa Montclare?'

Mike Wilson took a deep breath, as if to inflate himself for the long diatribe that was to follow. 'I'll tell you my interest. I represent the poor girl's parents. Let me tell you something – that girl died in this city and nobody seems to care. She left a lot of money, but nobody seems to know where it is. Her poor parents are devastated by her death, and I'm here to represent them and to recover for them what is rightfully theirs. It isn't much to ask, is it? You can't blame her mother and father for wanting to know where . . . I mean, what happened,' he corrected himself.

'The trouble is, nobody seems to have known anything about her! When I saw Rebecca's name under all those photographs,' and here Mike slipped back into an intimate tone again, 'I thought to myself, now there's someone who knew Tracy . . . I mean, Marissa! There's someone who could tell me something about her . . . you know, how much she was worth and all that.'

'As I told you, Rebecca is away,' Stirling said coolly. 'But even if she hadn't been, she would have been unable to help you. Rebecca didn't know Marissa any better than she knows any of the other media celebrities in this town.' He wanted to bring this meeting to an end. At first he'd been startled by the unexpected arrival of this little man who said he was an International Probate Researcher but who was obviously only interested in securing his percentage of whatever money Marissa had left. Now he had an instinctive feeling that he didn't want to become involved. There was something unpleasantly disreputable about Mike Wilson, and it didn't surprise Stirling that he was having a problem finding out about Marissa's background.

But Mike leaned forward conversationally in his chair, elbow resting on Stirling's desk, indicating he had no intention of leaving. 'This Sly Capra . . . he seems to be very rich. The second doorman I talked to, the one who pointed Sly out to me, said he'd set up Marissa in one of the biggest apartments. He said she'd been kept in real style.'

'You don't suppose,' suggested Stirling with a vicious thrust that caused him private amusement, 'that all the money really belonged to this man? That Marissa actually had no money of her own at all?'

For a fraction of a second Mike's face fell before he rallied. 'That's impossible. She was known to have a lot of money,' he said a trifle pompously.

'Who says?' asked Stirling blandly.

'I cannot reveal my sources,' said Mike, quoting one of the newspaper editors he'd spoken to, but he sounded less sure of himself.

'Do you know how she died?' Stirling probed, curious.

'She fell from a window.'

'You think she fell?'

Mike looked rattled, wishing he'd found out more before coming to see this gangling sharp-eyed man who sat behind a large cluttered desk and looked as if success had come easily to him. 'Well, of course she fell! I don't understand what you're getting at. I shouldn't be having all these problems, you know.' He sounded as if it was Stirling's fault. 'I've come to New York to wind up this young woman's affairs on behalf of her parents and all I'm getting is aggro. I thought she was supposed to be living with this old man, Sir Edward what's-his-name, and it's only by pure chance, and because I'm a very thorough person, that I actually discover she was living with someone quite different. At least, now that I've met up with this Sly Capra, I feel I'm getting somewhere. I'm sure he'll be able to help.'

'I wish you luck,' Stirling said drily. He was rising to bring their meeting to an end when he had a sudden thought. He had no use for the likes of Mike Wilson, but it would be on his conscience if he let Mike get himself into trouble. He knew, if Mike didn't, that behind Marissa's death lay an utterly ruthless killer with a motive as yet undiscovered. Stirling decided to speak out.

'I'd be careful if I were you when you meet this Sly Capra again,' he said, looking at Mike who was eyeing him with deep distrust now. 'There's more than meets the eye about Marissa's death and I'd be careful who you talk to. I'm not entirely sure it was an accident.'

'You mean she was bumped off for her money?' Mike demanded bluntly.

Stirling hesitated, unwilling to speculate. 'I'm not sure.'

'Well, I'll tell you one thing,' bragged Mike, 'unless she was married to Sly Capra, her parents are still her next-of-kin.'

'Sure. I'm just telling you to be careful.'

'Oh, I'll be that all right. Bye for now. I'll let you know how I get on.' His bravado seemed a bit forced to Stirling, who watched him as he strolled out of the Hertfelder Agency with a jaunty swagger; but the little man had taken on a challenge and he seemed determined not to let it beat him.

'I'm sure he'll pull through, m'dear.' Sir Edward's voice was kindly as he looked across Simon's bed at his ex-wife. 'He's young and strong, and it's miraculous what the doctors can do these days.'

Angela sat rigid with tension, dark shadows encircling her eyes which now looked sunken after two nights without sleep. She barely heard what Edward said. Watching Simon's face for a flicker of life, all her energies were concentrated on willing him to recover. In

140

any case, she thought fleetingly, Edward's presence was a comfort neither to herself nor to Simon. For a moment she wished she hadn't asked him to fly over. It was the doctor who'd suggested it.

'I think you should inform the young man's father, Lady Wenlake,' he'd said, as he'd stood looking down at her beloved boy.

And so Edward had come, bringing with him an aura of rich living, of expensive cigars and designer aftershave, of hand-made suits and shoes, of a jet-set existence she'd only read about; and above all, a loucheness and sexuality that still disturbed her after nearly thirty years.

'Simon's a strong chap,' Edward remarked, trying to cheer her up. They both looked at their son whose eyelids remained closed and whose mouth looked sulky even in repose. To Angela he was everything, the one male being who had never let her down or disappointed her. He was her compensation, she was sure, for having had a father who drank and a husband who philandered. Simon was the man she'd given life to and then moulded into a likeness of herself. The thought of losing him now was an agony she couldn't bear. Her nails dug deeply into the palms of her hands as she fought for control, while her mind was seized with panic. At that moment she felt a pressure on her arm and realized it was Edward's hand.

'Take it easy, old girl,' he was saying gruffly. 'They're doing all they can.'

Exhaustion and despair swept over her at the cliché. There had been so many banal things said in the past forty-eight hours. 'He's as well as can be expected.' 'He's in the best hands.' 'His condition is critical but stable.' Would they ever say he was better? That there was hope of him recovering?

At that moment Jenny slipped into the room, her arms full of flowers she'd picked in the greenhouse at Pinkney. With troubled eyes she surveyed the mass of bleeping equipment that surrounded her brother.

'How is he?' she whispered.

'There's no need to whisper, we're not in church,' Angela snapped. 'It's good for him to be stimulated by voices. Why have you brought all those flowers? They use up oxygen and the nurses will have to remove them every night.'

'I don't think they do that any more,' Sir Edward said gently. 'Trouble is, there isn't much space in this tiny room.'

Jenny looked crestfallen and stuffed the flowers on the window-sill as if she wanted to disown them. 'Is he any better?' ·

'He's about the same,' Sir Edward replied, and Angela winced as her ex-husband came out with another platitude. She'd heard them all now. 'No change.' 'Holding his own.' 'Too soon to say.' Closing her eyes she felt with a pang of guilt that it had crossed her mind that she'd rather it had been Jenny lying there than Simon.

'Did you have a nice rest, Jenny?' she asked.

'Yes, thank you.' Jenny looked surprised.

'The doctor does say Simon's responding to treatment,' Sir Edward interjected. 'It's just this damned spinal injury and concussion.' He had stood up and was moving restlessly around the small white room. 'It's not knowing how long it's going to take either, before he regains consciousness, that's so frustrating.'

'Yes, I know. It is,' Jenny agreed.

'You don't have to stay.'

They both looked at Angela, her words hanging between them in the air like accusatory arrows, their feelings of guilt at wanting to get back to their own lives showing in their faces. Quickly they sought to pacify her.

'Of course I'll stay . . .'

'Wouldn't dream of going . . .'

'There's no question of it . . .'

Angela silenced them both with a look. 'There's nothing you can do,' she pointed out, her tone quite reasonable. 'It's just a case of waiting until he comes round . . .' her voice trailed off. Then she added: 'There's no point in us all sitting here.'

She wants to be alone with Simon, thought Jenny with a flash of intuition. She doesn't really want Daddy and me here at all.

'Nonsense. Of course I'll stay,' said Edward stoutly. 'You can't sit here on your own.'

'Quite. We wouldn't dream of leaving you,' added Jenny.

'It's not really necessary,' Angela protested.

'Wouldn't hear of it, m' dear,' said Sir Edward, with equal determination.

And so they all stayed round Simon's bed, Jenny and her father slipping back to Pinkney just to make phone calls and attend to things, while Angela remained, accepting the occasional cup of coffee or sandwich but never leaving her son's side.

On the fourth day, Jenny was the first to hear a car coming up the drive as she and her father sat in the study drinking tea, before she left for the hospital again to take a turn at keeping her mother company.

'I wonder who that is?' Sir Edward asked, folding the *Financial Times*. 'Someone coming to call on your mother?'

142

Without Angela, who only came back to shower and change each morning, Pinkney House was more pleasant and peaceful than he'd ever known it, and he was quite enjoying his visit to his old home. Without Angela, he could almost have settled for a quiet life in England's lush countryside, he thought, instead of the frenetic pace of Manhattan; especially now that there was no Marissa at his side.

'I'll go and see who it is,' said Jenny, remembering Peters was off duty that afternoon. Getting up and going into the hall, she went to one of the long windows that flanked the front door and peered out. A familiar-looking car was parking in the drive. 'My God!' she shouted over her shoulder. 'It's Mummy . . . and she looks dreadful!'

Father and daughter looked at each other and Sir Edward seemed to grow a little older and a little greyer in that moment.

Rebecca, with her press pass safely in her purse, arrived early at Grosvenor House for the gala ball. The Prince and Princess of Wales were not due to arrive until eight o'clock, but as all the eight hundred guests were supposed to be seated by seven forty-five she guessed, rightly, that everyone would get there early. Filled with expectancy, she jumped out of the taxi when it dropped her off outside the large and famous hotel in Park Lane and found police already hovering about, roping off the entrance to the ballroom, checking everyone who entered and making sure no cars parked nearby. Specially trained police sniffer dogs had already searched the ballroom area of the building for possible hidden explosives, and to Rebecca's experienced eye security was going to be tight tonight. It reminded her of when the President and his wife were expected someplace.

Leaving her scarlet woollen wrap in the ladies' cloakroom, she surveyed her appearance critically in a long mirror. For a working girl, and probably the only female photographer tonight, she looked both businesslike and elegant. Her long slim black dress was slit up the back to allow her to move quickly and easily, and her black satin pumps were comfortable and not likely to come off. She'd once worn sling-backs on a job and had spent most of the evening trying to keep them on her feet. She'd also chosen a high neckline and short sleeves; with her camera bag slung from her shoulder she needed a dress that stayed in place and didn't reveal bra straps or too much cleavage. Lastly, she'd coiled up her long hair into a becoming chignon, to keep it out of the way, and decided on a pearl choker and pearl stud earrings as her only jewellery.

Before the action started Rebecca decided to reconnoitre the premises, so that she could become familiar with the layout. In her experience one could miss getting just the right photograph by not knowing where to go. Near the main ballroom entrance, a VIP suite had been set aside where the ball committee would be presented to the royal couple. Rebecca, who had a pass for this room, decided to check it out first. Brightly decorated in aquamarine with pink rose-patterned furnishings, it dazzled with crystal chandeliers and polished mirrors. In one corner, a cascading tumble of willow branches and pale pink peonies, myrtle, ferns and pure white lilies gave off a delicate perfume. On a side table, a bouquet of white roses lay ready to be presented to Princess Diana by the ball chairman's six-year-old daughter. It was in here that Rebecca, and a few other selected photographers, were to take pictures at the beginning of the evening.

She looked around, checking the available light from the chandeliers on her light meter but finding it too dim. She decided she'd have to use a flash. Regretfully she drew out her hand flash unit from her case. It gave such a hard light and created such heavy shadows that she avoided using it if she could. Then she had a brilliant idea.

She looked up at the ceiling and decided it was no more than nine or ten feet high. Perfect for 'bouncing' the light. She'd point her flash at the ceiling instead of at the Princess, and the reflected down light would be soft and evenly spread.

Having worked that out, she then explored the rest of the banqueting area. The ballroom was vast and surrounded on three sides by a wide gallery. It would be a very good vantage point from which to take the royal couple dancing, she decided, providing she used a telephoto lens.

On the fourth side of the gallery, two sweeping staircases led down to the ballroom where hundreds of round tables were set with pretty pink table-cloths and flowers and pink candles in silver candelabra. From the list of instructions Rebecca had received from the press office at Buckingham Palace, she knew that photographs could be taken of the royal couple entering the ballroom, but were not allowed while they were having dinner. How great it would be, she thought, to get a shot of Princess Diana coming down that grand staircase! The point was, though, which staircase? Would they choose the left or the right? She'd have to know in advance in order to be in the right spot.

Rebecca found a waiter who was polishing some glasses. 'Excuse me,' she began tentatively, 'can you tell me which staircase the Prince and Princess will be using when they come into the ballroom tonight?' She showed him her press card to prove she was a bona fide photographer.

'They're not using either,' he replied smiling.

'Then how . . . ?' She looked around, bewildered. There was no other way to get from the gallery down to the ballroom.

'They'll be making an entry by the bandstand,' he told her, in a quiet confidential voice. 'That way, they only have to walk across the dance floor which will be empty at that time, and then go straight to the top table.' He indicated a long table facing the bandstand on the opposite side of the ballroom, which was garlanded with swags of pink flowers.

Rebecca frowned, puzzled. 'Why is that? I'd have thought the stairs would be perfect for a big entrance.'

He nodded in agreement. 'Up to a point, but when they get to the bottom of the stairs they've got to get past all those tables with people at them in order to get across the room to their own table. It takes too long, you see. Princess Anne did it the other night, weaving her way in and out and round the tables with people jostling close, and it took too long and looked undignified. That's why the organizers tonight have decided on the royals making an entry by the bandstand.'

'So how,' asked Rebecca, intrigued, 'do they get from the VIP lounge upstairs, down to the bandstand?'

The waiter chuckled, delighted to be in the know, proud that several times a week he helped serve dinner in the presence of royalty.

'This way, ma'am,' he said. He led Rebecca across the ballroom, winding his way between the tables, until they came to the raised bandstand. Then he pushed back the heavy red velvet curtains that hung from the bottom of the gallery all the way around the room, and she found herself in a wide 'corridor' under the gallery, formed by the outer walls of the ballroom and the heavy curtains. He pointed to a small staircase.

'That leads from the gallery too,' he explained. 'They come down that way, the back way.'

'I see! Does everyone know this?'

He shrugged. 'Only the organizers and the security people,' he replied. 'They wouldn't want everyone to know or you'd get a crowd down here lying in wait.'

Rebecca nodded. 'I can see that. Well,' she smiled warmly, 'thank you for your help.' Then she hurried up to the gallery again, frantically planning the 'exclusive' shot of the Princess she so badly wanted to get. Now, if the other photographers didn't know which staircase was going to be used tonight . . .

The guests were starting to arrive, great clusters of them, the women in a dazzling array of colours and fabrics, their jewellery blazing, their expressions eager. On nights such as this charities could raise thousands of pounds as people happily spent money just in order to be present and to dine out on the experience afterwards.

Rebecca, keeping an eye on the time, took a lot of pictures and realized that rich socialites were the same on both sides of the Atlantic: eager to see and be seen, and to have their photographs in the shiny magazines.

At ten to eight, she presented herself in the VIP room, passing the scrutiny of two security guards and a press officer from Buckingham Palace.

'Please stand over here,' he told her, and she found herself with a television crew from the BBC and four other press photographers. She smiled quickly, introducing herself. They all smiled back and she realized they were a friendly bunch of professionals, out to get good pictures, just as she was. Only she hoped to go one better.

At eight o'clock precisely, there was a flurry of activity just outside the door of the VIP room, and Rebecca could feel a frisson of excitement tingle down her spine. She raised her camera and prepared herself to take pictures of not only one of the most beautiful women of the century but the future Queen of England. The television lights were switched on now, flooding the room with brilliance, allowing Rebecca to abandon her need to use a flash; and there, standing in the doorway, were the most photographed couple in the world: Prince Charles in an impeccably cut dinner-jacket, and Princess Diana in a slim-fitting white dress covered with thousands of pearls and crystal beads that glimmered as she moved, showing off her figure.

Rebecca barely remembered the next three or four minutes. She took picture after picture, exhausting the film in one camera and automatically switching to the second one that hung round her neck. In her shoulder bag was a third loaded camera, just in case.

'That's it,' she heard a man's voice say, quietly but clearly. At the touch of a button, the TV lights were switched off and everyone stopped taking pictures. The Palace aide signalled to the photographers to leave the room quietly so the reception could progress undisturbed, and Rebecca found herself in the lobby outside, amazed that it was all over so quickly.

'We've got time for a quick one,' said one of the photographers, glancing at his watch, 'before we get them going into the ballroom.'

'You're on!' said another, and four of them hurried off to the bar. The TV camera team had done their bit: there'd be a six to eight second showing during the nine o'clock news on BBC-1, and they had to hurry back to the studio with the film.

Rebecca didn't hang around. Walking briskly, she made her way to the gallery where people still stood in groups, drinking and laughing and in no hurry to go down to the ballroom which was already filling up. Through a microphone a red-coated toast-master was urging guests to take their places for dinner. Making sure the other photographers couldn't see her, Rebecca slipped along to the small hidden staircase and ran down it, coming out below the gallery a moment later. The area was deserted, save for a group of waiters who were hovering by the kitchen doors. As soon as the royal party were seated, they'd be given a signal and then dozens of them, each carrying a platter containing the first course, would fan out around the giant room as they served the hundreds of guests. Meanwhile all was quiet. Trying to keep calm and stop her fingers from shaking while she re-loaded her cameras, Rebecca waited, praying no one would come along and order her to leave. It was obvious the other photographers presumed the grand staircase was going to be used, and what a scramble there'd be when they discovered it wasn't!

Minutes passed and she grew anxious. Suppose there'd been a last-minute change of plan? Peeping through a gap in the curtains, she squinted into the ballroom where the atmosphere was buzzing with excitement. There was no activity by the staircases, although the photographers were now hanging hopefully about. Rebecca checked her cameras and flash once more. She was ready for perhaps the most exciting assignment she'd had so far in her career.

They came upon her so quickly and silently she was almost taken unawares. One moment she was alone under the gallery, cocooned between the wall and the floor-to-ceiling velvet curtains, and the next Prince Charles, with the Chairman of the ball, and Princess Diana with the Chairman's husband, were right there in front of her, smiling and chatting quietly to each other. They paused, and Rebecca could hear the beginning of a long drum roll and then an official parted the curtains. Through the gap she saw a flood of light as great arc lamps were switched on, directed at the royal couple as they entered the ballroom.

Prince Charles was the first to move forward . . . Rebecca started taking pictures, concentrating on the Princess who was following. Then she paused, and at that second someone pulled the curtains wider, looping them back into a graceful swag. For just a second Princess Diana stood alone, poised against the dark crimson drapery, her blonde hair and shimmering white dress caught by the brilliant lights – and then she turned and smiled at Rebecca. Holding her breath she clicked away as if her life depended on it, for

147

what seemed like an incredibly long moment, and then the Princess of Wales moved forward and the heavy curtains closed behind her, leaving Rebecca once again standing alone. While the band played the National Anthem, she hurried up the back stairs they'd just used and ran to the nearest pay phone.

'I've done it!' she yelled to Stirling when she got through. 'The most fantastic shots ever! What did you say? You bet your sweet ass they're exclusive! I gave all the other photographers the slip and got Princess Diana on her own . . . against red velvet drapes. They could have been posed shots in a studio, Stirling, they were so good! God, I can't wait to see the results!' She was quite breathless.

'Well done, sweetheart! I knew you'd do it,' he said warmly. 'I suppose there's no chance of my getting the films tomorrow?'

Rebecca glanced at her watch. She'd had a feeling that if the job went well Stirling might want the films even sooner than a courier service could get them to him.

'If you can send someone to JFK tomorrow lunchtime, I'll have the films on the first flight out of here in the morning,' she said. 'This is the flight number of the plane they'll be on. If there's any problem, call me.' She gave him all the details which she'd got earlier from the freight department at Heathrow.

A moment later she was grabbing her evening wrap from the cloakroom and heading out of Grosvenor House into Park Lane. A passing taxi was quite happy to take her to the airport and back, in return for a promised generous tip. 'I'd like the freight department for flights to New York,' she explained as they drove swiftly along the M4 in the darkness. Glad that she'd cashed a large amount of travellers' cheques earlier that day, she produced from her camera bag a specially reinforced envelope, on which she'd already written Stirling's name and address. Although it was going to cost her eighty or ninety pounds to send the film this way, she knew she could expect to earn thousands of dollars for her exclusive pictures.

Once at the airfield the taxi drove straight to the freight building, where she showed the man on duty the contents of the envelope before sealing it and filled in a form giving the necessary details for Customs.

'OK, I'll see it gets there,' said the official, who was helpful and friendly.

'Great. Thanks.' Rebecca hurried back to the waiting taxi. It was still only nine-fifteen. With any luck she'd be back at Grosvenor House by ten o'clock, just in time to photograph the royal couple enjoying the rest of the evening, not that she imagined she'd be lucky enough to get any more exclusive scoops tonight.

148

Mike Wilson arrived at the Hertfelder Agency, unannounced and uninvited, for the second time that week. He burst into Stirling's office as if he were being chased by someone he particularly wanted to avoid, and flung himself into the chair facing the desk. Stirling, who was examining the coloured transparencies of Rebecca's shots of Princess Diana, which had just come back from the laboratory, felt deeply irritated.

'Was there something you wanted?' he asked, without looking up. The pictures were every bit as good as Rebecca had thought they'd be, great full-length shots of Princess Diana that were technically perfect. Now he had to syndicate them world-wide, getting the best price he could, and the last thing he needed was to have his time wasted by the likes of Mike Wilson.

'I met Sly Capra's business partner last night,' Mike announced without preamble. 'Sly couldn't make it himself as he was tied up, but his partner was most helpful.'

Stirling looked up, startled. 'What's he like?'

Mike crossed his legs, folded his arms and seemed to settle down for a long chat. 'Very friendly,' he began.

'Where did you meet him?'

'He called me at my hotel.'

Stirling looked at him askance. 'He did?'

Mike licked his lips and tried to look superior. 'I told you I was hoping to set up a meeting. We had a drink in a bar and I learned a lot about the doings of Miss Marissa Montclare! Interesting stuff, I can tell you. Of course I pretended to know a great deal more than I did, to lead him on, you know. Anyway, although he couldn't actually tell me how to get hold of her money he promised to find out from Sly, and said he'd get in touch again. I'm sure he did know actually, but I'm going to have to work on him a bit more before he'll spill the beans. It's no problem, though. I can handle it,' he added boastfully. It occurred to Stirling that Mike was only telling him all this because he couldn't resist showing off.

'Did he tell you where all her money came from?' Stirling asked.

'Yes, he did. It's quite a story.' Then Mike dropped his voice to a low monotone so he couldn't be overheard as he repeated what he'd been told. Stirling listened with growing horror as his worst fears were realized. Now that he knew what . . . and who . . . was behind Marissa's death, he realized the great danger Rebecca was in. That Mike was telling him the truth he had no doubt. He would not have had the imagination to make up a story like this in the first place. But why the hell, Stirling asked himself, had Sly Capra's partner told him so much? Unless of course Mike, with his usual bragging, had given the impression he already knew everything and had merely been getting it confirmed?

Stirling jumped to his feet and rushing over to the safe in the corner of his office, grabbed a brown envelope and withdrew a batch of glossy prints. Selecting one quickly, he placed it on his desk in front of Mike.

'Is this either Sly Capra or his partner?' he asked urgently. If Mike could lead them to Marissa's killer he would also be leading them to the man who was threatening Rebecca.

Mike picked up the photograph of the waiter adjusting the curtains at the party. He spoke loftily. 'This is a waiter. Why should this be Sly or the man I met? It's nothing like either of them.'

'Are you sure?'

Mike looked affronted, as if Stirling were making fun of him. 'I can tell a gentleman when I see one, you know. This is nothing like Sly or his partner. This waiter looks like a forty-year-old Spaniard.' He tossed the picture back on to the desk. 'Why do you want to know?'

'I just wondered,' Stirling replied evasively. 'I like to be able to caption every picture on file.'

'What? Of a waiter? Where was it taken . . . don't tell me! Rebecca took this the night Marissa died, didn't she?' Mike jabbed the print with his finger. 'Was this waiter a friend of Marissa's too?' He'd long since ceased to call her Tracy. If no one in New York knew much about Marissa, they sure as hell didn't know anything about Tracy.

'I doubt it,' said Stirling. 'Tell me one thing: did this man you met refer to Marissa's death as an accident or a homicide?'

'An accident, of course,' Mike replied instantly. 'There's nothing to suggest otherwise, is there? She slipped and fell . . . that's what all the newspapers said, and that was the verdict brought in at the inquest.'

'Sure.'

'So why should anyone think it was murder?'

'It's been rumoured,' said Stirling shortly. He regretted having said so much. Mike would worry the question like a dog with a bone now.

'Are those more pictures taken at that party?' Mike was asking, pointing to the envelope which Stirling was still holding.

'Yup.'

'Can I see them?'

Stirling could think of no reason for refusing the request. 'OK. Help yourself.'

Mike shuffled through the photographs, pausing at the ones of Marissa he'd seen reproduced on the front pages of the newspapers.

'Dishy-looking bird, wasn't she?' He'd been a young man in the sixties and still spoke the lingo. Stirling was sure he'd also be wearing a gold medallion on a chain under his shirt.

'She was a beautiful girl,' agreed Stirling. 'She had that Monroe vulnerability.'

'Ah, there's one of that old bastard Wenlake,' observed Mike, pausing at a picture of Sir Edward welcoming some guests. He flipped through a few more and then let out a little cry of triumph. 'Here's one of Sly Capra! See? I told you he was a gentleman.'

Chapter Nine

Angela sank on to one of the hall chairs, her eyes red-rimmed and her voice catching. 'It's good news . . . and bad.'

Sir Edward looked grim. 'How bad?'

'He regained consciousness shortly after you left.'

'Yes?'

'But they don't know if he'll ever be able to walk again.'

'Oh, Christ.' Sir Edward sat down heavily, while Jenny stood there looking from one to the other, a creeping nervousness making her insides quake. 'When will they know?' she heard her father ask.

'His spinal column is badly bruised. Until that is better and the internal swelling goes down, he's paralyzed and they say there is a chance he may remain so. Only time will tell.'

Sir Edward slapped his forehead with the palm of his hand and swore under his breath. 'Of all the wretched luck! Damned horse!'

'It was a present from me,' Angela burst out, and then she started sobbing as if her heart would break. Jenny watched in astonished embarrassment. It seemed to her that Angela, unable to hide her feelings any longer, had burst the banks of some secret store of suffering which was now pouring out all at once. It was all the more amazing to Jenny because her mother loathed any show of emotion. 'So common,' she'd once said when one of their maids cried hysterically because her mother had died. Yet now here she was, expensive tweed suit rumpled, silk blouse undone at the neck, rocking herself backwards and forwards in a paroxysm of grief. Jenny looked away as her father went over and put his arms around Angela.

'Steady on, old girl,' he said gruffly. 'He'll probably be fine. Alarmist chaps, these bloody doctors.'

Angela leaned against him for a moment and Jenny remembered a time long ago, when she'd been a child and her parents had seemed to care for each other. She recalled how secure she'd felt then, believing nothing would change; but then there'd been the divorce and her safe little world had come crashing down. Now, for

153

some reason, as her father talked softly to Angela, she felt strangely left out and excluded. She'd had him to herself for so long that the presence of another woman close to him made her burn with secret resentment . . . even if it was her own mother. How would she have felt if Marissa Montclare had lived? she wondered.

Going over to the window she looked out at the wintry landscape. The lawns were stiff with frost, the grass like crisp white whiskers, and the bare trees were etched black against the heavy grey sky. A raven flew down and hopped about, pecking furiously at the hard ground. Jenny felt cold inside and very alone.

'I'll stay over here a bit longer, just until we're sure Simon is going to be all right,' she heard her father say. 'You can't be allowed to cope with all this on your own.'

'Thank you, Edward,' Angela replied.

To Jenny's surprise her mother sounded grateful, gentle even. Without a backward glance she climbed the stairs to her bedroom, leaving her parents together as they thought about their firstborn. The new term at Trevor House had already begun and she had to get back to work. Besides, she told herself, it was time she started living her own life now.

The clamour of bright young voices rose to an excited crescendo when Jenny entered her classroom the next morning. A junior teacher had been in charge of her class during her absence at Pinkney and she grinned when she saw Jenny.

'Am I glad you're back!' she exclaimed. 'Another few days of this and I'd have been a nut case.'

Jenny smiled, pleased by her reception. 'What a terrible noise,' she shouted to the children above the din, pretending to look shocked. 'I've never heard such a terrible noise in all my life!' She regarded her six-year-old pupils with mock severity. The racket subsided and there were a few muffled squeals and giggles as eager little faces looked up at her, knowing she was not really angry.

'Let's start again, shall we?' Jenny suggested. 'Good morning, children.'

They chorused back obediently. 'Good morning, Miss Jenny.'

'Please sit down at your desks and we'll begin with reading.' Jenny took her place at a table set diagonally across one corner of the large bright room and surveyed her pupils with affection. She had to admit they looked adorable in their winter uniform of wine red skirt and cardigan and crisp white blouse. Each child seemed to have glossy well-kept hair and their faces shone with good health. What fascinated her most was that each little girl was already stamped with an individual personality that would become more apparent as she grew older. In each one she could already see the future woman; the nice ones would get nicer and the mean ones would always be mean.

'Turn to page one of your reading books,' she commanded. 'You've all had this book as your holiday reading and now I want to hear how well you can do. Lucy, you can start. Nice and clearly now, so we can all hear you.'

A little girl in the front rose, blushing at being the centre of attention.

' "Roger the rabbit and Tommy the tortoise . . ." ' she began in her soft little voice. Jenny found her mind drifting as the child continued. When she'd got back to London last night, her parents in agreement that there was nothing she could do at Pinkney, she'd spent the night thinking long and hard about her future. Her father had been right about one thing: she had no idea how to have fun. Somehow she'd got locked into the lifestyle of a middle-aged spinster. If she wasn't careful she'd soon look like one too, she thought, regarding herself in her long bedroom mirror. She needed to lose weight, have something drastic done to her hair, and get herself some new clothes more suited to a twenty-three year old. Her legs were quite good, so there was no reason why she shouldn't start wearing mini-skirts. A New Look, that's what she wanted. A whole new look to go with a New Life. She'd give up teaching and get herself a job where she'd meet lots of bright ambitious young men and women like Rebecca Kendall who would inspire her to make something of herself. As yet she wasn't sure what she'd do, but suddenly she felt sure something interesting would turn up.

By the time she crawled out of bed the next morning to get ready for school, she felt exhausted but content. The long night of self-examination had swept away a lot of the bitterness she'd experienced yesterday when she'd felt pushed to one side by her mother and father. It was Simon who needed everyone's sympathy, not her. Feeling a great deal less sorry for herself, she hurried off to Trevor House, determined to bring about changes in her life.

The classroom was silent, and Jenny was aware the children were watching her and that Lucy had finished reading. She pulled herself together. 'That was excellent, Lucy. Your reading is much better than it was last term. Now, Amelia, I want you to read the next page aloud.'

Amelia rose with alacrity, her dark curls quivering as she prepared herself for her big moment. Amelia was a born performer and loved nothing more than showing off her talents.

' "Roger said to Tommy," ' she said earnestly, ' "you're a BAD BOY." '

Jenny tried her best to look severe. 'I don't think he did, Amelia,' she remonstrated. Amelia also had a talent for editing stories to please herself.

'He did!' Amelia replied with conviction. 'I know he did because Tommy *was* a bad boy!'

'Please read the story as it's written or you'll have to sit down, Amelia.' The little girl looked crestfallen and for the next few seconds Jenny could see the inner struggle she was having, trying to decide whether to abandon her own version of the story or sit down and miss her Big Moment. The tiny mouth tightened and the dark eyes flashed defiantly, but then, with a deep sigh, she decided to read the rest of the page as it had been written.

I shall miss all this if I give up teaching, Jenny reflected. I love children and I love being instrumental in opening up the world to them and sharing with them the adventure of learning; but what I need, she thought with sudden clarity, is to experience the adventure of learning about life myself, because at that I'm a novice.

The phone rang just as Rebecca was going to bed in her room at the Belgravia-Sheraton. It was Jenny.

'I wondered if you were free to come to dinner tomorrow evening?' she asked. 'I'm sorry I didn't get in touch sooner, but what with my brother's accident I only got back to London yesterday morning, and then I had to go to work.'

'How is your brother?'

'Not so good, I'm afraid. I'll tell you all about it when I see you. Are you free tomorrow?'

'Yes. Thanks, I'd love to have dinner. I've got heaps to tell you,' Rebecca replied.

'Seven-thirty then? I'll give you the address.'

The black taxi shuddered to a stop, its diesel engine rattling loudly. Climbing out, Rebecca found herself in a quiet Kensington street called Brunswick Gardens, tree-lined and elegant, the white stucco early Victorian houses exuding an aura of residential respectability and wealth. Number 12 had an imposing front door reached by a wide steep flight of white marble steps, on either side of which stood stone urns filled with small bay trees. This was where Jenny shared an apartment with a couple of friends. Rebecca had not expected to find anything so imposing or formal. It hardly compared with her converted warehouse in TriBeCa, she thought wryly, but then her income and that of her parents hardly compared with the Wenlake fortune. Pressing the brass bell marked 'J. Wenlake' she heard Jenny's voice almost immediately, crackling on the intercom.

'Come up.' The door buzzed loudly and Rebecca pushed it open. 'I'm on the second floor . . . er . . . I mean third as you'd call it in America.'

'OK, I'm on my way.' Rebecca entered a warm softly lit hall, the atmosphere delicately perfumed from a large Chinese bowl of pot pourri that stood on a gilt console table under a large mirror. In one corner was a small lift shaped like a gilded birdcage. Jenny was waiting for her on the landing outside her apartment door. She greeted Rebecca warmly.

'You look terrific, Jenny,' Rebecca exclaimed, unable to keep the surprise out of her voice. 'What have you done to yourself? Oh, I like your new hair-style.'

Jenny flushed, pleased. 'I had it cut and coloured this afternoon at Annie Russell's when I got out of school. D'you really think it's all right? They're supposed to be the best hairdressers in London.'

'It's sensational!' Jenny's hair had been streaked with golden highlights and layered so that it framed her face in short loose waves. She'd also put on some make-up, rather too heavily applied but still effective, and she was wearing a cherry red dress with a short skirt. 'You look fantastic. What's all this about? Got yourself a new boyfriend?'

'Not yet, but I'm working on it!' Jenny laughed. 'Come in and sit down. What would you like to drink?'

'Have you any coke?'

'Diet Coke. I want to lose at least fourteen pounds, so I'm afraid I'm not buying the ordinary Coke at the moment.'

'I must say,' Rebecca grinned in open admiration, 'you really are changing your image, aren't you? What's it all about, then?' She sat down on a chintz-covered sofa which was piled with armfuls of small tapestry cushions and watched as Jenny went over to the drinks tray. The living-room, though not large, was like a stately drawing-room in miniature, furnished with small but exquisite antique furniture, gilt-framed water-colours and some priceless Dresden figurines. To complete the English country house look that Rebecca was familiar with from photographs in magazines were large baskets filled with books and magazines, a gallery of family snapshots in silver frames and an impressive array of engraved invitations on the mantelpiece, some of which were for Jenny and some for her flatmates.

Jenny handed Rebecca her drink and then sat, feet tucked under

157

her, on the gros point rug embroidered by a Wenlake ancestor that lay in front of the fireplace. 'I want to change everything,' she said slowly. 'I want to change my looks, my job, my life, everything.'

'Wow! What's brought all this on?'

Then Jenny told her what her father had said, and how the events of the past few weeks had made her realize that she must stand on her own feet. 'It's even more important now,' she added, 'because Simon may not get better and then, of course, he'll need all the attention he can get from Mummy and Daddy.' She spoke without rancour or bitterness, but it was obvious to Rebecca that she'd subjected herself to brutal self-analysis.

Jenny continued: 'When Daddy said I was dull . . . ! Well, I admit I knew he was right.' She smiled wistfully. 'I hate dull people myself. Daddy actually said I could learn a lot from you and I'm sure he's right.'

'For heaven's sake, Jenny!' Rebecca looked embarrassed. 'Don't underestimate yourself. I'd say it was the system that was wrong, not you.'

'How d'you mean?'

'Well, aren't the upper classes very protected in England? Sent to exclusive private schools? Not allowed to mix with the hoi-polloi? Brainwashed from birth into believing they are different? I don't mean to sound rude but . . .'

'No, no, you're right. That's exactly how I was brought up . . . with the added pressure of believing I must only do a certain type of job and only marry a certain type of man.'

'Exactly.' Rebecca looked at her sympathetically. 'It's like being doomed before you start, isn't it? All choice is taken away from you, although most people would envy you your privileges and position. I think it's wonderful that you've come to grips with the problem so quickly and all by yourself. I've had friends who've had professional analysis for years because they weren't happy with the way things were, and they *still* don't know what to do with themselves.'

Jenny laughed, more relaxed now that she'd told someone what was on her mind. 'I've still got to think about a new career, though. Anything that will get me out of the rut I'm in. And I've also got to get myself an emotional life that is not dependent on my father. That's going to be the most difficult.'

Rebecca leaned forward, her voice encouraging. 'But you've taken the greatest step of all and that's realizing what's wrong in the first place. That's half the battle, Jenny. You're so positive. Coming to grips with the way you look is important too. It reflects a person's state of mind.'

Jenny beamed. 'I enjoyed having my hair done. Funny how something like that can make one feel so much better, isn't it? I must practise with my make-up, though.' She giggled quietly. 'Mummy's going to have a fit the next time she sees me.'

'I've got the most brilliant idea!' Rebecca exclaimed. 'When I get back from my trip to Paris at the end of the week, let's go into Hyde Park and I'll take some shots of you. Semi-fashion pictures, so that you can see for yourself how good you look.'

'That would be terrific. Are you sure it wouldn't be too much trouble? You're working so hard.'

Rebecca spoke with sincerity. 'It would be my pleasure.'

Dinner was simple, a ready-made fish pie from Marks and Spencer because, as Jenny explained, the hairdresser had kept her longer than she'd thought and she hadn't had time to prepare anything. But she'd also bought a deliciously ripe brie, some black grapes and a bottle of wine. Over the meal they sat at a round table in the dining recess of the room, talking as if they'd known each other for years.

'I haven't told you about the sinister message I received the day after my arrival, have I?' Rebecca remarked, helping herself to more cheese.

Jenny clapped her hand over her mouth in a childish gesture. 'Oh, I've been so busy talking about myself, I quite forgot the problems you've been having. I am sorry. What was the message?'

Rebecca, who knew it by heart, repeated it to her.

Jenny looked concerned. 'Was it from Jerry Ribis?'

'Who knows?'

'What does your boyfriend say?'

'Stirling, you mean? I've no idea. I haven't told him.'

'Why ever not?'

'What good would it do, Jenny? He's thousands of miles away and I don't think anything's going to happen until I get back to the States.'

Jenny thought about this. 'Why don't you let whoever it is have those wretched films back?'

'Then we'd never know who killed Marissa Montclare, or why. I never wanted to get involved in the first place, but now that I am I must see this thing through. My apartment's been ransacked and my darkroom wrecked; I've been followed and threatened, and I feel so damned mad I want to get whoever did it.'

'I can understand how you feel. More wine?' She topped up Rebecca's glass. 'Maybe you should report everything to someone higher up in the New York police than that detective . . . what's his name?'

'O'Hara.'

'Yes. There must be a chief-of-police you could go to? Someone in a superior position who would get to the bottom of the whole thing? If, as you said, O'Hara has been bribed, then you'll never get anywhere.'

Rebecca nodded in agreement. 'Don't I know it! The trouble is, I don't think we've got enough hard evidence.'

'Surely the threatening calls are enough? And the picture of the waiter in the window? The rendezvous in the Post Office?'

'No. That could all have been the work of a crank or a practical joker. Until we know why Marissa was killed, we can't even begin to figure out who did it.'

Stirling flipped over the large T-bone steak with an impatient gesture and turned the grill up higher. Then he opened a container from his local delicatessen and tipped out the ready-made salad on to a side plate. Lastly, he reached in the fridge and took out a bottle of Corona beer. He hated eating alone, even in the cosy atmosphere of his own apartment where the news programme on TV blared out in a corner so that he could keep tabs on what was happening in the world, even though the phone kept ringing, even though he was tired at the end of a hectic day. He was missing Rebecca more than he'd been prepared for, and having dinner alone was one of the things he was having difficulty adjusting to. Life was empty without her, all the more so because she'd stayed with him before flying to Europe and he'd gotten used to having her around when he went to bed, and finding her still there, warm and sweet, when he awoke in the morning.

He took a swig of beer straight from the bottle, wishing he had a wedge of lime to give it a tang, and wondered how he was going to persuade Rebecca to go on living with him when she got back. Of course, he reflected, if all the things Mike Wilson had told him that afternoon were true, even she'd see the sense in it. The point was, had they been true? Or was Mike still trying to impress, bragging about a situation of which in reality he had little knowledge? At the time, he'd believed everything Mike had told him, but now he was beginning to have doubts. The whole story of Marissa was so incredible he wondered if it could possibly be true.

He removed the steak from the grill and sat down to eat, then he glanced at his wristwatch. Rebecca would have arrived in Paris that afternoon. He'd call her as soon as he'd eaten and tell her what Mike had said. He'd also have to warn her that Marissa's death had not been an isolated incident, but a part of something much bigger and more sinister than either of them had imagined.

160

* * *

With Jenny in London, Edward and Angela found themselves alone together for the first time in eleven years. They took turns sitting with Simon. In the mornings Edward breakfasted in lonely splendour in the dining-room while Angela, uncharacteristically, had a tray in her bedroom. But at lunchtime and in the evenings they were forced to face each other across the polished table, and indulge in polite conversation because of the presence of Peters and the other servants.

Simon was still paralyzed from the neck down and the doctors had said it was too soon to say whether this would be a permanent condition or not, and so their conversation, stilted and uncomfortable, revolved around mundane things rather than the subject which weighed heavily on both of them.

What would happen if Simon were to be permanently confined to a wheelchair was something Angela refused to contemplate, and Edward contemplated but refused to discuss. If the worst came to pass, he thought, he'd fly the boy, by privately chartered plane to America where he knew he could get the best treatment in the world. When he mentioned this to Angela, she flew into a rage, asking if he wanted to kill their son?

'Stoke Mandeville is the best hospital in the world for back injuries,' she cried. 'He'll go there if he has to go anywhere. I won't let you take him to the States.'

The subject had been dropped and not mentioned again, but the strain on them both was severe as Edward tried to run the Tollemache Trust by telephone to Brian in New York, and Angela sat at Simon's bedside, watching for any change in his condition. Mentally he was totally recovered, though still in a state of shock, and all he wanted was to go home.

'I can't stay here,' he grumbled in a surprisingly strong voice, when they were both by his bedside one evening. 'You can hire a nurse to look after me, can't you?'

Angela hesitated, afraid of the responsibility. 'We must see what the doctors say.'

Edward agreed. 'Your mother's right, m'boy. We can't have you taking risks. You've been a bit bashed up, y'know. Got to take it easy for a while.'

'Mother can look after me,' Simon protested petulantly. 'You don't have to hang around.'

'Of course you can come home as soon as they say it's all right,' Angela cut in hurriedly, to avoid a scene. 'Meanwhile I can visit you every day and bring you whatever you need.'

161

'That's right,' Edward said stoutly. 'And why don't I buy you a nice car as your next birthday present? I'll get some details tomorrow; there's a lovely new BMW that's just come on the market, and cars are a lot safer than bloody horses, aren't they? Fred or Jones can drive you around, when you're better.'

Angela told him not to be absurd, preferring to indulge in her favourite fantasy in which Simon was hunting again and one day became Master of the Hunt, as she'd always planned. But later that evening, as she and Edward finished dinner in the candlelit dining-room after Peters had withdrawn to the kitchen, he spoke with blunt honesty.

'I'm all for keeping the boy's spirits up, Angela,' he conceded, 'but I think it's folly to let him think he may be able to hunt again.'

'Don't be such a wet blanket,' she snapped. 'Hunting is his life. He'll be distraught if he thinks he can never ride again.'

'That's what I mean.' Edward tried to be patient. 'Is it fair to let him think it's a certainty? Shouldn't we be preparing him for the fact that he may be a quadraplegic for the rest of his life?'

She jumped to her feet, throwing down her white damask table-napkin. 'Absolutely not!' she stormed. 'He must be given hope . . . anyway he *is* going to be all right.'

'Naturally I hope so, but it'll be harder for him to accept if we've let him think otherwise. Can't you see that?'

'All I can see is that your attitude could have a detrimental effect upon Simon,' Angela flared. 'It could even retard his recovery! Don't you dare suggest to him that he may never be able to walk again.'

'I don't propose to spell it out to him,' Edward replied mildly. 'I'm not that insensitive. I merely think the boy should be prepared. Gently, of course.'

'Well, I don't! And as he's out of danger now there's no need for you to stay in England any longer.' She walked towards the door where she paused and looked back at Edward, still sitting at the table, his white hair gleaming in the flickering light, his handsome face impassive. 'We don't need you here any more,' she said cuttingly. 'Please leave in the morning.'

Rebecca was staying at the Hôtel Eiffel Duquesne, on the tree-lined Avenue Duquesne near the left bank of the Seine. She could go out on to the balcony of her pleasant room on the fifth floor and look up the long straight stretch of the Avenue de Labourdonnais to the Eiffel Tower itself, towering majestically over the city skyline. In the twilight of the first evening, she could see the variegated grey rooftops and the silvery sculptured stonework of the magnificent old buildings of the city. This was her first trip to Paris. There hadn't been time when she'd visited Europe with Stirling, two years before, and now she couldn't wait to explore. Turning back into her room she perched on the edge of the bed and studied the schedule Stirling had fixed for her. It didn't leave much time for sightseeing.

The next morning, as a milky sun streamed through the windows and she sat up in bed enjoying croissants and café au lait, she made up her mind to leave the hotel early so that she could visit the Louvre before her first appointment, which was with Yves Saint Laurent in his design studio. At lunchtime she planned to get the métro to Montmartre and have a look at the Sacré Coeur, considered by some to be the most beautiful church in the world, and then she was due at the American Embassy at two-thirty to photograph the Ambassador. If she got through that session quickly, there'd be time to look at the Place Vendôme and some of the shops in the Rue de Rivoli before she was due to take some shots of Roger Vadim who was holding a press conference to discuss his newest film.

With no time to spare she showered and dressed quickly, checked her equipment and hailed a taxi. Caught up for the rest of the day in a whirl of activity she got only brief impressions of Paris between her appointments; of straight wide cobbled streets lined with trees, of lifesize statues gleaming white in the sunshine, of formal gardens where fountains sprang, dancing in the sharp breeze, and of cafés and brasseries exuding a warm welcome along with the aroma of Gitane cigarettes and garlic. Cars hooted at perilously balanced cyclists, and gendarmes blew shrill whistles as they tried to control the traffic with white-gloved hands. To Rebecca, Paris was an enthralling, dizzying place and she was glad she had some knowledge of the language. Back at the Hôtel Eiffel Duquesne at last, she flopped on to her bed, elated at having done everything she'd set out to do. Only then did she realize she was ravenous. There'd been no time to stop for food; every moment of the day had been spent taking pictures, for her private collection as well as on assignment, and sightseeing. Dozens of rolls of film lay heaped on the bed beside her, pictures that would show Stirling better than words ever could what Paris was really like.

'But now . . . food,' she said aloud to herself, running a brush through her hair. Down in the lobby she asked the concierge to recommend to her a good restaurant.

'L'Escargot, madam,' he replied immediately, and proceeded to give her directions in voluble French, his arms gesticulating wildly as he spoke. Then, to her relief, he produced one of the restaurant's business cards which had a map drawn on the back.

'Merci.' Rebecca took the card, studied it for a moment, and realized it was only about ten minutes walk away.

'*Bon appetit*!' he called out after her.

L'Escargot turned out to be a typical little French restaurant, with a red awning over the entrance, a scrubbed wooden floor, and small tables covered in red and white checked cloths. It was run by three middle-aged sisters who popped in and out of the kitchen in turn and, with much giggling, helped Rebecca translate the hand-written menu. Deciding to start with the traditional onion soup, and then go on to medallion of veal with braised celery and a basil sauce, she ordered half a bottle of Châteauneuf du Pape. She didn't usually drink, but tonight she felt like celebrating the success of her day.

The restaurant, which had been empty except for an elderly couple when she'd arrived, soon started to fill up. A large family, complete with grandparents and small children, took up three tables pushed together; a honeymoon couple, judging by their smart new clothes and lack of anything to say to each other, occupied a table by the window; four English tourists, asking for a pot of tea with their dinner, crammed themselves around a small table in the corner. Fascinated, wishing she could take sneak shots to capture this motley collection of diners, Rebecca observed all that was going on and wished Stirling was there to share it with her.

It was ten-thirty. She had another early start, this time photographing Princess Stephanie of Monaco who was launching a new fragrance, Stephanie, at a nearby hotel. Paying her bill she bade the sisters goodnight, and they responded with a shower of good wishes.

'*Bonne nuit*!'

'*Dormez bien*!'

'*Au revoir*!'

'*Bon voyage*!'

They giggled and jostled each other like overgrown schoolgirls.

'Good night,' laughed Rebecca. With a final wave she stepped into the street. It had grown much colder and the wind made her shiver. Buttoning up her leather bomber jacket she started walking back to the hotel, along pavements shadowed thickly by an avenue of plane trees, lit only intermittently by high ornamental bronze street lights. The Avenue Saint Dominique was deserted and silent now, with not even a passing car to break the solitude. Walking briskly Rebecca turned right into the Rue de Babylone, and then she heard it. A scraping sound that was not quite a footfall but she was sure had been made by a shoe or a boot. With her heart hammering, she stopped for a second and looked back over her shoulder. Behind her, slanting across the pavement like the bars of a giant prison window, lay the shadows of the trees. Beyond was the enveloping darkness. All was still.

Shrugging, she started walking again, reminding herself that this was Paris and not Manhattan. Only that afternoon she'd marvelled at the sense of freedom and safety she'd felt as she wandered around the city with two valuable cameras hanging round her neck, and her camera bag unzipped. That was something she'd never dare do back home. Nevertheless, she chided herself for forgetting the first rule she'd ever learned at her self-defence classes: never walk alone on an empty street at night.

The strange scraping sound had started again; scrape-thud, scrape-thud, like someone with a limp. In the distance she could see the brightly lit and busy Avenue au Duquesne. She must reach it quickly, get to where there were lots of people before the scraping footsteps caught up with her.

Breathing hard now, she started to jog, her leather boots pounding on the paving stones, the sound of her heart roaring in her ears. Scrape-thud. Scrape-thud. The sound was nearer now. Wondering how someone with a limp could keep up with her, she paused for a second to glance over her shoulder again. At that moment two of the long black shadows merged instantly into one, and the uneven footsteps halted. Rebecca wanted to scream but there was no one to hear her, so she continued running in the direction of the hotel as fast as her legs would carry her.

'We're going to learn how to make papier mâché today,' Jenny told her pupils, as she spread a sheet of plastic over a long table by the classroom window. Then she put out pots of glue, some one-inch wide paintbrushes, and a stack of newspaper which she'd already ripped up into small pieces.

'What's papier mâché, please, Miss Jenny?' Amelia asked, her eyes excited at the thought of doing something new.

Jenny laid a tinfoil dish in front of each child as they took their places round the table.

'Papier mâché is layers and layers of paper glued together to make a shape. You're all going to make papier mâché plates, and you're going to use these tinfoil dishes as your shape. When the glue is dry you can paint the plates beautiful colours, then varnish them and take them home. Won't that be nice?' She sat at the head of the table, ready to help and guide her little pupils as they learned another form of handicraft.

'Can I paint mine pink?' said Lucy. 'My mummy likes pink the best in the world.'

Jenny smiled. She loved to see them all going home at the end of the week, clutching the things they'd made, whether it was a painting, a piece of pottery or an ornament. She always imagined the warmth with which they'd be received and the hugs and kisses and absurdly exaggerated praise with which they'd be showered. The fact that her own mother had never greeted her own efforts with any enthusiasm when she'd been a small child always came back to her at these moments.

'Of course you can paint yours pink, Lucy,' Jenny replied. 'Now settle down and start.'

Within minutes a dozen little heads were bent over the table in concentration, as small hands wielded paste brushes and then placed and pressed with care the scraps of newspaper Jenny had prepared. There was hardly a sound in the room, except for the occasional heartfelt sigh when a piece of paper got stuck the wrong way. So absorbed were the children that they didn't notice when Jenny went to the cupboard to get some more old newspapers to rip up, or when, on glancing at one of them with idle curiosity, she let out a loud gasp. Her eye had caught a news item, no more than a column wide and six inches long. So utterly fascinated was she by the piece, dated eighteen months before, that it put everything out of her mind for the rest of the day and made her wish that Rebecca had not already left for Paris.

If he hadn't been carrying documents in his inner pocket, the police would have had a problem identifying the body. The head was unrecognisable, a bloodied pulp of broken teeth and splintered bone and bruised-black flesh, with dark rivers of blood trickling through the matted hair into the gutter where it congealed in clotting globules. The body lay inert, like a bundle of old clothes bunched up and tied round the middle as if ready to be despatched to a jumble sale. The hands, fingers spread like starfish, clawed the air in a spasm of helpless surrender.

It had been dusk when the young black waiter from the Arcos Cafe, on Sixty-Second Street, had slipped into the street for a quick smoke. Curious at first at the sight of the lumpy mass in the gutter, he had gone up to it and peered closer. A second later he was reeling away, vomit spewing from his gagging mouth, horror making him seize up so that he swayed, stricken, before staggering back to the doorway of the café. Even the police, arriving in a cacophony of screaming sirens and pulsating red lights, flinched momentarily, averting their gaze, appalled by the thought that one human being could inflict such brutality on another.

Later, at the local police headquarters the sergeant in charge of the case examined the possessions found on the victim's body. They included his passport, some travellers' cheques, a flight ticket, some loose change, a cheap wrist-watch and several of his own business cards, as well as other people's.

'He was British apparently,' observed the sergeant. 'Next-of-kin a mother who lives in Hackney, London, and a brother in Portsmouth. Have we any idea what he was doing in New York? From these business cards it doesn't look like he was on vacation.'

'There's a letter here,' said his second-in-command, who had been one of the first at the scene of the crime.

'Check into it, willya? And check with these people . . . a couple of newspaper editors, a photographic agency . . . all the people who gave him their business cards. They might be able to tell us something. So far, it looks like an unprovoked attack – nothing's been stolen and it seems he was jumped on from behind.'

'The police surgeon thinks the weapon was an axe.'

'I wouldn't be surprised.' The sergeant sounded weary and depressed. Crime, senseless violent wanton crime, had been on the increase in the past year with innocent people getting attacked every day. The city was rotting away from the core as far as he was concerned, and he longed for the day of his retirement when he could move away. He looked up at his second-in-command.

'Put Detective O'Hara on to this case, willya? Tell him to find out anything he can about this guy . . . what's his name . . . Mike Wilson. Let O'Hara get on with it. He's got the stomach for this sort of thing.'

Stirling came face to face with Detective Tom O'Hara for the first time the next morning. The policeman arrived at the agency unannounced, and warily Stirling agreed to see him, remembering he was the one who had dismissed Rebecca's theory as impossible.

'What can I do for you?' he asked, remaining seated behind his desk as O'Hara lumbered into the room. He sat down opposite Stirling, his heavy face flushed and with an expression of barely restrained anger.

'I believe you had a visit from an Englishman called Mike Wilson earlier this week?' O'Hara was watching him closely. Stirling saw no point in denying it.

'Yes, I did. Why?'

'He was murdered on a sidewalk not far from here, yesterday evening.'

Stirling felt the blood drain from his face leaving his skin cold. Less than forty-eight hours ago Mike had sat in that very chair, repeating what he'd been told by Sly Capra's partner. Who else had he boasted to? One thing was obvious: he'd learned too much for his own good.

'What happened exactly?' Stirling asked quietly.

O'Hara shrugged, the muscles of his great shoulders straining through his jacket. 'People get mugged every day. There's nothing unusual about this case but we have to make routine inquiries, you know.'

Like hell you have, thought Stirling, knowing this was going to be a game of cat and mouse.

O'Hara was persistent. 'So what did he want?'

Stirling's mind worked rapidly. Whatever happened, he wasn't going to let on that Mike Wilson had been looking for Rebecca; she must be kept out of this at all costs. So what should he say? To gain time he rose and strolled over to the percolator on a side table.

'Coffee?'

'No thanks.' O'Hara was watching him all the time, little bright eyes buried in a fat face swivelling to and fro while his head remained still. Stirling decided to stick as near to the truth as possible since there was no way of knowing how much O'Hara had already found out.

'Was he a friend of yours?' O'Hara asked suddenly.

'No. He turned up here wanting photographs of a girl called Marissa Montclare. Her parents had sent him over from England to get her things and any mementoes he could. I'd never met him before.'

O'Hara looked sceptical. 'Photographs taken by Rebecca Kendall, I suppose? Why should he want those?'

Stirling met the policeman's gaze levelly. 'They happened to be the last ones ever taken of her. It's obvious her mother and father wanted copies.'

'And you sold him some?'

'No, we're an agency. We sell only to magazines and newspapers.'

O'Hara's eyes continued to glitter. 'What else did he want?'

Stirling feigned surprise. 'Nothing else. What else could he want?'

'You tell me.' There was insolence in his tone. Stirling returned to his seat with his mug of coffee, which he placed with care on his cluttered desk.

'I'm afraid that's all I can tell you.'

'Did Mike Wilson say anything else? If he'd managed to collect Marissa Montclare's things, for instance?'

'He didn't say.'

'What . . . nothing? You must have talked about something, apart from her photographs. Did he say how long he'd been in New York?'

'No, but I gathered not long.'

'Did he say if he'd been able to contact any of her friends?'

'He didn't mention anyone,' Stirling lied. 'Look, as far as I'm concerned, Mike Wilson came here to get some pictures of Marissa Montclare and I wasn't able to help him.'

O'Hara wasn't finished. 'How did he know it was your agency that handled those pictures?'

Stirling was able to answer with complete honesty. 'He saw Rebecca Kendall's byline, and he asked a newspaper editor which agency she used for distribution.'

'He told you that?'

'Yes.'

Suddenly O'Hara turned away as if he were bored by the whole subject. 'That about winds it up then,' he said ponderously, making a move to leave.

'Do you know why he was killed?' Two can play this game, thought Stirling, remembering Rebecca's conviction that O'Hara had been bought.

The policeman shrugged again. 'Why is anyone mugged in the streets these days? There are several killings every week in New York, most of them committed by crack-crazed junkies with no motive beyond looking for a handful of dollars to pay for the next fix. I don't know why Mike Wilson got himself killed. I suppose he was just in the wrong place at the wrong time.'

And you don't give a damn, thought Stirling as he watched the large man stride out of his office.

When he had gone, Stirling thought back to the last time Mike Wilson had been in this very room, talking his head off as dusk had slowly settled on the city and the lights from a thousand office windows had pricked the darkness. Now Stirling felt burdened by a knowledge he wished he didn't have, the same knowledge that

169

undoubtedly had cost Wilson his life. Of that he was certain. And because Wilson's death had occurred in the same precinct as Marissa's, and O'Hara was in charge of both cases, Stirling began to feel apprehensive. Not least because both his office and his apartment were in that precinct too.

Chapter Ten

'Stirling, I'm sure I'm being followed.' It was lunchtime the next day, and a busy morning photographing Princess Stephanie, as she posed with large bottles of her new perfume at the press launch, had made Rebecca's fear of the previous night recede. Now, in broad daylight, she felt quite calm as she sat on her bed in the Hôtel Eiffel Duquesne and talked to Stirling. Briefly she told him what had happened.

'Shit!' he exclaimed. 'How much longer are you going to be in Paris?'

'I fly back to London tomorrow, and then . . .'

'Stay there. For God's sake, stay there.'

'What . . . in Paris?'

'No, London. Find somewhere different to stay this time. Not a big hotel, that's too obvious. Try and find the sort of place where no one will go looking for you. A taxi driver at Heathrow might be able to recommend a small private hotel.'

Rebecca pushed her long hair away from her face, and wondered why there was an edge of panic in Stirling's voice. 'But nothing happened last night,' she said reasonably. 'I was only followed, and then whoever it was disappeared. It may not even have anything to do with Marissa's death. It might have been a molester.'

'I doubt it,' Stirling said drily. He seemed to be weighing up every word as he spoke. 'Things have been happening here. I've found out a lot about Marissa and I don't want you coming back to New York right now. It's too damned dangerous. Believe me, you've no idea what's really behind all this.'

'What d'you mean? Are you all right?'

'I'm fine, sweetheart. I can't talk now because I've got a feeling my phones are being bugged . . .'

'You've got to be kidding! Why? Why should your phones be tapped?'

'Listen, Rebecca. We can't talk now. Call me when you get to London.'

'But . . .'

'Call me at the agency and don't say where you're staying. Just give me the number and I'll call you back from a friend's house, in case the agency phones are tapped as well. I may sound paranoid but this is no laughing matter.'

Rebecca had never heard him sound so serious. 'My God, Stirling, I don't believe this is happening! Listen . . . there are other things I haven't told you, things that have been happening to me.' She thought about Jerry Ribis at Kennedy Airport and the threatening message she'd received at her hotel.

Stirling broke in swiftly. 'Don't tell me now, it's not safe. Get to London and be careful, Rebecca. For God's sake, be careful.'

'OK.' She paused uncertainly. 'Is it really serious?'

'As serious as they come.'

That night Rebecca ate in the hotel where there was a cheerful café on the ground floor. From her table she could observe the comings and goings of the other diners. She found herself watching them curiously, wondering if any of them had a limp. But nobody looked suspicious and nobody seemed even to notice her. At last she went back to her room, and went out on to her balcony to observe the street below without being seen.

It was a cold night. People were hurrying to and fro along the frosty pavements, cars and taxis were driving past and everyone seemed to be going about their business in a normal busy way. Rebecca turned back into her room, still thinking about her experience the previous night. She was certain she'd been followed. It was a disturbing thought. Whoever had been ruthless enough to kill Marissa would kill again, and next time it might be her because of the photographs she'd taken on the night of the murder. But why was Stirling now involved? Perhaps he'd found out something – maybe the reason for Marissa's death? Without doubt both of them seemed possessed of a knowledge that put their lives in danger.

It was then Rebecca had the idea of asking Jenny if she could stay with her when she got back to London. This whole business had started with Sir Edward. Maybe the way to bring it to a conclusion was through Jenny and Sir Edward as well.

Rebecca hurried out of the arrivals building at Heathrow and joined the long line of people waiting for taxis. As it edged slowly forward, she kept looking around to see if she was being watched or followed, but no one seemed interested in anything except securing taxis for themselves, and she chided herself for being neurotic. Nevertheless, she took the precaution of getting into the cab and banging the door shut before giving the driver Jenny's address, just in case anyone should overhear her.

As it was Saturday, Jenny was at home. 'Come any time you like,' she'd said, when Rebecca had called her from Paris the previous day. 'I'll be out shopping first thing, getting in food for the weekend, but otherwise I'll be there all day.' Now, as the taxi stopped outside the large white stucco house in Brunswick Gardens, Rebecca was glad she'd thought of coming here. The security was good; it took two keys to get into the building, and there was also a video entry-phone for visitors. If she wasn't safe here, she wouldn't be safe anywhere.

Jenny opened her arms to hug Rebecca as she stepped out of the bird cage elevator. There was no mistaking the warmth in her voice.

'It's so good to see you. I'm dying to hear what's been happening and why you've got to go into hiding.'

Rebecca laughed. 'You make it sound so dramatic . . . but then I suppose it is really, at least according to Stirling.'

'What's happened?' Jenny led the way into the living-room where potted hyacinths in large bowls filled the room with their breath-taking fragrance.

'I won't really know until I call him from here,' Rebecca replied. A small bright-looking Filipino woman was vigorously polishing the brass fender. She rose as they entered, a smile spreading across her face.

'You want coffee?' she asked, in a voice that was pitched high as a child's.

'This is Marina,' said Jenny. 'We'd love some coffee please.' When she'd gone, Jenny whispered: 'She's an absolute treasure. Irons my things like a dream and doesn't mind washing up last night's dinner dishes.'

'You're lucky.' Rebecca sank down among all the little sofa cushions. 'I've never had anyone to clean, although I could certainly use the help, especially with Karen. You haven't met my roommate, have you? She's a fabulous person, but not exactly neat!'

Jenny laughed, her new hairstyle and black mini-skirt making her almost unrecognizable from the girl Rebecca had first met. 'I'm only tidy,' she said, 'because this is a small flat, and with three of us sharing it . . .'

Rebecca looked guilty. 'Are you really sure I'm not going to be in the way?'

'Of course not. It's lovely to have you,' Jenny replied sincerely. 'That's a put-you-up sofa you're sitting on and it's very comfortable.

You're welcome to stay as long as you like, especially as you're only in this dreadful position because of what happened at Daddy's party.'

'Thanks. I'm really grateful. I don't know what the hell's been happening, but Stirling seems to think it's serious.'

Jenny's smile faded. 'Daddy's still in London and I've asked him to dinner tonight. You must tell him everything. He might be able to help in some way.'

'I hope so.'

At that moment Marina returned, still beaming, with the coffee which she set down on a small table between them. As soon as she'd gone Jenny sprang to her feet and went over to the desk by the window. She took a newspaper cutting out of a drawer.

'I've been dying to show you this,' she said, handing it to Rebecca. 'I'm going to ask Daddy tonight if he knows anything about it.'

The headline caught Rebecca's eye first: 'Showgirl Hits £1.3 Million Jackpot.' She looked inquiringly at Jenny.

'Wait until you read the rest.'

A nineteen-year-old chorus girl has won 1,800,000 dollars (£1,350,000) after placing only three dollars in a Las Vegas slot machine. Topless dancer Tracy Handford hit the jackpot less than five minutes after she'd fed her money into one of the Golden Palm Casino's fruit machines.

'Suddenly bells started ringing!' she said. 'When I realized that four golden nuggets had come up I nearly fainted with excitement!'

Asked if she'd continue performing in cabaret at the Golden Palm, she replied, 'No way. I'm a millionairess now.'

Rebecca put down the cutting, her expression stunned. 'Well! What do you know? That's the most bizarre thing I've ever heard. So that's how she got all her money, and yet . . .' She paused, her brows furrowed. 'She was worth more than that! I know how expensive those Trump Tower apartments are, and then there were her clothes which were all designer label, and her furs and jewels. Jenny, she was worth several million dollars. Some people said she was as rich as your father. That was the whole thing, what caused so much of the gossip. Everyone wanted to know how she came to have so much money.'

174

'Then she must have been a prostitute,' Jenny said bluntly.

'Her clients would have to be Arab oil in that case,' Rebecca commented drily. 'Can I use your phone? I want to call Stirling.'

'Of course.' Jenny handed her the mobile phone and turned to leave the room, muttering something about seeing if Marina was getting on all right.

'There's no need to be so tactful,' Rebecca called after her. 'I'm only giving Stirling this number without saying where I am, and then he'll call me back later.'

Jenny came back into the room and looked at her blankly. 'Why can't you say where you are? Doesn't he know you're staying with me?'

'No, and I can't tell him because he thinks his phones are being tapped, and it's dangerous to talk.'

'My God!' Jenny's mouth dropped open.

'That's why . . .' Rebecca broke off and spoke into the phone. 'Stirling? Hi! It's me.'

'Hi, sweetheart!' She'd dialled his private line at the agency and he'd answered immediately. 'Are you OK?'

'I'm fine. I'll give you my number . . .'

'Don't say where you're calling from,' he reminded her urgently.

'I know.' She gave him Jenny's number, omitting the prefix 071-code as that would pinpoint it as being in the United Kingdom if anyone should happen to be listening. 'How long before you can call me back?'

'Give me an hour, will that be OK? Are you going to be there for a while?'

'I'll be here permanently,' she told him.

'Good. I'll be as quick as I can, sweetheart.' There was a click and then silence. Rebecca looked at Jenny. 'I hope he calls back soon. I'm dying to know what's going on.'

'I wonder if he knows about Marissa winning all that money?'

Rebecca got up and went to look out of the window. The quiet residential street was empty except for a black cat who jumped up on to a garden wall and then disappeared among the shrubbery of a typical London garden.

'Whatever he's found out, there had better be a good reason for my having to go into hiding, because it isn't my style at all,' she remarked softly.

Stirling belted his heavy winter coat and put on thick gloves. 'I'm going out for a while,' he told Minah, his assistant. 'If anyone calls, take a message and say I'll be back in a couple of hours.'

'Sure.' Minah looked up from her word processor, and smiled. Petite, with skin like polished ebony and frizzy hair that was now a curious shade of copper since she'd tried to dye it blond, Minah was one of the most cheerful girls Stirling had ever known. She was also extremely efficient and managed the company's accounts with tact and precision. A girl I can trust, Stirling reflected as he left the office, and yet he didn't dare, for her sake. Recently, he'd discovered that knowledge, of the wrong type, could put a price on your head. It was best little Minah was kept in the dark.

He took the subway to Brooklyn Bridge, and then walked the short distance from the station to his friend Bill Bateman's apartment, on Spruce Street. Bill was someone else he could trust, but right now he didn't want to put his friend in danger either.

'Can I use your phone?' he asked, as soon as Bill had invited him in. Bill gave him a penetrating look, and said: 'Yeah, sure,' without asking any questions.

'Thanks.'

'Want a beer?' Bill led the way into a large cluttered living-room that doubled as an office. He ran a small PR agency, promoting mostly restaurants, and on his desk were a stack of press releases, sample menus, and a large mock-up for an advertisement extolling the charms of 'Leoni's, New York's finest Italian Restaurant'.

Having committed to memory the London number Rebecca had given him, Stirling picked up the phone, while Bill slipped quietly into the adjoining kitchen, closing the door after him.

Rebecca answered at once. 'Stirling, what's been happening for God's sake?' she demanded, as soon as she'd told him she was staying with Jenny. Then she added, 'Did you know Marissa Montclare won over a million dollars in a slot machine at the Golden Palm?'

'Yes, and I've learned what was behind her murder too.'

'How?'

'Someone called Mike Wilson who was over here from England, making inquiries on behalf of her family, came to see me. He was looking for you actually.' Then Stirling told Rebecca about the visits he'd had from Wilson and that he had been brutally murdered. 'O'Hara is trying to make out it was just a random mugging, the same way he insisted Marissa's death was an accident, but I don't believe a word of it. I think he's covering up again.'

'You mean Mike Wilson's death occurred in O'Hara's precinct too?'

'That's exactly what I mean. Some coincidence, huh? Wilson

176

also recognized the man who killed Marissa when he saw the photographs you'd taken at the party. His name's Sly Capra.'

Rebecca sighed in relief. 'My God, you mean he was able to identify the waiter? Then can't you just go straight to someone else in the police?'

'It wasn't the waiter,' Stirling cut in. 'Sly Capra is a well-dressed, pleasant looking guy in his early thirties. You photographed him talking to a blonde girl in a group with some other people. The point of all this is that Wilson was obviously killed because he knew too much. Now I know too much and so do you. You see what I mean?'

'Yes, I do,' Rebecca replied slowly. 'You especially are in danger if the police know Wilson went to see you.'

'They do. O'Hara was here yesterday. I hope I got rid of him, but I'm not sure.'

'Stirling, could you do something for me?'

'Sure. What is it?'

'Could you send me a copy of that picture I took of Sly Capra? I'd like to see what he looks like.'

'No problem.' Stirling reached for a pencil and pad among the clutter on Bill's desk. 'Where shall I send it?'

When Rebecca had given him Jenny's address she said: 'I have a feeling this man may also go under the name of Jerry Ribis.'

'Who the hell is Jerry Ribis?'

As Rebecca told him about Jerry giving her a lift home after Sir Edward's party and then phoning her to ask her out, Stirling could feel himself grow tense with a mixture of fear and irritation.

'Why didn't you tell me about him before?' he burst out. 'Have you heard from him again?'

She told him about the incident at the airport. 'There was also a nasty message left at my hotel, which I kind of figured out he'd sent.' Then she repeated, as if the words were forever engraved in her mind, what the message had said. 'And, as I told you, I'm sure I was followed in Paris the other night.'

Angry, hurt, and most of all frightened, Stirling felt as if something in his head was going to explode. 'For fuck's sake, why didn't you tell me all this?'

'I can look after myself,' he heard her reply, 'and what could you have done about it, anyway?'

'That isn't the point!' He knew he was being unreasonable but the thought of her being in danger, and then being too damned independent to mention it, filled him with fury. 'Did you tell the British police you'd had a threatening note?' he demanded.

'I told no one. I think I'm safe as long as I stay out of O'Hara's

177

precinct, but I've got to go home sooner or later, Stirling. I can't stay in hiding forever.'

'Jesus Christ, be sensible! There's a vicious killer out there, Rebecca. Mike Wilson was hacked to pieces with a hatchet! Do you want that to happen to you?' He thought of her beautiful face with its perfectly symmetrical features and her long silky hair. 'You will stay in hiding until I say it's OK for you to leave,' he shouted.

'I will do as I like,' Rebecca retorted. 'I'm seeing Sir Edward this evening and I'll tell him everything you've told me. I think it's time we worked out a plan, and he might be able to help. After all, he's got contacts, money, and he knew Marissa. He may even be in danger himself, without realizing it. I'm not going to run away from this thing, Stirling. I want to see Marissa's murderer caught.'

'At the risk of getting yourself murdered. Are you crazy?'

'I'm not crazy,' she replied, 'I'm just sick of feeling as if I'm being watched and followed all the time, and I'm sick of feeling the police don't believe me, even when my apartment's been ripped apart.'

'That's O'Hara, not the whole police force.' Stirling had never heard her sound so angry.

'OK, so it's only O'Hara, but he just happens to be the one in charge. It's time we did something. It's time we went over O'Hara's head.'

'We will, when I've got a bit more evidence together, for God's sake!' Stirling's anger matched hers now. Of all the goddamn obstinate women, he thought, slamming down the receiver. When Bill came back into the room, he was sitting slumped in a chair by the phone, his long legs sprawled before him, his dark hair ruffled.

'Here.' Bill handed him a bottle of Miller Lite.

'Thanks.' In silence, Stirling opened the ice cold beer. Then he let out a long irritated sigh.

'Sounds like you've got problems,' Bill observed cheerfully.

'Have I got problems!' echoed Stirling. 'I've got so many problems I don't know which one to tackle first.'

'If it's a woman, buy her a present, and if it's business, never give a sucker an even break.'

Stirling grinned. 'The woman's too far away, and anyway she's one lady who can't be bought. And as for the business – well, I've just got to be careful not to get myself stitched up.'

Sir Edward arrived shortly after seven, an elegant figure in a pale grey Savile Row suit, his silvery hair brushed smoothly, exuding a faint aura of expensive cologne.

'Good to see you again, m'dear,' he exclaimed, as Rebecca stepped forward to shake hands. 'How are you? What are you doing in England?'

Before she had time to reply, Jenny cut in. 'She's been having the most awful time, Daddy. That's why she's staying with me, sleeping on the sofa. It's fearfully cramped for her but at least it's safe.' There was a ring of authority in her voice that neither Sir Edward nor Rebecca had heard before; it was as if she'd suddenly discovered her self-confidence and was determined to demonstrate it.

'I don't understand.' Sir Edward looked from his daughter to Rebecca. 'Why do you have to be in a safe place?'

'Sit down and I'll pour you a whisky, then we'll tell you all about it,' said Jenny. 'Rebecca's life is in danger, and it's all because of Marissa Montclare.'

Sir Edward looked deeply startled and Rebecca felt a twinge of annoyance. It was *her* story for a start, and surely the subject of Marissa was still a painful one for Sir Edward?

'Certain things have come to light,' she said quietly. 'It's a long story, but I may accidentally have taken pictures at your party of the person who . . .' She paused, wondering if Sir Edward still believed Marissa's death had been an accident, or if he had at last come to terms with the truth.

'The waiter you asked me about?' he asked immediately.

'No,' replied Rebecca, 'this is an accomplice, a man in his thirties who is called either Sly Capra or Jerry Ribis?'

Sir Edward shook his head. 'I've never heard either name before. Do you really think Marissa was killed?' Some of his savoir-faire had deserted him. He looked old and a little crumpled. 'If you took a picture of the murderer, I suppose he must have been brought to the party by someone else. Hateful modern habit, the way people drag along their friends to other people's parties.' He snorted in disgust. 'What do the police say?'

'Not much so far,' Rebecca replied bitterly. 'Have you heard of a man called Mike Wilson?'

'Ah.' He took a gulp from the whisky Jenny had given him. 'There I can help you.' He told her how Wilson had barged his way into his office demanding to know what Marissa had done with her money. 'Damned cheek! Why do you ask?'

Rebecca began to explain, but then with a startled cry her hand flew up to her mouth. 'I've just remembered something!'

They both looked at her with surprise.

'What is it?' Jenny asked.

'Do you remember,' Rebecca asked, leaning forward and looking at Sir Edward, 'that you thought Marissa had said something about a "spy" just before she died?'

Sir Edward's pale eyes were troubled. 'Yes, I believe I did.'

'I remember you saying you thought she might be a spy, Daddy,' Jenny cut in.

'Yes.' He still sounded doubtful.

'Well, I think she was talking about Sly . . . Sly Capra, not a "spy" at all. I think he turned up unexpectedly at your party and she was scared and tried to tell you.' She could recall every detail of those last few minutes of Marissa's life: the babble of talk and laughter in the crowded room, the air a hazy blue from cigar smoke; Marissa in her black sequinned mini-dress tugging at Sir Edward's arm, fear in her eyes, desperation in her manner; and he so jovial and hearty, laughing with his friends and not listening.

Sir Edward sat in the chintz armchair in Jenny's drawing-room, gazing into space.

'You could be right,' he said at last. 'She could well have said "Sly" and not "spy". Oh, God almighty!' He crashed the whisky glass down on the table beside him and covered his face with his hands. 'I wish to God I'd listened to her and then none of this would have happened.'

Jenny sprang forward, her arm round his shoulders. 'Don't blame yourself, Daddy.'

He refused to be comforted. 'I feel I'm to blame in some way,' he retorted.

Rebecca and Jenny looked at each other, remembering what Stirling had said on the phone earlier.

'Did you know,' Jenny asked, 'that she won the jackpot in a casino in Las Vegas?'

'Or that she was in business with Sly Capra? And that was why she was so rich? Her winnings from the jackpot were only a small part of what she was probably worth at the end,' said Rebecca, adding, 'but I think the business arrangement went sour and that's why she was killed.'

Sir Edward handed Jenny his empty glass to be refilled. 'What sort of business arrangement?'

Rebecca looked at Jenny again, hesitating before saying the words that would strike fear in Sir Edward's heart. Words that could mean ruin to him if he had, even unwittingly, been involved. Words that could bring the Tollemache Trust crashing down.

The offices of Lawson, Martin & Grant were housed in a shabby building in Belsham Street, where the slums of East London seemed unchanged since the turn of the century. By day street markets selling vegetables, fruit, fish and cheap clothes brought an influx of people who haggled and argued at the price of the goods in response to the 'Roll up, roll up' bawl of the cockney vendors. By night, when the barrows had been wheeled away and the pubs were full of beer-drinking locals, rotting garbage and litter lay strewn in the gutters, sniffed over and devoured by rats with long tails, which, when disturbed, slithered down their burrows beneath the old buildings, sharp of eye and rippling with fat.

It was in these insalubrious and low rent surroundings that Steve Wragg, who now ran the company, discussed with his partner, Gary Thomas the death of their erstwhile colleague Mike Wilson. More than that, they were trying to decide whether it was worth sending someone else to New York to try and locate Tracy Handford's fortune.

'Myself, I think it's a waste of time,' Thomas commented.

'It's a pity Mike got himself killed before he'd even found out what she'd done with her money,' Wragg agreed. 'If we do decide to send David, it means he'll have to start from scratch.' David McNee had only been with them for six months and had come straight from university. Interested in genealogy, and unable to get a decent job, he had decided to work for Lawson, Martin & Grant until something better turned up. Ever since childhood he'd shared his working-class mother's fascination with the great families of Britain, and it was his ambition one day to get a job on a publication like *Burke's* or *Debrett's Peerage*, or even *Who's Who*, tracing the lineage of the aristocracy.

'There's a lot of money involved, though,' said Thomas. 'I don't think we can afford *not* to send someone. We'd have to put him on a tight budget, though.'

At that moment they were joined by John Massey, who had been with the firm for such a long time he could even remember the original Lawson, Martin and Grant. 'Are you talking about the showgirl's money?' he enquired, lowering himself on to one of the worn leather seats.

The others nodded. 'If we could only ascertain how much she left, it would be easier,' Wragg said.

'It was several million pounds,' said John Massey.

Wragg looked at him pityingly. 'We don't know that for certain. We only decided, on spec, to do this job because we knew we could charge a good percentage if we got lucky, but we don't know how much we're actually talking about.'

'Then it's a pity Mike Wilson's luck ran out,' Massey's voice

181

cracked drily. The others looked at him suspiciously, wondering what he was getting at.

'It was his own damned fault for walking in a dangerous area at night,' Wragg snapped, then added thoughtfully, 'It's a pity that both Sir Edward Wenlake and his ex-wife were so unhelpful.'

'Especially as Mike said he was on the brink of finding out something, the last time he phoned,' added Thomas.

'I wonder what it was?' Wragg mused.

'You'll never find out now,' said old John Massey with a hint of malice.

'We will if we send David over,' Wragg insisted.

'Perhaps we'd better then.' Thomas still sounded reluctant, yet the thought of passing up a nice percentage was unthinkable.

'Shall we tell him now?'

'I suppose so.' The last of Thomas's resistance crumbled.

'John,' said Wragg, 'fetch David, will you?'

The old man rose slowly, used to being ordered around by the younger ones.

'I think we're doing the right thing,' said Wragg, 'and it'll please Mr and Mrs Handford to know we haven't given up trying to get Tracy's money for them in spite of Mike's death.'

Thomas ignored the touch of sanctimoniousness in his colleague's voice and thought about young David McNee. When he was told he was going to New York the poor bugger would think all his Christmases had come at once.

When the letter arrived informing Mavis and Bert Handford of the untimely death of Mike Wilson, they received the news with equanimity. They'd never really believed he'd get any money for them anyway, because they didn't believe their Tracy had ever had any. She'd sent them a few pounds now and again, for little treats like, but as Mavis assured her husband when she read that her daughter had been a millionairess, she'd have sent them more if she'd been that rich. There'd never been anything mean about their only child; she even used to share her sweets with them.

'We don't need the money, do we, luv? It won't bring her back,' Bert observed.

'You're right,' Mavis agreed. 'Nothing will bring our Tracy back now.' And then she looked over to the 1930s yellow-tiled fire-place. Beside a vase of plastic flowers on the mantelshelf stood the snapshot of Tracy that the *Margate Echo* had returned. They'd put it in a fake silver frame so that now she was immortalized forever, her white tutu stiff around her legs, her smile coy as she balanced on the

182

garden wall. That was the way they liked to remember her: a bright pretty little girl, full of promise and brimming with ambition. ''I'm goin' to be famous one day, Ma,'' she'd often said.

Their Tracy had been innocent and sweet and loving. This Marissa Montclare had been someone else, a person they'd never known who had nothing remotely to do with them, a flashy chorus girl who'd kept bad company. Tracy would never have brought disgrace on her family whereas Marissa must have been a tart to end up the way she did. In their minds the two were completely unconnected. That was why they weren't interested in this David McNee or anyone else going to New York, and that was why they weren't interested in the money.

To have been otherwise would mean they had believed in the existence of Marissa Montclare.

Rebecca spoke succinctly. 'Insider trading, Sir Edward. That's what Marissa and Sly Capra were involved in.'

He sat forward in his chair, alarm etched on every line of his face, his eyes registering panic. 'Insider trading?' he repeated.

She nodded. 'I'm afraid you're not going to like this, Sir Edward, but Marissa was set up in that Trump Tower apartment by Sly Capra for the sole purpose of getting to know powerful businessmen from whom she could wheedle information about share deals and takeover bids.' As she spoke, a part of her was wondering how a man as brilliant and successful as Sir Edward could have fallen for the oldest trick in the world.

'Oh, my God.' He sank back as the full impact of her words sank in. 'I trusted her. That would explain a lot of things,' he added hollowly.

'Like the takeover of the Mackenzie Machine Tool Company?'

Sir Edward groaned. 'We wondered who was buying up all those shares, just before the takeover went through.'

'Yes. From what Stirling said, Sly is part of a drug running gang, who want to find a way of laundering money, while making a profit at the same time, and Sly acted on information given to him by Marissa. She would pass on details of any business deals she heard about and he would invest her winnings from the jackpot, plus his own money. Of course he bought and sold shares in various nominees' names so the dealings couldn't be traced back to them, but there seems to be no doubt that they made a fortune between them.'

Like a tired old dog with toothache, Sir Edward shook his head and took another gulp of whisky. 'I wonder what went wrong? Why did he kill her?' There was pain in his voice. 'She was so young.'

Jenny leaned forward and touched his arm. 'Don't get upset, Daddy. I'm sure Marissa meant no harm.'

He spun on her with sudden anger, his eyes blazing. 'Of course she meant harm!' he roared. 'She made up a whole lot of lies to deceive me. She got me to talk about the various deals the company was involved in and she used that information to help some gangster make a fortune. Don't tell me she meant no harm!'

He closed his eyes, seeing in his mind Marissa's exquisite platinum beauty and remembering her sweet innocence and understanding. Marissa, he reflected, was the type of girl who'd been born to relieve men of their burdens. He'd thought her the perfect woman to come home to at the end of the day. Within her presence he'd always been able to unwind and relieve his body of the pent-up longing that had plagued him all day, for he was a man to whom sex was vital.

Curling up beside him afterwards, she'd always asked him about his day at the office, and as he'd recounted the various deals and coups he'd brought off, he'd felt flattered by her interest. Fool that he'd been, he'd even thought seriously of marrying her! And all the time, instead of yielding herself in surrender, she'd been secretly capitalizing on his confidences.

He flushed darkly. Now he must adjust to an entirely new picture of what had really happened, with all its dark overtones. Unwittingly, he'd been involved in insider trading on a grand scale and he might still have to pay the price for his foolish indiscretions.

'How did you find all this out?' he growled, looking at Rebecca.

'You said that a man called Mike Wilson had been to see you?'

Sir Edward nodded.

'He also went to see my agent and boyfriend, Stirling Hertfelder, because he'd seen my byline under Marissa's pictures and thought I might be able to help him. He thought I was a friend of hers.' Rebecca paused and took a deep breath, trying to remember in chronological order everything Stirling had said on the phone. 'It seems,' she continued, 'that Mike went to her apartment in the Trump Tower and found that it was actually owned by Sly Capra. Mike then told Stirling he'd had a meeting with Sly's partner, and had learned that Sly and Marissa had got together when she'd won the jackpot at the Golden Palm. Apparently he made a proposition to her, promising substantially to increase her winnings if she entered into a business arrangement with him. We all know now what that was.'

Sir Edward drained his glass and handed it to Jenny. 'Go on,' he said to Rebecca.

'Apparently,' she continued, 'Sly Capra had millions of dollars at his disposal to invest, and was looking for the right sort of girl to become his business partner. She had to be classy as well as bright, acceptable in New York society, and she also had to be willing to go along with him. As far as Stirling could gather from Mike, everything went well for a time and the Mob thought highly of Sly's "discovery".'

'Then what happened?'

Rebecca shook her head. 'That's what we don't know. Something must have, though. Tell me, where did you meet Marissa?'

'At a charity dinner. She was with some people I know.'

'That would figure. That's how she got on to the society circuit.'

'Well, doesn't that about wrap everything up?' Sir Edward sounded weary.

Rebecca spoke forcefully. 'It certainly doesn't.'

'Why not? It's all over, isn't it? Now that she's dead?'

'Sir Edward, Mike Wilson was hacked to death whilst walking along a sidewalk in Manhattan, shortly after his meeting with Sly Capra's partner. Stirling is sure his phones are being bugged. I'm being threatened, followed, and I've had my apartment ransacked . . . I think our lives are in danger. Both Marissa and Mike's murders took place in the same precinct, both cases are being handled by a detective called Tom O'Hara, and I'll bet my life that he's in their pay otherwise why would he insist that both deaths were accidental, for God's sake!' Her voice had risen as she spoke and her dark eyes were blazing. 'We've got to do something,' she added vehemently, 'before we wind up dead in the gutter too!'

Chapter Eleven

Brian Norris could feel his blood pressure rising as he looked across his desk in the offices of the Tollemache Trust – the young man from England was asking awkward questions about Marissa Montclare. Like a nightmare he couldn't awaken from this Marissa business kept coming back to haunt him, just when he thought he'd settled the media, quietened the gossips and persuaded everyone there was nothing to worry about. The girl was dead . . . and yet she wouldn't lie down. Shimmering like a siren on the rocks of his impending downfall, drawing him inexorably and relentlessly back to the scene of the disaster so that the company must surely flounder and be damaged with each new disclosure, she seemed to still beckon him although he did his best to wriggle away.

Edward's absence in England left him exposed and vulnerable. Marissa hadn't been *his* girlfriend or *his* responsibility in life, and she certainly had nothing to do with him in death. Angry with Sir Edward for causing this embarrassment, and worried that any further scandal would cause shares in the Tollemache Trust to take another dip, he turned in fury on David McNee from Lawson, Martin & Grant.

'I have no idea what she did with her money,' he raged, 'and Sir Edward wouldn't know either. Why should we? Do you ask every Tom, Dick and Harry where they bank? Who their brokers are? If they have any deposit accounts? Why should we know what the wretched girl did with her money? She was nothing more than a guest at a New Year's Eve party. Now, get out of here and stop wasting my time. It's got nothing to do with us.'

Brian rose dismissively, indicating the door with his plump little hand, his rotund body bristling more with fear than indignation.

David McNee felt himself blush. He'd been totally unprepared for the hostility which the mention of Marissa Montclare's name had aroused, and he was taken aback by this tirade from the stout little man who sat behind his enormous desk.

'OK, OK, I'm going,' he said, backing away and leaving the

luxurious office. Depression mixed with humiliation hit him with the force of a sledgehammer, making him realize that Manhattan was not the glamorous city he'd seen on so many television movies. When he'd first been told he was being sent to New York, he'd been thrilled.

'It'll be a cinch,' he'd told Wragg and Thomas with engaging confidence, when they'd given him all the details the day before his departure. 'New York – that is, Manhattan – is a much more compact area than London. It's much easier to find your way around and I'm sure I can get help from the various banks in tracing this young lady's money. If that fails, there are always the credit card companies. I bet she only used plastic for shopping.' He spoke patronisingly, showing these dreary old men how sophisticated he was; practically a yuppie. He'd have this whole affair wrapped up in no time.

'You know Manhattan?' Wragg asked politely, although he thought it unlikely. McNee was a fresh-faced lad who'd done reasonably well at university but his family were hard up. Trips to the States would surely have been a luxury beyond him on a grant.

McNee answered with a touch of cockiness: 'I know all about Manhattan, how it works and all that. I can find my way around without any problem.' He didn't add that a friend of his who worked for Air India had lent him one of their publications, *New York in Flash-Maps*, which listed everything from the subway system to Greenwich Village restaurants, and was packed with useful information.

'Don't worry,' McNee continued, 'I'll crack this one easily. Money doesn't just vanish when someone dies. For example, who paid for her funeral? They must have used her money, mustn't they? They'll know where she banked. I wonder why Mike Wilson ran into problems?' His voice was slightly disparaging. 'And surely she must have had medical insurance? Now, was that paid by banker's order, or credit card, or cheque?'

Wragg had to admit privately that perhaps a university education had its advantages. Mike Wilson hadn't been nearly as clued up as this. At first, after what had happened to Mike, he'd felt he might be sending a lamb to its slaughter. Now he was convinced he was only instructing a piranha to go after a shark.

Twenty-four hours later, David McNee was boarding a British Airways flight, convinced he was going to conquer Manhattan, take it by the scruff of the neck and force it to offer up the simple matter of how to lay his hands on Marissa Montclare's fortune . . . for the benefit of her parents, of course, although Wragg had promised him a percentage of whatever they took. He was also determined to have a ball.

Three days later, panic was beginning to shaft him. Supposing he was unable to trace Marissa's money? As he trudged along the densely populated streets surrounded by buildings a mile high, making him feel as small as a beetle at the bottom of the Grand Canyon, while tons of metal thundered past in a never-ending stream, it dawned on him that this mission might prove to be impossible. His very first undertaking on behalf of Lawson, Martin & Grant, and he was about to fail! Despair drenched him in nervous sweat.

Wherever he'd been, he thought, doors had been slammed in his face, both metaphorically and physically. For once his boyish charms had cut no ice. Sometimes he thought about Mike Wilson, and at those moments he'd be careful to keep to well-lit crowded places wishing that Mike was still around to help. In his last report he had said he was on the verge of finding out all about Marissa and who she'd been living with. Now David was going to have to begin again from scratch and he didn't know where the hell to start.

Rebecca awoke the morning after Sir Edward's visit with a splitting headache and a feeling of nausea.

'You poor thing,' Jenny sympathized as she hurriedly gathered her things together for school. 'Will you be all right on your own? I'll be back by four o'clock. I'll write down the doctor's telephone number on the pad by the phone. Ring him if you feel any worse. He's awfully nice.'

Rebecca sat on the edge of the sofa-bed in the drawing-room, where she'd spent a restless night, and pulled the blanket around her shoulders. 'Don't worry, I'll be fine. I'm not usually ill. It's probably just a stomach upset.'

'There's a lot of 'flu going around. Keep warm and drink lots of liquids.'

'OK.' Rebecca heaved herself to her feet and smiled wanly. 'You'd better go or you'll be late. Honestly, I can look after myself.'

'If you're sure.' Reluctantly Jenny turned to leave. 'Help yourself to anything you want.'

'Thanks.' When she had gone Rebecca went to the kitchen for a glass of water, fighting the great waves of nausea that were sweeping over her, leaving her weak and dizzy. 'Damn,' she cursed, hating being ill and wishing she was in her own apartment in TriBeCa where everything was familiar and she could do as she

189

liked. She searched in the bathroom cabinet for something to settle her stomach, but at that moment the bile rose in her throat and she was violently sick.

'What the hell . . . ?' She leaned over the lavatory, feeling the strength drain from her limbs, her head pounding as if someone were stabbing her with a knife. Karen had attacks like this. Migraine, she called them.

Well, whether it's a migraine or something I ate, Rebecca reflected as she tottered back to the sofa, I sure hope it eases up soon. I have plans to make and things to do and I haven't got time to be ill. But within a few minutes of getting back into bed she was fast asleep.

The sun, reflecting on the Chippendale mirror above the fireplace, woke her two hours later. Gingerly at first she stretched and raised her head. Then she sat up slowly. To her surprise she felt better, hungry even. The migraine seemed to have lifted. Thankfully she got out of bed and decided to have a shower. Then she made herself a cup of herb tea and decided to take a walk to clear her head.

An hour later she was walking briskly down Kensington Church Street on her way to Kensington Gardens. It was a brilliant gold and blue morning, and as she turned up the narrow pathway that led into the park she noticed in the distance a beautiful Tudor building of mellow pink bricks and cream stonework, with an imposing porticoed entrance. Set in the lush parkland of Kensington Gardens, it stood majestically against the skyline, the brass clock in the tower gleaming in the sunshine, the long elegant windows veiled in white muslin.

Rebecca recognized it at once as Kensington Palace, the home of several members of the royal family who lived in apartments there. She remembered it had been built in 1661 by Sir Christopher Wren, who had built St Paul's Cathedral, and from the books she'd read she knew it was steeped in history. Fascinated, she crossed the private road that lay parallel to the Palace, known by the locals as 'Millionaires Row', and noticed with surprise that only two policemen stood on duty near the entrance. Surely security was tighter than this? In the distance, by a statue of Queen Victoria, and divided by only a brick wall from the Palace gardens, Londoners were going casually about their business, walking their dogs, pushing their children in prams, enjoying the unexpected bonus of a bright winter's day and seemingly taking for granted that they were within yards of where royalty lived.

At that moment, something happened that made Rebecca catch

her breath and reach automatically for her camera. For a moment she couldn't believe what she was seeing. Two small blond boys on red bicycles were pedalling vigorously along the private road in front of the entrance, watched over by a nanny and a tall burly-looking man. They were Prince William and Prince Harry, the sons of Prince Charles and Princess Diana, trying out, she supposed, their Christmas presents.

Jamming the telephoto lens on to her Leica and checking that it was loaded with Kodachrome 64 film, she quickly calculated the exposure and shutter speed and then moved quietly forward, unable to believe her luck, knowing that there wasn't a member of the paparazzi who wouldn't give his right arm to be in her shoes at that moment. To have got a good shot of Princess Diana was wonderful, but to be able to capture her enchanting sons on film was a real scoop. Syndicated world-wide by Stirling, these shots would be worth thousands of dollars too. Clicking the shutter continuously she took shot after shot as the little Princes, unaware of her presence, wheeled their bikes around in circles, grinning and shouting at each other. Against the perfect backdrop of the late mediaeval palace, the pictures were going to be terrific.

At that moment, as if sensing someone was coming too close, the plain clothes policeman spun round, saw her and then said something to the nanny. Rebecca managed to get a final shot of Prince William's face as he concentrated on turning his bike around before they all disappeared inside the palace. It had been a magical few moments and she couldn't believe her luck at having got pictures of the future King of England, playing like any other child. Wait until Stirling hears about this, she thought, hurrying back to Jenny's flat, her walk in the park forgotten. She'd call him up right away and ask if he wanted the film put on the next flight out of Heathrow.

A courier from Federal Express was standing on the doorstep of Jenny's building when she got back. He looked as if he was waiting for someone to come to the door.

Rebecca was the first to speak. 'Can I help you?'

He glanced at the envelope he was holding. 'Kendall?' he inquired.

'That's me.'

'Sign here, please.' He thrust his clipboard towards her.

'Thanks.' The label on the envelope said it was from the Hertfelder Agency. It must be the photograph of Sly Capra that Stirling had promised to send her. As she let herself into Jenny's flat, she ripped open to the envelope, expecting to find a picture of the man she knew as Jerry Ribis.

Pinkney House seemed unbearably empty and silent when Edward returned to London. Angela had urged him to go, saying quite fiercely that there was no point in his staying now that Simon was out of danger; but once he'd gone, a growing sense of isolation made her realize how comforting it had been, in spite of everything, to have had both him and Jenny home for a while. Now she had to face the future, and whatever it held, alone. Although Simon was out of danger there had been no improvement in his condition. Every day she drove over to the hospital in Andover to sit with him, and every afternoon she realized there was no change; he was still paralyzed and his legs still had no feeling.

'It's impossible to say how long it will take,' the doctor explained one afternoon, 'and you must prepare yourself for the fact, Lady Wenlake, that your son may never be able to walk again.'

Angela had driven home from the hospital that evening gripped by depression. If only she had someone to talk to, she thought, as she parked the car round the back of the house, near the stables. If only she wasn't so utterly alone in this great mansion, with just Peters and the other servants hovering in attendance, watching she was sure for a crack to appear in her armour. When she went up to her room to change for dinner, she slipped into the bedroom that had been Edward's and was instantly assailed by a lingering waft of his aftershave. It still seemed to pervade the room like a presence, and as she looked at the bed he'd slept in, and the pillow where his head had rested, she was overcome by a feeling of emptiness.

Life seemed to have slipped away from her without her realizing that the time was passing, and now although she couldn't be considered old, the best was over and would not come again. Jenny had grown up and left home, sliding out of the picture almost as if she'd never been, leaving no mark behind; and Simon might now be an invalid, his life reduced to the confines of a wheelchair almost before he had begun to live – bound to her side for ever, as she'd always wanted, but not in this way, oh God, not in this way. Was this the answer to her prayers that she and Simon would always remain close, sharing Pinkney, sharing their lives? Was this the doing of the Almighty she'd prayed to, begging him to keep Simon from going to live with his father in America?

She turned to leave the spare room, hugging her stomach with her arms, for the pain she felt was physical, deeper than tears, more wrenching than sobs. As she entered her own room she found a comforting fire had been lit in the grate, and her dark red velvet caftan laid on the bed, ready for her to change into for dinner.

Crouching before the flames, she extended her hands to the warmth but the ache inside would not go. All she'd ever wanted was to share the good things in life with her beloved son: Pinkney and the beautiful surrounding grounds, the animals they both loved, the pleasant social life they led. In time, if this accident hadn't happened, Simon would have got married and had children and there'd have been a new heir to inherit the Wenlake title. There would have been a future for her too, helping to bring up her grandchildren in the lovely ancestral home that had been in her family for generations.

Now the only future Angela could visualize was one of Simon as an eternal invalid, deprived of a normal life as she pushed him around the estate in a wheelchair. Automatically she slipped on her velvet dress and brushed her hair with short sharp strokes, wondering all the time if it wouldn't have been better if he had died.

She felt no shame at the thought. His suffering, as he lay there inert, his poor limbs cold and useless, was pitiful to see. And, oh, how bitter were his eyes! Only this afternoon he had looked at her as if he hated her because she'd told him how she'd walked into the village the day before. That she had the use of her legs and he didn't made him so resentful she could feel the animosity coming at her in great waves. She'd wanted to weep with guilt, wishing the accident had happened to her instead, wishing with all her heart she could take away his pain and helplessness; but Simon had lain there with his sulky mouth, brooding on his misfortune, and she was overcome with the feeling that it was all her fault.

She looked at her reflection now in the dressing-table mirror, as she fixed her pearl earrings, and raged with silent misery against everything that had conspired to bring about this situation. But nothing took away the feeling of impotence. She wanted to lash out, to hurt Edward for being a rotten husband and a hopeless father; to vent her spleen on Jenny for being plain and dull and healthy while Simon was so sick; she wanted to scream at the injustice of it all, and as she sat there wondering how she was going to endure the rest of her life she knew that there was something that had to be done. Something only she could do.

Angela took a shawl out of her wardrobe, and putting it round her shoulders picked up the flowing skirt of her long velvet dress and hurried down to the library. From her purse she took a bunch of keys, and selecting a slim antique one unlocked one of the drawers in the large pedestal desk that stood in the window. Opening it slowly, she withdrew the old semi-automatic Luger revolver her father had taken from the dead body of a German soldier during the Battle of the Somme in the First World War. It was a 1908 model,

9mm calibre with a four inch barrel, the mark of the German eagle alongside its serial number still visible on the side. She'd always meant to donate it to the Imperial War Museum as a relic of historic interest, but now she was glad she'd kept it.

Holding the Luger in her left hand she snapped the uniquely designed magazine with its eight cartridges into place. Then she slipped the revolver into her evening bag, and without a backward glanced hurried out of the library.

It was a face Rebecca had never seen before, the face of a good-looking man in his thirties, with dark shining hair and a deep tan that made his teeth look dazzlingly white. He did not remotely resemble Jerry Ribis, she thought, studying the picture. Sly Capra appeared to be talking to a skinny blonde in a stretch Lycra dress and a blaze of rhinestones, and he was dressed much more smartly than Jerry, in a sharp tuxedo with a white carnation in the buttonhole. Rebecca let the picture drop on to the sofa beside her while she sat deep in thought. Then she looked at her watch. It was already nearly two o'clock in the afternoon. Jenny would be back from school in a couple of hours and she had a lot to do first.

'I'm flying back to New York in the morning,' she announced as soon as Jenny returned from Trevor House. 'It's been wonderful of you to let me stay here but I must get home. Things aren't adding up and I've got to find out what it's all about.'

Jenny looked at her with pale bewildered eyes. 'Are you well enough to travel? This morning you were really sick.'

'I'm fine. After a couple of hours' sleep I felt much better. Then I went for a walk and got some shots of the Royal Princes, and the picture arrived from Stirling. Now I feel terrific! Take a look at this.' She handed Jenny the photograph.

'So this is what Jerry Ribis looks like,' Jenny remarked.

'That's the whole point – it's not Jerry! It's one of the shots I took by natural light at the party. Frankly I don't even remember taking it, but this is the man identified by Mike Wilson as Sly Capra. I think he's one of the people responsible for Marissa's death.'

Jenny looked awestruck as she examined the photo. 'He doesn't look like a killer, but then I don't suppose I know what a killer looks like.' She peered closer. 'I've met the girl he's with. Daddy and I were at the same table at a big charity ball a couple of years ago.'

'Who is she?'

Jenny shook her head. 'I can't remember her name, although Daddy probably will. She was with her husband when we met, but it wasn't this man.'

Rebecca sat forward, her elbows resting on her knees. 'This is fascinating. I wonder if she brought Sly Capra to your father's party, or if he came with someone else. Of course you know what all this means?'

'What?'

'It means several people were involved in killing Marissa. We've got the waiter, opening the window,' she counted them off on her fingers, 'there's Jerry Ribis, who I'm convinced had something to do with it, and then there's this man, Sly Capra, who set her up in society in the first place . . . and maybe this woman's involved as well!'

'My God,' said Jenny. 'Well, I suppose it would figure. How scary! What are you going to do?'

'I'm going to ask your father who this woman is, and when I get back to New York I'm going to go and see her.'

'Why don't you fly back with Daddy tomorrow morning? You'd be company for each other and you could ask him then.'

'Good idea.' Restlessly, Rebecca got up and started pacing around Jenny's prettily cluttered drawing-room. Slim, in black tailored trousers and a black and white sweater, her face looked pinched and pale.

'Are you sure you're well enough to go?' Jenny asked.

'Really, I'm fine.'

'Stirling will be thrilled you're going back.'

'I'm not telling him. He'd be furious and what's the point? He's probably being followed too, so I plan to lie low for a bit when I return and do some investigative work on my own. It will be better for him if he doesn't know I'm back.'

'Where will you stay?'

'In my apartment, where else?'

'That's not a good idea, Rebecca. Stay with Daddy. He's got a guest suite which I always use, and I know he'd like you to be there. The security in his building is very good, and Scott and Maria live in so you'd never be on your own at night.'

'Oh, Jenny, that's sweet of you, but I couldn't possibly impose on your father.'

'Nonsense.' Jenny sounded brisk. 'You wouldn't be in this mess if it hadn't been for Daddy. I'll call him now, get him to arrange for you to be on his flight in the morning, and tell him you'll be staying at his apartment.'

'Are you sure?' Rebecca asked. She had always taken such pride in being independent from the moment she'd arrived in New York, four years ago, and this seemed like admitting failure.

'Of course I'm sure,' Jenny said positively. 'The situation is too dangerous for you to be living on your own.'

'I must say, Mike Wilson's murder has put a different light on it all. These people are obviously prepared to do a lot more than just threaten.'

'I wish I was coming to New York with you.'

'You'll be over at Easter, won't you?'

Jenny brightened. 'I certainly will. I'm leaving Trevor House at the end of this term and now that I've decided to go, I can't wait. I've no idea what I'm going to do, but whatever it is, it has to be more exciting.'

'I'll take those pictures of you when you come over. I'm sorry there hasn't been time since I got back from Paris, but we'll go into Central Park and make a real session of it. OK?'

'That would be great. I hope I'll have lost some more weight by then, too.'

'Your make-up is good.'

Jenny giggled and looked at herself in the mirror above the fireplace. 'One of the other teachers said I was putting too much on, so I've tried to tone it down a bit.'

Rebecca put her head to one side and looked at Jenny as critically as if she'd been assessing a model. 'Ummmm. With your peaches and cream skin, you don't need much. You've got very good bone structure.'

Jenny's eyebrows shot up. 'Have I? Mummy always told me I was plain, and Daddy . . . well, Daddy . . .' her voice faltered.

'All parents are too close to their children to see the wood for the trees,' Rebecca said briskly. 'Let's do some shopping in Bloomingdale's and Bergdorf Goodman when you come over and we'll surprise them all.'

Sir Edward and Rebecca took their seats in the front row of the first-class compartment of the Pan Am Boeing 747 early the next morning, fussed over by the airline staff who were obviously in awe of the famous financier. Eager hands offered them a champagne breakfast, newspapers, magazines, rugs, pillows, eye shades and soft slippers. Sir Edward accepted everything with smiling graciousness, but Rebecca stuck to her usual mineral water and nothing else. Once airborne, she drew the photograph of Sly Capra out of her hand luggage and showed it to Sir Edward.

'Do you know who this man is?' she asked.

He shook his head. 'Never seen him before, but I know the girl.'

'Yes, Jenny told me you knew her. What's her name?'

'Um . . . Oh, I'm so bad at names.' He reached into an inner pocket and drew out a slim address book. A moment later he gave a grunt of triumph. 'Here it is. Theresa Bendotto.'

'This picture was taken at your party. I presume you invited her?'

He thought for a moment before replying. 'Yes, I did. Theresa and Manuel Bendotto give a lot of money to charity, and I thought they'd be helpful with some of the causes I support. Come to think of it, though, I don't remember seeing them that night; not that I remember much about that evening anyway, as you know,' he added drily.

'You've no idea who this man is then?'

'No.' Sir Edward looked at her inquiringly. 'Should I?'

'It's Sly Capra.'

He gave an involuntary gasp and snatched the photograph out of her hand. Then he studied it for several minutes without saying anything. Rebecca could see his mind was in a turmoil as he looked at the face of the man he'd been told had killed Marissa. After a while Rebecca broke into his thoughts.

'Can you tell me how to get hold of this Theresa Bendotto?' she asked.

'They've got an apartment on the East Side, near the United Nations Headquarters. I'll give you the address.'

'Thanks. I think I'll go and see her on the pretext of taking her picture for an assignment. Manhattan Hostesses, or Best Dressed Women, or something like that.'

'You'd do better if you angled it towards charities,' Sir Edward advised. 'As I said, they're very generous because they know that's the way to social climb. They'll do anything in the name of charity.'

Rebecca smiled knowingly. 'Then I'll say I'm doing a feature on Beautiful Benefactresses.'

Sir Edward smiled. 'That should get you in anywhere. Will you ask her outright if she knows Sly Capra?'

'I'll play it by ear, but I have a feeling she brought him to your party instead of her husband. Could she be connected with the Mafia?'

Sir Edward looked shocked. 'My God, I don't think so, but how can one tell? Anyone with money can infiltrate society these days. One has no way of knowing who people really are.'

'Where the hell is Rebecca?' Stirling slammed down the phone, his feelings of anxiety surmounting his frustration and anger.

Minah looked up from sorting through a pile of photographs. 'Anything I can do, Stirling?' Her beautiful black face showed concern.

Stirling swore. 'I've been trying to get hold of her for two days now

197

and there's no reply from the place where she's staying in London, and yet I know three girls share the apartment. I've left messages on the answering machine, too, but she hasn't got back to me.'

'Maybe she's been very busy. She's sent back some great shots on this trip, hasn't she?' Minah suggested. 'Perhaps she's got caught up on another royal scoop?'

'Ummm.' Stirling scowled, unwilling to explain why he was so worried. The last contact he'd had with Rebecca had been a couple of days before, when she'd called him up to say she'd taken some pictures of Princess Diana's sons. It wasn't like her not to stay in contact or respond to messages.

When Minah took her lunch break, he called Rebecca's parents in New Hampshire. He'd had the phone checked for bugs and none had been found, so it was safe to make personal calls.

'I'm sorry, dear, but Becky hasn't been in touch,' her mother told him when he got through. 'Isn't she still in Europe?'

'That's right. Don't worry, Mrs Kendall. I'm sure I'll catch up with her soon.' Stirling tried to sound casual. There was no point in alarming Rebecca's family.

'Well, if she calls us I'll tell her you're trying to get in touch with her. When are you both coming for a weekend again?'

Stirling was fond of Pam and Douglas Kendall and he and Rebecca always enjoyed staying at the historic old house on the edge of Lake Winnispesaukee. The Kendalls were a warm and intelligent family, and the house seemed to overflow with books and music, stimulating conversation and good humour.

'Just as soon as we can make it,' Stirling responded with sincerity. 'I'll be in touch.'

'Give her our love if you speak to her first. Goodbye, dear.'

'Goodbye.' When Stirling hung up, he reflected that a lot of Rebecca's strength and confidence were the result of her parents' loving and supportive attitude. They'd given her a sense of self-worth that nothing could diminish.

Stirling dialled Karen's office number next. Perhaps she'd heard from Rebecca, he hoped.

'Why should I have heard anything?' she asked bluntly when he got through. 'You must know where she is?'

'I know where she's staying, but she never seems to be there,' Stirling said shortly. Then he added: 'Is everything all right with you?'

'You bet! I've met the most gorgeous guy called Geoffrey. He's in advertising, and so dishy you wouldn't believe!'

'That's nice.'

'Yes, you and Rebecca must meet him. We'll get together when she gets back. Have there been any more developments, by the way? Any repercussions from her leaving the wrong films at the Post Office? I miss hearing all the latest about the on-going saga of Marissa Montclare.'

He decided to take her into his confidence. 'I haven't heard from Rebecca for two days now and I'm worried. She usually calls me every morning. She's been receiving more threatening messages, you know, and she thinks she was tailed in Paris. I insisted she go into hiding when she got to London, but I didn't expect her to hide from me, for God's sake.' He gave a shaky laugh.

'Aren't you being a bit dramatic? You know how independent Rebecca is. I've never met anyone so self-sufficient. I don't believe whoever killed Marissa would try and kill Rebecca, do you?'

Stirling told her about Mike Wilson.

'Jes-us!' Then there was a stunned silence before Karen exclaimed: 'Why don't you get police protection? This really is serious, Stirling.' It was as if she'd only just grasped the situation could be life-threatening. 'Hey! Supposing I was seen, watching in the Post Office that day? What if they come after me?'

Stirling tried to soothe her. 'I shouldn't worry too much if I were you. Just keep a look out for anything unusual.'

There was silence on the line while Karen digested this. Then she said: 'Geoffrey isn't going to believe his luck!'

'Why?'

'Because I'm moving right in with him tonight! It beats staying with my sister. I'm scared, Stirling.'

Typical, he thought. Trust Karen to be both self-obsessed and man-mad at the same time. Aloud he said genially: 'You do that Karen. I'm sure Geoffrey's a very lucky guy.'

'You bet your ass he is!'

Vaguely, Stirling wondered why Rebecca had chosen Karen as a roommate. They couldn't have been less alike.

Later that day, unable to concentrate on work, Stirling went over to Bill's apartment, arriving on the doorstep with a large pizza and a six-pack of Corona beer. Bill's face was a study of horror and pity when he saw the provisions.

'Dear God, a pizza? Stirling, my old buddy, if I'd known you wanted to eat we could have gone to Leoni's or Tio Pepe's or Fu Tong. I do their public relations, remember? I'm allowed freebies for myself and my friends!' He took the pizza from Stirling and laid it with mock reverence on his kitchen table.

Stirling ignored Bill's banter, his tall lean frame filling the kitchen as he ran his hands nervously through his hair. 'I've got to talk to you.'

'Surely we can talk in a restaurant?' Bill reasoned mildly.

'No, not really. This is serious stuff, and I want to ask your advice. I'm sorry to do this to you, but if I don't talk to someone I'll go crazy.'

'OK, but let's ignore that disgusting-looking pizza for the moment and just have a beer. Perhaps we can eat out later.' Bill led the way into his living-room where the clutter was greater than usual. Since his divorce, he'd been looking after himself and it showed. Clearing to one side a stack of press releases headed 'Tio Pepe Restaurant', he waved for Stirling to sit on the sofa while he himself perched on the edge of his desk. 'So what's your problem?'

Stirling flopped, his long legs seeming to stretch halfway across the room. Then he told Bill the whole story, ending up with the visit Mike had paid him before he'd been murdered. 'Now I can't get hold of Rebecca in over two days, and I'm going crazy thinking that something has happened to her.'

'Woah! Steady!' Bill sounded as if he were trying to soothe a runaway horse. 'To begin with I wouldn't worry about Rebecca. That's one woman who has always been able to look after herself.'

Stirling frowned. 'Even so . . .' he protested.

'Hang on a minute. That story you just told me about Mike Wilson having a meeting with Sly Capra's partner, and being told all about the insider trading scam he had going with Marissa, and then getting murdered because he knew too much . . .'

'Yes.'

'You're probably right, but there's one fatal flaw to your theory.' Bill's charmingly ugly face was alive with intelligence. 'Why should this man tell Mike Wilson anything? And why tell him all these things only to have him bumped off a few hours later for knowing too much? It doesn't make sense.'

Stirling nodded. 'I absolutely agree, and yet I'd swear that everything Wilson told me was true. Personally, I believe he bluffed Sly's partner into thinking that he knew a great deal more than he did, and by accident hit the nail on the head. That was why he had to be eliminated. His wild guesses may have been true, but Sly's partner wouldn't have had any way to know Mike was only guessing.'

'You really think Marissa and Sly Capra were doing a number on Sir Edward Wenlake?'

'Actually it doesn't surprise me at all. Looking back, the whole picture fits. All the unanswered questions about Marissa's wealth and position become clear when you realize what she was up to. It's also a fact that she won the jackpot at the Golden Palm in Las Vegas, and that was when she seems to have become involved with this gang.'

'They probably own the casino in the first place. I wonder if they fixed for her to win so they could use her?' Bill added thoughtfully.

Stirling looked doubtful. 'On one-armed bandit machines it would be impossible. Now if she'd been playing roulette or black jack, you'd have a point. The question is, what do I do now? Where do I go from here?'

Bill tugged thoughtfully at the blue silk cord and tassel that held one of the Quo Vadis menu pages together. 'Why not go to the source, to where it all began?'

'How do you mean?'

'Take a trip to Las Vegas and try and find out as much as you can about Marissa's life before she won the Jackpot. She must have had friends, known other dancers! Try and find out what made her tick, and it might lead you to something. You might be able to piece together this whole mess and get to the bottom of it.'

Stirling sucked in his lower lip, then hauled himself to his feet and restlessly prowled the room, his hands deep in his pockets. 'That's a good idea, but I can't do anything until I find out what's happened to Rebecca.'

'Nothing's happened to Rebecca. She's probably partying in London, having the time of her life.'

'I hope to God you're right.'

'Of course I'm right! Now stop worrying and let's eat.' Bill cast a good-humoured glance in Stirling's direction. 'Let's bin that god-awful pizza and have a decent dinner! How can you possibly stay calm on a diet of junk food?'

Stirling grinned in spite of himself. 'OK, you win. What's it going to be? "The best of Italian cooking" or "authentic dishes from the Orient"?'

Chapter Twelve

The ice sparkled and glittered like chips of crystal between the ancient cobbled stones of the courtyard, as Angela, her wrap pulled tightly around her, picked her way across them, stepping carefully so as not to slip. Above, a clear moon cast its chilly light on a deserted countryside and in the distance a dog barked in sudden agitation, as if it sensed something was about to happen and by barking could give warning.

Clutching her bag tightly she took the path that led to the outer buildings beyond the high-walled kitchen garden, passing on her left the large greenhouse that loomed dark and glassy now, nursery to a thousand seedlings that would one day fill the herbaceous borders with blooms. On either side of the path, high hedges of speckled laurel rustled as a sharp breeze sprang up, sending freezing gusts around her feet. In the distance she could hear the soughing of the wind in the trees.

Nothing must stop me now, Angela thought as the lights from the house receded into the distance and the wildness of the night foreshadowed the storm that was to come. This is something I have to do, because my soul will know no peace until it is done.

At last she reached the out-houses, which bore the date 1610 cunningly worked in contrasting coloured bricks on the clock tower. On top, a weather-vane vacillated and shuddered as the wind, growing in strength, whipped across the roof of the buildings. Angela stood listening, making sure none of the staff had followed her. No one must be allowed to stop her now. Then she opened her bag and slowly drew out the Luger. It lay heavy and cold in her hand, the instrument that would help assuage her guilt.

For several moments she stood looking down at it, contemplating the repercussions of what she was about to do. Some people were going to think she was mad, unbalanced, distraught, but she didn't care. Let them talk! She'd been through so much in the past few weeks, first with the humiliation of Edward's notoriety and then Simon's accident, that she was beyond caring.

203

With steady hands she undid the safety catch of the revolver, and dropping her bag on to the frosted grass verge stepped towards the out-buildings.

A minute later a shot rang out, echoing in the darkness, awakening the rooks in the nearby trees so that they croaked nervously, alerting each other to danger. The gale, bringing with it lashing rain, reflected the violence of the explosion as if the elements were condemning the wilful act.

'Rebecca!' The relief in Stirling's voice echoed down the line. 'Where the hell have you been? I've been going out of my mind with worry.'

'I'm staying at Sir Edward's apartment.'

'Oh? I didn't know he had an apartment in London. Why aren't you still at Jenny's?'

'Not in London, Stirling. I'm here . . . in New York.'

'You're *what*?'

'Yes.'

'For Chrissakes!' Stirling yelled. 'Why didn't you tell me? What are you doing here? Don't you realize you're in O'Hara's precinct? Oh, Rebecca!'

He only calls me by my full name when he's angry with me, she thought, but it was what she expected. 'What sort of a welcome is that?' she asked, trying to keep it light.

'I'll tell you what sort of a welcome it is: you've had me scared to death! What the hell are you playing at?'

'I'm not playing at anything! I knew you'd get upset about my coming home and that you'd try to stop me, but I've got to get to the bottom of this business, Stirling, and I'm not going to do that by running away! I could have gone back to my own apartment,' she added defiantly, 'but Sir Edward and Jenny insisted I stay with him because the security is better than at my place.'

'But you had no right to come home at all! I told you to stay . . .'

Rebecca cut in icily. 'You don't tell me what to do, Stirling. I'm my own person and always have been. This is my home town, just as much as it's yours, so stop talking crap.' She was angry too now. How dare he treat her as if she were a child.

'But what are you doing? Don't you realize these people are dangerous . . . that they'll stop at nothing? You're out to lunch if you think you can take them on single-handed, with not even the police to offer protection.'

'I have my own enquiries to make. I've got a lead, and I want to pursue it.'

'What sort of lead?'

'You know that picture of Sly Capra at the party? Well, in an hour's time I'm seeing the blonde he's with. If you're interested in finding out how I get on, why not meet me for lunch at Sandolino's at one o'clock?' She sounded cool and confident and it infuriated him.

'Rebecca, for God's sake! Where does she live? You could be walking right into a trap. You mustn't go.'

'I've made the arrangements.'

'Then let me go with you.'

'No, Stirling. I got into this thing in the first place and I'm going to see it through. Don't worry,' she added more gently, understanding how he felt but still determined to go ahead and do it her way, 'I'll be all right. This woman and her husband are friends of Sir Edward and they're great social climbers. I'm hardly likely to get bumped off in their duplex. Think how bad it would be for their image.'

'I still don't like it,' he said grudgingly.

'But are you going to meet me for lunch?'

She sounded flippant now, as if she were doing nothing more serious than going to Bloomingdale's to buy some clothes.

'I suppose so, but for God's sake be careful.'

'I'll be fine. See you later.' There was a click. She'd hung up.

'Fuck!' Stirling swore, slamming the phone down in frustration, wondering how he was going to get through the morning until he saw her again.

Sir Edward had told Rebecca that Theresa and Manuel Bendotto's apartment was on the East Side. Although she knew the area, she was unprepared for the magnificence of their home situated in a block on Mitchell Place. She was whisked up to the twelfth floor by one of the uniformed doormen who patrolled the imposing entrance, and then greeted by a young English butler who offered her some refreshment.

'I'd like some coffee, please,' she replied, putting her camera bag down and looking around. Although it was a grey wintry morning the large drawing-room she'd been shown into was filled by a peachy golden glow, glittering with crystal and perfumed by great bowls of pink roses. Pink silk brocade covered the walls and was echoed in the French gilt furnishings. A priceless tapestry rug covered the polished floor, and apple wood blazed in the white marble Louis XV fireplace. Through the filmy voile curtains that festooned the long windows, Rebecca could see the East River, flowing turgidly along.

Into this bower of pink opulence came Theresa Bendotto, a few minutes late, skinny in a tight white woollen dress with long sleeves and a skirt so short it hugged her thighs. Her blonde hair was wound up into what looked like a casual topknot, an effect which Rebecca guessed must have taken a hairdresser an hour to achieve, and her make-up was immaculate. As she came forward, her left hand hovered over the pearls round her neck and the large pink diamond ring had slipped around as if too large for her bony finger.

'Hello,' she greeted Rebecca. 'I'm sorry to have kept you waiting. So many calls, you know, from all over: Bermuda, Acapulco, Hawaii. I don't know, it never seems to stop. We have so many friends. I hope you've been offered some refreshment? Now, where do you want to take these pictures? Are they for a magazine?' Without bothering to wait for answers, Theresa Bendotto rattled nervously on, a constant smile fixed on her face, revealing perfectly capped teeth.

'I think this room would be perfect,' Rebecca replied. From her point of view it was. It told more about Mrs Manuel Bendotto than anything else could: her love of luxury, her fixation with pink, her predeliction for fripperies, and of course her great wealth. Rebecca decided to photograph Theresa sitting on one of the brocade sofas, surrounded by the white satin cushions, vases of roses, and with mirrors and chandeliers sparkling in the background.

A pot of coffee was brought on a large ornate silver tray, and the butler's white-gloved hands poured it into fine china cups. Rebecca set up her telescopic tripod and chattered inconsequentially in order to get Theresa to relax.

'You have a beautiful place here. Did you design it yourself?' she enquired ingenuously.

'Oh, yes, of course.' Theresa's eyes flickered nervously around the room and Rebecca knew she was lying. 'I've also designed my husband's office. It's been photographed for a magazine as a perfect example of contemporary interior design.'

'That must give you great satisfaction,' Rebecca said seriously. Theresa squirmed slightly on the sofa and gave a false smile. Rebecca decided to move on to a subject that would make her less uptight.

'I believe you work very hard for various charities?'

'Oh, I do. I work very, very hard,' Theresa trilled. 'Nobody realizes what hard work fund-raising is! I'm chairman of the Fantasy Flower Ball which is to raise money for Cancer Research.'

'How wonderful,' Rebecca said genuinely. 'Now, Mrs Bendotto, if you could look this way – oh, that's fantastic! Hold it, just like that, while I get a shot!' Rebecca's flattery soon had Theresa Bendotto beaming with pleasure.

Rebecca had been waiting for the right moment to put her plan into operation and she reckoned it was now or never.

'I have photographed you before, you know. Do you remember?'

Theresa looked puzzled, her narrow forehead puckered. 'I don't think so . . .'

'I may even have the shot with me,' Rebecca continued, delving into her camera bag. 'Yes. Here it is! Taken at a party.' She purposely didn't say which.

Theresa took the photograph from her. 'Goodness, I don't remember this being taken! What a mess my hair looks! Has it appeared in any magazines?' Being in magazines seemed to be more important to her than anything, thought Rebecca.

'No, it hasn't been published.'

'When was it taken?'

There was a pause, and then Rebecca said quietly, 'On New Year's Eve.'

For a moment Theresa's eyes were expressionless and then she shot Rebecca a startled look. 'Oh, New Year's Eve? At Sir Edward Wenlake's party? I remember now, but I still don't recall this picture being taken. I bought that dress specially for that night. I don't think I've worn it since. Do you think it's a bit short? Manuel said he thought it was a bit short, especially as there were going to be so many older people there. I wish I'd known you were taking this . . . I'd have done something with my hair.' She was still frowning at the picture.

'Were you still there when the accident happened?'

'You mean when that chorus girl fell from a window?' She looked vague. 'I think so.'

Without looking up, but watching Theresa's reactions through the viewfinder lens of the Hasselblad, Rebecca continued: 'That's your husband with you in the picture, I suppose?'

'No, that's not Manuel.' She peered closer and Rebecca realized her eyesight was bad. 'I don't know who it is, but he's quite dishy, isn't he? What made you think he was my husband? Manuel couldn't go to Sir Edward's party because he was in bed with 'flu, so I went with my sister instead.' Suddenly she looked up suspiciously, scrawny as a bird. 'Why do you ask? You're not going to put this photograph in a magazine, are you? My husband doesn't like me being photographed with other men.'

'No, this picture is not for publication,' Rebecca assured her placatingly. 'I just thought it would amuse you to see it.'

Theresa handed it back to her, a touch coolly. 'I wouldn't want Manuel to see it.'

Rebecca slid the print back into her case. 'No problem. Now, if you could look up, turn your shoulders to the left a bit . . .' Coaxingly, hiding her disappointment at having drawn a blank, Rebecca humoured Theresa until she was in a good mood again, this time talking about her favourite dress designers. It gave Rebecca the opportunity to slide in another leading question.

'It was awful what happened at the party, wasn't it? I suppose Marissa Montclare must be greatly missed by her friends.'

The heavily mascaraed eyes were impenetrable. Theresa shrugged her narrow shoulders. 'I wouldn't know. We moved in different circles.'

Rebecca feigned surprise. 'Oh, I thought she was a friend of yours? Everyone who knows Sir Edward well seems to have known Marissa too.'

The essence of the remark was not lost on Theresa. 'Oh, well, we met her often through dear Sir Edward,' she cooed, 'but I wouldn't say she was actually a friend. I mean . . . you know . . . she did come from a very different background. Manuel and I could never understand what an aristocratic English gentleman like him was doing with a girl like that.'

Rebecca's mouth tightened but she said nothing. When she left the Bendotto's apartment ten minutes later she knew she'd wasted her time. It was a coincidence that Theresa Bendotto had been photographed talking to Sly Capra and nothing more.

It was not yet noon, too early to go to Sandolino's, so Rebecca hailed a cab. She wanted to check out her own apartment. When she arrived, she hurried up the front steps of the building, bumping into her neighbour from the first floor, the choreographer, who came bounding out.

'Hello, dah-ling!' he greeted her breezily. 'Long time no see. Been shacking up with the boyfriend?'

Rebecca grinned. 'I've been in Europe, I only just got back. How are things? Any excitement since I've been away?'

'Depends what you mean by excitement, my sweet.'

'Rape, murder, arson, burglary,' she joked.

'Nothing worth stealing in this dump, dah-ling. I keep my jewels close to my body.'

'What jewels?' she laughed.

'The crown jewels, what else, my sweet? Every queen has her crown jewels!' With a wave he was off, running down the street looking deceptively boyish in his track suit.

Rebecca's apartment was exactly as she'd left it and for a moment she longed to move back and resume the pleasant life she and Karen had shared there for the past year or so. The sitting-room was deserted and cold now, as if it needed the sound of voices and the warmth of bodies to inject fresh life into it; their bedrooms looked small and bleak with clothes hanging limply in the closets; the little kitchen, once so cheerful with its high red stools and poppy-patterned mugs, now sulked in the grey light that filtered through the window. She turned away and went into the darkroom, which still stank of formaldehyde. Until the insurance money came through she couldn't afford to refit it and replace all the equipment. Meanwhile it was a depressing sight.

For a moment she felt quite nauseous from the suffocating smell as she looked at the stained walls and floor and the ruined boxes of printing paper. So much of her life had been centred in this small room and now it lay wrecked. Sadly, she returned to the living-room. There were some messages on the answering machine, and with a feeling of dread she sat down and switched it on.

The first message was from a well-known magazine editor, suggesting they meet for lunch; then there was a call from an old school-friend from New Hampshire, asking if Rebecca could put her up for the night. There were several messages for Karen from a variety of young men who had names like Teddy and Max, Davie and Johnnie; all leaving their numbers, all asking Karen to call them back. Then there was a click, and Rebecca stiffened with fear as the warm pleasant voice of Jerry Ribis filled the room.

'Hello, Rebecca. This is Jerry. I hope you enjoyed your trip to Europe. How about lunch one day? I'll call you again and let's get together real soon. Bye.'

They came running from the house, sprinting through the rain in the darkness, shouting to each other in speculation. Peters reached the stable block first, with Jones the gardener just behind him. Following on their heels were Ruby and Heather, panting so that their breath curled into the freezing air like smoke.

'One of the stable doors is open,' Peters shouted. 'Where's that light?'

Jones thrust the battery powered torch forward. ' 'ere. Can you see anything?'

Peters snatched the torch from him and shone its bright white beam through the open door.

'Shall I dial 999?' Ruby asked excitedly, her curly hair plastered to her head by the rain.

'Quiet, girl! No need to bring in the police unless we have to,' Heather admonished. 'Her Ladyship wouldn't like it.'

Peters stepped forward, filling the gap in the open stable doorway, smelling the sweet scent of hay as he swung the torch around.

' 'ere, Mr Peters,' said Jones, 'wot's 'appening?'

The others could tell by Peters' rigid stance that something was very wrong. When he spoke it was in a tight voice.

'Go back to the house. There's nothing to be done. Now go back.'

Heather and Ruby peered at each other in the darkness, their faces wet, wondering what was wrong. And then they looked at Jones. He shrugged his shoulders and turned up the collar of his jacket.

'Do as I say. Go back to the house,' repeated Peters. Uncertainly, they started shuffling away, not so sure-footed in the dark now that the emergency seemed to be over.

'Shall I dial 999?' Ruby asked again.

'No! For goodness' sake don't do that.' Peters spoke urgently. 'Go away.'

When they'd left and he stood alone again, he became aware of noises he hadn't noticed before. Gentle snortings and snufflings from the adjoining stables, the occasional clop of a hoof on cobblestones, the swish of a tail. Then he stepped forward, his heart contracting with pity and pain at the sight that met his eyes.

Angela Wenlake crouched on her haunches by the side of Clover, the roan mare that had been her Christmas present to Simon, the horse that had thrown him and accidentally rolled on him.

'There, girl, there,' Angela was saying softly, stroking its neck. 'That wasn't too bad, was it? There, there.' Her diamond rings winked in the semi-darkness as she gently smoothed the silky hair, repeating the gesture over and over while her voice continued to speak soothingly and comfortingly. But Peters, his torch directed at the horse's head, had already seen the dark round bullet hole, dripping blood, that pierced Clover's forehead between the laid back ears, and the sad eyes that gazed opaque in death.

'Am I glad to see you!' Stirling swept Rebecca up in his arms, his anger vanishing the moment he saw her arriving at Sandolino's. He pressed his cheek against hers and hugged her close. 'It's wonderful to have you back, Becky. I have missed you.'

Rebecca looked laughingly up into his face. 'That's better! I thought you were never going to speak to me again. I've missed you too, by the way.' She reached up to kiss him on the mouth.

'I've made a reservation,' he announced, as they entered the restaurant together. 'Tell me about this morning. I've been worried sick about your going off to see this woman.'

Rebecca shrugged. 'I'm afraid it was a waste of time. It was just a coincidence that I photographed her with Sly Capra. She doesn't know him, and she wasn't a friend of Marissa's either.'

'Well, thank God for that is all I can say,' Stirling retorted. 'At least you're still in one piece.'

'And hungry! Can I have the chicken-stuffed tortillas in chilli sauce, with roasted corn-on-the-cob?'

'You can have anything you like, my sweetheart.' He reached across the table and took her hand. 'I've really been worried about you, you know.'

'There's no point in worrying, Stirling. Life must go on. Obviously I'm being as careful as I can, and my self-defence classes have made me much more confident. There's nothing else we can do. By the way, Jerry Ribis knows I'm back in town.'

'The man you think is also Sly Capra?' Stirling sounded tense.

'No, he's not. I meant to tell you that I've never seen the man in the photograph you sent me. Jerry looks quite different.'

'But he's watching your every move! Perhaps he's Sly's partner? The one Mike Wilson met? What makes you think he knows you've returned to New York?'

'Because there was a message from him on my answering machine when I went to my own apartment just now.'

Stirling looked ready to explode again. 'You went . . . ? What the hell were you doing at your apartment, of all places? I thought you were supposed to be staying with Sir Edward?'

'I am. I just wanted to check out my own place and I had some time to kill before lunch.'

'And why aren't you staying with me? There's nothing wrong with the security in my building.' He sounded angry now.

'I didn't want you to know I was coming back because I knew you'd try to stop me.'

'Oh, for God's sake! What did this Jerry Ribis say in his message?'

'He welcomed me home and suggested we meet for lunch some time.'

'Oh, I see. All very cosy! And I suppose you're going?'

'Don't be ridiculous. Of course I'm not going,' she retorted. 'I don't know what his game is, but I know he's up to his ears in this business, and either he or Sly Capra, or the waiter for that matter, pushed Marissa out the window that night. I wish I'd taken a picture of Jerry too. How are we going to bring this thing to a head, Stirling? I'm sick to death of being spied upon, never knowing what's going to happen next.'

He reached over and took her hand. For a change his voice was coaxing. 'Before we do anything, darling, you're moving back to my place. Today. What on earth possessed you to stay at Sir Edward's?' He sounded genuinely hurt.

Rebecca squeezed his hand. 'I'm sorry. You know how I hate being fussed over.' Her tone was conciliatory though. 'It seemed like a good idea when Jenny suggested it. I'm still hoping Sir Edward may be able to help me track down these people.'

'I think it's unlikely, Becky. He's far too protective of himself and the Tollemache Trust to want to get more involved than he has to. So you'll move back in with me tonight?' His eyes were filled with longing now, and her heart skipped a beat.

'Yes. I'll move back tonight.'

'God, I love you, Becky.'

'So you should!' she quipped. 'Where else are you going to find a talented, hardworking, successful, beautiful, rich career girl . . . who can heat up a frozen dinner for two?'

'Let me help you into the house, m'lady,' Peters' voice was shocked. Never in all his life had he seen anything so dreadful as the sight of his autocratic employer sitting crouched over the dead horse as she continued to talk to it. The pistol still lay on the velvet of her outspread skirt. He took it quickly, slipping it behind the manger in case she tried to use it again. By torchlight the stable was an eerie place. He wished that Fred who looked after the horses had been around, but he and his family lived in a small lodge by the entrance gates to Pinkney House.

'I think we'd better get indoors, m'lady,' he said. 'It's very cold out here and you'll catch a chill.'

Angela Wenlake didn't answer. Looking at her pale, finely lined face he wondered if she'd even heard. Was she aware of what she'd done? Her well-manicured hand continued to stroke the mare's neck but her eyes looked blank, as if she were sleep-walking. Peters tried again.

'M'lady, it really is time we went back to the house. Come along now. I'll help you.'

This time Angela looked up as if he'd spoken for the first time, a half-surprised, half-annoyed expression on her face.

'You can call the knacker's yard in the morning,' she said, in a perfectly ordinary voice, rising as she spoke. Wisps of straw clung to her dress. She brushed them off fastidiously. Then, unaided, she walked briskly in the direction of the house, with Peters following awkwardly behind.

As she entered the hall she turned and looked calmly at him. 'You can serve dinner in ten minutes please.'

'Certainly, m'lady.'

'And I should be grateful if you and the rest of the staff would refrain from gossiping about what happened tonight.'

'Of course, m'lady.'

Then Angela turned and walked up the stairs to her bedroom without saying another word. Peters hurried into the kitchen where Jones, Heather and Ruby stood huddled, trying to get dry in front of the Aga cooker.

'What's happened?' Heather asked fearfully.

Peters' deferential and precise manner evaporated with Angela's departure upstairs. In his customary way when with his own sort, he ended every statement with a question.

'She's only sodding well flipped, hasn't she?'

'What d'you mean?'

'She only went and killed Mr Simon's new horse, didn't she?'

'Eh, I don't believe it.' Jones and Ruby joined Heather in a series of astonished gasps.

'Well, you'd better.' Peters sounded grim. 'I've got to call the bleeding knacker's yard in the morning, haven't I?'

Back at the agency, Stirling sent Minah out to do some shopping for him, giving her a list that included large fresh shrimps and a variety of cheese and fruit, crusty bread and a bottle of wine. He wanted Rebecca's first night back at his apartment to be romantic and perfect, and so he also asked Minah to get some flowers and chocolates, a box of candles and Rebecca's favourite crystallised pears.

'Just one more thing,' he said as he scribbled on the memo pad again, 'get a bottle of Beautiful by Estée Lauder, will you? It's the one in a pink and gold box. It's Rebecca's favourite perfume.'

Minah grinned, showing perfectly even white teeth. 'Sure thing, boss! Anything else?' Her black eyes sparkled. 'The odd diamond ring?'

Stirling grinned back. 'Maybe next week.'

At five-thirty, he turned up at Sir Edward's apartment with Minah's purchases in the trunk of his car. Rebecca was ready packed and busy writing a 'thank you' note to leave for her host.

'OK, darling?' Stirling asked, helping her with her cases.

Rebecca smiled back at him, happy they were together again. 'I'm fine, Stirling.' Together they went down in the elevator and out on to the sidewalk where the doorman helped load her luggage into the car.

'What's all this?' she asked, eyeing the profusion of provisions and flowers in the trunk.

'Tonight's dinner.'

She looked up at him, round-eyed. 'Are we entertaining?'

'Nope. Just you and me. I got in all the things you like.'

Touched, she turned and reached up to kiss him. He clasped her in a bear hug. As she looked over his shoulder she saw a car cruise slowly past, the driver watching them out of the side window.

'What is it?' Stirling felt her stiffen, but as he turned to look the car sped off. 'Who was that?'

Rebecca's face was white. 'Jerry Ribis.'

They had eaten supper and drunk the delicious bottle of chilled Chablis. Now, as they got ready for bed, Rebecca realized how much she'd missed Stirling. Her body ached for him as she watched him undress, the sight of his tight round buttocks and muscular thighs filling her with desire. Quickly, she slipped out of her own clothes, conscious of her breasts tingling with longing for his touch, and her insides dissolving with heat. She wanted him and she wanted him now. There was no time for showers and getting into bed, no need for preparation and foreplay. It had been over three weeks since they'd made love, and now she was burning for him with all the excitement she'd felt the very first time years before.

A feeling of limpness and weakness engulfed her as she reached out for him. At once Stirling had his arms around her, sensing her need, supporting her as he pushed her back against the bedroom wall.

'Oh, Stirling,' she whispered, closing her eyes, feeling his body pressed against hers, feeling him enter her with one glorious and triumphant thrust so that, impaled, she clung to him, her arms round his neck, her feet not even touching the ground. For a moment she thought she would faint at the exquisite sensation which flooded her body. Then she relaxed against him, giving herself to him in a rush of passionate love.

Without a word Stirling brought them both to a climax until they leaned, breathless and exhausted, against the wall. Then, with his last ounce of strength, he picked her up and carried her over to the bed.

214

'You're staying with me forever,' he whispered, still holding her in his arms. 'I'm never going to let you go again.'

Rebecca snuggled closer, too spent to argue. She loved being with Stirling. He turned her on and satisfied her and she knew she was tremendously lucky, but she wasn't prepared to give up her independence yet. There was too much to achieve; too many things she wanted to do. As soon as it was safe she'd go back to living in her own apartment – but in the meantime, why start an argument? She kissed his neck and told him again how much she loved him. Content then, he fell asleep in her arms.

'England must have agreed with you,' he observed as they showered later.

Rebecca looked at her reflection in the mirror, and saw how clear and radiant her skin looked and how glossily her hair hung down her back. 'I can't think why,' she remarked, 'unless it was the cold damp weather.'

'It's not that,' Stirling observed, giving her bottom a playful smack. 'You've put on weight.'

After Stirling had gone to the agency the next morning, Rebecca lingered over her coffee, reading the *Herald Tribune*. It was something she liked to do each morning, part of the pattern of her working day. Sometimes one of her own photographs had been reproduced, and then she paused to revel in her byline; but mostly she just went through the newspaper to get ideas for events she might cover. Most interesting were the small news stories, because they could sometimes be developed into good photographic features. Today there were the usual news items: comments on the rising balance of payments, the strengthening dollar, President Bush's latest statement on the economy. In Europe, Mrs Thatcher was having another contretemps with President Mitterrand of France, Mikhail Gorbachev was gaining popularity. Communism was collapsing, and Princess Diana was pictured visiting an AIDS clinic and shaking hands with the patients.

Rebecca skimmed down the various news columns to more local stories. An artist in Kentucky had modelled a 'geo-physical globe' measuring six feet in diameter with a price tag of $36,000 – which would make a good picture, she thought – and a footballer who had been fired from the Phoenix Bulls was quoted as saying: "I'm too young to retire and not rich enough, either." Nice human interest feature there, reflected Rebecca, turning to the back page where the International classified advertisements were listed. It was while she was glancing under the various headings of Real Estate,

Employment, Escorts & Guides and Business Services that she saw an ad under the single heading Wanted. To her astonishment she read that anyone who had been connected with the late Marissa Montclare should contact the box number provided, in order to learn something to their advantage.

Chapter Thirteen

Sir Edward also saw the advertisement in the *Herald Tribune* that morning and was consumed with curiosity. Immediately he asked his faithful secretary to contact the box number, acting under a pseudonym.

'I want complete discretion, Elsbeth,' he told her as he gave her the details. 'Think up a suitable false name, and for God's sake don't let on you've got anything to do with the Tollemache Trust.'

'I quite understand, Sir Edward. I'll use my cousin's address in Brooklyn. Shall I say I was a friend of Miss Montclare's?'

Sir Edward looked at the plain bony woman with her dingy skin and drab clothes. It was on the tip of his tongue to say: 'As long as they never see you', for to imagine she and Marissa as friends was impossible. Instead he said tactfully: 'Maybe a friend of her family. If you're asked, say you lost touch with her a couple of years ago.'

'Do you know what it's about?'

'I imagine she left a will and they're trying to contact the beneficiaries. That's the usual reason for this sort of ad.' Then he thought about Mike Wilson, hacked to death on a sidewalk because he had tangled with Marissa's associates and he felt a pang of guilt. 'Don't agree to meet them on any account. As soon as you get a reply, bring it to me. I won't involve you beyond that.'

'Very well, Sir Edward.'

When Elsbeth had returned to her office, Sir Edward buzzed Brian Norris on his intercom.

'Come into my office for a moment, will you?'

A minute later Brian bounced into the room. 'What is it?' he demanded, dropping into the leather chair facing Sir Edward's desk.

In the past few weeks he'd abandoned all thoughts of trying to step into Edward's shoes by bringing about a boardroom coup. It was too risky, and his plans to try and take control of the Tollemache Trust could easily backfire. Although convinced he could do the job, he was dealing with a wily old bird who also happened to

217

have the luck of the devil. Sir Edward had turned out to be a natural survivor, one of those people born under a lucky star. In trying to displace him, Brian could well be the one who ended up out in the cold. Edward also had the class system to back him, thought Brian bitterly. If it had been himself who'd been the centre of a scandal involving a showgirl young enough to be his granddaughter, he'd have gone down without trace. As it was, Sir Edward had emerged only slightly bruised by the affair, and with his bum in the butter as usual.

Sir Edward handed him the *Herald Tribune*.

'Take a look at his.' The advertisement was circled by a red ball-point. Brian read it silently and then exclaimed.

'Bugger! Will this thing never go away?'

Sir Edward looked surprised. 'You haven't been troubled by anything since the night Marissa died,' he pointed out in a pained voice.

'The hell I haven't!' Brian told him about the recent visit from David McNee of Lawson, Martin & Grant. 'He was ferreting about for information, trying to trace the money Marissa had left. Of course I sent him packing.'

Sir Edward nodded slowly. 'He must have taken over from the chap who was here before from the same company.' He wished he was good at remembering names. 'Anyway,' he continued, 'do you think we should contact this . . . what's his name?'

'David McNee.'

'Warn him that he might be in danger?'

'In danger of what?'

Sir Edward remembered that Brian probably hadn't heard that Mike Wilson had been murdered. He shrugged. 'Oh, I don't know,' he said casually. 'It's an unpleasant business.'

'I say we should mind our own business,' Brian replied tartly. 'Don't you know what this scandal nearly did to us?'

For a moment Sir Edward closed his eyes, knowing better than Brian what this whole affair had nearly done to the Tollemache Trust, and what it could still do if ever it came out that there had been insider trading going on. Even now, although Marissa was dead and the likelihood of a leak was small, he awoke in the middle of the night in a cold sweat of panic. For him, it seemed, the nightmare would never end. But this was something Brian didn't know and must never find out. To Brian, the greatest worry had been that the shares had dipped before recovering and becoming steady again.

'I know we had a sticky patch,' Sir Edward said evenly, 'but that's behind us now. People have short memories and our acquisition of Busby's Breweries, two days ago, has put us right at the top of the heap again.'

A disgruntled Brian went back to his office, but Sir Edward remained at his desk deep in thought, regretting now that he'd asked Elsbeth to respond to the advertisement. The more he reflected on it, the more he realized he might have placed her in danger just to satisfy his own curiosity. At that moment an important call came on the line from Tokyo, and then he had a meeting followed by a business lunch with the head of the giant Prinnie Corporation, and it was late afternoon before he remembered he wanted to tell Elsbeth to forget about replying to the advertisement.

But she was a conscientious secretary. She'd already composed a nice little letter, written by hand because she thought that looked genuinely amateurish, on plain writing-paper, saying she was an old friend of Marissa's parents and could she be of help in their inquiries? She'd signed it 'Ruth Warner' and had taken the precaution of mailing it in her lunch hour in a public post box instead of sending it through the Tollemache Trust mail room.

Rebecca's pictures of Princess Diana and two the little princes began appearing on the cover of some of the more popular magazines, filling her with pride as she walked down the street and saw them stacked up on the newsstands. They had reproduced brilliantly, in dazzling colour, and as she'd hoped the one of the future Queen of England looked as good as a posed studio shot.

When she arrived at Stirling's office he was busy on the phone, talking to another photographer. But he signalled her to sit down, blowing her a kiss at the same time. When he hung up he jumped to his feet and came round from behind his desk. Rebecca had bought several of the magazines which she handed to him.

'They look great, don't they?'

'Fantastic. You're a clever girl.' He stooped to kiss the top of her head, his voice filled with admiration. 'I love the ones of the little princes, obviously having a ball on their new bikes.' He looked down at the magazine covers, knowing that the pictures would soon be appearing all over the world, making thousands of dollars for Rebecca.

'That trip to Europe was worthwhile, wasn't it?'

'It certainly was,' he agreed, 'and the credit is all yours. I could never have fixed for you to get pictures like this. They're real scoops.'

'Well, thank goodness for the British Royal Family! They've probably made a lot of photographers rich.'

219

'You can say that again. The going rate for a real sneak shot, say of Princess Diana looking luscious in a bikini, is ten or fifteen thousand dollars.'

'You're kidding!' Rebecca looked amazed.

'I'm not.'

'I'd no idea they were that valuable. Mind you, mine are nice complimentary shots; ones I don't think anyone in the Royal Family would object to. I'm not sure I'd be keen to do really sneaky shots, even for that sort of money. It's awfully unfair to them, isn't it? I'd be furious if someone plastered me, caught offguard, all over the newspapers.'

'Not everyone has your scruples, sweetheart. The paparazzi would dangle a camera on a fishing rod through a bedroom window if they had the chance.'

'Isn't that awful?'

Stirling shrugged. 'It's the price of being royal, and belonging to one of the richest families in the world.'

'Can I go to Europe again, Stirling? If it hadn't been for Jerry Ribis and being threatened and everything, I'd have really enjoyed myself. Next time, you must come too.'

'I've got a small trip planned for us before then.'

Rebecca looked at him inquiringly. 'Where to?'

'Las Vegas.'

'Why?' Then she looked at him suspiciously 'Has this anything to do with Marissa Montclare?'

'Yup. My friend Bill suggested it. I was telling him all about this business, and he said we should go back to the beginning; find out all we can about Marissa before she came to New York; before she won the jackpot, even.'

'I think that's a wonderful idea.'

'Then how about flying down tomorrow for a couple of days? You don't have anything scheduled, do you?'

'Not a thing.'

'Great. I have a story all worked out. You'll be doing a photo-feature on cabaret dancers; getting them backstage, putting on their make-up, getting into costume – you know what I mean.'

'At the Golden Palm Casino where Marissa worked, I suppose?'

'That's right.' Stirling dialled the number of his travel agent as he spoke. 'And that makes it business, a tax deductible expense.'

'You would think of that,' Rebecca laughed. The idea of a trip to Las Vegas with Stirling delighted her – providing Jerry Ribis didn't follow them there too.

*   *   *

220

Angela Wenlake arrived at the hospital shortly after two o'clock to find Simon asleep. His luncheon tray lay untouched on the trolley by his side. Worried, she looked down at him and noted how much weight he'd lost. Even the nurses who tried to spoon-feed him were unable to persuade him to eat. All he wanted to do was sleep, and when she'd visited him yesterday she'd been unable to tell him about Clover because he slumbered so deeply she couldn't rouse him. He doesn't want to face what's happened, she thought with a flash of insight, that's why he's taking refuge in sleep. But she wanted to talk to him today. She had to tell him about his horse, because she knew he'd feel better when he'd heard what had happened . . . just as she did.

Fred the groom had cleaned out Clover's stable and now it stood empty, never to be occupied again. She would sell the other horses, and tell the Hunt to hold its Meet somewhere else in future. As far as she and Simon were concerned horses were a thing of the past, never to be mentioned again after today.

His eyes flickered at that moment and he looked up sleepily at his mother. 'Hello,' he said groggily.

'Hello, my darling.' Angela gripped his useless hand. 'How are you feeling?'

'About the same.'

'You haven't eaten your lunch?'

'The food's revolting. When can I come home? You know I hate it here. It's not fair that I should have to stay.' His voice had a whining quality and his eyes were filled with self-pity.

'Soon, I hope, darling. Soon,' said Angela. 'Meanwhile, you'll be glad to hear that that wretched Clover is no more.'

Simon looked at her with startled bloodshot eyes. 'What d'you mean?'

'I mean she's dead.'

His eyes grew wider and he tried to lift his head off the pillow. 'Dead?' he whispered.

Angela smoothed the sheet under his chin. 'That's right, darling. I shot her. I had to do it. That horse caused your accident and I had to get rid of her.'

'You . . . you . . .' Simon choked on the words and looked at his mother as if he was scared of her. Then his eyes welled up with tears, and within seconds he was crying as if his heart would break.

'Simon!' Startled, Angela jumped to her feet, alarmed at the way he'd taken the news of Clover's death. She'd expected him to be grateful but instead here he was, bawling his eyes out like a small child. She rang for the nurse, worried he might do himself harm.

'How . . . could . . . you . . . ?' Simon gasped between sobs. 'I loved that horse. I was going to ride her again as soon as . . . as soon as . . .' He couldn't finish the sentence. It was as if, by killing the horse, his mother had also killed his hope of ever recovering.

'My darling.' She was appalled by his reaction. A nurse came bustling into the room, all starch and efficiency.

'Now then, what's going on?' She looked from mother to son for an explanation.

'He's upset because . . .' Angela began, but Simon cut in, the words wrenched from his throat.

'You stupid bitch! How could you do such a thing? Get out! Get out! I never want to see you again!' In a paroxysm of grief he cried hysterically, rolling his head about on the pillow while the rest of his body remained immobile.

She shrank back, hurt and bewildered. 'I only . . .' she began, but the nurse took her by the arm and pushed her gently through the doorway.

'Better to leave him for a bit,' she advised briskly. 'Why don't you go and get yourself a cup of tea while I see to him?'

A moment later Angela found herself standing alone in the corridor, ignored by doctors and nurses as they hurried about their work. Never before in her life had she felt so rejected.

It was dawn in the city where time has no meaning, where night is day and day doesn't exist and where there are no clocks anywhere to tell visitors whether they should be waking or sleeping, lest it distract them from the main purpose of their visit: gambling!

Rebecca had been to Las Vegas before, to cover the wedding of an internationally famous filmstar for world-wide distribution. She thought of the city as a glittering image thrown up by a malevolent desert that sought to lure and tempt the weak and the unwary; a flashing neon nightmare of a place where the promise of riches so often turned out to be as arid and fruitless as the sand the town was built on.

Stirling had booked them a suite at the famous El Cortez, the oldest hotel in Las Vegas, 'right on Glitter Gulch' as the advertisements said. Climbing out of bed the first morning, Rebecca went quietly to the window and looked out. Below, all the lights of the city blazed as they had done all night, vying now with the rising sun but still unquenchable.

'Come back to bed, sweetheart,' Stirling mumbled sleepily. He rolled on his back, feet sticking over the end of the bed, hands behind his head. He looked at Rebecca standing naked in the dusty dawn light, her long hair falling over her shoulder. 'Why are you up so early?'

'I couldn't sleep.' She turned back into the room, letting the curtains close again, shutting out the light. Then she climbed back into bed and snuggled into his side. Stirling put his arms around her and held her close.

'Are you all right, Becky?'

'I'm fine.'

'I love you.' He nuzzled her neck, sucking the lobe of her ear while his hands stroked the smooth planes of her back.

'I love you too,' she replied, then turned her head away and seemed to push him from her, although the movement was gentle.

'What's wrong?' Stirling knew her so well that he was aware of the slightest change in her moods.

'Nothing.'

'Let's make love again.' Twice the previous night he'd taken her and made her his, and now he could feel himself becoming aroused again. The softness of her skin and her musky smell always drove him crazy. He wanted her now as badly as he'd wanted her last night.

'Not now,' she whispered, closing her eyes. 'I want to go back to sleep.'

'I thought you couldn't sleep?'

'I couldn't, but now I feel tired.' She rested her head on his shoulder, sweetly, like a child.

Stirling clenched his teeth and wondered what he was going to do with his erection. It was unlike Rebecca not to want to have sex, no matter what time of the day or night it was, and last night she'd certainly been as keen as he. Her hand was resting in his now, a slim tanned hand, with well-kept almond-shaped nails. She never wore any rings and he wondered idly, as he willed his ardour to subside, how a ring, a gold wedding ring, would look on her finger.

Later, as they had breakfast, Stirling suggested that they make their way straight to the Golden Palm as soon as they'd eaten. Rebecca, having declared herself starving when she awoke the second time, broke off a piece of croissant and considered the suggestion.

'We could, but I doubt we'll find anyone who's connected with the night club at this time of day, and I don't particularly want to watch the gambling, do you?'

Stirling shook his head. 'I agree, but it might be worthwhile, just in case we find them rehearsing. It's the dancers we want to talk to, isn't it?'

'You're right. What time is the show?'

Stirling consulted the brochure he'd got earlier from the hotel concierge, listing all the places of entertainment.

'Here we are,' he said, and then read aloud: ' "Cabaret and Lounge Acts. The Golden Palm Casino. Dinner and Cabaret Performances Nightly. Thirty Dollars (with fresh trout or prime rib of beef as an entrée). Dinner served at 6.30 p.m. The two-hour musical extravaganza commences 8 p.m. See the loveliest girls in town." '

'Wow!' he added mockingly, squinting at a photograph of a shapely brunette, adorned by a few beads and feathers. 'Get a load of that! Just look at those tits!'

Rebecca cast her eyes to heaven. 'Men! Why are you all crazy about big tits!'

'Oh, I like legs too,' Stirling protested, 'and you've got great legs.'

'Thanks!' Rebecca laughed good-humouredly. 'Pity about being flat-chested, I know, but I'm glad you approve of my legs!'

'You've got sensational tits. Small but sensational,' he assured her with a wolfish grin. 'I adore them to bits!' He leaned across the breakfast table and grabbed her hand. 'I would have shown you just how much I adore them this morning, but you went back to sleep.'

'I know.' She shook her head. 'I was wide awake one moment, and then suddenly I couldn't keep my eyes open. I must have been more tired than I realized.'

'We'll make up for it tonight.' Stirling's look made her pulses quicken. Then he was the businessman again, the agent who had to get things organized. 'Let's go to the Golden Palm and ask to see the entertainments manager. We can talk about your feature on cabaret dancers. From there we'll have to play it by ear.'

'Oh, I hope we find someone who knew Marissa,' Rebecca exclaimed. 'If we draw a blank here, what do we do next?'

He looked serious. 'We do not go sniffing round her apartment in the Trump Tower, that's for sure, unless we want to end up like Mike Wilson.'

Rebecca said nothing. She hadn't told him that before leaving New York she'd replied to the advertisement in the *Herald Tribune*.

'Mummy, you sound peculiar. Is anything the matter?' Jenny propped the telephone receiver between her shoulder and jawbone, and carefully took the new dress she'd bought out of its wrapping-paper. It was a cocktail dress made of black velvet with flounces of green and black shot taffeta round the knees. It had cost her a small fortune but now that she'd decided to change her image it seemed cheap at the price. To go with it, she'd bought some Charles Jourdan black suede shoes with diamanté buckles.

'I want you to come home this weekend,' Angela was saying.

'Is Simon worse?'

'Not exactly.' Her mother sounded evasive. 'Come on Friday night, will you . . . in time for dinner?'

'OK,' Jenny replied, trying to hide her reluctance. She much preferred to stay in London at the weekend when it was always gloriously quiet and deserted. She liked to potter about her flat, reading all the newspapers and watching her favourite programmes on television.

When she'd replaced the phone, she went into her bedroom and almost reverently hung up the dress on the outside of her wardrobe. Easter was only four weeks away and she wanted to buy as many new clothes and accessories as she could afford, so that she could really surprise her father when she arrived in New York. She'd even been to the Joan Price Face Place in Chelsea, to learn what cosmetics she should use and how to apply them.

Looking at herself in the mirror now, she had to admit the transformation was extraordinary. With her new hairstyle, gold-tipped and loosely flicked round her head, and her warmly glowing make-up, she looked both young and chic. She also felt all dressed up with nowhere to go!

It was a long time since anyone had asked her out, and although she and her flatmates gave at least one dinner-party a week, it was always for chums as far as she was concerned, rather than potential boyfriends.

Angela was already sitting in the drawing-room, changed for dinner and sipping her customary Manhattan cocktail, when Jenny arrived on Friday evening having driven down from London through pelting rain. Feeling tired and cold, she longed to have a hot bath and get into bed, but there was her mother, waiting to dine formally and no doubt engage in small talk.

'You've had your hair cut,' was the first thing Angela said.

'Yes, it was getting in my way before,' Jenny replied shortly. 'How is Simon?'

'He's in rather a bad way. That's why I wanted you to come home this weekend. I want you to talk to him.'

'Me?' Jenny looked startled. Simon had never listened to her and she couldn't imagine why he would now. Unless he was so ill he'd listen to anyone without protesting.

'The paralysis is no worse, is it?'

225

'No. It's his state of mind. Do you want a drink?' Angela had gone over to the tray of drinks in the corner of the drawing-room, and was helping herself to another Manhattan from the silver cocktail shaker.

'No thanks. What's the matter with his state of mind? He's bound to be very depressed, you know,' Jenny reminded her.

'It's more than that,' Angela replied slowly. 'I got rid of Clover, and he's very upset about it. I thought he'd be glad.' She resumed her seat on the sofa in front of the fire, without looking at Jenny.

'Well, buy Clover back then! If that's what he wants it's easy, though God knows what he's going to do with her.'

'I can't. She's dead.' Angela's voice was so low as to be almost inaudible.

Jenny's voice was scandalized. 'You didn't have her put down, did you?'

'I shot her myself.'

'You . . . !' Jenny looked at her mother in horror, her hand clasped to her mouth. Angela detected the same fear in her eyes that she'd seen in Simon's when she'd told him what she'd done.

'Oh, stop being so ridiculous,' Angela snapped, suddenly angry. 'I've shot horses before! I had to shoot my favourite hunter when he broke a leg. I was only twenty at the time, but it was the only thing to do. God, girl, you'd think you'd been brought up in a town instead of the country! You're like those Animal Rights Activists – all sentimentality and squeamishness.'

'How could you?' Jenny felt nauseated. 'No wonder Simon's upset. Oh, Mummy, what a dreadful thing to do.'

Angela's eyes blazed. 'I might have known you'd never understand. You never back me up, do you? I asked you down this weekend so you could talk to Simon; tell him Clover's death is for the best. He doesn't want to be reminded of what happened every time he goes near the stables, does he?'

'I think he's already going to be reminded of what happened, every day of his life, because of his condition,' she replied drily. 'You shouldn't have taken the law into your own hands and got rid of Clover like that. What about Bunty and White Socks and Paddy?'

'I'm selling the others.' Angela sounded as if she was doing someone a favour. 'But I gave Clover to Simon and it was up to me to take her away again.'

'But not this way.' Jenny covered her face with her hands for a moment. Not a great lover of horses, she nevertheless felt badly at the thought of a young and healthy animal being put down unnecessarily. 'Simon will never forgive you, especially if he makes a full recovery,' she added.

At that moment Peters came into the drawing-room to announce dinner.

'Thank you, but I'm going to my room,' Jenny announced. 'I don't want any dinner.'

'Jenny!' Angela looked furious. 'Of course you must have dinner.'

She picked up her jacket and bag and turned to leave the room. 'No thank you,' she said politely, and then without a backward glance walked out into the hall and headed for the staircase. As she climbed the red-carpeted stairs, she felt exalted by her own bravery in standing up to her mother. The change in her was not just on the surface, showing itself in trendy clothes, but deep within her too.

Early the next morning, while Angela was still in her room, Jenny jumped into her car and drove to the hospital in Andover to see Simon. When she arrived, she asked the nurse on duty whether it was all right to go into his room.

'Of course. Your mother's not with you, is she?' The nurse had a merry twinkle in her eyes and she was grinning broadly.

'No, I'm on my own,' Jenny replied, looking confused.

'That's OK then.' She lowered her voice. 'Simon's told me never to let his mother in to see him when he has another visitor.'

'But who else comes to see him . . . ?' Jenny began. The nurse raised her eyebrows knowingly, as if they both shared a secret.

Hurrying along the polished corridor to room 12B, Jenny tapped lightly on the door.

Simon replied in a breezy happy-sounding voice that she'd never heard before. 'Come in.'

Jenny opened the door and saw him, propped up on pillows, with a very pretty dark-haired girl by his side. She had her arm round his shoulders and it looked as if they'd been kissing.

'Jenny! What the hell are you doing here?' he asked, startled. The girl by his side, whom Jenny recognized at once, smiled. It was Charlotte Cowan who lived nearby, and whom Jenny had suggested would make a good partner for Freddy Wareham at the Hunt Ball.

'Hello, Simon. Hello, Charlotte,' said Jenny, beaming. So this was why Simon didn't want his mother admitted when he had 'visitors'. Amused, she pulled up a chair and sat on the other side of the bed. 'It's nice to see you again, Charlotte. I'm glad you're here to cheer Simon up.'

'Thanks, Jenny. You're looking marvellous! What have you done to yourself?'

'Nothing much.' Jenny laughed, pleased. 'So how are you, Simon? Sorry I didn't bring you anything, but I slipped out of the house before Mummy was up, and I didn't have time.'

He eyed her suspiciously. 'So she doesn't know you're here? Are you going to tell her?'

Jenny knew what he meant. She shook her head. 'I've got my case in the car, and I'm driving straight back to London when I leave here. I may tell her I popped in to see you but I won't mention you had a visitor.'

'Why are you here?' He still didn't sound sure of her.

'Because I wanted to see you,' Jenny replied honestly, 'and I wanted you to know that I abhor what Mummy has done. I think it's unforgivable and I'm just so sorry. It's a real shame.'

Simon averted his eyes, gazing into the distance as if he found the subject of Clover's death too painful to discuss.

'Yes. Well,' he muttered. There was a pause and then he said: 'At least I have Charlotte.'

'I'm very glad about that,' Jenny said with genuine warmth. She'd always liked Charlotte. She was intelligent, strong, and would stand no nonsense from Simon or anyone else. If he had been lucky enough to secure her as a girlfriend it could be the making of him.

'So how long has this been going on?' she asked, helping herself to some grapes from a bowl on the bedside table.

He looked sheepish. 'Since the Hunt Ball, I suppose. Freddie never had a chance. I knew as soon as Charlotte arrived that she was the girl for me. Damned fool not to have realized it sooner.'

Charlotte grinned engagingly. 'I've had a crush on Simon since I was eleven,' she admitted, turning to look fondly into his face, 'and from now on, whatever happens, we're going to be together, aren't we?'

'That's right. But for God's sake don't tell Mother!' Simon said to Jenny. 'Charlotte has agreed to marry me, even if I'm in a wheelchair for the rest of my life. But it will mean changes at Pinkney and we want to think the whole thing through before Mother knows, don't we, poppet?'

'That's right,' she agreed, squeezing his hand.

'Well, you can count on my discretion,' Jenny promised. 'I think it's the most wonderful news I've ever heard and I'm really thrilled for you.' Already she could see how Simon had changed. Gone was the sulky self-importance and the whingeing manner. In spite of his terrible disability he seemed to be coping cheerfully.

Jenny didn't stay long. She could see that they wanted to be on their own and in the afternoon he'd have Angela to contend with. Driving back to London, forty minutes later, she thought about the future and what it held. With her living in New York, and Simon bringing a bride back to Pinkney, she wondered what Angela would do.

As soon as they'd had breakfast, Rebecca and Stirling walked down the dusty Strip, past all the famous casinos where blackjack, keno, craps, poker, baccarat and roulette were endlessly played. Where lines of one-armed bandits whirred and clicked, jingling and tinkling as people fed money into the metal mouths and pulled the chrome levers until their arms ached.

Rebecca thought of Marissa, putting in her money, pulling the lever and then watching for the row of matching nuggets to click into line: and then the avalanche of coins that must have poured out, overflowing, cascading, gushing in a torrent of clattering silver and copper. What a moment that must have been for Marissa! So much money. More than she could ever have dreamed of. Did she scoop it up in handfuls? Did the management of the Golden Palm rush forward with buckets, while the casino's security closed circuit TV cameras recorded what had happened? Did Marissa shriek or feel faint or just triumphant? She was rich at last, beyond her wildest dreams, and she must have thought it was the beginning of a new life for her.

'I wonder exactly what happened when she won the jackpot,' Rebecca said aloud.

'That's what we're here to find out,' Stirling replied, knowing exactly what she was talking about. He took Rebecca's arm and hugged her to his side. 'Come on, sweetheart, the Golden Palm's over there on the other side of the Strip.'

She saw a large pink building of hideous proportions and vulgarity, the entrance flanked by massive fake palm trees that glittered with gold paint in the morning sunshine. The courtyard in front was paved with pink concrete slabs from which sprouted more fake palms. Without saying a word to each other, Rebecca and Stirling crossed the Strip, dodging the traffic, and entered the casino through the revolving doors.

Inside it was all gold palms and turquoise velvet-padded walls, with gilded ceilings and burnished lamps that filled the lobby with a blaze of light. They went through more revolving doors to the left, and found themselves in the casino which was crowded with gamblers, although it was only ten-thirty in the morning. Some were playing poker, roulette or blackjack, while others concentrated on games of baccarat where the stakes were high and the turn of a card could ruin a punter or make him very rich. And down one side were the inevitable rows of fruit machines, pinging and rattling like a swarm of metal locusts, driving Rebecca crazy with the repetitive sound of money being dropped into the slot, and the whirring of the wheels as the handles were clanked again and again.

'Look at those faces,' she whispered to Stirling. 'They look mesmerized. What a great picture that would make!'

He looked along the lines of people, mostly middle-aged women, who sat on high stools as if they'd been set in cement, their eyes glued to the elusive pictures of different fruits being jerked into position.

'What a way to pass the time,' he observed, shaking his head. 'They say the gambling industry in Las Vegas is valued at about two billion dollars a year. As far as I'm concerned they're welcome to it.'

'I agree. Let's get out of here. We'll see if we can find the entertainments manager.'

Together they left the gaming room and went back to the brilliantly lit lobby. Opposite them were brass-studded turquoise velvet doors. Pushing them open, they found themselves in a wide corridor that wound round to the left. The walls were painted gold, the carpet turquoise, patterned with yellow palm trees. As they walked along they looked at the life-sized coloured photographs of cabaret dancers that hung, gilt-framed, along the walls. Rebecca noticed they were all typically stereotyped glamour shots, showing lots of white teeth, large breasts, abundant hair, and fixed expressions. So similar were the photographs, that they could almost have been of the same girl in just a change of costume.

Then she grabbed Stirling's arm, and pointed to a particular picture of a girl in scarlet feathers and rhinestones, her platinum hair framing her face, her dazzling smile out-shining all the other girls. The name Tracy Handford was painted on a little plaque below.

'Well, what d'you know?' Stirling said slowly.

'So that proves she worked here,' Rebecca observed. 'I wonder why her picture's still hanging on the wall.'

'I suppose there was no point in taking it down when she left.'

At the end of the corridor there were more brass-studded velvet doors. Stirling strode forward and opened them, and they found themselves in the semi-darkness of a vast restaurant, with what seemed like acres of empty chairs and tables. At the far end was a large dimly lit stage. The place seemed deserted.

'Let's go,' he said, making his way between the tables. Rebecca followed close behind. At that moment they heard a man's voice coming from the wings. He sounded angry.

'That third number will have to go. It's fucking shit! The scenery's tacky, the costumes are lousy, and as for Juno and Maybelline . . . their act gives a whole new meaning to the word "amateur". They're the most crappy double act that ever hit town.'

'I know, I know,' said another voice wearily.

Stirling and Rebecca moved nearer the stage. Stirling called out: 'Hi, there.' There was complete silence, and then two men in velour track suits emerged from the darkness of the wings.

'What do you want?' one of them demanded. 'No one's allowed in here until the dining-room opens at six o'clock.'

Stirling smiled charmingly. 'I wonder if you could help us? This is Rebecca Kendall, the famous photographer. She's come all the way from New York because she's doing a photo-feature on cabaret dancers around the world.'

'That's right,' Rebecca said, jumping up on to the stage and stretching out her hand in greeting. 'I'm doing the girls at the Moulin Rouge in Paris, La Dolce Vita in Rome, and I'd really like to take some shots of the girls from the Golden Palm. Can you give us permission?' She looked from one to the other with a coaxing smile.

One of the men walked off, shrugging his shoulders, but the other grabbed her hand and shook it. Under the working lights his curly blond hair gleamed like a halo.

'Hi! I'm Gabriel Latimer, the choreographer. Nice to meet you.' Then he shook hands with Stirling. 'I'm sure we can arrange something. I'll have to get clearance from the management but I don't suppose there'll be a problem.'

'Of course, I'd like to take pictures of you with the girls,' Rebecca added flatteringly.

Gabriel's expression brightened. 'Sure. It'd be a pleasure. Are you coming to see the show tonight?'

Rebecca hesitated, looking at Stirling.

'Come as my guests,' Gabriel suggested. 'The show starts at eight. Afterwards I'll take you backstage and you can meet the girls and take some pictures then.'

'That would be great,' said Stirling. 'Would Rebecca be allowed to take any pictures during the show?'

'That's strictly forbidden, unless she's in the wings.'

Rebecca smiled. 'OK.'

'Fine. I'll see you tonight. I'll book a table in your name . . . Kendall, did you say?'

'Yes.'

Gabriel turned to move away, but Rebecca felt compelled to say something more. 'I used to know one of your dancers,' she began lightly.

'Oh, yeah? Who was that?'

Rebecca watched Gabriel's face closely. His blond eyebrows were almost invisible, and his bright cloud of hair formed a nimbus round his head, making him look like an old painting of a saint.

'Tracy Handford, also known as Marissa Montclare,' she said quietly.

In a second his expression changed, the saintly look vanished and an expression of knowing relish filled his face. 'My! Wasn't her death just something, my dear?' He sounded like an old woman all set for a good gossip.

'Are you coming, Gabriel?' complained the other man from the outer darkness. 'There's still a helluva lot of work to be done.'

Gabriel leaned towards Rebecca and Stirling in a conspiratorial manner. 'I always knew that girl would come to no good. I warned her, you know, but would she listen?' He cast pale fronded eyes to heaven. 'My, but was she heading for trouble! Look, I must rush now but I'll see you tonight, OK? I'll join you for a drink before the show begins.' With a wave of his hand he loped off towards the wings, the golden aureole round his head bobbing away until he vanished into the enveloping darkness.

Rebecca drew in a deep breath. 'You know something? I think we've just scored a bull's-eye.'

Chapter Fourteen

David McNee congratulated himself on the brilliance of his idea. Why hadn't Mike Wilson thought of it? Instead of running round, chasing after people, why not make them to come to you? Mike might have been alive now, David thought smugly, if he'd had more brains. Having endured for the past ten days a chronic lack of his customary self-confidence, he now felt elated. He was going to succeed . . . indeed was halfway to succeeding in his mission to recover Marissa's money. He could just picture the welcome he'd receive when he returned to London. Everyone at Lawson, Martin & Grant would congratulate him on his clever handling of the affair. 'Bright young man, always knew he'd succeed.' 'An asset to the firm, he'll go far.'

Of course, he'd never tell them what a bad time he'd had at the beginning, being insulted by Brian Norris and snubbed by everyone else. He'd never tell them how he'd nearly died of worry and misery or about the dreadful sense of failure that seemed to confirm his darkest dread in life – that he was a loser.

No, he'd sweep into the offices of Lawson, Martin & Grant, his head held high but with a becoming expression of modesty on his face, and he'd tell them, lightly of course, that it had been a piece of cake. He'd offer token apologies for having taken so long, but he'd explain that he'd had to exercise his sense of timing. One couldn't just rush at such a delicate situation, could one? Then he'd give them all the necessary documentation. He might even ask if he could visit Marissa's parents and tell them himself that he'd recovered their daughter's money. How grateful they'd be! What a wonderful person they'd think he was!

David felt so good about himself at that moment that he decided to go into a bar and buy himself a drink. A vodka and tonic, perhaps, to celebrate the fact that he'd cracked it. Well, very nearly. Well, almost. It was just as matter of time now, he was sure.

He chose a table by the window of the Go-Go Bar, and while he waited for his drink to be brought drew from his pocket the cause of

233

his exultation. Three letters . . . all in response to the advertisement he'd put in the *Herald Tribune*. Three people who had replied to his box number, saying they knew Marissa Montclare and would of course be interested in learning anything to their advantage. David unfolded them and read them again. One of them, he was convinced, would surely know all about her estate. There was a letter, handwritten on plain white paper, signed 'Ruth Warner', which said little but he thought sounded hopeful. There was a more interesting one, typed on a sheet of blue writing-paper with an address in downtown Manhattan, signed by someone called 'Rebecca Kendall'. The third, which was also typed, but gave no address, only a telephone number where the writer could be contacted. It suggested they meet. It was signed 'Sly Capra'.

Rebecca crouched in the wings, trying to avoid the paraphernalia of ropes and pulleys, scenery and curtains, as the famous Golden Girls of the Golden Palm Casino came high-kicking downstage in a dazzle of glittering rhinestones and snowy ostrich plumes. Boom-boom went the drums as the large orchestra swelled to the bump-and-grind rhythm of the music and the cymbals crashed and the saxophones shrilled. Boom-boom echoed the drums, pulsing out the beat, filling the auditorium with a thrusting, stomping, surging sensuality that made Rebecca gasp, taking her breath away. The sheer sexuality of the scene was overpowering as the dancers pranced and high-stepped, reminding Rebecca of the famous Lipizzaner horses of the Spanish Riding School in Vienna. The contours of their bodies were highlighted by a million twinkling beads as their long legs swung effortlessly above their heads and their feathers oscillated with each movement. Linking their arms in a long line, they resembled frothy sparkling waves, pounding powerfully up a beach.

This was the finale of the two-hour show, and Rebecca wanted to get a picture that would encapsulate the essence of the glamour and glitter, the forcefulness of the choreography, and the absolute professionalism of the dancers who must, she thought, have been drilled by Gabriel as if they'd been soldiers on parade. There was something thrilling she admitted to herself, having been very sceptical at the beginning of the evening, at the thought of watching a lot of semi-naked show girls prancing about; at the sight of perfectly matched dancers moving in perfect unison, legs rising and falling as if they'd been pulled by one master string, heads swivelling to left and right with the precision of metronomes.

At last the performance came to an end, and with a glorious

swishing rush of crimson velvet the curtains closed. Rebecca moved out of the wings, the thunder of applause still ringing in her ears as the girls scurried back to their dressing-rooms.

'Enjoy the show?'

Rebecca spun round and found Gabriel standing just behind her.

'It was fantastic,' she replied. 'Honestly, I'd no idea it would be anything like this. I've got some wonderful pictures, I think.'

'That's great. Let's get your friend and we'll go visit the girls in their dressing-rooms. I told them a famous photographer was going to take their pictures tonight.'

'The girls must work very hard,' Rebecca remarked as they made their way backstage through a maze of scenery and props. 'Have most of them been with you for a long time?'

'Some have been with me three or four years, others less. I suppose you know most of them come from Europe. England especially.'

'No, I'd no idea. Why is that?'

Gabriel shrugged. 'Search me. Even in Paris, at the Folies Bergère, most of the girls are English.'

'You're right. The Bluebell Girls, of course!'

Stirling joined them by the stage door, and then Gabriel led them up a steep flight of stone stairs. Giggles and raucous laughter filtered from behind closed doors, and Rebecca sensed a great feeling of camaraderie among the performers. There was even the pop of a champagne cork in the distance, and a burst of song from the floor above. How happy Marissa must have been working here, Rebecca thought, as they followed Gabriel down a corridor. It would have been gruelling work, of course, requiring great discipline, but judging from the fact that her photograph was still displayed in the lobby, she must have been one of their star dancers. There'd been no time to mention her to Gabriel again but now, sensing the evening was slipping by, she was anxious to fix a time when they could meet and she could question him thoroughly.

'Are you free for lunch tomorrow?' she asked guilelessly, giving Stirling a knowing look behind Gabriel's back. 'I'd like us to talk more, and I'd like to get some shots of you on your own, away from the Golden Palm perhaps?'

'Fine.' He seemed pleased to be asked. 'Now, here we are.' Without ceremony he knocked on a dressing-room door, opening it as he did so. 'Hi there, girls! You were good tonight! Nice house too. Now I want you all to meet Rebecca Kendall, the very very famous photographer!' There were giggles all round, including from Rebecca. 'If you're good, my darlings, she'll take your picture,' he added.

For the next fifteen minutes, while Gabriel and Stirling stood watching in a corner of the long narrow dressing-room, Rebecca shot roll after roll of film, fascinated by what lay beneath the heavily made-up faces and exaggerated false eyelashes they wore: probably girls who were as vulnerable as Marissa had been, from simple backgrounds and humble beginnings. They offered her a glass of wine in a plastic cup, and with much fluttering of eyes and flashing of smiles offered one to Stirling too.

'You're lucky,' remarked a tall redhead, perching on the edge of the long dressing-table covered with make-up and powder and blending brushes. Behind her, the long mirror was edged with electric light bulbs which blazed unflatteringly. It crossed Rebecca's mind that if one looked good under these cruel lights, one would look good anywhere.

'Why am I lucky?' she asked the redhead, whose name was Samantha.

'You've got a regular guy in tow.' She winked knowingly.

'But there must be a line of men waiting to take you all out after the show,' Rebecca protested. 'Fantastic-looking girls like you? You could have your pick, I'm sure.'

The redhead looked back at her in amazement. 'Are you kidding? I haven't had a decent date since I arrived here eighteen months ago.'

It was Rebecca's turn to look astonished. 'For God's sake, why not?'

'All the guys around here are like Gabriel . . . gay. Or else they're straight and married and so schmucky you wouldn't want to know! I'm just here for the money.'

A petite blonde with fragile-looking features joined in the conversation. 'That's right. I've got a boyfriend back in Manchester. As soon as we've got enough money to buy a house, I'm off. There's no one around here I'd marry.'

'What about Tracy Handford? Was she here for the money?'

There was a chorus of surprise from the girls. 'Tracy?' they asked. 'Did you know her?'

'Yes, I knew her,' Rebecca replied. 'Not very well, but I photographed her several times, mostly at New York parties. What was she like when she worked here?'

'She was sweet. Ever so kind, a lovely person,' said the English blonde with the boyfriend in Manchester.

'Yes,' agreed Samantha. 'Everyone liked her. She was a brilliant dancer. A really popular person.'

'So what happened when she won the jackpot on the fruit machine?'

Samantha took a swig of wine and settled herself more comfortably on the dressing-table, her long legs splayed elegantly before her. 'She was terribly excited, of course. Talked of all the things she'd do with the money. Then almost immediately things started to go wrong. She met up with someone called Sly Capra who promised he could double, even triple, her money. He wanted her to go to New York where he said he'd set her up in a swish apartment. It was to be a business deal; she wasn't having an affair with him or anything.' Samantha sounded vague. 'Anyway, that was it! She left here and we didn't hear from her again, that is until we read of her death in the newspapers, and found out she'd changed her name. What a terrible thing to happen!' She sighed deeply, and lowered her voice. 'It was Gabriel, you know, who told the press her real name was Tracy Handford and that she came from England. At least he didn't let on how she'd got so much money. But how could she have slipped and fallen out of a window?'

As briefly as she could, Rebecca explained what in her opinion had really happened. 'I'm here to try and find out something about her life before she came to New York,' she explained. 'I want to talk to people who knew her well, knew who her friends were; that sort of thing.'

'My God!' Samantha sounded shocked. 'She was such a sweet girl. She wouldn't have hurt a fly. Tracy and I came to work here at about the same time. She shared an apartment with some of the other dancers, downtown, and I lived just off the Strip, but we used to chat a lot. She'd tell me about her family and how they sacrificed so much in order for her to become a dancer.'

'Did she keep in contact with them?'

'No, not really. She'd send them the odd postcard. Then, when she won all that money, she wanted to send some to her family, but this man, Sly, he forbade her to tell anyone what their business deal was. He wouldn't even let her tell her parents she'd got all that dough.'

Rebecca looked surprised. 'Why did she go along with that?'

'She told me it would be worth her while in the long run to keep in with Sly. He was going to help her make loads more cash and she said, eventually, she'd be able to go back to England with a real bundle. She planned to buy her parents a big house and everything then,' Samantha replied.

'So Tracy planned to ditch Sly eventually?'

'Sure. As soon as she'd made her pile she was going to go home.' Samantha looked distressed, 'Poor Tracy. I can't believe she was murdered. How awful for her parents.'

Rebecca pressed on with her questioning. 'How did she come to meet Sly Capra?'

'He came backstage one night after the show. She had to work out her contract before she could leave, and he turned up, asking for her by name.'

'What happened then?'

'He took her out to dinner that night, and for several nights after. She wouldn't tell us exactly what the deal was, because he told her she mustn't talk, and she seemed worried and unsure at first. Then I suppose he persuaded her it was all right, because by the end of the week she'd cheered up and then she couldn't wait to go to New York with him.'

'Were they lovers?' Rebecca asked.

'No way. She said he wasn't her type. That it was just a business arrangement.'

From her camera case Rebecca drew out the photograph of Sly Capra talking to Theresa Bendotto. 'Is this the man?'

Samantha pounced. 'That's him! Smooth-looking, isn't he?'

Rebecca slid the picture back into its envelope. 'Was there anyone else who came to see her around that time. Did this man Sly Capra have a partner for instance?'

Samantha screwed up her nose in thought, and was just about to shake her head when she suddenly remembered something. 'Yes! That's right! Another man did come to talk to her one evening. But I think he must have been a competitor, not a partner, because she said he didn't want Sly to know he'd been to see her.'

'Was he a man in his late twenties or early thirties, with a boyish type of face and short brown curly hair?' Rebecca asked.

'Yes, he was! Do you know him?'

'His name is Jerry Ribis and he's an accomplice of Sly Capra. Between them they probably bamboozled Marissa into doing whatever they wanted.'

Rebecca and Samantha talked for a few minutes longer, and then Rebecca rose to leave. 'Thank you for giving me your time.'

Samantha swung her long fishnet-clad leg down to the ground. 'It's been a pleasure. I hope I've been a help.'

Rebecca smiled politely, not wanting to say that she hadn't learned anything she didn't already know. Together, she and Stirling left the Golden Palm by the stage-door and started walking back to their hotel.

'Well, I haven't learned anything useful,' she told him, taking his arm, 'but somehow I feel closer to Marissa. I know a bit more about her than I did, and she sounds like she was a very nice person.'

238

'Just naive,' he commented.

'Probably,' Rebecca agreed slowly, 'but of course we don't know what sort of bait Sly and Jerry used to get her to agree to go along with their scheme.'

'Maybe the angel Gabriel will be able to tell us more at lunch tomorrow.'

Rebecca dissolved into laughter. 'With that blond hair, he does look like an angel, doesn't he?'

But at lunch the following day, he had little to add to what Samantha had said, except that his attitude was less sympathetic and more salacious.

'I'm not saying she was promiscuous – don't get me wrong,' Gabriel told them, 'but with those looks, my dear, it was just a matter of time before she got into trouble. All along I guessed she'd been murdered. She was too sweet, too innocent for her own good.' He looked at them with wide blue eyes. 'But she soon caught on, didn't she? From what I read in the papers she was doing very nicely, thank you, with that titled English businessman. Maybe, in the end, she asked for it.'

David McNee decided to ask the three people who'd replied to his advertisement to meet him in the lobby of the Inter-Continental Hotel on East Forty-Eighth Street. He couldn't ask them to go to where he was staying because it was far too shabby for the impression he wanted to give, which was that of a prominent businessman from a flourishing UK company of international probate researchers. He needed to be seen against a background that suggested style, wealth and success. He cased the Inter-Continental Hotel one morning and decided it was perfect. The large gilt aviary, set in the middle of the entrance lobby and filled with exotic birds that sang loudly but not too often, was very classy. He liked the way it set off the Victorian opulence of the place with its buttoned leather chairs and sofas, and great arrangements of flowers. He also thought the gallery that ran down one side, where light refreshments and drinks could be served, was a perfect setting for confidential business meetings.

David wrote to Ruth Warner first, suggesting they meet three days later at eleven o'clock in the morning. He'd like to have made the appointment for sooner, but he wasn't sure how long it would take for his letter to be delivered to her address in Brooklyn. Then he left a message on Rebecca Kendall's answering machine, suggesting they meet the next day at four o'clock. Lastly, he called Sly Capra and spoke to a young woman he presumed to be a secretary.

She said it would be quite convenient for Mr Capra to meet him at the Inter-Continental at eleven-thirty the next morning.

Well pleased, David put the three replies back into his cardboard folder along with the various notes he'd made during his stay in New York, most of which were refusals to aid him, and then he left the public pay phone from which he'd been making his calls and started to walk downtown back to his own hotel. He had his report to write, and he would couch it in glowing terms.

One day, he promised himself as he hurried along the cold windy sidewalk, I'll make sure I'm rich enough to stay at a hotel like the Inter-Continental, not just meet people there for a cup of coffee.

Rebecca and Stirling had returned from Las Vegas late that evening, and gone straight to his apartment. She felt tired and irritated that their trip had not been more successful and in no mood for Stirling's light-hearted banter.

'Come on, sweetheart,' he said coaxingly, 'cheer up. Don't let this Marissa business get to you!'

'How can I help it?' She spun on him angrily. 'You won't let me stay in my own place. You spend your time warning me to be careful – don't go here, don't go there . . . all the time! How can I expect to be cheerful when I'm threatened constantly on one side and over-protected to the point of suffocation on the other?' She knew her remarks were unfair but tonight she felt like lashing out, so great was her frustration.

Stirling's face hardened. 'Now you're being silly,' he retorted. 'If you want to get yourself bumped off, go back to your damned apartment then! For God's sake, Rebecca, stop all this pseudo-feminist nonsense! You're being a pain. You know we're dealing with the Mafiosi. What mercy do you think they're going to show you if they catch up with you?'

Rebecca sat in sullen silence, as if she was spoiling for a fight. 'But we've reached stalemate! We're not getting anywhere. We're just going round and round in circles, and I'm sick of it. If we even had the police on our side it would be something. Someone, somewhere, has got to have the evidence that would put Sly Capra, Jerry Ribis and the waiter away for life.'

'Being impatient and acting impulsively isn't going to bring that evidence to the surface, though.'

'I'm not being impulsive,' Rebecca argued. 'I just want to see some action.'

'The only action you're seeing tonight sweetheart, is going to bed with me.' Stirling's good humour rose to the surface again, and catching the drift of Rebecca's perfume, he suddenly wanted her. He stretched out his hand and placed it round her wrist.

She pulled away. 'Don't patronize me.'

'I'm not patronizing you. I want to make love to you. Is that so dreadful?' His smile was attractively lopsided as he leaned forward to kiss her.

Rebecca looked both fretful and cold. 'Not tonight, Stirling. I'm tired and I've got stomach cramps.' She rose from the sofa, almost as if it was an effort. 'I'm going to have a long hot bath now, and then I want to sleep.' Without another word she turned and left the room. Stirling frowned, partly with annoyance, but partly puzzled. It was unlike Rebecca to behave in this way. Then he thought about the stress she'd suffered ever since the night Marissa had died. It was no wonder the strain was beginning to show. Maybe he'd suggest they go away for the weekend, perhaps to her family in New Hampshire. If she doesn't have a break soon, he thought worriedly as he went around the living-room turning out the lights, she's going to crack up.

Rebecca awoke first the next morning, all dewy-eyed and rosy-cheeked, like a small child who has slept deeply. She turned gently in the bed so as not to disturb Stirling, and watched him as he lay there. She'd been really mean the previous night, she reflected, and now as the dawn showed its grey light round the bedroom curtains, she tried to figure out why she'd been so bad-tempered. Overtired, she supposed, and strung out; anyway she felt wonderful this morning and snuggled closer to Stirling, longing to show him how much better she felt, anxious to make up to him for her irritability of the previous night. He stirred, as if he sensed her watching him, and then opened his eyes. A moment later Rebecca was kissing him all over his face with a flurry of light kisses.

'Sorry . . . sorry,' she said between kisses. 'Sorry for being such a pain! I love you.'

For answer Stirling rolled closer, taking the feather-filled white duvet with him so that they both vanished beneath a snowy mound of bedding.

'Oh, darling.' He returned her kisses, putting his arms around her and placing one of his long muscular legs over hers. 'I love you too.' Rebecca had taken his face in her hands and was kissing him slowly and lingeringly now, flicking her tongue into his mouth, pressing herself against him so that he became instantly aroused. He kissed her deeply then, stroking her breasts, whispering words of love, and she wound her arms and legs around him, holding him

241

tightly. Her mood of the previous night had swung to feelings of passionate love, and her desire for him was strong. When Stirling entered her, they became a part of each other, knowing every move the other would make, aware of every sensation the other was feeling. They had made love thousands of times, and yet on each occasion it was as if they could reach a greater depth of feeling and find something wonderfully new. Holding her as if he could never bear to let her go, Stirling poured his love and his life into her, while Rebecca cried out in delight.

Afterwards they lay still, the bedroom tranquil and quiet, the hum of the traffic muted as it sped past hundreds of feet below. Stirling was the first to speak.

'I'm so glad you're here with me.'

'I'm glad too,' Rebecca replied sincerely. Last night she'd longed to go back to her own place; however much she loved Stirling she found it claustrophobic to be with him, or with anyone for that matter, on a constant basis. But this morning she was glad to have awakened in the same bed, happy that he lay beside her, so that they could make love as soon as they awoke.

'Don't you think we should make this a permanent arrangement?' he asked.

Something in Rebecca's mind snapped shut, rejecting the idea, wishing he hadn't mentioned it. 'No, I think I must get back to my own apartment when this is over,' she replied lightly. 'I've got to fix up my darkroom as soon as I get the insurance money, and I really miss not being able to potter around, developing and printing some of my stuff.'

'That's not a good enough excuse. If we lived together we could get a bigger apartment than this one, and I could build you a new darkroom.'

It was the old argument and she wished he wouldn't keep asking her to give up her own place. 'We'd lose something of ourselves if we lived together,' she said tensely, determined to try and avoid an argument, but nevertheless anxious for him to know she hadn't changed her mind.

'I know, I know . . . our independence and freedom and our own space,' he said in a reasonable voice. 'But life is full of compromises, Becky, and just think what we'd gain. To live with someone you love is the most wonderful thing in the world. I miss you like hell when you're not with me.'

Rebecca smiled. 'I miss you too, but that makes being together all the better, doesn't it?'

Stirling sighed, and rolling on to his back gazed up at the ceiling.

242

'I'll never be convinced,' he said. 'Life is too short to be wasting it by being apart.'

'Oh, come on!' She propped herself up on one elbow and looked at him. 'We see each other three or four times a week and we frequently spend Sundays together. What more do you want?' she added in a joking voice.

Stirling turned his head and looked at her directly. 'What I want,' he said clearly, 'is to have you with me all the time, and I'll succeed one day. You can bet on it – even if I have to marry you!'

As soon as David McNee saw a dark-haired man in his late twenties, well-dressed and of medium built, come through the revolving glass doors of the Inter-Continental Hotel, he knew instinctively that his eleven-thirty appointment had arrived. Not only was the man alone, he was looking around as if expecting to meet someone. David left the table on the side gallery, where he'd taken up his position ten minutes before, and hurried forward.

'Mr Capra,' he gushed, extending his hand. 'I'm glad you could make it.' He led the way back to the table and gestured for his guest to sit down. 'Would you like some coffee?'

'Thanks.'

'I expect you know why I wanted to meet you,' David continued, feeling suddenly unnerved by the way Sly Capra was looking at him. The eyes were so penetrating David instinctively knew there would be no hiding-place from this man if ever he was on the wrong side of him. He opened his file, fumbling for his notes so that the replies he'd received to his advertisement fell on to the table.

'Allow me.' Deftly, with neat tanned hands, the man scooped up the papers and handed them back to David, but not before he'd glanced at the letter that lay on the top.

'Most kind. Thanks.' Confused, David then ordered coffee from the waiter and proceeded to explain his reason for advertising. 'It's very good of you to meet me, Mr Capra, and I hope you'll be able to help me.'

The man drank his coffee and glanced up at David. 'Is that it?'

He nodded, his sang-froid evaporating under the scrutiny. 'Would you be able to help me trace Marissa Montclare's money for her parents?'

'No way. I came here today because your advertisement suggested you had information about Marissa Montclare. I didn't realize you were trying to get hold of her money. I'm afraid I'm unable to help you.'

Disappointment hit David like a body blow. 'You can't help me find out what happened to her fortune?'

'I'm sorry.'

'I see.' David sat in contemplative silence for a moment. 'I wonder what I should do now,' he said at last.

'If you want my advice you'll go home. Go back to England and tell your boss Marissa's money went to pay off all her debts.'

'Yes, but . . .' David wondered why Sly Capra was providing him with a ready-made excuse.

'Look, buddy. I know this town and you don't. I knew Marissa and you've never laid eyes on her. I know my way around this place because I was born here, and I'm telling you, you haven't got a cat's chance in hell of recovering Marissa's dough.' He made a dismissive gesture with his hand, and his words were like a warning to David. 'Get lost, buddy, or you'll regret it.'

'Yes, but . . .'

The man rose. Although not tall, he seemed to tower over David. His voice was low, and he spoke with sudden ferocity.

'Get lost, d'you hear me? Get outta here and make it damned quick! This is my territory, pal.' He turned away and hurried down the steps to the lobby. A moment later he was being swept round in the revolving doors through which he vanished into the street.

An hour later, in a small office in a building on Fifty-Ninth Street and Second Avenue, an urgent meeting was taking place among a small group of men. One of them was being questioned.

'Mine wasn't the only reply to the advertisement,' he said. 'There was one from Rebecca Kendall, too.'

'Shit!' said the interrogater. 'How are we going to get rid of that dame? She's poking her nose into everything.'

'I'll have to set up a meeting with her. Put an end to her trouble-making once and for all.'

The interrogater spoke again. 'Take O'Hara with you when you meet this Kendall woman. He'll be able to persuade her to mind her own business.'

'OK. I will.'

Rebecca studied the gilt-edged invitation card that had been sent to the Hertfelder Agency, addressed to both herself and Stirling.

'We've been invited to a fashion show and party afterwards, at the Museum of the City of New York,' she observed, perching on the edge of his desk. 'It's next Wednesday, and it's in aid of Cancer Research. You will come, won't you, Stirling?'

244

He shook his head. 'You know I hate that sort of thing; all small talk and dead bits on toast, and people I'd cross the street to avoid. Anyway, Wednesday's my night for playing squash.'

'We don't have to stay long,' Rebecca coaxed.

'Why do you want to go? Charity galas are no more your scene than mine.'

'But I could get some great pictures,' she protested. 'Look who's supplying the clothes: Oscar de la Renta, Bill Blass, Carolyne Roehm, Adolfo, Scaasi, Giorgio Armani. It's going to be a big night, Stirling.' Suddenly she brightened. 'Look, you don't have to come. I don't mind going on my own as I'll be working.'

'No way.'

'What d'you mean . . . no way? Of course I can go on my own. It's not as if there were a sit-down dinner or dancing or anything! Look, it says "Champagne Reception, 7.30 pm. Fashion Show, 8.15 pm. Buffet Supper, 9 o'clock." There's no reason why I shouldn't slip along for a couple of hours to cover the evening.'

'I'm not letting you go out on your own at night, Becky. It isn't safe. If you really want to go, I'll cancel squash and come with you, but you're not going alone.'

'Stirling, nothing is likely to happen to me in front of three hundred people at the Museum of the City of New York!' she joked.

'You can't be sure of that. Who would have thought anything would have happened to Marissa at a highly respectable private party given by Sir Edward Wenlake in his own apartment? Anyway,' he added, 'it's the getting there and the coming home again that's risky.'

'I could hire a car and a driver,' she pointed out.

'I won't let you do it, sweetheart. I'd never have a moment's peace. We'll go together.'

'It'll mean you having to wear a tuxedo?'

Stirling shrugged. He was notoriously fond of informal clothes and never wore suits.

'I'll survive.'

Rebecca leaned across the desk and kissed him affectionately. 'We'll have fun, darling. Lots of champagne, good things to eat. Look, the invitation says all the refreshments have been donated by Party Planners Incorporated. They're the top catering company in New York. You can't get much smarter than that.'

Stirling laughed, happy to indulge her. 'OK, OK. We'll have a night on the town and I'll dress up like a dummy.'

'What shall I wear?' She read the invitation again. 'I'll be pretty

245

busy taking pictures, so it had better be the little black number I wore when I went to that ball in London.'

'Whatever you wear, you'll look great,' he assured her.

The next day Rebecca returned to her own apartment in TriBeCa to collect some more clothes and pick up any messages there might be on her answering machine. Threatening calls she could do without, she reflected, as she wound back the tape, but she hadn't been to her apartment for several days now and she hoped she hadn't missed anything important. As usual, there were a dozen calls for Karen from a variety of young men, but nothing for herself until she heard a man's voice. He gave a name she'd never heard before.

'This is David McNee and I want to thank Rebecca Kendall for her letter in reply to my advertisement in the *Herald Tribune*. I suggest we meet at the Hotel Inter-Continental on East Forty-Eighth Street, tomorrow, that's Tuesday the twenty-seventh, at four o'clock. I hope that will be convenient. Thank you. Goodbye.' The English voice spoke haltingly and awkwardly, as if he wasn't used to leaving messages on answering machines.

Rebecca glanced at her watch and swore. Today was the twenty-eighth. She'd missed the vital appointment by twenty-four hours! How could she have been such a fool as to give this number when she was never at her apartment? On the other hand, to have given either Stirling's or the agency's number would have meant telling Stirling what she'd done, and he would have been furious. She looked up the number of the Inter-Continental in the phone book, and hastily dialled it.

'I'm afraid we have no Mr David McNee staying here,' she was told by the receptionist a few minutes later, in answer to her query.

'Thanks,' Rebecca replied, disappointed.

'That's OK, mam. Have a good day.'

It's already too late for that, Rebecca thought, preparing to leave her apartment once more with a stack of clothes over her arm. Who the hell was this David McNee, and what had he wanted? There was only one way she could contact him now and that was through the post office box number he'd given in his advertisement. As soon as she got back to Stirling's place she'd write him another note, explaining why she'd missed the appointment and suggesting another date for them to meet.

David McNee hadn't hung around. Badly scared by Sly Capra's tone and manner, he booked himself on the next flight out of New York which took off at eight-thirty that night. Full of righteous indignation, he was bursting to tell the partners of Lawson, Martin & Grant just what they could do with the job of retrieving Marissa Montclare's fortune! How dare they send him into a situation that had already lost them one of their senior employees? Not only was the whole of New York a den of iniquity, he assured himself as he ordered a glass of beer while waiting in the departure lounge at Kennedy Airport for his plane to be called, but there was more than met the eye about that showgirl's death. He nodded vehemently, still shaking from anger and fear.

He was sure now that she was in with the Mafia. They'd killed her and Mike Wilson, and he sure as hell wasn't going to hang around waiting for them to bump him off too! Sly Capra's words of warning kept coming back to him: 'Get lost, d'you hear me? Get outta here and make it damned quick! This is my territory.'

David was sorry he'd never got to meet Rebecca Kendall, but although he'd waited nearly two hours for her, making each fresh cup of tea he ordered last as long as he could, she'd never turned up. He'd never get to meet 'Ruth Warner' now, either. Still, what Sly Capra had said had probably summed up the whole position, and for all he knew Rebecca and Ruth could well be tied up with the Mob, too.

Once seated in Row K of the Pan Am jumbo jet, he began to relax and feel better. He ordered a brandy from the stewardess when she came around with the drinks trolley, and re-thought what he'd say when he got back to the office. Perhaps it was still possible to turn the story around a bit, so that he came out of it looking like a hero rather than a wimp? He could say that Sly had threatened him and vowed to kill him if he continued with his enquiries. He could say he'd unearthed a massive underworld plot, of which Marissa was a part.

Pleased with this embellished version, David ordered another brandy, and thanked his lucky stars that he'd got away from New York before any serious harm befell him. By the time he'd worked out what he was going to tell Lawson, Martin & Grant he was sure they'd think very highly of him for having handled such a dangerous situation with skill and coolness.

Stirling hired a chauffeur-driven car to take them to the fashion show and pick them up afterwards. 'If we're going, let's go in style. Anyway, parking will be impossible,' he said. When they arrived, there was a long line of limousines dropping off the cream of New York society. The women, anxious to see and be seen, were posing at the Museum's entrance although it was a freezing night, so that the waiting photographers would get a glimpse of their jewellery and couture evening dresses.

'There's a bigger fashion show going on among the audience than there'll ever be on the catwalk tonight,' Rebecca giggled, as she checked her camera in the lobby, being one of the few photographers privileged to have been given a pass to take pictures inside the building. 'I'd better get busy.'

'Yes, *Women's Wear Daily* and *Town and Country* have already asked for your pictures, and with so many international celebrities here I think we can sell some to the European magazines too.'

'Great!' Enthusiastically, she started taking pictures of the more famous guests: Jackie Onassis in a simple black dress; Elizabeth Taylor in a blaze of diamonds; Gloria Vanderbilt looking elegant and chic, while a string quartet played in a corner of the flower-filled lobby and waiters handed round champagne amid the effusive cries of greeting that filled the air.

At eight-fifteen the guests were invited to move into an adjoining gallery where a catwalk had been set up, surrounded by row upon row of little gilt chairs with red velvet seats. In the front row, two had been reserved for Rebecca and Stirling, giving her an uninterrupted view so that she could photograph the models as they paraded past. She reloaded her camera then paused to look around, making sure she hadn't missed anyone important.

'It isn't every night you find so many celebrities under one roof,' she whispered.

Stirling nodded. 'A lot of the pictures you've taken tonight can go on file, then when one of these celebs does anything interesting or scandalous, I can send a print straight over to the picture desks of the newspapers without delay.'

'And we can make a lot of money for having exclusive shots on hand!' she added.

Stirling's dark eyes glinted with amusement. Four years ago Rebecca hadn't been so interested in the commercial side of photography. 'Quite,' he agreed.

At that moment the lights dimmed, plunging the gallery into darkness, and then a blaze of dazzling spotlights burst down upon the catwalk while pounding rock music filled the air. Startled, the sophisticated audience sat on the edge of their seats, craning their necks as the royal blue silk curtains at the end of the catwalk parted and two models stood there, bathed in the brilliant lights. Both wore white, one a beaded ball gown that shimmered as she moved, the other in a swathed cocoon of silk, draped Grecian-style.

There was an explosion of spontaneous applause, and then as the

248

music throbbed loudly and clouds of vapour from a dry ice pump sent swirling mist around their feet, the models moved forward slowly and sensuously, their sleek heads groomed so that there was not a hair out of place, their make-up as perfect as painted masks. Moving with the grace of gazelles, they came languidly forward while Rebecca clicked away, getting dramatic back-lit shots.

'Aren't you glad we came?' she whispered a few minutes later as more models appeared, this time dressed in ice blue evening dresses, one in satin, the other in chiffon. Within a few moments six more models filed out, each in a darker shade of blue, until the final pair appeared wearing sapphire velvet and brocade. Then all ten girls came on together, forming a perfect range from the palest to the darkest of the colour. Wild applause greeted this tableaux, and then started all over again when it became apparent the producer of the show had taken each colour of the spectrum and was showing a range of clothes in every possible shade and tone of that colour.

Pale lilac to darkest amethyst, delicate pink to lusty red, primrose yellow to deep gold; all the colours imaginable were there, until forty-five minutes later, for the finale, sixty models lined up on the catwalk, forming a dramatic rainbow, while the thundering music was almost obliterated by applause. People jumped to their feet, shouting 'Bravo'. The clapping reached a crescendo when the producer and each of the top designers came on to take their bows.

'What a night!' Rebecca observed when it was over, her face flushed with excitement. 'What a spectacle! That's the most amazing fashion show I've ever seen!'

'It wasn't bad,' Stirling grinned, 'the girls were certainly pretty.'

'Oh, really!' She grimaced, pretending to look disapproving. 'You weren't supposed to be looking at the girls.'

'Well, I sure as hell didn't come to see the dresses. Let's go get some supper before the locusts descend.' Already they could see the diamond-encrusted guests scurrying in the direction of the buffet in the adjoining gallery, as if they hadn't eaten for days.

'You're on.' Rebecca slipped her Leica into the camera case that hung from her shoulder. 'I have to go to the ladies' room, but you go ahead and get us something to eat. I'll join you in a minute.'

'Is there anything particular you'd like?' They'd already had a peek into the gallery where supper was to be served and had spotted great platters of salmon, lobster, soft-shelled crabs and giant shrimps, cold collations of various meats and large bowls of exotic salads.

'Get me whatever you're getting for yourself. You know the things I like.'

'OK.' He squeezed her hand as they pushed their way through the crowds. 'Don't be long.'

'I won't.'

The long wide corridor leading to the ladies' cloakroom was deserted as Rebecca walked briskly between the life-size statues that lined it on each side. Dark, except for the overhead spotlights that picked out the curves and contours of the marble figures, it resembled a hushed and shady aisle as her high heels clicked loudly on the stone floor. As she walked, her shadow cast and recast itself on the ground before her and in the distance the sounds of the party became fainter. Then out of the corner of her eye, beyond the statues, she saw a movement. A white-coated figure was emerging silently from the shadows. In that second Rebecca felt a fear so deep she stood frozen, unable even to scream, her mind spinning in a spiral of terror as the figure came steadily towards her.

'NO!' The word was wrenched from her throat, tearing at her vocal cords. 'NO!' Something gleamed in the man's hand. Almost fainting, she tried to remember what she'd been taught: go for the eyes . . . but was she strong enough to hurt this man she could see so clearly now? He'd been strong enough to push Marissa out of a window, so surely he'd be able to overcome her efforts at protecting herself? She screamed now, loudly and desperately, overwhelmed by the despairing knowledge that no one would hear her. Three hundred yards away a party was going on and everyone was having a good time, and she was about to be killed and no one would even know.

I won't let it happen was the only thought that seared her mind. Then, throwing down her camera case, she launched herself in an explosion of arms and legs at the waiter she'd photographed on New Year's Eve.

Chapter Fifteen

Jenny drove down to Pinkney for her last weekend in England. It had been the most hectic week of her life: leaving Trevor House, doing last minute shopping and packing, and assigning her share of the flat to the teacher who was taking over her job and had nowhere to stay in London.

Now, as she turned off the motorway into a quiet country road, she realized how emotionally as well as physically exhausted she was. Leaving her pupils had been the worst part, especially when they'd arrived on her last morning with little presents and cards, and had clung to her as she kissed each of them goodbye. For a dreadful moment she doubted if she was doing the right thing, wondering what on earth the future held for her, especially in New York where the pace of life was fast and the going tough. But now she knew she'd made the right decision. This was a turning point in her life, and it hadn't come too soon. There was nothing to keep her in England, she reflected with a tinge of regret, and there was no one here she cared for enough to make her want to stay.

At last Pinkney House came into sight, as beautiful and solid a building as ever, with wisps of smoke coming from the chimneys. Parking her car, which she intended leaving here when she went to the States, she went up the stone steps to the massive front door and pushed it open. The hall was deserted.

'Hello? Mummy? Anyone at home?' she called out.

Peters came hurrying from the direction of the kitchen. 'Ah, Miss Jenny.' He beamed in greeting. 'I'm afraid Her Ladyship is out. She's gone to the village, but I don't think she'll be long. Is there anything I can get you?'

Jenny blew on her chilled fingertips. 'I'd love a cup of hot chocolate. And, Peters . . . ?'

'Yes, Miss Jenny?'

'My luggage can stay down here in the hall, ready to be put into a taxi on Monday morning when I leave for the airport. I'll only need my overnight bag taken upstairs.'

'Very well, miss. Is there anything else?'

'That's all for the moment, thank you. I think I'll sit in the library.'

'Yes, miss. You'll find Mr Simon there, miss.'

Jenny looked startled. 'Is he home? How is he?' Without waiting for an answer she hurried across the hall and opened the library door. Had Simon recovered the use of his limbs then? All along she'd known it was a possibility, but surely her mother would have told her? A moment later her hopes were dashed, and she prayed the disappointment didn't show in her face as Simon looked up and saw her. He was sitting in a wheelchair by the fire, watching television.

'Hello! I didn't know you were home.' Jenny tried to keep her voice cheerful. 'When did you leave the hospital?'

Simon looked older and much more mature than before the accident. He turned and smiled at her, and for once his expression was friendly. Gone was the arrogance and puppyish display of self-importance that had previously marred his character.

'A few days ago,' he replied. 'I've got the use of my hands and arms back.'

'Simon! That's wonderful! God, I'm glad. How about your legs?'

He shook his head. 'Dead as dodos so far. No feeling at all, but at least I can feed myself and write and turn the pages of a book; not that I'm much of a reader, but it's time I got into it.' For once there wasn't a trace of self-pity in his voice.

Jenny came closer and sat in the chintz-covered chair by his side. 'How's Charlotte?' she whispered conspiratorially.

Simon grinned. 'The greatest girl in the world! Now that I'm home she comes to visit me but Mother has no idea we're planning to get married! Sometimes I'm able to telephone her if I'm left on my own, and that's the only chance we really have for private conversations.'

'When are you going to tell Mummy? You can't keep it a secret forever.'

Simon glanced towards the door to make sure they were not being overheard. 'Quite soon, I think. Maybe at Easter. I've told Mother I want to have a look at the family jewels, for insurance purposes I've said, and right now she's pandering to my every whim!' He laughed, but not unkindly. 'I actually want to choose a ring to give Charlotte.'

'Mummy has lots of jewellery. You'll have quite a choice.'

'Would you help?' He looked at her hopefully. 'I haven't much idea about these things but I think Charlotte would like a ring with an emerald. Mother said she'd get the jewellery out of the safe tomorrow morning.'

'OK. If I admire a ring especially, you'll know that's the one I think is the nicest,' said Jenny, grinning. Peters entered the library at that moment, with a cup of steaming frothy hot chocolate on a silver tray, which he placed on a side table near her.

'Is there anything I can get you, Mr Simon?' he inquired.

'No thanks, Peters.'

As soon as they were alone again Simon turned to Jenny. 'Tell me, why are you going to live in New York?'

'I don't know that I am going to live there, I mean permanently. I'm going for at least a year, but then, who knows?' She shrugged. 'I'll have to see what happens.'

'You certainly look a lot better these days,' Simon remarked, with brotherly candour. 'Charlotte couldn't get over the change in you when she saw you at the hospital.'

'I've been inspired by an American girl I know, called Rebecca Kendall. She's really helped me shape up and want to do something with my life.'

'Not one of your father's birds, I hope?' For a second she saw the old sneering Simon again and realized, at that moment, that somehow their father must have hurt him very much.

'No, of course not,' she replied quietly. 'She's a famous photographer and more or less lives with the agent who has helped her to get where she is today. She's fantastic, Simon. I felt like a drippy schoolgirl beside her when we first met, although she's not much older than I am. It was Rebecca who made me decide to get out of the rut I was in.'

'Well, make sure your father doesn't hold you back when you get to New York.'

'Our father, Simon,' she corrected him gently. 'I don't think he's ever held me back. In fact, I think he's given me more opportunities than most girls of my age.'

He shook his head sagely. 'The wrong sort of opportunities, Jen. He's kept you tied to him like a little girl, instead of letting you have your independence. Oh, you've had a great time when you've stayed with him, doing all sorts of grown-up things, but it's been in the role of a sort of proxy girlfriend and hostess, hasn't it? It would have been better if he'd given you the money to travel around the world with a friend of your own age.'

Jenny frowned, troubled. 'Actually, I agree, Simon, and I think Daddy knows it too now. He was really quite nasty to me the last time I stayed with him. Told me I was dull, that I didn't know how to have fun, I felt a real drag by the time I came home.'

Simon chuckled. 'Join the club, my dear!' he said in a mocking voice. 'When I was sixteen he told me I was a fool, that I'd never amount to anything, and that I was a deep disappointment to him. Is it any wonder I don't care a damn for him either?'

'I never knew.'

'Oh, yes, he has a fine way with words; harsh ones when he doesn't get everything his own way, and charming ones when he wants something. Up to now you've only seen the charming side of him, because he wanted you to be his little pet. Bloody nearly gave you a father complex while he was at it!'

'A father complex?' Her eyes widened.

'Of course.' Simon's expression was sympathetic. 'I'm not the utter fool I sometimes appear to be, you know. Why haven't you had a string of boyfriends, for instance?'

'I don't see . . .' Jenny protested.

'It's because, out of vanity and even jealousy, Father has always wanted to keep you to himself. Rather in the same way that Mother has tried to keep me to herself,' he added in a low voice.

They sat in silence for a long moment, each deep in thought. Then Jenny spoke.

'You're getting out from under, aren't you? You're going to marry Charlotte . . . and what's going to happen to Mummy?'

'Hush!' Simon put his fingers to his lips. 'I can hear her car. She'll come bursting in here in a moment, so let's be talking about something else.'

'OK. But can we talk later, Simon? We've never really talked before,' Jenny asked.

'Yes. Maybe tonight, when I've been settled in bed. I sleep in the study now, you know. Can't make the stairs in this damned contraption.'

Jenny nodded understandingly, knowing she'd never be as brave as he was under the circumstances. 'I'll come and see you then,' she whispered.

The library door opened and there stood Angela, slim and elegant in a tweed suit the colour of heather, with an amethyst silk scarf knotted loosely at her throat.

'You've left your car by the front door, Jenny,' she said immediately. Her tone was accusing. 'Would you kindly take it around to the garage? You know I hate cars cluttering up the drive.'

Jenny rose, composing her face into a bright smile. 'Hello, Mummy. How are you, Mummy? Nice to see you again, Mummy,' she said sarcastically. Angela flushed scarlet and her eyes sparked.

'I'll have none of your impudence!' she snapped. 'Simon must be kept quiet.'

254

'Simon is just fine,' Jenny replied smoothly. 'I'll move my car when Peters has put my luggage in the hall.'

'Why the hall? Why can't it be taken to your room?'

'There's no point, when it's going to be loaded straight into a taxi on Monday morning.'

Angela clicked her tongue with annoyance, then went over to Simon, resting her hands on his shoulders and gazing down into his face. 'How's my boy?' she asked tenderly.

Simon caught Jenny's eye over his mother's shoulder and for a split second brother and sister nearly burst out laughing. It was a classic example of what they'd been talking about. Just in time Simon controlled himself. 'Fine,' he said breezily. 'When are we having lunch? I'm starving.'

As Jenny left the room, she glanced back at the figure of her mother, bending over Simon, and for a moment she felt a pang of sorrow for both her parents, wrong though they were in their attitude towards their children. The birds were about to fly from the nest. Simon would get married, and for the rest of his life put his wife before his mother. Jenny was about to step into the real world and leave her father behind, in his. Being parents must be tough, she thought as she went up to her room, and learning to let go must be the most difficult part of all.

The next morning Angela brought several large jewel cases into the library and set them down on a low table in front of Simon's wheelchair.

'I can't imagine why you want to see all this stuff,' she remarked good-humouredly. 'You must have seen it all before.' But she patted his arm affectionately.

'I know, but I've never seen it all together before. What's in this case?' With hands that were growing stronger every day Simon opened a large flat dark blue leather case. Inside, lying on a bed of deep blue velvet, was a diamond necklace, designed in linked lovers' knots, with a large drop diamond between each bow.

'I wore that to the Hunt Ball. There's a matching tiara but I haven't worn that for years. This is quite pretty.' Angela showed him a diamond and ruby bracelet. 'It belonged to my mother. Of course, all this will be yours one day, my darling.'

Simon looked at her stubbornly. 'You must leave half to Jen.'

Angela's lips tightened. 'Her father will give her all the jewellery she wants. These are family pieces. Some, like these sapphire and diamond earrings, have been in my family for several generations.'

'Jenny is family,' Simon remonstrated obstinately. 'You can't cut her out, Mother.'

'She has done little to deserve anything.'

He ignored the remark. Instead he said jokingly: 'Of course, it wouldn't be me who would get all this stuff anyway. It would be my future wife.'

'Your . . . ?' Angela caught her breath, and looked away.

'Go on, Mother, say it!'

'Say what?'

'Who's going to marry you in your condition?'

Her flush deepened, staining her neck a deep crimson. 'I would never, in a million years, say such a thing.'

'But you must have thought it!'

'Oh, my darling.' Angela sounded deeply distressed. 'You mustn't be so bitter. I shall be with you always, you'll never be alone. Is that what all this is about? Wanting to torture yourself by looking at things that will never be worn by a wife of yours?'

Simon averted his head so that she could not see his expression. At that moment, Jenny came hurrying into the room, slim and vibrant-looking in jeans and a heavy blue sweater that matched the pale colour of her eyes.

'What?' she exclaimed. 'Have you started looking at the goodies without me?'

Angela ignored her, still hovering anxiously over Simon.

'What have we got here?' Jenny asked flippantly, opening several jewel cases at once. A blaze of diamonds, emeralds, sapphires, rubies, amethysts, coral, pearl and aquamarines lay exposed on the table, a veritable Aladdin's hoard of gems worth a king's ransom.

'Do be careful, Jenny!' Angela chided fretfully.

'Wow!' Simon remarked, impressed. He started picking over some of the pieces. 'Are you sure this is all fully insured?'

'It is not only insured, it's kept in a safe in the strong room in the cellar. Any thief would have to blow up the house to get to it.'

Jenny was opening more cases with reckless abandon, until the whole table-top was covered with a profusion of jewels more valuable than she could imagine. As she did so, she carried on a running commentary, seemingly to herself. 'Ummm. That's quite nice, though I don't know when you'd wear it. This is pretty. That brooch is a bit too big to wear, isn't it? Ah, this is beautiful. What a strange bracelet . . .' And so on, while Simon watched closely.

'Really, Jenny,' Angela protested. 'Put everything away now. We're really not interested in your opinion on every single piece of jewellery.'

Simon spoke suddenly. 'Mother, why don't you give Jenny something as a farewell present? Those pearls would suit her, or perhaps those diamond earrings? After all, as we've just agreed, I'm not going to have any use for them myself.' His smile was sly.

'No!' Jenny exclaimed, embarrassed. 'I don't want anything. I was merely curious to see what there was.'

'Edward can get her some pearls if she really wants any,' Angela said coldly. 'Now, for goodness' sake, let's get everything put safely away.'

'Don't worry, it won't take a moment.' Swiftly and surely, Jenny replaced necklaces and earrings, brooches and bracelets, ropes of pearls and the fabulous diamond tiara, but not before she had made sure that one small square jewel case, containing a ring mounted with an exquisite flawless emerald, surrounded by diamonds, had been slipped by Simon into his pocket.

'There!' She announced cheerfully. 'It didn't take long, did it?'

'Are you sure you've packed everything away?' Angela asked. 'You're so careless and you do everything so fast.'

With mock exaggeration, Jenny got down on her hands and knees and examined the surrounding area. 'No stray diamond necklaces? No missing tiaras? No, Mummy, there's nothing there.'

'Oh, stop being so silly , and help me carry everything down to the cellar.'

'OK.' Jenny picked up some of the boxes, holding them to her chest. 'Lead on, MacDuff! To the dungeons we go!' Giggling, and giving Simon a knowing wink, she turned to follow her mother out of the room.

'Thanks, Jen,' he whispered.

It was early Monday morning and a thick freezing mist lay over the gardens and beyond them the fields and copse that surrounded Pinkney House. Jenny was up early, slipping into the study to see Simon before their mother came down. Peters had brought them both some coffee and had returned to the kitchen, remarking: 'Them two seem to be thick as thieves, don't they?'

Jenny sat on the edge of Simon's bed. 'Mummy will never find the ring behind those books,' she whispered.

'Thanks for hiding it for me. The nurse who comes each day undresses me. I was worried that either she or Mother would find it in my pocket.'

'When will you ask Charlotte to marry you? When will you give her the ring?'

'As soon as Fred leaves.'

'Fred the groom? What's he got to do with it?'

Simon leaned back against the mound of pillows that propped

257

him up and eyed his sister speculatively. 'You didn't know that when Fred found out Mother had shot Clover, he gave in his notice? Said he could never work for someone like her.'

Jenny's eyes widened in astonishment. 'Really? Fred is such a mild little man, I can't imagine him standing up to Mummy. Has she sold the other horses yet?'

'No, and I won't let her. Fred came to see me when Mother was out the other day. He's found a girl who lives nearby who is willing to come here every day to look after them. He's got himself another job at a training stables in Newmarket.'

'I still don't see what any of this has got to do with you asking Charlotte to marry you.'

'Fred will be leaving his house in the grounds here, won't he?' Simon paused to let his words sink in.

'Yes. So? Oh!' Jenny clapped her hand to her mouth. 'The lodge, you mean? Oh, my God, Simon, you couldn't! You couldn't do that!'

Simon smiled drily. 'Why not? I honestly couldn't expect Charlotte to share this house with Mother, could I? It wouldn't be fair.'

Jenny looked stunned. 'So you're going to make Mummy live in the lodge?'

Simon let out a bellow of laughter. 'No. At least, not right away. Charlotte and I will have the lodge done up, and it will suit us fine. That is, until we have children and then we'll have to move in here, and at that point Mother can move into the lodge.'

'Have children? You mean if you get back the use of your legs?' Jenny asked, looking embarrassed.

Simon shook his head. 'There's nothing wrong with me in that department. I asked the doctors, and one way or another I'll be able to have children.'

'Oh, that's wonderful. Does Mother know that?'

'Not yet. In fact there are a lot of things she doesn't know yet!' Thoughtfully he gazed into the blazing log fire that Peters had lit for him soon after dawn. 'In a funny sort of way, I'm going to miss you, Jen,' he continued. 'We haven't always got on; it infuriated me that you seemed to reject us in favour of Father, but I don't suppose that was your fault. Anyway, I want you to know that no matter what happens, you'll always be welcome wherever my home is. In time, I hope it will be here. That may make it awkward for you with Mother, if she's in the lodge, but I hope you'll stay with Charlotte and me. She's always liked you and I hope you and she will be friends.'

'Of course I'll come and stay with you,' she said stoutly. 'We

258

victims of a broken marriage and selfish parents have to stick together, you know,' she added jokingly to lighten the atmosphere.
'And you promise you'll let me know when you get engaged?'

'Try and stop me,' he laughed. 'I'll be taking a half page advertisement in *The Times* and *Telegraph*. To hell with the Court Circular!'

Jenny laughed too, glad to be leaving Pinkney on such good terms
with her brother.

Two hours later, as watery sunshine struggled to permeate the
clouds, Jenny waved cheerfully out of the taxi window to her mother
and Simon, who'd been pushed to the front door in his wheelchair.

'Take care of yourself,' Simon called.

'You too,' Jenny shouted back with a broad grin. 'Say goodbye to
Charlotte for me and give her my love!'

'I will.'

'Remember to keep in touch.'

Simon's smile deepened. 'You'll be the first to know.'

As the taxi swept down the long drive, Jenny saw her mother turn
inquisitively to Simon.

'Know what?' Angela demanded.

Through the back window, Jenny watched as mother and son
seemed to argue about something, and then the taxi turned left, out
past the gates and into the main road, and Pinkney was lost to sight.

How I wish I could be a fly on the wall, Jenny thought, smiling to
herself, when Simon tells Mummy he's planning to get married.

An agonizing pain down one side of her head brought Rebecca
slowly back to consciousness. Her first thought, through the loud
buzzing in her ears, was to struggle to her feet before the waiter
finally killed her. She willed her eyes to open and her limbs to move,
but a black swamp seemed to be drawing her down to the hard stone
floor, so that she felt paralyzed. With terrifying certainty, though,
she knew that if she didn't get up he would stab her with the knife
she'd seen glinting in the darkness. With a detached sense of fear she
wondered why he hadn't already done so. She mustn't delay. Every
second was crucial. With all the strength she could summon, she
clenched her fists and was about to raise her arms in a final attempt at
lashing out through the black fog that surrounded her, when she
heard her name spoken urgently.

'Rebecca. Rebecca!'

She fought harder, unsure how long she'd been unconscious, desperate now to overcome her assailant. Opening her mouth to let out
the scream that seemed caught in her throat, she made one more
violent effort, but arms encircled her, holding her tightly, and the

voice which she now recognized was repeating her name.

'Rebecca, sweetheart. Rebecca.'

'Stirling?' she muttered uncertainly, opening her eyes.

'It's all right. Everything's OK. Just take it easy.'

Her mind was clearing rapidly now and so was her vision. Several white-coated waiters were hovering around as she lay in the shadowy corridor, and Stirling was kneeling by her side.

'Where is he . . . the waiter?' she whispered urgently.

'Being looked after.' He gazed at her with concern. 'You need a doctor.'

Slowly and painfully, her head pounding and a trickle of blood running down from her temple, Rebecca sat up, supported by Stirling. 'He came out of those shadows,' she said brokenly. 'He had a knife.'

A worried-looking waiter handed her a clean table-napkin which had been soaked in icy water. Taking it, she gingerly dabbed at her head, wincing in pain. Then she looked anxiously to Stirling.

'They won't let him go, will they?'

'Don't worry, everything's under control,' he assured her. He'd been summonsed from the supper room moments before by a waiter who had seen him earlier in the evening with Rebecca, and who now told Stirling that she'd attacked one of their colleagues in the corridor that led to the ladies' powder room. He spoke hurriedly as he led Stirling to the spot.

'I think she must have thought he was someone else, because she jumped on poor old Sam Kelly like a ton of bricks! I was just behind him and I saw what happened. We were on our way to the supper room with more cutlery when your young lady went berserk. Started yelling and scratching like an alley full of cats! Sam had an awful job defending himself, because he was so surprised. Then she slipped and went crashing down and I think she hit her head on one of the statues.'

Stirling started running, and by the time he arrived in the corridor the injured waiter was reeling around, his hands covering his face, saying he was blinded, while three others hovered around him trying to see how badly he was hurt. Still and inert on the floor lay Rebecca, blood seeping from her head.

'Call an ambulance,' Stirling commanded. As he cradled Rebecca in his arms, he glanced across at the injured waiter. He'd taken his hands away from his face and in that moment Stirling realized the enormous danger Rebecca had been in.

Rebecca was sitting up in bed in Doctors Hospital, glaring at the physician with a mixture of disbelief and shock. She'd spent the past thirty-six hours having tests to make sure the blow to her head hadn't caused any serious injury, and now here was the doctor giving her the most unlikely and surprising piece of information.

'You can't be serious!' she said, incredulously.

'Why not?' Doctor Fleming was a fatherly-looking man with twinkling eyes and a kind smile. 'What's so strange about a healthy young woman like yourself being pregnant?'

'Well, it's just that . . . it's just . . .' she floundered. 'I don't want to be pregnant, and I thought the coil was safe. I didn't mean this to happen.'

'I see,' he replied conversationally, plunging his hands into the pockets of his white coat. He didn't seem in the least shocked by her reaction.

Rebecca continued fretfully, 'I'd like children one day but not yet. I don't even want to live with my boyfriend or get married right now.'

'Ummmm.' Dr Fleming went over to the window of her small hospital room and looked out.

'I mean, I love my boyfriend and all that, and there's no one else I'd like to have a baby with. But not now . . . not yet.'

His smile was understanding. 'We can't always choose the timing for these things to happen,' he said. 'I think, when you get used to the idea, you'll change your mind.'

Rebecca sighed. 'How far pregnant am I?'

'About nine weeks.'

'Nine weeks! My God, I'd no idea. My life has been so hectic I hadn't even noticed . . . although I have had a couple of bad headaches and I have been feeling a bit nauseated at times. Is that all part of it?'

Dr Fleming nodded. 'Undoubtedly. You may get bouts of lassitude too, when all you want to do is sleep, and after this blow to the head you must rest up a bit. Take it easy for a couple of weeks.' His smile deepened. 'Will your boyfriend be pleased?'

Rebecca grimaced. 'Oh, sure. He'll be over the moon. He'll definitely want us to get married now, just when I thought it was safe to go back to my own apartment.' She plucked at the sheet with restless fingers. 'How could I have let this happen?' she demanded crossly.

'In the usual way!' he laughed. 'Now, you're going to rest, eat sensibly and take your vitamins. And,' his mouth twitched, 'there are to be no more punch-ups.'

'I still don't believe this is happening.' She shook her head slowly. When she was alone again she thought about having a baby, and how it would curtail her independence. Her career was at the stage where if she continued she'd become one of the country's leading photo-journalists. As it was, she could now command a high price for her pictures, and certain top editors had come to depend on her to produce the perfect photograph whenever the occasion demanded. She couldn't let all that go! She owed it to herself to remain in a position where her work appeared regularly in all the leading newspapers and magazines, and her byline 'Photo by Rebecca Kendall' was one people respected. Feeling annoyed with herself for ever letting this happen – who the hell said the coil was safe? – she lay in bed, wondering when to tell Stirling. The sooner the better, she supposed. Get it over with. He'd be thrilled of course. No doubt about that. He'd probably make a wonderful father too. Nevertheless . . .

She was dozing when he came to visit her later that day. Opening her eyes as soon as she felt his presence in the room, she smiled sleepily, her pregnancy forgotten for the moment.

'Hi,' she whispered lazily.

'Hi there, and have I got news for you!' Stirling replied, kissing her.

Rebecca opened her eyes wider. 'What's happened? Has the waiter been charged?'

'You're never going to believe this.' He pulled a chair forward and sat close to her bed. 'The waiter, Sam Kelly, is in the clear. He had nothing whatever to do with Marissa's death.'

'I *don't* believe it!'

'I didn't believe it myself at first, but I've been in touch with the chief of police because I wasn't going to be sweet talked by a nerd like O'Hara. It's true though. I actually went to the trouble of checking it out myself with the two catering companies involved, De Vere's and Party Planners. The man you attacked is absolutely innocent.'

Rebecca's hand flew to her mouth, aghast. 'But he came for me in the corridor. He had a knife in his hand.'

Stirling shook his head gently. 'Under the same circumstances I'd have reacted exactly as you did. You saw the man we've assumed from the beginning was Marissa's murderer, and he was walking towards you when you were alone in a deserted part of the museum, and he had what looked like a knife in his hand. In fact he had *several* knives in his hand, and some forks too, because he is a bona fide waiter, and he and others were on their way to the buffet with some extra cutlery. He wasn't going to attack you. There are witnesses who saw what happened, and it was you who went for him.'

'Because I thought . . . oh, Stirling, am I getting paranoid?' Rebecca asked, distressed.

'No, sweetheart. As I said, I'd probably have done exactly what you did. The trouble is, we all jumped to conclusions because you happened to take a shot of him opening the window out of which Marissa fell.'

'I still don't understand why he's not a suspect?' There was still doubt in her voice.

'I'll explain. Until recently Sam Kelly was a freelance waiter and butler who used to be hired for a lot of parties given by the top people. He joined Party Planners, about six weeks ago. He has the highest references, otherwise they wouldn't have taken him on. Some time last autumn, while he was still freelancing, he was approached by a friend of his who works for De Vere's. The friend's wife had just had a baby and he'd promised her he'd spend New Year's Eve at home, so he asked Sam Kelly to stand in for him at Sir Edward's party, without De Vere's knowing. It's a company rule that staff are not allowed to put in substitutes if they're ill or can't work, so this guy would have been given the chop if it had got out. That's why De Vere's didn't recognize Sam Kelly when you showed them his picture.'

Amazed, Rebecca leaned forward. 'Is that why his white jacket didn't have De Vere's logo embroidered on the pocket?'

Stirling nodded. 'He was wearing one of his own that night.'

'But he did open the window?'

'Yes. One of the guests complained of the heat, so he opened the window and then went back to the kitchen.' He paused to let his words register. 'That's where he was, with half a dozen other waiters from De Vere's, when Marissa fell from the window.'

'My God, and all along I was sure it was him.'

'So was I,' Stirling agreed. 'Foolishly, I think in the circumstances, he slipped out the back entrance of Sir Edward's apartment before the police arrived, because he didn't want to get his friend into trouble by being there. Of course he'd no idea you'd taken his picture or that we suspected him of killing Marissa.'

'This is really all true, Stirling?'

'Absolutely. There are witnesses to prove he was in the kitchen when it happened, and he's also described the man who asked him to open the window as being in his early thirties, well dressed, dark haired, and with a pleasant manner.'

'So we're back to Jerry Ribis again, aren't we?'

'Or Sly Capra.'

Rebecca spoke decisively. 'I must apologize to Sam Kelly. What an awful thing, Stirling! Did I hurt him badly? Oh, I feel dreadful about it now.'

'He's all right, sweetheart. You made a good attempt at scratching his eyes out, but there's no permanent damage. He's a nice man, and I've persuaded him that accepting a gift of some cash would be preferable to suing you for assault.'

'Oh, I hadn't thought of that! What a mess I've made of everything.' She leaned back in the narrow hospital bed, her brows puckered. 'I've beaten up the wrong man, the killer is still on the loose, and we're no nearer to finding him than we were at the beginning.' Her mouth tightened unhappily. Knowing her as well as he did, Stirling suspected there was something else troubling her.

'What else is wrong?' he asked gently.

She looked at him wistfully. 'I'm pregnant,' she said, and burst into tears.

'Becky! My darling! That's wonderful! Here, don't cry, sweetheart. Why didn't you tell me before? It's the most fantastic news I've ever heard.'

'I suppose you'll want to get married now,' she wept.

'Hey, there, sweetheart. Don't get upset. It's going to be all right, I promise you. You don't have to do anything you don't want to do.' Keeping his arms around her, he let her cry until her sobs subsided. Then she dried her tears and looked at him, shamefaced.

'I'm sorry.'

'Don't be sorry, Becky. I love you . . . I understand. I hope we can get married now, for the sake of the baby.' Stirling kissed her tenderly, cupping her tear-stained face in his hands.

She shook her head. 'It shouldn't be like this. When we first met, years ago, I longed for you to ask me to marry you. I dreamed about it all the time. But we're so happy now and we've worked out such a good lifestyle between us, each having our own space, that I don't want anything to change. What are we going to do with a baby?'

'Ever heard of nannies?' he teased, his grin lopsided. 'Ever heard of apartments big enough for two people to be able to give each other enough space? And have you ever heard of working mothers? Career women . . . with children, you know?'

Rebecca smile wanly. 'Do you think it's going to work?'

'Of course it's going to work! We'll get married when you're ready and not before, and you can pursue your career as much as you've always done! We're going to make it work, Becky, because we love each other so much and we can have a wonderful life together.' He kissed her lips gently. 'You don't think I want to be married to a *hausfrau*, do you? If that were what I wanted, I'd never have gone out with you in the first place.'

She giggled weakly, kissing him back. 'I'm not exactly domesticated, am I?' she admitted. 'I'm a terrible cook and I hate cleaning.'

'But you're wonderful in bed,' he murmured between kisses, 'and you're beautiful and talented and hard-working and successful . . . and you're going to produce the baby of the century!'

She laughed outright. 'We may have to employ a housekeeper as well as a nanny!' she warned.

'With the amount we're both earning, why not a butler and chauffeur as well?'

Rebecca left the hospital the next morning, having been passed as totally fit. She'd also been given several pamphlets about pregnancy and childbirth, instructions on eating and resting and a supply of vitamin pills.

'To think I've come to this!' she moaned as she got into Stirling's car. 'My God, the next thing will be prenatal classes instead of my self-defence! Whatever became of Action Woman?'

Stirling kissed her swiftly. 'Action Woman's not going to be idle,' he assured her. 'I've got an assignment for you at the end of the week, if you're up to it.'

'Of course I'm up to it. What is it?'

'Taking some photographs of Jesse Jackson while he's in town.'

'No problem.' Rebecca settled herself in the bucket seat as the car moved slowly along East Eighty-Sixth street in the last throes of the rush hour. Stirling was dropping her off at his apartment on the way to the agency and she was looking forward to a quiet morning spent phoning various friends and contacts.

'Don't forget to call your parents and tell them you're home,' Stirling reminded her as if he'd guessed what she was planning.

Rebecca smiled. '*Your home*,' she said. 'Not my home . . . yet. My home is still in TriBeCa.'

He looked at her out of the corner of his eyes. 'OK, my home,' he said equably.

When he'd dropped her off, Rebecca hurried across the lobby to the lift, which would take her to the eighteenth floor. Once inside the apartment, she unpacked the few things Stirling had taken to the hospital for her, and then settled herself in the living-room with a cup of coffee and her address book. It was so good to be out of the hospital and back in familiar surroundings that she felt relaxed and happy. Perhaps living with Stirling wasn't going to be so stifling after all. Perhaps having a baby was even going to be fun.

When the phone rang she picked it up immediately. Thinking it must be Stirling telling her he'd arrived at the agency, she spoke gaily.

'Hi there, sweetheart.'

In the silence that followed, she realized it wasn't Stirling. 'Who is this?' she demanded sharply.

'Fancy you thinking I was that waiter.' The strange robotic voice, unearthly and eerie, came over the telephone line like an alien spirit. Suddenly she realized it *was* a robot's voice and not someone trying to disguise himself. Recently she'd watched a TV programme, that showed people who had been born dumb being able to communicate by typing what they wanted to say into a special computer, which was able to speak for them. What a brilliant tool, she thought, for a criminal who didn't want his voice recognized. She remembered that it was also possible to link the computer to a telephone. Now that they'd eliminated the waiter as a suspect, was she to visualize Jerry Ribis or Sly Capra sitting at a keyboard, operating it with the assurance of one who knows that no vocal analyst would ever be able to discover who had spoken?

'What the hell do you want?' Fear and anger made her voice harsh. Her knees were shaking and she felt icy cold. Jerry, she was sure it was him, must have watched her leave the hospital and known the moment she'd arrived at Stirling's apartment. Her eyes flew to the window. There were no curtains on it because Stirling liked maximum light. She could see straight across the ravine that separated skyscraper from skyscraper, to the office block opposite that housed a large insurance corporation.

Her eyes skimmed the hundreds of windows, picking out men at their desks, many on the phone; groups of men gathered round a table; men talking to women colleagues; men drinking their morning coffee. Men looking at their computer screens, their hands on the keyboard. There were dozens of them. From ground level up to the twentieth floor there were scores of men working at computers. Jerry, if it was Jerry, could be almost any one of them. Dark hair, pleasant nondescript face, neatly and conventionally dressed; they all looked like that. From a distance she couldn't be sure if she could see him or not. None of them were looking across to the windows where she sat, but then Jerry wouldn't, would he?

Rebecca dropped on to the floor in front of the sofa, so that she could no longer be seen and started crawling towards the door. The voice in her ear spoke again, sending a fresh shock wave through her.

'I'm going to teach you a lesson . . . a final lesson for meddling in what doesn't concern you. The end will come quickly and very unexpectedly, so don't think that by taking precautions you will be able to escape.' Metallic, hollow, and yet frighteningly real too, the voice twanged on. By now, Rebecca was sitting on the floor of Stirling's small lobby, out of sight of anyone who might be watching from the building opposite.

'I'll see you in hell first!' she yelled into the receiver, but her words were barely spoken when there was a click, and silence. The caller had hung up.

Sir Edward looked thoughtfully at Jenny as they dined out together on her first night back in New York. He'd booked a table at the fashionable Le Cirque and now as Jenny sat on the banquette facing him she felt a greater sense of self-confidence than she'd ever known before. It was very different to feeling merely grown up, she reflected. That had been like playing a game, pretending she was a sophisticated hostess and woman-about-town, while all the time she really felt like a little girl who had borrowed her mother's clothes for the evening. Now, as she sat quietly in a becoming red dress with brass buttons, her hair softly framing her face, she felt for the first time that she really knew who she was.

'I'd no idea until I came to England, when Simon had his accident, that you didn't exactly hit it off with your mother,' Sir Edward was saying.

Jenny chose her words with loyal care. 'It's not exactly that I don't hit it off with Mummy, we're just very different types. We've nothing in common, so we have no shared interests. The trouble is I always seem to annoy her because I'm not Simon! He's her favourite and always has been, from the moment he was born.'

'A lot of mothers and sons are strongly bonded,' Sir Edward observed, 'just as a lot of fathers and daughters are.'

'Like us,' said Jenny, smiling, glad now that she felt more relaxed about her relationship with him. Facing the fact that she'd been so dependent on him once but had somehow lessened her dependency without loving him any less.

'Like us, my pet,' he agreed.

'I've got something to tell you actually.' Jenny sipped her glass of Perrier and looked directly into the eyes that were so like her own.

'Something good, I hope?'

'I think so. I've left Trevor House, Daddy, and I'm out to seek adventure in the big wide world. Hence the new hair-style and clothes and make-up, not to mention the loss of about eighteen pounds.'

'I thought you were looking different.' He cocked his head on one side to examine her more thoroughly. 'Ummm. You look very nice, very nice indeed, but are you sure you've done the right thing in giving up teaching? What else can you do?'

She felt stung by his words, as if teaching small children was all she were capable of. 'I did take a shorthand and typing course when I was eighteen, and I can do book-keeping,' she protested mildly. 'I'm not a complete fool, you know. I'll look around and see what there is.'

He sounded doubtful. 'It would look like favouritism if I found you a job in the Tollemache Trust, but on the other hand, if you plan to stay in New York we'll have to think of something. I can ask around . . .'

Jenny cut in swiftly. 'Oh, I wouldn't want you to do that, Daddy. I'll find something, and I'd rather do it on my own.' She could see he looked relieved. 'There is just one thing, though,' she continued, 'may I stay with you until I can afford to rent myself a small apartment?'

'Of course, my pet! I wouldn't let you do anything else. You must stay with me permanently. New York can be a dangerous place for a young woman on her own.'

'Rebecca Kendall seems to do all right,' she reminded him. 'I thought I'd give her a ring, actually. She promised to take some pictures of me.'

'That'll be amusing. Why don't you invite her to dinner? She's a great girl. Full of spark.'

'We'll have to ask her boyfriend too,' Jenny pointed out. She hoped her father wasn't getting a thing about Rebecca. It would spoil their newfound friendship. 'It'll be nice to see her again. I really enjoyed having her to stay with me in London. Have there been any more developments about that man, Sly Capra, since you returned?'

Sir Edward jumped as if he'd received an electric shock, and his skin flushed darkly. 'Keep your voice down, for God's sake!' he whispered furiously. He glanced round at the other tables to make sure no one could have overheard her. The tables at Le Cirque were always placed close together and one had no idea who one's neighbours might be, except that they were bound to be people one knew.

Jenny blushed, taken aback by his anger. 'I didn't mean . . .' she whispered.

'We'll continue this discussion when we get home,' he muttered coldly.

Chapter Sixteen

'I'm sure it's Jerry, you know, making these calls,' Rebecca said as she lay in bed beside Stirling. 'All along I've been certain he's the one who's been pursuing me.'

'Why should he?' Stirling twined a long strand of her hair around his finger and then kissed it. 'It was Sly you photographed at the party, not Jerry.'

'Perhaps he's acting for Sly. I wish I knew what the hell to do next.'

'I think you should go away and stay with your parents. This whole thing is getting out of hand and it's obvious Sly Capra and whoever he's working with are not going to ease up. It's not safe for you to stay in New York.'

Rebecca rolled on to her side and looked at him. 'When will you accept the fact that if Sly Capra – or Jerry Ribis for that matter – is out to get me, he'll do it wherever I am? Remember how I was followed in Paris? Received a threatening message in London? I'm not safe anywhere, so I might as well stay here. What I really need is police protection.'

'I know, but we're obviously not going to get that as long as O'Hara continues to maintain that Marissa's and Mike Wilson's deaths were accidents and your robbery was just another break-in. We haven't got a shred of evidence that would stand up in court.'

'What am I supposed to do, then? Get myself genuinely attacked before anyone will take me seriously?'

'You're not going to take any more risks – like answering strange advertisements in newspapers regarding Marissa, that's for sure!' Stirling retorted. He'd been furious when she'd told him that she'd missed meeting someone who might have given her a lead on the dead girl. 'You've got to take care of yourself now, sweetheart, and if you go to your parents, they'll see to that.'

'I haven't told them I'm pregnant yet,' she said in a quiet voice. Stirling looked at her sharply, wondering just how much she really minded about having a baby.

'D'you think they'll be pleased, or shocked because we're not married?' he asked.

'I expect they'll be thrilled, partly because they like you so much, and they'll also see this as a way of getting me to settle down,' she replied, smiling. 'They're longing for us to get married.'

'So? When shall we do it?'

Rebecca moved restlessly. 'Please don't pressure me, Stirling. With this hanging over me, I'm becoming obsessed with tracking down Sly Capra and Jerry Ribis and proving their guilt. Until I do that I can't think of anything else.'

'We can't put it on the back burner forever,' he said gently. 'The baby is due in seven months. It's not like a job you can shelve until it's convenient.'

'Don't I know it, but right now I want to concentrate on one thing at a time. September is ages away.'

Stirling said no more, aware that apart from the strain she was under, she'd become very moody since she'd got pregnant. One minute she was sweet-tempered, the next irritable. Another time she'd be supercharged with energy, and an hour later utterly exhausted. Holding her hand now, as she fell asleep, he felt the best thing he could do was to be as understanding and supportive as possible. With any luck this unbearable situation with Sly Capra wouldn't last forever.

The next morning, Rebecca had a call from Jenny. 'How lovely to hear from you,' she exclaimed. 'How are you? When did you arrive in New York?'

'Yesterday lunchtime. Daddy took me out to dinner last night, and I've been busy settling in. For good this time. I've given up teaching.'

'That's great, Jenny. We must get together. When are you free?'

'I've absolutely nothing booked at all,' Jenny admitted honestly. 'How about lunch today?'

'Fine. I haven't forgotten I promised to take some pictures of you, too.'

'Then why don't you come here and I can show you all the new clothes I've bought? They cost me a fortune! I'd like you to choose what I should wear for the pictures.'

Rebecca laughed. 'I can hardly wait. I bet you're looking terrific.'

'I've lost another six pounds since you last saw me and I don't think the result's too bad,' Jenny giggled self-deprecatingly.

When Rebecca arrived at the Wenlake apartment at lunchtime, she and Jenny greeted each other effusively, and she gave a whoop of admiration when she saw Jenny's figure.

'You look marvellous!' she exclaimed warmly. It was true. The weight loss had brought a definition to Jenny's features too, revealing high cheekbones and a clear jawline. Her light make-up and gold-tipped hair gave her an almost incandescent glow, but more than anything Rebecca noticed the self-confidence and happiness that radiated from her friend.

Jenny laughed with pleasure. 'For some reason I feel much younger.'

'That's because you're dressed for your own age group, and not your mother's. Let's see this wardrobe of yours. We could take some pictures this afternoon, if you've nothing else to do,' Rebecca added, seeing Jenny's eager expression. It obviously meant so much to her to have changed her image that Rebecca made up her mind to do a mini fashion session instead of portrait shots.

After Scott had served lunch, during which Rebecca told Jenny the latest developments concerning Sly Capra and Jerry Ribis, they went through Jenny's new wardrobe. 'The rooms in this apartment make a perfect backdrop for fashion photography,' Rebecca remarked, unloading her camera case and setting up her telescopic tripod. 'Let's have you in that black velvet cocktail dress, standing in the doorway. We'll put these flowers on the table, here, and switch on the lights.' Quickly, and with an assured touch, Rebecca rearranged the setting for the pictures. Jenny got into position, self-conscious and awkward at first, but as Rebecca showed her how to stand and pose in various positions she seemed to slip naturally into graceful stances, as a professional model will do, and she had the knack, Rebecca noticed, of generating a really vivacious expression as soon as the camera started clicking.

Rebecca took rolls and rolls of film, taking Jenny in suits and day dresses, party clothes and a beautiful layered evening dress of pink and white organza, caught round the waist with a wide belt of pink velvet.

Two hours later the session was over, and they both flopped exhausted into armchairs.

'I can't thank you enough. I've never had so much fun,' said Jenny sincerely. 'D'you think they'll come out all right?'

Rebecca didn't want to raise her hopes in case she was disappointed. 'I think we've got some pretty good stuff,' she replied cautiously. 'I'd like to take some more, in a couple of days, in Central Park. Natural shots, with no make-up and you wearing just jeans and a sweater. How about it?'

Jenny gave a little wriggle of excitement. 'What fun! I say, let's have some tea, shall we? Or would you rather have coffee?'

'I shouldn't drink too much caffeine. May I have herb tea?'

'Of course.' Jenny rose and pressed the bell in the wall by the fireplace.

'Doesn't caffeine agree with you?'

'It used to, but recently it's made me feel sick and my heart pounds.'

Jenny's eyes widened. 'Why?'

'Well, it's not general knowledge yet. In fact I haven't even told my family, but I'm going to have a baby.' Rebecca smiled ruefully.

'A baby! How fantastic! You must be thrilled!'

'I suppose I will be when I'm used to the idea, but right now I'm not so sure. It means giving up so much, like my own apartment which I adore, and – oh, just the general feeling of freedom!'

'But Stirling's gorgeous, isn't he?' Jenny protested. 'My God, if I had a man like that in my life, I'd have a baby tomorrow! You don't know how lucky you are.'

'It sounds like you want to marry him yourself,' Rebecca joked. 'Oh, I'm sure everything's going to be fine, but I don't feel a hundred percent.'

'Is that why you were ill that morning when you were staying with me in London?'

'It must have been. I'm also worried, Jenny, worried sick all the time. Since the incident at the fashion show, I'm beginning to wonder if I'm not losing my sense of judgment; getting paranoid even. OK, it *was* the waiter I'd photographed, walking towards me out of the shadows, but I should have seen he was carrying a handful of cutlery and not a murder weapon. I should have realized he'd have pounced first, if he'd been about to attack me . . . and I should also have realized there were other waiters just behind him.'

Rebecca shook her head, and put her hand up to her face, covering her eyes. 'He could have been blinded if I hadn't slipped and fallen just as I was about to have another go at his face with my nails.' She looked down at her well-manicured hands. 'I'd no idea I could do so much damage.'

'But you haven't been imagining the threatening phone calls!' Jenny protested. 'Anyone would have attacked that waiter, in your position. Can't you get away and have a break? Even for a short while?'

Rebecca shook her head. 'I don't want to. I have the feeling that if I go away Stirling will try to stop me from coming back until this business is over . . . if it ever is over. It seems like years since Marissa died, and yet it's only just over three months. Three months of being scared sure can take the bloom off a girl's cheeks.'

'I wish there was something I could do. I'm sure Daddy could

272

bring pressure to bear, but when I asked him about Sly Capra last night, he was furious! I know we were in a restaurant, but he refused even to talk about it when we got home. He's scared of everything coming out, isn't he? The insider trading and all that?'

'It would ruin him if it did,' Rebecca said drily. 'I can understand him wanting to keep everything under wraps, but something's got to give, some time.'

Later that afternoon, she took a cab to the agency and gave Stirling the films she'd taken. 'These are for private use, as a present to Jenny,' she told him. 'Could you get the lab to do contacts? Then I'll choose half a dozen shots to blow-up.'

'No problem.' His dark eyes searched hers lovingly. 'Would you like to go out to dinner tonight? Make a change from carry outs and cooking?'

Rebecca came around behind his desk to where he was sitting, and putting her arms round his neck pressed her cheek against his. 'Do you really want to take an old meanie like me out to dinner?' she asked, something wistful in her voice.

Stirling reached behind him and clasped her by the calves. 'This old meanie, yes!' he quipped. 'With the best legs in the business . . . how can I resist?'

She kissed him on the neck. 'I don't deserve you.'

'You're right, you don't! Never mind, I can take it.' He turned his head, so that his mouth was close to hers.

Rebecca pressed herself closer. 'I want you . . . now,' she whispered. 'Oh, Stirling, I'm hot for you.'

He was surprised. Swings of mood were one thing, but it was the first time she'd ever suggested they have sex in the office.

'Why not?' he whispered back, feeling himself instantly aroused. 'I'll tell Minah I don't want to be disturbed.' Springing to his feet he delivered the message to his secretary, and then locked the door, just to make sure.

Rebecca came to him with outstretched arms, her lips parted, her eyes glowing. 'Take me quickly,' she breathed.

He took her in his arms, kissing her deeply, feeling the tension in her body as she moved her hips against his groin, her eyes closed now, her hands stroking his head, his neck, his face.

'I love you,' he whispered back, lifting her skirt, sliding his hand inside her panty-hose. She gasped as he touched her, rotating her pelvis against his probing hand, pressing herself down so that he thought her orgasm must be near.

'Are you sure I can't hurt you now?' he breathed softly, as he released himself from his trousers and pushed her gently back against his desk, so that she lay among his papers and photographs.

'No . . . no, you can't hurt me.' She shook her head in longing. 'Come inside me, darling. Now! Oh, please, now.'

With a thrust he entered her, wedging himself between her thighs, his hands on either side of her, taking his weight.

Rebecca raised her face to his, her eyes dark now, her breath coming fast. Kissing her again, he started moving back and forth, increasing the speed as her breathing quickened. He could feel the tumescence and moisture surrounding him as he plunged deeper, trying to be gentle because of the baby, but desperate to make her his, desperate to satisfy her need and his own.

Suddenly she convulsed so violently she nearly displaced him, but he held on to her tightly, gripping the floor with his feet, managing to stay inside so that they seemed locked together in a rhythm he didn't dare let go of. A few seconds later, as he pulsed and throbbed with a violence that matched hers, he felt himself black out for a moment. Then he held her close until the strength returned to his legs.

'Oh, my God,' Rebecca said in a muffled voice. 'It's never been like that before, has it?'

'No, I don't think it has. Are you all right, my sweetheart?' Stirling took her face in his hands, looking down at her with tenderness.

She smiled back. 'I feel wonderful. It's just what I needed, I was so strung out before.' She paused for a moment. 'Let's not go out to dinner tonight after all.'

'Why not?'

She gave a wicked smile as she looked into his eyes. 'Because it would be nice to stay at home and do it all over again,' she whispered.

Two days later, Rebecca and Jenny spent the morning in Central Park, while Rebecca clicked away on two cameras, one loaded with colour film, the other black and white.

'You're a natural, did you know that?' she said, as Jenny flung back her head, laughing, her hands in the pockets of her tight-fitting jeans. 'We're getting some great shots.'

Jenny laughed again, obviously enjoying herself. 'Shall I lean against the back of this bench?' she asked, taking up a pose that looked perfect for the camera and yet was entirely natural.

'Good. Turn a bit to your left,' Rebecca said encouragingly. 'Now look up. That's it. Now turn and look right into the lens. Good. Good. A bit more of a smile. Wonderful.'

Smoothly, as if she'd been doing it all her life, Jenny took up one pose after another. She didn't seem to have a bad angle, no matter which way she looked, thought Rebecca.

At last the session came to an end. They were sitting on a bench, discussing photography, when Rebecca suddenly gripped Jenny's arm.

'Don't turn round now but I think there's someone in the bushes, over on your right,' she whispered. 'Someone's watching us.'

Jenny looked scared. 'Can you see who it is?'

'No, but keep your head turned this way and keep talking to me.' As she spoked she slipped the telephoto lens on to her Leica. 'I'm going to take a close-up of whoever it is, but I want to surprise them so they won't duck out of sight.' Then with a swift movement she raised the camera, and looking through the viewfinder took shot after shot, moving the lens from left to right until she'd covered the area.

'I knew it!' she muttered under her breath.

'What is it? Can you see who it is?'

'No, but as soon as I started taking pictures there was a movement among the bushes, and whoever it was got out of there.' She swore, her eyes still scanning the undergrowth.

'Do you think you got a shot of them?'

'I can't be sure, not until I get the film developed. OK, let's go.' Rebecca swung to her feet, camera case hanging from her shoulder. 'I've rather gone off Central Park now,' she said with an attempt at flippancy. 'Let's go to the agency and get Stirling to buy us lunch.'

When they told him what had happened, he grimly took Rebecca's films from her. 'I'll have these developed,' he said. 'Let's hope you've got something on film that will give us a lead.'

When Rebecca got back to Stirling's apartment later that afternoon, there was a message on the answering machine for her to call Karen. They'd been in touch several times since Rebecca's return from Europe, and had been trying to make a date for lunch to suit them both. When she got through, her friend gave a squeal of delight.

'Becky! Thanks for returning my call. We're frantically busy here, but my boss is going to be out of town on Friday so I can take a longer lunch break. Are you doing anything?'

'No, Friday would be fine. Where shall we meet?'

'Why not pick me up at my office? Then we can go to some place close by, depending on how we feel. I'm dying to tell you about Genghis!'

'Who?'

'Genghis, my new fella. He's gorgeous.'

'You can't really know someone called Genghis!' Rebecca laughed.

'Why not? His mother had a thing about Genghis Khan, and so she called him Genghis Rock Maximilian Flaherty.'

'I don't believe it! Where do you find them?'

Karen answered indignantly: 'He's a wonderful human being. Very kind and thoughtful. You'll love him!'

'I'm sure!' Nothing's changed, Rebecca thought with nostalgic amusement. She actually missed Karen and her string of boy-friends. Aloud she said: 'Twelve-thirty on Friday, then?'

'Great. And by the way, is there any chance of our getting back to TriBeCa soon? Staying with my sister is cramping my style.'

'Not so that it's noticeable!' Rebecca rejoined. 'I'll tell you what's happening when I see you on Friday.' She decided to wait until she saw Karen before mentioning the baby.

'OK. Twelve-thirty on Friday. I'll look forward to it.'

Stirling flipped the prints of Rebecca's shots of the bushes in Central Park on to the coffee table when he got home that evening. 'No luck, I'm afraid,' he said. 'I can make out the dark outline of someone, but it's impossible to see who it is.'

Rebecca picked up the photographs and examined them closely. 'Hell, you're right. It's impossible to recognize anyone in these. What a drag.' Irritably, she tossed them down.

'Great shots of Jenny, though,' Stirling said cheerfully. 'Has she ever thought of going into modelling?' He was moving restlessly round the living-room as he talked. In spite of his apparent good spirits Rebecca knew he was more worried about Jerry Ribis and Sly Capra than he was admitting.

'I don't think so,' she replied. 'I think she's got potential but I didn't say anything to her in case it raised her hopes.'

'I've half a mind to show these pictures, and the other ones you took of her, to the editor of *Vogue*. What d'you think?' Stirling picked up a magazine that lay on the window sill and then put it down again without looking at it. He turned towards Rebecca, who was watching him. 'Oh, Jesus, I can't concentrate,' he burst out suddenly. 'Has anything else happened today?'

'No, nothing,' she replied. 'I made a few calls . . . I'm meeting Karen for lunch on Friday, but that's all. Come and sit down, Stirling. You're making me feel edgy, prowling around like a caged lion. Let's discuss Jenny. Yes, I think you should show these pictures to *Vogue*. I think, with a bit of experience, she could have a great career. She's a natural.'

He came and sat on the sofa beside her and together they studied the shots. 'OK,' he said at last, 'I'll have some of the best ones blown-up and we'll see what we can do.'

'It could be the answer to her problems,' Rebecca said thoughtfully.

On Friday morning, she awoke feeling tired and rather nauseous. It happened from time to time now, but if she rested she usually recovered by mid-morning.

'Stay in bed,' Stirling advised, handing her a glass of plain soda-water. 'This will help, and try and go back to sleep.'

'Thanks.' Wearily she wondered how many mornings were going to be spoilt by her pregnancy. She hated feeling unwell, and resentfully leaned back against the pillows sipping the water.

'Shall I cancel Karen?' Stirling suggested.

Rebecca shook her head. 'No. I want to see her. I haven't told her about the baby yet, and we've got to decide what to do about my apartment. We can't leave it standing empty indefinitely.'

He kissed her gently on the cheek. 'Call me at the office if you need anything.'

'I will. Sorry to be such bad company.' She looked up at him gratefully. 'I'm sure I'll be OK in an hour or so.'

'Stay in bed if you're not. You can always see Karen another day.'

Leaving the bedroom quietly, with the curtains still drawn to shield her eyes from the dazzling March sunshine, he crept out of the apartment, double locking the door after him.

Rebecca snuggled down for a nap. When she awoke, two hours later, she felt recovered and refreshed. It was half-past ten; time for breakfast and a leisurely shower before she set off to meet Karen. In the kitchen she pressed fresh orange juice and made herself some toast. Funny, she reflected, how pregnancy can make you feel sick one moment and starving the next. After her shower she spent some time deciding what to wear. The trouble was that all her pants were too tight round the waist now, and regretfully she realized she'd soon have to go shopping for maternity wear. Meanwhile a pretty yellow suit with a pleated skirt still fitted. Tying her long hair back into a ponytail with a yellow and green scarf she was just about to leave the apartment when the telephone rang.

'Hello?' she said, answering it.

'Is this Rebecca Kendall?' asked a man's voice.

'Who is this?'

'Well, my name's Genghis Flaherty. I'm a friend of Karen . . .'

Relief swept over her. 'Oh, yes. Hi! Is she having to cancel lunch?'

'No, not at all,' he said swiftly. 'You were supposed to pick her up at her office at twelve-thirty, weren't you?'

'Yes.'

'She's awfully sorry she couldn't call you herself, but she had to take some contracts to a client over on Fifty-Ninth Street and Second Avenue, and there's been some hitch in signing them so she's still there. She wondered if you could go there to pick her up, instead of her own office?'

'Sure. No problem.'

'I'll give you the address.'

'Thanks.' Rebecca reached for the pad and pencil.

'I hope this doesn't inconvenience you too much?'

Karen is right, she thought. This young man, improbably called Genghis, sounds charming.

'Not at all,' she assured him. 'I hope we get to meet some time,' she added.

'I'm sure we will. Perhaps the four of us could have dinner one night? You and your boyfriend and Karen and I?'

'That sounds like fun.'

Automatically slinging her camera bag over her shoulder, Rebecca left the apartment a couple of minutes later, and started walking along the sidewalk as she looked for a taxi. Overhead the sky domed crystal clear and there was a feel of spring in the air. For the first time in ages she felt full of well-being and happiness. Maybe having a baby wasn't so awful after all. Maybe getting married wouldn't wipe out her independence as she'd feared. After all, there was no one in the world as understanding as Stirling, and she knew she loved him as she would never love anyone else. Her step quickened with a feeling of anticipation. Everything was going to be all right after all. She could feel it in her bones.

At that moment she saw a cab and hailed it. Giving the driver the address, she settled in the back, looking forward to her lunch with Karen. The cab stopped outside an old building which, at some time in the past, had been divided into offices. Genghis had said Karen had taken some documents to the real estate company on the third floor. She looked at the row of brass bells by the intercom. Yes, there it was. Neary and Assinder Partnership. Real Estate Agents. She pressed the bell and a moment later a girl's voice answered.

'Can I help you?'

'I've come to pick up Karen Rossini. I believe she's in your office.'

The receptionist sounded bright and cheerful. 'Come on up.' The door buzzed as the lock disengaged, and Rebecca pushed it open and entered a long narrow hall, elegantly furnished with a grey carpet and a console table on which stood a vase of flowers. Walking to the far end, she got into the waiting elevator and pressed the button marked three. Slowly and smoothly it rose up through the building and when she alighted she found herself in a small lobby. Opposite her was a door on which were painted the words: 'Reception'.

It swung open effortlessly. Entering she found herself in a large square office. There were two desks facing the door. One was occupied by Detective Tom O'Hara and the other by Jerry Ribis.

'Damned good pictures, of course, but then Rebecca only takes the best,' said the editor of *Vogue*. 'I think we should do a feature on Jenny Wenlake and use some of these shots.'

Stirling leaned forward eagerly. He might have been in the business for years, but he still got a thrill out of closing a deal. 'That will please Rebecca. She thinks Jenny shows promise as a model.'

'It can't hurt to be the daughter of Sir Edward Wenlake either!' the editor replied drily. Then she added: 'In fairness, though, I do think she's got star quality. I'll recommend her to a top agency and she could go far. We might use her for the October issue. We're doing a big bridal spread with wedding dresses from all the top couture houses. The English Rose look is going to be all the rage this fall.'

'That's fantastic,' Stirling replied, genuinely pleased.

They shook hands as Stirling rose to go. It wasn't often he went to see the magazine editors in person, but there were exceptions, and *Vogue*, being all-powerful, was one of them.

When he got back to the office, Minah handed him a message. 'It's from Karen Rossini,' she explained. 'She was expecting Rebecca to pick her up from her office for lunch, and she wonders what's happened? Rebecca hasn't shown up.'

Without a word, Stirling strode into his own office, trying to quench the sudden feeling of sick dread that swept over him. He picked up the phone and dialled the number of his apartment. There was no answer. Even the answering machine hadn't been turned on, although he and Rebecca always switched it on when they went out. Of course Rebecca might be sleeping deeply or she might be ill . . . Next he dialled Karen's office number. 'Karen Rossini, please,' he snapped abruptly.

When he got through, he didn't mince his words. 'Stirling here. What exactly were your arrangements with Rebecca for today?'

'She was supposed to pick me up at twelve-thirty and then we

279

were going to have lunch somewhere nearby. It's no big deal, Stirling. I just wondered what had happened?' Karen sounded unperturbed.

'Which restaurant were you going to?' Stirling's shortness sounded brutal.

'We hadn't actually decided. We agreed to wait and see what we felt like. If we'd wanted a place that's good for fish we'd have gone to . . .'

'Are you sure she understood that?' Stirling cut in.

'Sure, I'm sure.'

'Is there any chance Rebecca could be waiting for you in some restaurant right now?'

Karen sounded bewildered and a little scared. 'No. What's the matter? Maybe she just forgot.'

Stirling's voice was tight. 'Rebecca didn't forget. Something's happened. If you hear anything from her – anything, Karen – call me at the office, will you? Leave a message with Minah if I'm out. OK?'

'Yes, OK, but I'm sure she's all right, Stirling, unless you think . . .' Her voice seemed to freeze on the line.

'That's exactly what I'm afraid of.' He hung up and hurried into the adjoining office. 'I'm going out again,' he told Minah. 'If Rebecca contacts you, find out exactly where she is and what's happening.'

'Is something wrong?' Minah's exquisite black face looked up anxiously.

'I think there probably is,' Stirling replied succinctly. Then he had a sudden thought. 'Have you got Sir Edward Wenlake's number? Good. Get it for me, will you?' There was just a chance Jenny might be able to throw some light on Rebecca's whereabouts. When he got through, Scott answered.

'I'm afraid Miss Wenlake's out, sir. I'm not expecting her back until later this afternoon. May I take a message?'

Stirling thought rapidly. 'Has a Rebecca Kendall been in touch today, d'you know?'

'Not that I know of, sir. I do know the young lady, but she hasn't been here for several days.'

'And she hasn't telephoned?'

'No, sir. I've taken no calls from Miss Kendall.'

'Thanks for your help.'

With his mind in a turmoil, Stirling flung himself out of the agency and started running the three blocks to his apartment. Please, God, let her still be in bed, he prayed, as his feet pounded on the pavement and his chest felt tight with the exertion. Please, God, let this be a false alarm. Let her be in bed, asleep, feeling sick, anything, as long as she's safe. But with a sense of dark foreboding, he knew it wouldn't be so.

Rebecca faced the two men. Her first thought was: Karen has betrayed me. Tricked me into coming here today. She's been involved all along.

O'Hara and Ribis had risen from their seats and were coming towards her now, walking around the side of their desks.

Rebecca stood her ground, sizing them up, her jaw tense and her eyes watchful. She might have been able to take on one of them single-handed but two was impossible, especially as O'Hara must weigh over two hundred and twenty pounds.

Jerry Ribis spoke first. 'I'm sorry about this, but we had to get you to come here, Rebecca. Come and sit down. We want to talk to you.'

So they're going to talk before they kill me, she thought numbly. In silence she sank into the chair and waited. Bereft of words, she could only stare with loathing, as the two men returned to their desks.

'It's been necessary to put a tap on Stirling Hertfelder's home phone,' Jerry began. 'That's how we knew you were lunching with Karen Rossini, today. We used the only ploy we could think of to get you to come here.'

Rebecca's mind was beginning to clear. So Stirling's phone was tapped after all! She found her voice again as another thought occurred to her, something far more vital. 'So Karen's not involved with you?'

'No way.' It was O'Hara who answered. He rested his beefy arms on the desk in front of him, and Rebecca noticed again how the back of his hands were dark with hair. She averted her eyes, unable to look at him without revulsion. 'You've been giving us a hard time, getting in our way,' O'Hara continued. 'You've been asking too many questions, sticking your nose in where it ain't wanted. It's got to stop.'

Jerry shot O'Hara a warning look, as if he was saying too much. 'Let me explain to her,' he said quietly.

'You've been determined to prove Marissa Montclare was murdered, haven't you?' O'Hara continued, ignoring Jerry. His tone was belligerent.

'Yes, I have, because I'm sure she was,' Rebecca said hotly. Now that she was cornered a strange feeling of strength was gradually growing within her. She felt she had nothing to lose. There would be no more looking over her shoulder, wondering what the shadows held. She was face to face with the enemy, and the worst that could happen was that they would prolong the suspense before they killed her.

'Of course you're quite right,' Jerry said. 'She was murdered by someone called Sly Capra who is a drugs dealer, in a big way. He got a waiter to open a window at Sir Edward's party, and then managed to grab her and drag her behind the heavy velvet drapes and then push her out.'

'While you watched,' Rebecca said bitterly.

'No, I was in the same room as you when it happened. You may not remember, but I followed you into the dining-room when you started taking pictures. Then I gave you a lift home.'

'I remember. You've been following me ever since.'

'Sometimes I have, and sometimes I haven't. On occasions it was me: at Kennedy Airport when you were flying to Europe or in the park the other day, for instance, but at other times it was undoubtedly Sly Capra.' Jerry had risen as he talked, going over to a coffee percolator in the corner. On the table beside it was a tray laid with three cups and saucers and a container of milk. 'Coffee?' he asked politely.

She shook her head, wishing they'd get to the point. Was she supposed to sit through a resumé on how Sly Capra had befriended Marissa at the Golden Palm after she'd won the jackpot, and had then persuaded her to come to New York so she could seduce rich businessmen into telling her their business secrets?

'There's not much I don't know about what's been going on,' she said coldly.

'But a little knowledge is a very dangerous thing,' O'Hara cut in. He acknowledged the cup of coffee Jerry placed before him with a curt nod of his head. 'You've been poking into business that doesn't concern you, and you could screw things up for all of us. D'you want to end up like that English asshole, Mike Wilson?'

Rebecca stiffened, gritting her teeth, forcing herself to look at O'Hara, eyeball to eyeball. Suddenly there were flickering black and white spots before her eyes, like a television screen when there is no transmission, and a wave of nausea threatened to engulf her. She clenched her fists in her lap, digging her nails into the palms of her hands until the pain cut like a shaft of light through the fog that was closing in on her.

'Perhaps I will have some coffee,' she said, surprising herself by the calmness of her voice. Then she bent down as if to adjust the

282

buckle on the front of her shoe, forcing the blood back into her head as she hunched her shoulders tightly; another trick she'd learned in self-defence classes.

'Of course,' she heard Jerry say as if from a distance. 'Do you take cream and sugar?'

'Both,' she managed to answer. By the time he placed the coffee in front of her, she was able to straighten up slowly, realizing her vision had cleared. She was bathed in sweat, though, and her clothes felt cold and clammy as they clung to her. Then the strong hot coffee scorched a path down to her stomach, making her feel better, and she knew the fainting fit had passed.

'Are you all right?' Jerry asked, eyeing her doubtfully.

'Fine,' Rebecca said firmly.

'Then I think we'd better start explaining things to you. As Detective O'Hara says, your meddling is very dangerous.'

She sat listening, thinking there was nothing more detestable than a bent cop. Jerry Ribis was bad enough, but a policeman like O'Hara, who was prepared to suppress evidence and turn a blind eye to murder, was something so low and utterly disgusting that she felt sick.

'You may not realize this,' Jerry was saying, 'but I'm in the police force too.'

Now I'm up against two corrupt cops instead of one. Not that it makes much difference, she thought bitterly.

'I'm an under-cover agent for the FBI. O'Hara and I have been trying to get evidence on Sly Capra and his associates,' he was saying.

Startled, Rebecca blinked, not fully taking in what he was saying. 'What?'

Jerry smiled his mysterious smile again. 'We're detailed to get evidence on Capra that will stick, not only for the murder of Marissa Montclare but for half a dozen other crimes as well. You thought we were in with him, didn't you?'

Bewildered, Rebecca looked from him to O'Hara and back again. 'You're not?' she asked uncertainly.

'Damn right we're not,' cut in O'Hara. 'When I lay my hands on that motherfucker I'll pin a whole string of murder raps on him – enough for a one-way ticket to Sing-Sing, no matter how many fancy lawyers he hires.'

'But . . .' Rebecca's head was spinning. There were a hundred questions she wanted to ask; a thousand things that didn't add up. It struck her that this could be another trick too, to lull her into a false sense of security.

'I've been after Sly for a long time now, even before he approached Marissa in Las Vegas,' Jerry was explaining. 'Sometimes I've pretended to be him, to someone who didn't know what he looked like, and on other occasions I've said I was his business partner in order to find out what I could . . . like with Mike Wilson. I knew he was sniffing around and I wanted to know if he'd found out anything interesting.'

'Then you bumped him off?' Rebecca exclaimed, aghast.

Jerry looked shocked. 'Of course not! That was one of Capra's people. They'd guessed that Mike Wilson had found out a lot more than they cared to let him know. They killed him. I felt really bad about that. I should have told him I was with the FBI, not Capra's partner, and I should have told him to get out of the country right away. But of course I couldn't blow my own cover and Mike Wilson was one hell of a motor-mouth. If he hadn't gone bragging to your boyfriend, he might be alive now.'

'But you let him put Stirling in danger,' Rebecca protested. 'What protection did you give him? How did you know Sly Capra wasn't going to have him killed too for knowing too much? Have you any idea what we've been through. Do you know I keep getting threatening calls? Did you know I was followed in Paris? Why weren't Stirling and I given police protection?'

O'Hara regarded her caustically. 'You were, both of you, although you didn't realize it. We had a round-the-clock watch on you both.'

Rebecca's mouth fell open and she looked at him with unbelieving eyes. 'But I never saw anyone.'

'Why should you? The whole point of police protection in these circumstances is to smoke out the threat to you. We wanted Sly Capra to show his hand. Give us evidence we could use. D'you think we'd have got that if we'd laid on armed cops to hold your hand in public, day and night! We didn't want Capra to know we suspected *anything*, get it?'

'So that's why you insisted Marissa's death was an accident?'

'Uh huh!' O'Hara agreed blandly.

'Was it your doing that a verdict of accidental death was brought in at the inquest?'

'That was a bit of luck for us, and temporarily for Capra, as it turned out,' Jerry interjected. 'Sir Edward Wenlake and his Vice-Chairman, Brian Norris, were so anxious to hush up the whole thing, in order to avoid a scandal, that they played right into our hands. Both of them swore she'd slipped on the polished floor and fallen. Sir Edward didn't even realize I was at his party that night, he was so drunk.'

284

'Tell me something.' Rebecca leaned forward, her mind in a turmoil, the questions she wanted to ask tumbling over each other. 'You went to Las Vegas to see Marissa, didn't you? After she'd been approached by Sly Capra?'

Jerry nodded.

'Did you warn her what she was getting into?' Rebecca persisted.

'I couldn't. I had to get her to talk; find out from her what Capra had asked her to do. We had her tailed from then on, as we gathered information about Capra's activities. We thought she'd come to no harm, of course, as long as she and Capra were partners. He needed her too much.'

'Then what went wrong?' Rebecca closed her eyes for a moment, as if to blot out those last moments of Marissa's life; those moments when, obviously frightened, she'd tugged at Sir Edward's arm, trying to tell him something. Then the terrible echoing scream that seemed to go on and on, so that Rebecca still felt it was inside her own head.

'She'd double-crossed him,' said Jerry.

'Marissa double-crossed Sly Capra?'

He nodded. 'Everything was fine at first. She was having a very good time. He'd set her up in this ritzy apartment, full of nice paintings and furniture. He bought her clothes and jewels to wear, and before long Sir Edward fell in love with her. I believe she was really fond of him too. I imagine, for a girl like that, his title and position were a real turn on. And she wanted to be as rich as him one day.

'Anyway, as you probably know by now, the deal she had with Capra was that he'd invest her winnings, along with his own money, on the tips she'd given him. Then they'd both do well. Capra's as crooked as they come, but there is a sense of honour among thieves and they do stick by each other. I don't think Marissa would have come to any harm if she'd played it straight with him. At that time we were investigating him for importing and selling drugs, but of course after the events of New Year's Eve, all that became secondary to the murder rap.'

'How did she swindle him?' Rebecca's voice was almost awestruck.

'At first she passed on details of deals the Tollemache Trust was involved in, and with insider knowledge she and Capra were able to do some very profitable trading. But Marissa was a greedy girl. She became upset that Capra was making so much more money than herself. Of course he had ten times as much to invest in the first place, but she didn't seem to see it like that. So she started feeding

285

him false information, and then with her own money, and with the help of a broker recommended to her by Sir Edward Wenlake, she did her own insider trading, cutting Capra right out of the picture.'

'She must have been very bright,' Rebecca exclaimed. 'I wouldn't have a clue how to buy and sell stock and take advantage of take-over bids and that kind of thing.'

'Marissa was nobody's fool,' Jerry agreed. 'At that time, she was with Sir Edward virtually day and night. No doubt unwittingly, he taught her every trick in the book. When she died she must have been worth three or four million dollars. No wonder Mike Wilson and David McNee were desperate to get their hands on it for her family.'

'David McNee?' Rebecca repeated. 'Do you know him? I was going to meet him, but I missed the appointment.'

Jerry smiled. 'I know! I saw your reply to his advertisement when his folder fell open. That's what prompted us to get you here today. We felt forced to tell you what was going on, for your own safety.'

'You went to meet him? At the Inter-Continental Hotel?'

'Yes. I wrote to him and signed myself "Sly Capra", and when I turned up that's who he thought I was. He knew nothing, so I advised him to get the hell out, for his own good.' Jerry laughed. 'I scared the shit out of him!'

'This is an incredible story,' said Rebecca. She still felt dazed and shocked, and knew it would be some time before she could rid herself of her fear of Jerry and O'Hara.

'Do you know what has become of Marissa's money?'

Jerry spread his hands, shrugging. 'We have no idea. She practically emptied her bank account a couple of days before she died, but we don't know what she did with the money. I have a feeling she realized Capra was on to her and she was desperate to hang on to her nest-egg, no matter what happened.'

'Pity she wasn't more interested in hanging on to her life,' O'Hara remarked lugubriously.

'I don't think she ever imagined Capra would turn up at Sir Edward's party,' said Jerry. 'We'd been tailing him all evening, wondering what he'd do, and when he made his way to the Wenlake apartment, I must say we were pretty surprised. He was taking a terrific risk. I thought he'd just gone to scare her. I didn't see how he could harm her in front of a couple of hundred people in a private house.' His voice dropped. 'I was wrong. He started chatting with a woman called Theresa Bendotto . . .'

'I went to see her because I'd photographed Sly with her,' Rebecca interjected.

'We know,' said O'Hara.

Jerry continued, 'Then Capra went to the men's room and I got one of my agents, posing as a guest, to follow him. Somehow Capra gave him the slip . . . and the rest you know.'

'Poor Marissa,' Rebecca said quietly. 'So it was revenge on his part?'

'Yes, and of course it suited him to have her die in Sir Edward's apartment because he hoped the scandal would bring about a massive drop in the price of the Tollemache Trust stock so that he could buy in cheap. Then, when it all blew over and the shares went up again, he could sell out at a profit.'

Rebecca shook her head, stunned by the revelations. Then she asked: 'Why did you trick me into coming here today? Why are you telling me all this?'

'To tell you to keep your trap shut,' O'Hara said shortly. Jerry shot him another glance. They might be working together, Rebecca thought, but O'Hara's partner was obviously uncomfortable with his rough style.

'For your own protection,' Jerry explained. 'We really want you and Stirling to lie low until we've got this sewn up. You're both in real danger, you know, and you are hampering our investigations. Protecting you both is also taking up police resources.' He paused, and Rebecca continued to regard him quizzically.

'Having got to know you better in the past few weeks than perhaps you realize,' continued Jerry. 'I knew you wouldn't give up on seeing Marissa's murderer caught unless we told you all the facts. That's why you're here today. I know you will tell your boyfriend everything, but naturally this is not to go any further.'

Rebecca nodded. 'I understand. How long will it be before you can arrest Capra?'

'Christ only knows,' burst out O'Hara. 'Jerry's right. Unless you back off you could screw everything up for us.'

'I do get the message, Detective O'Hara,' Rebecca said coldly. He might be on the level but she would never like him. She turned to Jerry. 'What about Jenny Wenlake?' she asked. 'She knows everything that's been going on so far because I've told her. So does Sir Edward. Are they safe?'

'Don't worry, we'll continue to keep an eye on both of them, but please don't mention anything we've talked about today, especially that I am really an undercover agent,' he said. 'You are still the one in most danger because of that photograph you took of Capra on New Year's Eve. As for Miss Wenlake, I don't think she's at risk at all. I mean, she's not likely to expose anything that would harm her father or his business interests, is she?'

Chapter Seventeen

Jerry arranged for a car to take Rebecca back to Stirling's apartment.

'I'd rather go to the Hertfelder Agency. I want to see Stirling'.

'We'd rather you didn't,' said Jerry. 'We'd like you to stay indoors and not move around the city any more than you have to. The security at your boyfriend's apartment is good because there's only one entrance and one elevator. Believe me, we have them watched twenty-four hours a day. Go back there, please, and stay there. I'm afraid we'll also have to continue to tap the telephone in case Capra calls you again. We're anxious to know where he's making the calls from.'

Rebecca looked frustrated. 'But what about my work? What about things like shopping for food? I can't be a prisoner, confined to a three-roomed apartment. You can't expect me to stay indoors permanently!'

'You got any brains, you'll listen to us,' O'Hara snapped. 'We don't want another stiff on our hands because you refuse to act sensibly.'

'But if you're giving me police protection!' she exploded angrily. The two men regarded her silently. 'How long am I supposed to go into hiding?' she added more quietly.

'I hope it won't be for long,' Jerry said. 'We're nearly there. It may be only a matter of days before we make arrests. That's why we wanted to explain things to you without delay; we're at a delicate stage of the operation, and we were scared that if you were kept in the dark you would do something that would jeopardize our chances of success.'

'You're also going to have to think up a good excuse for missing your lunch date with your friend, Karen today. We don't want her to know anything at this stage,' said O'Hara.

Rebecca thought for a moment. 'I could say I didn't feel well. I overslept and didn't wake up until . . .' She glanced at her wristwatch. 'My God, is that the time? Three-fifteen?' She shrugged, 'Oh, well, when I tell her I'm pregnant, I'm sure she'll understand.'

Jerry's eyebrows shot up. 'Pregnant?' he repeated. 'I didn't know that.'

'Unless you've got Stirling's and my bedroom bugged as well, there's no reason why you should,' she replied crisply. Jerry, she observed, had the grace to blush.

'Of course we haven't got his apartment bugged,' he said hastily, 'only the phone.'

'Right then.' Rebecca rose, feeling suddenly very tired. Her back ached and so did her head. 'Can I go now?'

'Sure.' Jerry rose too, and came around the desk. 'I'm sorry we had to trick you into coming here today, but it was the only way of getting you on your own without arousing Capra's suspicions.' He smiled contritely. 'Are you sure you're OK?'

'Yes.' Rebecca looked around the room, at the framed photographs of various buildings. 'This really does look like a real estate office.'

'It is . . . for today,' O'Hara said shortly. 'By tonight it will have gone.'

'Can I call Karen from here?'

O'Hara pushed the phone towards her. 'Go ahead.'

'Thanks.'

Unaware that Karen had already been in contact with Stirling, she was startled when her friend gave a shriek.

'Rebecca! Where in God's name have you been? Stirling's going out of his mind. He went back to the apartment to see if you were all right, and you weren't there. He's called me about six times to see if I've heard anything. At the moment he's calling up all the hospitals . . . I even think he called the cops. Where have you been?' Her voice was so loud O'Hara and Jerry could hear every word. Rebecca looked at them questioningly.

'Say you got involved in taking some important pictures. Say it was a scoop!' Jerry whispered urgently.

'Can you ever forgive me, Karen?' Rebecca said smoothly, taking his cue. 'A scoop absolutely fell into my lap. I've been taking pictures all morning and I got an exclusive too. I'm terribly sorry. If there'd been anyway I could have contacted you, I would have.'

'Then why didn't Stirling know you were on an assignment?' Karen demanded querulously.

'I couldn't contact him, for the same reason I couldn't contact you,' Rebecca lied. 'I got caught up totally unexpectedly.' She cast her eyes to heaven as Jerry and O'Hara watched her tensely. 'Karen, forgive me, and I'll call Stirling right away. We'll make another date for lunch, OK?'

'Of course it's OK, but put Stirling out of his misery,' Karen chided. 'The poor man seems to think you've been murdered, like Marissa. He's frantic.'

'I will, I will. Don't worry,' Rebecca promised. When she hung up she turned to Jerry. 'I'd better get hold of Stirling.'

'For God's sake, do! Tell him you're all right, you can't explain everything now but say you'll meet him back at his apartment in twenty minutes,' said Jerry. 'I'll come with you. I want to ask him exactly which police precincts he's phoned and who he's talked to. This was supposed to be an undercover operation,' he added, trying to suppress his irritation.

'Yes,' interjected O'Hara. 'Now the whole fucking police force knows that something's going down.'

Stirling got back to the apartment first, still not convinced that everything was all right. Rebecca had sounded very guarded on the phone, as if she were afraid of saying too much, and he was desperately worried about her. When her key turned in the lock, he bounded forward and then pulled up short when he saw she had someone with her.

'It's OK, Stirling. This is Jerry. He's with the FBI,' she explained hurriedly when she saw his expression.

'What the hell . . . ?' Stirling looked at Jerry suspiciously.

'It's all right, I'll explain everything in a minute,' she said. 'Jerry just wants to ask you who you've called to say I was missing? He's working undercover and no one must know where I've been this morning.'

Stirling relaxed when Jerry produced his identification. Although he still looked wary, he told him which police stations and hospitals he'd called.

'It's only natural I was worried,' he added defensively.

'That's OK. I'll deal with it now.' Jerry smiled briefly, but wearily. 'I've got to go, but this building is well covered and I'll keep you informed of events. Meanwhile, stay here, Rebecca. Don't go out, and if you get any more of those calls try and keep them talking as long as possible. I think they're made from Capra's headquarters and so far we haven't got a line on where it is.' He turned to leave. She followed him to the door.

'Thanks,' she said, suddenly feeling grateful. O'Hara she detested and always would, but Jerry was different. Now that it had really sunk in that he wasn't the enemy, she couldn't help looking upon him as a protector. 'Where can I contact you if I have to?' she asked.

'You can't,' he replied flatly. 'But don't worry. I'll stay in touch.' Then he was gone, the apartment door shutting quietly behind him.

'Well!' Rebecca turned and looked at Stirling. 'Have I got a lot to tell you!'

Rebecca woke in the middle of the night, realizing even before she was fully conscious that something was deeply wrong. In the dimness of their bedroom, she could see Stirling's outline lying beside her in the double bed. As she rolled over to reach out and touch him, she knew what it was.

'Stirling!' her voice was loud, agonized. 'I'm bleeding . . . I think I'm having a miscarriage.'

In a second he was awake and had turned on the bedside light. 'Are you sure?'

'Yes . . . it's bad. I'm afraid to move.'

He reached for the phone. 'I'll call an ambulance. Hang in there, sweetheart.' He held her hand tightly as he gave the emergency service the address.

Rebecca lay on her side, her knees drawn up, her face pinched-looking. 'Can you get some towels from the bathroom,' she whispered. 'I'm so sorry, Stirling. So sorry.'

'It's not your fault, sweetheart,' he assured her. She sounded so apologetic, like she'd miscarried on purpose, it broke his heart. 'If anyone's to blame it's Jerry Ribis and that damned O'Hara for giving you such a shock yesterday.'

He brought the towels to her, then wrapped a sweater round her shoulders. She was shaking all over now, and her skin was pale and clammy. Struggling into trousers and a sweater himself, he pushed his feet into sneakers, ready to accompany her to hospital. Then he sat down on the edge of the bed.

'You're going to be all right, sweetheart,' he kept repeating. 'Thousands of women miscarry the first time. You've had a shock and you've been under a great deal of strain. It's not surprising, really.'

At that moment the doorbell rang. With relief, and surprised at the swiftness of the paramedics, Stirling rushed to the door and opened it. A man dressed as a janitor stood there. In his hand was a mobile phone.

'I'm with Ribis,' he said briefly. 'We picked up your emergency call a minute ago. I thought you'd like to know we've made sure the ambulance is on its way. Top priority. It should be here in a couple of minutes.'

'Thanks,' Stirling said gratefully.

'I hope your lady will be all right.'

'Yes . . . er . . . thanks.'

'We'll be keeping an eye on her when she arrives at the hospital. We'll see that she's given a private room and there'll be a couple of our people on duty all the time.'

'Thanks. Do you mind if I go back to her now? Can I leave you here, so you can let the paramedics in as soon as they arrive?'

The man nodded. 'Go right ahead.'

Rebecca was weeping when he got back to her. 'It wasn't that I didn't want the baby,' she sobbed.

'Oh, I know it wasn't, sweetheart.' Stirling felt his own eyes sting and brim with salty tears, knowing that the child whose birth he had so been looking forward to was being swept away, and that there was nothing either he or Rebecca could do about it. He put his arms around her. 'There will be other babies,' he reassured her tenderly. 'You and I have only just begun our lives together, Becky. There will be as many babies as you want in the future. We have a whole long wonderful life to look forward to, my sweetheart.' For answer she squeezed his hand, wanting to believe him.

When the paramedics arrived, moments later, they wrapped her in blankets and put her in a special chair, as a stretcher would not have fitted into the elevator. Stirling followed with a heavy heart, locking up the apartment behind him. He'd never forgive Ribis or O'Hara for this.

Jerry Ribis came to visit Rebecca in hospital the following afternoon. He was carrying a bunch of white tulips which he laid tentatively on the bedside table. He looked at her apprehensively.

'I really am sorry,' he said, and from his expression Rebecca thought he seemed genuinely distressed. 'I wouldn't for the world have had this happen. What do the doctors say?'

She smiled wanly. 'The good news is, there's no reason why I shouldn't have more children.' Then, taking pity on him, she added: 'They also said this often happens with a first pregnancy and it's nothing to worry about. It could have happened even without the shock I had yesterday. Remember, I survived the incident in that museum when I staged a one-woman boxing contest. If I can survive that, I can survive anything.' She still felt shaky and weepy, but she was determined to try and keep her spirits up.

Jerry looked relieved. 'That's true. Look, if there's anything you want, anything I can do for you, please let me know.'

'Thanks. I just wish this whole damned business was over. How much longer will it be?'

He pursed his lips. 'I can't say, but not long.' He made a move to go, not prepared to say any more. 'Take care of yourself. I'll be in touch.'

'Thanks,' Rebecca said again. 'Good luck,' she added.

Stirling took her back to his apartment the following morning, insisting she rest in bed. He'd filled the freezer with all her favourite food and drink, bought all the latest magazines and a couple of new novels for her to read, and had even managed to arrange a bunch of roses in a vase on the bedside table. Rebecca burst into tears as soon as she realized how much he'd done to welcome her home.

'It's all right.' Stirling took her in his arms and held her close. 'Don't cry. Everything's going to be OK, you'll see.'

'I know. Oh, I know.' She clung tightly to him. 'It's just that I love you so much, and I'm so sad about that baby . . . and my hormones are buzzing around all over the place, making me feel dreadful, and I want to stay with you forever.'

Carefully, Stirling took her tear-stained face in his hands and looked down at her. 'You've never said that before.' His voice was husky.

'I know, I know, and I was wrong! How could I have been such a fool?' She looked up at him and suddenly she was smiling through her tears. 'I love you, Stirling, and being with you is the most important thing in the world. I know that now.'

'Becky.' He said her name softly, his dark eyes looking searchingly into hers. 'Oh, I'm so glad. It's all I've ever wanted, just to be with you for the rest of our lives.' Then, more softly, 'You'll never know how much I love you.'

Rebecca pressed herself closer. 'We'll be wonderful together, won't we?'

He nodded. 'Truly wonderful. I feel sure of you now, too.'

'What do you mean? You've always been sure of me, haven't you?' She dried her eyes, and gazed up at him.

Stirling chose his words with care. 'If we'd been married before this happened, I'd always have had a sneaking feeling that perhaps you'd only married me because of the baby. Now I know you really want me for myself.'

'Oh, I do, Stirling, I can't imagine . . . I don't even want to try and imagine . . . what life would be like without you.'

He grinned suddenly, that boyish lopsided grin that always set her heart hammering. 'Lady,' he teased, 'you're never going to get the chance to find out. We're going to get married, move into a large apartment with your own darkroom, and we'll set Manhattan on its ear before you have time to say Jumping Jack Flash!'

294

Rebecca laughed for the first time in days. 'Why do I suddenly feel much better?' she demanded, letting herself be tucked up in bed. 'Being looked after like this is heaven.'

Stirling stooped to kiss her. 'I've got to go to work now. You know the rules, don't you? Don't answer the door to strange men, and don't go out.' He spoke banteringly to hide the seriousness of his words.

'I know. Don't worry. I've had enough excitement to last me a lifetime.'

When he'd gone, she turned on the television and settled down to watch an old movie, but the warmth of the room and the softness of the large bed were so seductive, she closed her eyes, letting her thoughts drift. Ten minutes later she was fast asleep.

In a shoot-out in Brooklyn earlier today, during which a policeman was shot, a gang known to have been involved in a large-scale drugs racket, was rounded up. Police sources say one of the men killed, Sly Capra, was wanted for the murder of Marissa Montclare, the twenty-year-old show-girl and companion of Sir Edward Wenlake of the Tolle-mache Trust, who fell from his apartment window on New Year's Eve . . .

Rebecca shot upright in bed, startled, convinced for a moment she'd been dreaming. Then she looked over to the television and saw pictures of a blood-splattered body sprawled on a sidewalk before paramedics and police filled the screen in a burst of frantic activity and shouting. As she watched, spellbound, the commentator gave more details and then up flashed one of Rebecca's photographs of Marissa, taken on the fatal night.

'Surveillance of Sly Capra and his family has been going on for the past six months,' continued the voice-over, as film was shown of the restaurant where the shoot-out had taken place. 'The dead man, son of Amos Capra, who jumped bail several years ago after his arrest for the famous Brooklyn Bank robbery, fired several shots, wounding a police officer, before he was fatally shot himself. That is the end of this newsflash.'

The screen froze on a shot of an ambulance pulling away from the Pelican restaurant on Castle Hill. Immediately afterwards the screen was filled with a commercial for a shampoo.

Stunned, Rebecca continued to watch with unseeing eyes for several minutes before she reached for the phone. When she got through to Stirling, he stopped her in mid-sentence.

'I just heard,' he said.

'I can hardly believe it! Now that it's all over, it seems unreal. I never guessed it would end so suddenly, did you? Or so violently.'

'It's a nasty business. No doubt Sir Edward will be reeling from the exposure.'

'This means we're out of danger, doesn't it.'

'I'd wait until Jerry gives us the word,' Stirling advised. 'They've got Sly Capra but there may be others involved with him who'll be out for blood now.'

'I hope Jerry's all right. I hope he wasn't the policeman who was shot,' Rebecca observed. 'Come home soon, sweetheart, then we can watch the news together.'

'I'll get back as early as I can.'

When Rebecca had hung up, she turned her attention back to the screen again, switching channels, enduring quiz shows and endless commercials, while she waited for more news. It had all come to an end with such suddenness that she didn't dare believe the months of fear were over. On impulse, she called Karen at her office.

'You mean they've got Marissa's murderer?' she shrieked. 'When did this happen? Does it mean we can go back to the apartment now? What a relief! Wait 'til I tell Genghis!' She chattered on, asking and answering her own questions in a gushing torrent of words.

'I couldn't tell you everything before,' Rebecca explained. 'The reason I had to miss our lunch on Friday was because the police got hold of me and told me I had to stop trying to investigate Marissa's murder by myself. Apparently, not only was I in danger but they were afraid my meddling would screw up their efforts to catch Sly Capra. I'm sorry I had to lie to you.'

'That's OK. It's all so exciting! So our burglary really was them, as you thought? Who took the package from the Post Office when I was supposed to be watching?'

'One of Sly Capra's people. Jerry Ribis told me they are such smooth operators, they even had one of their people working in the Post Office. We didn't stand a chance of catching them ourselves.'

'What about all those threatening phone calls? Was that Sly Capra?'

'Possibly, but there again it might have been one of his gang, acting on his orders,' Rebecca replied.

'Wow!' Karen drew out the exclamation into a long thoughtful sound. 'Genghis will be fascinated when I tell him all this. I think he thought we were a couple of neurotic dames, but he'll have to change his mind now. Oh, I can't wait to get back to the apartment. It seems like years since we sat up all night, talking about men and dishing the dirt!'

At that moment, Rebecca realized just how much she'd changed since the dreadful happenings of New Year's Eve; she'd experienced danger and the threat of death, the prospect of motherhood and the loss of her baby, and she'd finally realized that life was better if you shared it with the right person. She knew now, with total clarity, that independence wasn't everything.

'Karen,' she said, 'we have to talk. There are a lot of things I have to tell you, including my plans for the future.'

Karen answered intuitively, 'If you're thinking of giving up the apartment, can I take it over from you? I might want to share it with Genghis.'

'Sure. Let's meet. I promise you I won't stand you up, this time.'

'You'd better not,' Karen joked.

Rebecca and Stirling watched television that night, digesting the biggest news story of the day. Jerry Ribis's photograph was flashed on the screen as he was described as one of the FBI's leading undercover agents, who had planned 'Operation Star Quest' to break up one of New York's most sophisticated drug rings.

'This is a great day for law and order,' said Robert Young, a director of the FBI, in an interview. 'We have managed to infiltrate the Capra family, one of New York's main drugs dealers, and we will be working on documents recovered from our raid on the Pelican Café, their Brooklyn headquarters, which may lead to further arrests.'

Then there was the now famous and familiar photograph Rebecca had taken of Marissa, posing and smiling in a doorway, only an hour before she died.

'Sly Capra was wanted for the murder of showgirl Marissa Montclare. It is now thought they were involved in insider trading on a large scale and that a subsequent falling out between them led to her death,' announced a voice-over, as exterior shots of Sir Edward's apartment building and the window from which she'd fallen were shown.

Rebecca shuddered as the television camera zoomed in to feature the window in close-up, and then pictures of Sly with his father, brothers, two uncles and a group of henchmen filled the screen.

'They were hoodlums operating a billion dollar drug racket,' the voice announced impassively. 'The death of Sly Capra and the arrest of his family is a major blow against crime in New York and in the rest of the country. This is just the start of our all-out war against drugs.'

As the news story came to a dramatic end, Stirling let out a long low whistle. 'Jesus, isn't that something?' he said, shaken.

Rebecca closed her eyes for a moment, then looked candidly at him. 'If I'd known all that at the beginning, I don't think I'd have been so brave! I wonder if Sir Edward's going to be involved now? If they've found papers about the Tollemache Trust's part in Marissa's share dealing, he could be in serious trouble, couldn't he?'

Stirling stroked his chin thoughtfully. 'It would depend on whether Sir Edward was able to prove he had knowledge of what she was up to or not. He didn't benefit himself from the transactions, and that will help. If not, of course, he'll be completely washed up and disgraced. He might even be brought up on criminal charges.'

'I hope for Jenny's sake nothing happens. She's just finding herself and something like this would really demoralise her,' Rebecca remarked. 'I must call her up tomorrow. See how she is.'

Stirling nodded. 'She's got a good career ahead of her as a photographic model, thanks to you. It would be a shame if that got messed up now.'

The next day, all the newspapers carried the story of the shoot-out. Rebecca scanned them to make sure there was no mention of Sir Edward before she called Jenny.

'I'm fine,' Jenny said cheerfully in answer to her inquiry. 'So is Daddy. I think it's quite a relief to him to know they've got Marissa's killer.'

It suddenly struck Rebecca that the FBI might still be tapping Stirling's phone; if so any talk of insider trading might incriminate Sir Edward.

'We can't talk now,' she cut in hurriedly. 'Why don't you come over for some lunch? I'm at Stirling's apartment and I'd love to see you.'

'That would be great.'

No sooner had Rebecca hung up, than the phone rang. It was Jerry Ribis. For a moment she felt quite shy, wondering whether to congratulate him or not. In the past twenty-four hours he'd become a media hero, for it was his bullet, shot at point-blank range from a 0.38 calibre semi-automatic, that had inflicted the fatal wound on Sly Capra.

'How are you doing?' he was asking conversationally.

'I'm fine. How are you?'

'Feeling a lot happier today. You've obviously heard what's been happening. I just called to say there's no need for you to worry any more. We've rounded up all the key people, so you're no longer in danger. Sly Capra was the one out for your blood, because you'd photographed him at the Wenlake party. The picture you took

298

placed him conclusively at the scene of the crime.'

'But how did he know I'd taken them in the first place?' Rebecca asked curiously. 'In fact, how did *you* know I'd taken them?'

'It was O'Hara actually. When you brought him those photographs of the waiter, you had a whole lot of other pictures with you as well, didn't you? And O'Hara promised to show them to his superior, at your insistence if I remember rightly.'

'That's true.'

Jerry cleared his throat as if embarrassed. 'We . . . well . . . we sort of let it get around, that we had a shot of Capra. We hoped it would make him show his hand, make a move. Of course,' he added hastily, 'as soon as we did that we gave you protection, without your knowing it.'

'Thanks,' Rebecca said drily.

'Anyway, it's all over now, and you're quite safe.'

'Er . . . yes,' she said uncertainly. She felt shaken and slightly betrayed to realize that she'd been used, without her knowledge, in a plot to entrap a criminal.

'I did check up on you personally as often as I could,' said Jerry placatingly. 'Anyway, thanks for everything. You've been more help in all this than you'll ever realize.'

That weekend, Rebecca and Stirling rested quietly in his apartment, making plans for the future and slowly unwinding from the dramas of the past few months. Jenny came to luncheon looking radiantly pretty, reporting that her father had heard nothing from the FBI and was beginning to think it would all blow over; and Karen came to supper, telling them she'd finished with Genghis, but would still like to rent the TriBeCa apartment for herself and a new guy called Kip.

By the beginning of the following week Rebecca and Stirling felt that life was at last back to normal. She had started to work again, glad to be back in the swing of things and longing for Stirling to find her interesting assignments.

'I don't know about interesting, but this might be amusing,' he said one morning, as she sat in his office going through her work schedule. She picked up the letter he'd flipped across the desk. It was from the public relations officer of a new 'underwater world' that had just been built next to the famous New York aquarium, on Coney Island. They wondered if she'd like to be the first photographer to take shots of it?

'Here's the brochure they sent,' Stirling added, handing her a highly glossy leaflet. 'It's not open to the public yet, so this could be a scoop. They suggest you get a shot of a group of kids looking at the fish. Something to inspire the tourists, no doubt.'

Rebecca skimmed the pages of information. ' "Enjoy a totally new experience",' she read aloud. ' "Gain an unsurpassed vision of life at the bottom of the sea, as you pass through the surging surf and on to the rocky reefs. See hundreds of rare fish in their natural habitat as you move freely about among them. Thrill as sharks pass within inches of you!" Hey, what *is* this?'

Stirling laughed. 'It's an underground aquarium designed by Ross Sheenan, an Australian diver and explorer. Basically it's a Lucite tunnel through which you walk. The tunnel is built at the bottom of a giant aquarium, so all the fish are swimming around you and you can see them from every angle.'

Rebecca grinned with delight. 'God, how fabulous! Count me in. I'm a child myself about this sort of thing.'

'So am I,' he admitted with a sheepish smile. 'I shouldn't really take the time off but I've a good mind to come with you. Shall I arrange for us to go . . . let me see,' he consulted his appointment book, 'the day after tomorrow? In the morning? They say they'll provide a group of schoolchildren for you to photograph. You should get some fabulous shots.'

'A little boy, nose to nose with a killer whale?' Rebecca joked. 'I wonder if I'll be able to use a flash? Lucite has such a reflective surface it might not work. Anyway,' she shrugged cheerfully, 'I'll take all my equipment. I'm really looking forward to this.'

They set off in Stirling's car, crossing over Manhattan Bridge to Coney Island, and taking Flatbush Avenue which led to Prospect Park. Then they headed along Ocean Parkway until they came to the waterfront and a large sign saying 'Ross Sheenan's Underwater World'.

'I'll give you a hand with all your stuff,' Stirling said as they got out of the car.

'Why don't we have a look first, then I'll know what I need,' said Rebecca, hitching her regular camera bag over her shoulder. 'I'd like to take pictures with just the available light, if it's bright enough. If not, we can always come back for the flash unit.'

'OK.' He slipped his arm around her waist, as they strolled towards the entrance. 'I feel as if we're on vacation, don't you?'

'Ummm.' She giggled. 'Like a couple of day-trippers.'

They were met by the public relations officer, a pretty blonde girl in her mid-twenties, who introduced herself as Dorothy Shiffert.

'Welcome to Sheenan's Underwater World,' she gushed, giving

each of them a limp handshake. 'Would you like to come this way?' Ushering them down two flights of stairs, she led them to a large underground lobby, complete with a restaurant and a souvenir gift shop in which the owner was unpacking shells and coral jewellery and a variety of toy animals, in preparation for the official opening by the Mayor of New York, two days hence. Chattering non-stop, she told them all about Ross Sheenan.

'He's an inventor as well as being a famous explorer and deep-sea diver,' she enthused. 'Let me show you this.' Briskly, she led them into a large ante-room adjoining the lobby, where a dozen videos were being shown on screens around the walls. Each depicted marine life. One, of a wrecked ship at the bottom of the sea, showed a diver picking gold coins out of a casket.

'Is that Ross Sheenan?' Rebecca asked.

'I don't know . . . it might be,' Dorothy replied. Then she giggled. 'With the goggles and the breathing apparatus, it's difficult to tell, isn't it? This audio-visual presentation,' she continued in a voice that made Rebecca realize the girl had memorized her lines off pat but was likely to be thrown if asked a question she wasn't prepared for, 'lasts fifteen minutes and is highly educational. A total of a hundred and seventy-two fish can be observed and it also shows a variety of sea plants.'

'I see.' Rebecca caught Stirling's eye and nearly laughed out loud. It wasn't the first time they'd come across a PR person who recited like a parrot.

Undaunted, Dorothy took them through to a mock-up of rocks and caves and little pools. 'In this rock-pool area we have crabs and crayfish. Look, there's a lobster, and of course we have shrimps.' She dabbled her long painted nails in the water, but was careful, Rebecca noted, to keep her fingers away from any snapping claws. 'Now, your underwater experience *really* begins here,' she announced, in a breathy voice, leading them to the dimly lit entrance of a tunnel, eight feet high and ten feet wide. As they stepped on to the moving conveyor that ran along one side of the tunnel, it slid forward and the green waters of the Atlantic closed in around them, threshing with a surf so turbulent it swished and pounded in their ears, turning the water to lacy foam and spinning fragments of seaweed above their heads.

'That's some pump,' Stirling observed practically, fascinated by how realistic the effect was. Rebecca didn't hear him. Wide-eyed, she let the conveyor sweep her slowly and gently forward into deeper greener waters, where golden sand lay on the 'seabed', lit by hidden lights as if dappled by beams of sunlight penetrating the clear

301

waters. A pretty grey angel-fish swam delicately about and a red moki and brightly coloured parrot-fish cruised tranquilly past. A shoal of tiny iridescent fish, glittering with every colour of the rainbow, appeared from behind a swaying sea plant, making her gasp in delight, and through a group of long-spined sea-urchins, yellow perch zig-zagged about, showing off their dazzling colour.

Then through the water, cutting it smoothly and swiftly like the blade of a knife, a shark shot forward in deadly silence. It was heading straight for Rebecca. Involuntarily, she screamed and ducked, and then looked up, embarrassed, as it swam over her head to the other side of the tunnel.

'My God!' she gasped. 'For a moment I forgot where I was!'

Stirling looked at her with a sympathetic twinkle in his eyes. 'It is very realistic down here,' he agreed. 'You really do feel you're at the bottom of the sea.'

They continued along the subterranean passage, sometimes using the conveyor, sometimes stepping off to have a closer look at something as the tunnel curved gently to left and right before finally forming a large circle, so that the exit and entrance were one and the same.

Stirling, working out everything mathematically in his head, guessed they were fifty feet below ground level, and that the total length of the tunnel was a thousand yards.

Dorothy Shiffert continued to recite her well-learned monologue, explaining how the aquarium, which was adjacent to the sea, was constantly being refilled through a series of filters and pumps by fresh seawater.

Stirling listened, interested in the technicalities, but Rebecca was in a world of her own. Like an excited child she hurried from side to side, looking at blue starfish and speckled Trunkfish, shy Hawksbill turtles and wriggling eels. It would be necessary to use her flash unit, she decided, because the available light was not bright enough. Especially, she thought, as the tunnel was actually constructed of hundreds of curved sections joined together which were not noticeable to the naked eye but when caught by a flashlight would form glittering arches, spoiling the underwater illusion.

'Everything OK?' Stirling asked. 'Shall I get the flash unit from the car? You're going to need it, aren't you?'

Rebecca nodded. 'I'll have to be very careful how I angle the three heads to avoid getting bad reflections but I think I can do it. I'll use the Rolleiflex on the tripod, linked to the flash unit, and I'll hand hold the Hasselblad for any close-ups I can get of the fish.' She was indicating what she meant when she stopped, her eyes widening. A

302

large circular-looking object, five foot in diameter and black against the aquarium lighting, slithered over the top of the tunnel, and with a swirling flapping motion, flopped down on to the sandy bed on the far side, its long whip-like tail trailing behind it.

'What the hell was that?' Rebecca asked. There was something incredibly evil-looking about the head, which jutted out of one side of the plate-shaped body.

Dorothy sounded surprised. 'It's a Sting-ray!' she said, in a voice that implied everyone should know that. 'They've got a barbed dorsal with venomous spines . . .'

'You mean that long tail?' Rebecca interrupted.

'. . . they eat crustaceans and fish,' Dorothy continued, 'but of course they could kill a person with their tail. They can literally shock you to death.'

Rebecca looked at her askance. 'You're not kidding!'

'Once the aquarium had been constructed,' said Dorothy, 'we literally opened the floodgates and in came the sea, bringing with it a lot of marine life. Of course we can never empty the aquarium. The more water we might try to remove, the more would come in, but our pumps and filtering plant do ensure it is all replaced by fresh water every twenty-four hours.'

'But you have imported a lot of fish, haven't you?' Stirling asked.

'Oh, of course, from all over the world.'

While Stirling fetched the flashlight unit from his car, which consisted of three flash heads, each mounted on telescopic tripods, Rebecca asked Dorothy to have the moving conveyor switched off so that she could set up. There were several maintenance men in white overalls working on the electrical switchboard in the main lobby. Dorothy went off, teetering on her high heels, to give them instructions.

Rebecca decided to mask the flashheads with white gauze filters to minimize any reflection, and to take the shots looking straight into the side of the tunnel. When Stirling and Dorothy returned, she quickly set up the lights, linking them electronically to the Rolleiflex so that when she pressed the shutter release button, the lights flashed in synchronisation. Then she worked out the exposure and shutter speed with an electronic light meter.

'The schoolchildren should be arriving any minute,' Dorothy said. 'There are ten of them and they're all quite small. Five and six year olds. Where would you like them to stand?'

'Close to the side of the tunnel, looking in,' Rebecca replied. 'I hope to get them in silhouette. All we need then is for some interesting fish to pass by at the right moment.'

'How many visitors do you expect to attract?' Stirling asked Dorothy.

'About a million in the first year,' she replied confidently. 'Then we hope to build.'

Rebecca glanced at her wristwatch. 'Can we get started?'

'I'll go and see if the children have arrived,' said Dorothy, teetering off once again.

'I'll go with you,' Stirling announced. Then he mouthed to Rebecca: 'I'll try and hurry things along.' She nodded. Once she was ready to do a job she hated hanging around. Too much delay could make a whole project go cold on her.

Leaning back against the brass handrail that ran along the side of the tunnel, she contemplated three Spotted Rays, their angular fins spread out flat, so that it seemed they flew through the water like a formation of aircraft. Beyond a shoal of carp glided effortlessly by. It was quiet and very peaceful in the tunnel with only the fish for company, swimming mesmerically to and fro.

Rebecca was unaware at first of the man in white overalls walking towards her. He was in his mid-thirties, dark-haired and thickset. He trod silently on the now stilled conveyor, the green waters giving his skin a sickly tinge. Then she heard the faint clank of a metal pail handle and, turning, saw only that he carried a bucket, covered with a white cloth.

I wonder what they feed the fish, she thought absently, glancing in the man's direction. Only then did she sense something familiar about his face, as if she'd seen it somewhere before. Only then did she begin to feel uneasy as he drew close to her, his eyes fixed on her. Only when he lifted an automatic revolver, black and lethal-looking, with a silencer, from out of the bucket did she realize she'd been caught completely offguard. The man was the image of Sly Capra.

For a long moment they seemed to stare at one another as if time had been suspended while all around them the fish glided to and fro, gathering together in oppressive masses, darkening the waters. A thousand thoughts stormed her panic-stricken mind. Who had set this trap? This plan, for her to be caught alone by this man, in this claustrophobic tunnel submerged under millions of gallons of shark-infested water? Someone had arranged for her to be here today for one purpose and one purpose only: to kill her.

This was no crazed maintenance man in clean white overalls who faced her now, his gun held two feet away from her chest. This man was one of Capra's associates, even perhaps a member of the Capra family, though hadn't Jerry said they'd all been arrested? With

304

pounding heart, she stared back at him, praying that Stirling would return in a moment, praying that . . .

Oh, my God, the children! she thought in panic. Stirling and Dorothy had gone to the lobby to meet the ten schoolchildren for her to photograph. Somehow she had to prevent them from coming into the tunnel.

The man spoke. 'You're going to pay for what you did.' His voice was as thick as dark treacle and his eyes were cold and expressionless. 'You should never have taken that picture of Sly. Without it the police would never have got him.'

'I . . .' The words stuck in her throat. Where was police protection now that she really needed it? Where were Jerry and O'Hara? 'I . . .' she began again. She'd had nightmares like this, when she wanted to scream and nothing would come out. When she'd opened her mouth to yell and been struck dumb.

'They won't hear you, the surf pump is too loud.' He sounded contemptuous.

'Please . . . the children! A group of children will be here in a moment,' she begged.

'Too bad.'

Then she heard it. The faint click of the safety-catch being released. She didn't stop to think. With all her strength she threw the Hasselblad at the man. Two pounds of finely turned metal and glass hit him a glancing blow on the wrist, causing his hand to jerk upwards. At that moment he pulled the trigger.

Rebecca jumped back involuntarily as the bullet ripped into one of the overhead joins of the Lucite tunnel. With a splintering crack the seam split, opening, dislodging the section so that an explosion of water gushed through the gap in the curved ceiling. The three flashheads on her camera sprang to life at that moment, popping and blazing with a life force of their own, maddening in their repeated action as the Rolleiflex to which they were linked went crashing to the ground. Then the lights crashed too, fizzing and spitting as they hit the water.

The man went down next, knocked over by the force of the jet of water that hit him as the crack widened. Rebecca saw the revolver swept out of his hand as she clung to the brass rail for support.

Fish were flapping all round her legs now, cold scaly creatures, no longer beautiful without the effective aquarium lighting, bumping into her and each other so turbulent were the dark waters around her feet. An eel wriggled past, making her gasp in disgust.

The man managed to get to his feet, hauling himself up by the brass rail, trying to brace himself against the gushing overhead torrent that seemed to be pinning him to the floor.

Rebecca struggled against a strong tide to make her way towards the exit, but the water was rising all the time, coming up to her thighs, increasing in volume. The gap was widening every second as the section of Lucite became more dislodged. Like the bursting of a dam, the flood threatened to engulf everything in its path.

She glanced over her shoulder; the man was on his feet again and had started to follow her, but at that moment a black disc, five feet in diameter, began to slither through the crack, slowly at first and then in a rush of flopping quivering fins. The man never saw it coming. It landed on him and wrapped itself around his head and shoulders like a great slimy cape. Then, as Rebecca stood transfixed with horror, the hideous spiked tail, laden with poison, started to whip the man in a convulsive frenzy. Rebecca had one last glimpse of his face, exposed for a moment as the Sting-ray lifted its fins, and saw that it was contorted in agony.

A second later he disappeared under the water and was swept away as the tunnel started collapsing, section by section, the seas of the Atlantic surging in, no longer held back by any restraints. In thirty seconds the water would reach the roof of the tunnel and then spill out into the lobby. Rebecca launched herself forward, and started to swim for her life.

Now she was part of the hurtling maelstrom that was being forced back towards the lobby by the force of the incoming sea. Half drowning, she was oblivious to the dreadful tossing and tumbling mass of fish that surrounded her, until, out of the corner of her eye, she saw a shark. It nose-dived close to her body and shot ahead of her. A second later another one followed.

They were near the exit now. She raised her head and could see that the lobby was already awash, people dashing around in helpless confusion. In another few minutes the place would be flooded.

'Stirling!' Rebecca screamed with all her strength, although she couldn't see him. 'Stirling! Get the children away! There are sharks!' The moment before she felt a searing pain in the back of her head, she caught a glimpse of his ashen face looking towards her in stricken horror, and then the foaming water around her seemed to be turning pink, and a feeling of warm lethargy was sweeping over her and she couldn't hang on any longer. The effort was too great. Delicious darkness was engulfing her, taking away the fear and the pain. Thankfully she surrendered to it.

Epilogue

Summer had come at last to Pinkney, a little late but all the more lush because of it. The gardens around the house and at the edge of the forest were ablaze with roses and lilies and lavender, and bright pink geraniums filled the old stone urns on either side of the front door.

Walking slowly, with the help of a stick, Simon made his way across the lawn with Charlotte by his side. They'd announced their engagement the previous week. On her left hand the emerald ring glinted in the morning sunshine.

'You're walking better every day, aren't you, darling?' she observed. 'By July, you'll be able to throw away the horrid old stick.'

He smiled, his face much leaner since the accident, so that he'd completely lost the pretty-boy look. 'It's wonderful, isn't it? I hardly need it now, but I'm afraid of falling over until my legs are stronger.'

'They soon will be, I promise.'

Simon paused to turn and look at her. 'I couldn't have done it without you. You know that, don't you?'

Adoringly she gazed up into his eyes. 'All I ever wanted in life was to look after you,' she whispered.

'We're going to be very happy, aren't we, my pet? Especially now my mother's decided to live in London.'

'Yes, I was so surprised when she said she was letting us have this place to ourselves. Do you think she'll be happy in town?'

Simon nodded briefly. He didn't want to cast a shadow over Charlotte's happiness by telling her that his mother had said she would find it too painful to stay.

'A hive can never have two queens, my darling,' Angela had said firmly. 'It simply wouldn't work and I've had you to myself for so long, I cannot bear the thought of sharing you with a wife.'

Angela's devastating honesty had shocked Simon, but he had respected her for it. And with cheerful bravery she had added that it was never too late to make a new life for one's self.

'Pinkney was always going to be yours, anyway, Simon. Enjoy it now while you're young, as I did. I shall get myself a lovely big penthouse in Eaton Square. I've always liked the idea of a penthouse, so chic, and there will be a spare room for you and Charlotte, when you want to spend a night in town.'

Simon had thanked her, feeling ashamed for a moment that he'd ever planned to get her to move to the lodge by the gates. If there had been a Dower House on the estate it might have been different, he reflected, but in his heart of hearts he knew the present solution was better.

He took Charlotte's hand. 'I actually think Mother's going to have a ball in London,' he replied with honesty. 'I heard her on the phone yesterday, telling friends what her plans were, and I think she's going to have one hell of a social life.'

Charlotte laughed. 'Then we'll be the country bumpkins! Oh, Simon, we're going to have such a wonderful life.'

Jenny sat for a long time looking at the newspaper in silent wonder. 'The Face of the Decade', said the headline above the photograph, a head and shoulder shot that Rebecca had taken on their first session in Central Park. It showed her laughing, her head thrown back. 'A natural study of a great natural beauty', ran the caption. The story went on to compare her with the other great natural English beauty of the last decade, Princess Diana.

At that moment Sir Edward came into the library where Jenny was sitting. He'd already seen the newspaper and had told her breezily it was 'a jolly good show'.

'Still looking at yourself?' he joked.

'You do realize what this means?' Jenny asked. 'Already the phone has been ringing all day with offers of work. My new agent is ecstatic. She says I'm made! By this time next year I could be earning as much money as Jerry Hall.'

'Ummmm. Great.' He seemed preoccupied. 'Want a drink?'

'No thanks.' Jenny waited, knowing he'd tell her sooner or later what was on his mind. Since he seemed happy she concluded it couldn't be bad news. Nothing more had been heard of the insider trading fiasco, and the Tollemache Trust was still flourishing.

'Jenny,' he said at last.

'Yes, Daddy?'

'I've got someone coming to dinner tonight . . .' He paused awkwardly.

Jenny looked at him, wondering why he suddenly seemed embarrassed. 'Yes?' she said encouragingly.

'Well, dammit, it's a lovely young woman I've met. Her name's Juliette Valentino.'

She looked suddenly enlightened. 'So what's her real name?' she asked crisply.

Sir Edward looked up, perplexed for a moment. 'Real name?'

'Forget it.' Jenny rose, smiling. 'I'm going out to dinner with a bunch of friends, to celebrate my new career. Tomorrow, I'll be looking for an apartment of my own, and then you can have your girlfriends stay overnight as much as you want.' She spoke indulgently, as an older person might to a teenager. 'You need the place to yourself,' she added.

'Yes . . . well . . .' Sir Edward paused uncertainly, suddenly realizing he was no longer in command of the situation.

'Have a good time,' she called over her shoulder as she left the room.

Mavis and Bert Handford regarded the slip of paper from Lloyds Bank with deep distrust. The figures: $3,654,000.00, handwritten under the section marked 'USA Currency – Total Amount' represented a sum that seemed unimaginable to them. Yet this was the amount Tracy had placed in a dollar deposit account, with instructions that if she had not withdrawn it by the beginning of June, it was to be transferred to her next-of-kin, Mavis and Bert Handford.

The fact that their Tracy had so much money to leave in the first place, staggered them. The added fact that she must have feared something would happen to her between December, when she gave the bank these instructions, and the following summer, left them with an eerie feeling, as if she had reached out from the grave and touched their lives again.

'What are we going to do with it all?' Mavis asked. 'It's like winning the pools . . . only more so.'

'It won't bring our Tracy back, will it?' Bert said. 'But it's nice to know she was thinking of us at the end, isn't it?'

'Very nice,' said Mavis. 'But then she always was a good girl.'

There was still snow on the highest of the mountain peaks, but in the Valley by Lake Winnispesaukee a gentle breeze, warm and embracing, played with the rushes and rippled the surface of the water. Sitting in the picturesque garden of one of New Hampshire's oldest and most historic houses, Stirling watched the activity on the lake. People were sailing with bright spinnakers billowing in the sunshine, and a cruiser, packed with tourists, cut a steady course straight across the water, leaving in its wake a trail of foamy wash. Along the banks, more people swam and picnicked and children ran around, shrieking and laughing with the sheer joy of being alive.

Stirling had been coming to this place for years now, ever since Rebecca had first brought him to meet her parents. He loved its tranquillity and the simple beauty of its orchards and dairy farms. There were rare birds to watch too, and wild flowers to gather. When he left to go home to New York on a Sunday night, he always felt refreshed, as if the invigorating air had blown away the cobwebs from his mind and given him renewed energy.

This is where Rebecca grew up he reminded himself. It is here her roots were laid, and it is from here she got her strength and courage and the ability to see clearly. To be, above all, straightforward. Qualities that were rare these days, he reflected.

It had been her courage that had made her think of the children's safety the day Sly Capra's brother had trapped her in the underground aquarium; her bravery and presence of mind that had averted an even greater tragedy. That day would be imprinted on his mind forever, that and the revelations that had followed. When Jerry Ribis told him that one of Sly Capra's brothers had escaped, Stirling guessed at once what had happened. Paulo, crazed with the knowledge that Sly, whom he'd worshipped since childhood, had been shot dead, had set out to get Rebecca.

The aquarium, designed by the Australian diver Ross Sheenan, and given his name for the sake of respectability, had been owned by the Capra family. It was to be used as a base for smuggling drugs into New York by sea. They'd built a jetty where boats could drop off supplies of 'food' for the fish, and where cocaine and heroin could be stored in metal containers, guarded literally by the sharks in the tanks. Dorothy had been given orders to invite Rebecca to take exclusive photographs before the place was opened to the public, and in all innocence had gone along with the plan.

'But Paulo would have been caught,' Stirling had protested. 'How would he have got away with it? What would he have done with Rebecca's body if he hadn't died himself in the collapse of the tunnel?'

Jerry's answer had nearly caused Stirling to throw up. Paulo's own body, or what was left of it when the sharks had finished with him, was unidentifiable except for the teeth.

Sitting now, months later, in the rose-filled garden that belonged to Rebecca's parents, Stirling shuddered as if an icy wind had suddenly blown up from the lake like a ghost of the past. As long as he lived he would never forget the events of that day.

Sensing someone coming out of the house and crossing the lawn, he turned and saw the tall slim figure of Rebecca coming towards him. Her tanned face was smiling and she stretched out her hand to take his as she dropped on to the grass beside his chair.

'OK, sweetheart?' He looked at her lovingly.

'Great! I've been telling Mom all about our honeymoon in Europe. She couldn't believe the things we ate in France!' Rebecca threw back her head, laughing. Only her eyes have changed, thought Stirling. They are the eyes of a much older woman.

'Did you tell her everything else we did?'

She gazed at him with mock severity. 'When a girl grows up,' she said, 'there are some things she never tells her mother.'